Fearin' the Banshee

A Novel by **Aidan Red**

Copyright

Fearin' the Banshee

Copyright © 2018 by Aidan Red

All Rights Reserved

Revision Date 9/21/18

Published by Red's Ink and Quill, Wichita, KS

For information on other works by Aidan Red, Science Fiction and Fiction, published or forthcoming, visit RedsInkandQuill.com or AidanRedBooks.com

eBook ISBNs:

978-1-946039-30-9

1-946039-30-6

Softcover ISBNs:

978-1-946039-31-6

1-946039-31-4

To my family and friends that have supported me and have made the challenge of creating and bringing life to my stories so rewarding.

¤-¤-¤-¤-¤

My many thanks to my editors and cover designer.

-¤-

Content Editing by **Trenda London**,
http://ItsYourStoryContentEditing.com

-¤-

Copy Editing by **Amy Jackson**,
Copy Editing and Proofreading, http://AmyJacksonEditing.com

-¤-

Cover by **Aidan Red**

Mary Gorden awoke and found she was alone. What was left of her past had been stripped away in a few seconds of pure terror! Her identity had vanished, and she did not know herself or what her future would be. Her memories and longings took advantage of her weakness, and her despair held her captive in her grief. She was angry! Angry over the hand that fate had dealt her; angry that she was the one that survived; angry that she was trapped in her new, terrifying reality.

Contents

Contents Continued

Prologue
Thursday, April 9

Cali was ready when the lunch bell rang and the children hurriedly left her classroom. With her own air of anticipation, she followed the last of her fourth-grade charges out and closed the door behind them. With a quick pass through the teachers' lounge, where she collected the picnic basket she had prepared at home that morning and the cold drinks from the refrigerator, she hurried out the side door to the lot where her car was parked. She waved at two other teachers as they left on their own lunch breaks.

The day was unexpectedly spectacular for early April in southern Michigan, and Cali tried very hard to let the bright, sunny postcard sky and the soft, fresh scents of cherry blossoms, daffodils, forsythias, and lilies buoy her spirits. And today, especially today, she wanted to be her happiest for this special lunch.

It had been in the middle of October when she and Bobby had their big quarrel over how his job was stealing him and his attentions away, how knowing the dangers in what he was doing was frightening and caused her great worry. Of course, he said he was sorry for the slights and worry and that he would try to be better at home. And to prove it, he set aside lunchtime on every Tuesday and Thursday of the week, just for the two of them. When the weather was bad and did not cooperate, they met at the Main Street Brewing Company, Charley's Tavern, or her favorite, The Mediterranean Gardens; and when it was good, they met in the park and had a quiet picnic for two.

She glanced at her watch as she left Elderwhite Elementary school's parking lot, turning onto Mt. Vernon Avenue, up the back way on Elderwhite Boulevard and then east onto Lutz Avenue. She had an hour and fifteen minutes and knew by taking Madison she could make it across to State Street and their favorite park on South University in less than five.

When she turned off of State Street, she saw him, Lieutenant Robert Marrow, smiling and waiting in his starched and pressed Ann Arbor Police uniform, proudly guarding an open parking spot. He waved and stepped up on the sidewalk as she pulled up and backed into the spot, paralleling the curb.

She unbuckled her seatbelt as he opened the passenger door and reached in to take the basket. He returned her bright smile.

"What a beautiful sight on a wonderfully beautiful spring day," he said, and caught her hand.

"Thank you, kind sir," she said, blushing as she pulled her door handle. "Has it really been three years today, Bobby?"

His smile deepened. "Yes it has. Come on. I saved a very pretty spot," he said, and stood up beside the car.

The windshield exploded, showering her with shards of glass. A loud pop echoed in her ears and her mind stumbled, trying to process what she was seeing and hearing as her husband stiffened and fell against the car. Then he collapsed, falling backwards, and dropped the basket.

More loud pops! Stunned, she watched as he fell away from the car in slow motion, bright red splotches appearing across his chest and torso. A large man stepped up beside the car, a gun in his hand pointed at her husband where he lay on the ground. The gun kept firing and she heard herself screaming as she fumbled with the door handle.

Then the man leaned down and looked into the car, catching her with his dark eyes under a deeply furrowed brow. He pointed the gun at her and her heart stopped!

The gun did not fire and the man cursed, his heavy accent slurring his words. His face—beneath red hair and framed by a short-trimmed red beard—scowled, and something fell out of the bottom of the gun. He stood back and reached into his pocket.

Cali shoved her door open and ran as fast as she could, across the street, away from him, screaming for someone to help. More pops filled the air and she pushed herself. *Faster! Faster!*

Pain exploded in her left arm and she spun around, jerked off balance. Stumbling, she knew she was hit, but she could not stop. She had to run, she had to! *He has a gun! He's trying to kill me! More pops!* The man ran between the cars and into the street, chasing her. She stumbled again and lunged for the sidewalk, hoping the cars would give her some protection.

Pop, pop, pop! Something huge, felt like a truck, hit her multiple times and slammed her to the ground. The world went black.

Dazed, she opened her eyes, jostled, her head hitting the ground; blurry people, lots of people, all around her, shadowy, lifting and touching, their hands, rolling her back and then forward. Bewildered, she could not remember them, who they were, where they came from. She could not hear them talking, yet they looked strangely familiar; some in funny uniforms, some not. They were fuzzy and unfocused. The brightness of the day slowly dimmed and they were silently consumed by the invading blackness...

¤-¤-¤-¤-¤

The blond woman was screaming and clawing madly at the driver's side door handle, frantically trying to get out of the car when the gunman leaned into the open passenger door, pointed his pistol at her, and squeezed the trigger.

Nothing! He looked at the gun and squeezed again. Nothing!

Einri stood up and thumbed the release; the empty magazine dropped out of the pistol as his free hand dug deep into the leg pouch of his cargo pants.

The woman was out of the car, running across the street as he shoved the full magazine into the butt of the pistol. He chambered a cartridge and fired two quick shots over the top of the car. She saw him over her shoulder and kept running. He darted around the back of the car and ran into the street after her.

He fired again and she spun around and stumbled. He smiled and fired again, and again in rapid succession as she slipped between two parked cars; she fell forward and disappeared behind them. Her screaming abruptly ceased.

Einri stopped in the middle of the street when the woman fell. He smiled again, knowing his shots had hit her, twice at least, maybe more. He moved to look between the cars and saw her, facedown on the sidewalk next to the storefront, her back and arms covered with blood.

He saw the people running toward her, coming from both directions, right and left, and he swore. He could not get close enough to shoot her one more time—a final shot to make sure.

Quickly glancing up the street and back toward State Street, he heard the wail of sirens filling the air. He stuffed his pistol in his pocket, turned, and hurried away from the gathering crowd. At least he had stopped that nosy police lieutenant and had silenced his wife. It did not matter that she was young and pretty; he could not let her live to finger him.

Einri turned at the corner and disappeared into the chaos of the people running to the scene.

Monday, April 13

Einri followed a middle-aged couple up the hill, across the still damp grass from the cemetery drive. He was surprised at the small number of people attending the funeral: eight police officers in uniform to carry the coffin from the hearse to the gravesite, and a dozen more paying their respects. Six couples attended that Einri did not recognize, and one private investigator and two detectives that he did.

The day was again a sunny one—the first since Friday, when a spring warm front had moved in and dampened everything for two days with the associated rains. But Einri actually wished it had kept raining, which would have been to his benefit; raincoats and umbrellas. Today he wore a brimmed hat and sports coat to match the style of the early thirties working crowd; the visible portions of his short trimmed beard and his eyebrows were temporarily blackened to help his disguise.

The gathered people and the uniformed policemen stood to one side of the coffin. A minister read a scripture and said a prayer. Einri listened to the soft comments and conversations between the people, hoping to hear anything about the policeman's wife; any comment that might suggest she was still alive.

But what he overheard eased his foreboding; two couples exchanged heartfelt concerns over her death and the senselessness of it all. One mentioned that a police officer was always in harm's way, at one time or another, but to kill his innocent wife was just heartless.

4

Einri smiled to himself, thinking how little they knew. He had worked many different angles and studied his many different schedules to find a time and situation when Lieutenant Marrow would be suitably inattentive. It was only when he was with his wife that he was distracted adequately.

After the coffin was lowered into the grave and the policemen saluted, the people began to disperse. Someone asked the minister about the wife's funeral, and the minister replied it was scheduled for Wednesday and that it would also be a closed casket funeral due to the extensive disfigurement caused by her injuries.

Einri followed a different couple down the hill to the drive and heard the man tell the woman that he had heard she died on the operating table, the gunshot wounds being too severe. Einri decided he would risk being identified again and attend the graveside services on Wednesday. Just to be sure.

Fearin' the Banshee

One

Friday, September 18

"This is it?" Mary Gorden asked in defiant desperation. "This? A big two-story house with four bedrooms? I know I looked at pictures of a couple, but what in the devil's name am I going to do with this?"

Her voice had pitched, growing louder until she forced herself to stop, inhale, and look out through the dining room window at the overgrown backyard, rising up into the wooded hillside.

"Of course this is it. It's nice," the woman in the navy blue skirt and hip-length suit jacket said as she followed Mary down the front hallway and into the dining area.

"Nice?" Mary did actually shout in surprise as she turned and stared at the woman.

"Yes. And in time, you will make it yours. You'll be comfortable here. I just know you will. And if you need—"

"I don't want to be comfortable here! I don't want to be here! What I want is for the police to find him!" Mary snapped back to the view of the yard. "It's been five months! Five! I want to go back ho—"

"This is your home now!" the woman asserted herself over Mary's tirade. Then she nodded and inhaled a deep breath herself, the tensions of the morning affecting them both. "I know. I really do know how you feel. But you know you can never go back. As unfair as it is, that's over."

Mary's stare challenged the woman's reinforcement of what they had talked about so many times. Slowly, Mary let her shoulders droop and turned back to the scene through the window.

"When I woke up in the hospital, the first time, I couldn't figure out who I was or where I was. I couldn't move my arms, I couldn't talk. No words would come out when I tried. It scared me beyond words, the not knowing, not being able to ask, the utter isolation.

"I remember a second time when I woke up, but it was dark and the memory is just a haze. I still couldn't talk, but there was a woman there dressed in scrubs, fiddling with an I.V. bag. That's when I knew where I was, but I still couldn't remember why. It was the third time I woke up that I remembered."

"Was that the day you met Ms. Gray?" The navy woman kept her tone soft, trying to stay pleasant, but her concern was genuine.

"It was the next day, I think. The doctor explained what had happened to me after…" Mary inhaled deeply and fought to hold back the tears. "He confirmed I was a widow after he explained how badly I had been injured, how close I had come to…dying…too…"

The navy-suited woman waited in silence and Mary could feel her eyes on her back.

"He told me it had been just over a month that day…since they brought me in. It seemed like the blink of an eye. Five surgeries on just that arm, two for my shoulder, and I don't remember how many to fix the damage the other two in my back did." Mary paused, remembering the shock of his explanation. "It took another two weeks before they got me on my feet, and with a special cane and a nurse, I could finally go to the bathroom like a real person."

"Ms. Gray," the navy woman explained, "said the doctors had expected you to start walking sooner. One of the nurses told her you just weren't trying."

Mary made a cynical chuckling sound that caught in her throat. "They only cared about fixing the machine and moving it out of their ward. They didn't care about how I felt, how hopeless it all is. There's no real reason to try. Nothing to look forward to. Nothing!"

Mary was taciturn but slowly continued. "Even after I was moved into rooms under the program's control, the nurses just looked for physical response. They knew they really couldn't fix what was wrong with me. They knew…"

"They knew you had to do it, Mary. Not them. They could not make you better. You have to do that. Your psychological therapist talked to you about that."

"Yeah. And Ms. Gray kept saying that. They also said they had to move me, get me out of the hospital. They never said why, but about the end of my second month, I was moved to a small place in Lansing. My arm was still in a cast and all I had was a cane to use to try to walk. A different nurse came and stayed with me three days at a time, then they would change. They were always new and asked the same questions when they started, except for one—a younger one that came back a few times on the rotation schedule. Whichever one was on duty on Fridays took me to the doctors for progress checks."

"When did they remove your cast?"

"End of the third month. After that, the doctors only wanted me to walk so I could get about without the cane or a walker." She shook her head and turned to look at the navy woman. "After I could do that for about a week, the doctors told me I was fine and that someone would follow up with me each year. They were finished with me and the program went to work on finalizing my move to a new place—this place. That was last week, and here we are, handed off like a sack of dry goods needing a place to be stored."

"You're not—"

"I am!" Mary shouted. "This is no better than being put away, set on an out-of-the-way shelf and stored for a—"

"No, Mary! It is *not*. And you know it." Navy held Mary's eyes firmly. Then, in a softer voice, she continued. "You've been given a second chance. So few get one, and even though it is and will continue to be hard for you, you must try to start over. I know how unfairly life has treated you, but you can survive this."

"Why is it taking so long?" Mary asked in a more civilized tone, trying to hold her emotions in check.

"I don't know why," the navy woman said. "We've been over this so many times. They've spent over two years trying to catch him and no one knows where he is. But that is not for you to worry about. He has no idea where you are, and that's the key, Mary. He doesn't know! And that gives you time. Time to—"

"'Scuse me, Ms. White," a man in smudged jeans and wearing a light-weight jacket said as he stepped into the doorway from the hall. He looked at Mary and then at Ms. White. "Sorry to interrupt. Everything's unloaded from the truck and put in the rooms like they're marked. Is there anything else you need for us to do?"

Ms. White turned, took the clipboard he handed her, and shook her head. "No. Thank you. I think that is all we need." She signed the top sheet and handed it back to him.

"Yes, ma'am," he said, nodding his thanks as he tore a duplicate page off the clipboard and handed it back. Then he turned and left down the hall and out through the front door.

Mary followed Ms. White into the living room. She absently looked around the furnished room, stopping when she saw the small assortment of boxes stacked near the fireplace.

"Your personal things and the rest of the boxes are upstairs in your bedroom. The one across the back of the house," Ms. White added, seeing where Mary's gaze had stopped. "Can I do anything else before I go?"

"Yeah. Lots. So you're really just going to deposit me here, a depressed and frustrated widow in Nowhere, USA, in the middle of the mountains, and leave me?" Mary glared at Ms. White.

"I will be back next weekend, end of the month. We will set up a regular schedule for me and my visits at that time." Ms. White opened her purse and took her car keys out. "You have my number and you have Sheriff Martin's phone number. You have a house phone and a cell phone, so call me if something happens that I need to know about. Otherwise, I will see you next week."

"So that's it?"

Ms. White hesitated and looked at her. "You know I can't stay but, like we talked, if you feel strongly about not being alone, I can arrange for someone—"

"No. I don't want to be alone, but I really don't want strangers hovering over me twenty-four seven like they have been. Like we talked, that's definitely not what I want."

"I know you want your old life back, even with the problems, but we don't have that option. Work on things this next week and we'll see how you do. We'll talk about it when I'm back."

Ms. White smiled—or at least it looked to Mary like she tried to, but the weight of the situation was really nothing to smile about. "Take some walks. Go out and see the town. Meet a few people, even if it's just making a trip to the grocery store or the library. You're able to do that now, so please try. Can you do that?"

Mary shrugged her shoulders. She was angry with Ms. Gray, Ms. White, with the whole witness protection program, and mostly with her specific situation. "We'll see," was all Mary said, and Ms. White nodded, then turned and stepped out onto the wide, covered porch that stretched across the front of the house.

"Yes, I guess we will," she answered, and walked to her car in the side drive. "You've come a long way, Mary. Try to keep moving forward, one step at a time. Before you know it, this will all be behind you. Things will get better."

"I doubt it," Mary mumbled to herself, and shook her head as Ms. White backed out, started down the street, and turned right at the first corner.

Fearin' the Banshee

Two

Devlin O'Brien walked along the narrow grass verge surrounding Dale Osborne's house and outbuildings, a seemingly untouched island amid a sea of blackened prairie where last night's wildfire swept across six hundred acres along the west side of Highway 24. He was following Sam Delany, the chief of Roosevelt's volunteer fire department, as they met with the other three fire crews, inspecting the aftermath.

"Got a little close here on the east side," Dev, as he was known by his friends, remarked as he gestured to the nearness of the black earth and ash where it had almost succeeded in reaching the back of Dale's house.

"Sure did," Sam agreed. He pointed to another group of men looking at one of the barns. "Rick says the Miller place wasn't so lucky. They saved the house but they lost two of the three outbuildings."

"Miller? They aren't farmers or ranchers, if I remember right," Dev said, half aloud.

"No." Sam nodded. "They aren't. He works nights in Buena Vista. Just lives on his acreage."

"How about the Houstons?"

"It got them and the Samuels before the first crews were able to respond." Sam's expression turned hard and he looked back down the valley in the direction the fire had come from. "Mike from the Chaffee County Sheriff's Office is investigating the source. He hasn't reported any findings yet, but..." Sam looked back at Dev and shrugged. "How's Mandy doing this morning? I was surprised you had her in the truck with you."

"She's fine." Dev smiled and shook his head. "Tired, of course. I tried to get Marti to come and stay with her when I got the call, but it was too late. So I just bundled the scamp up and made her sleep in the truck. At least I got her fed and to school on time."

"Not much else you could do." Sam nodded and pointed to the group from Leadville. "Keep looking around. I need to talk to Chief Riley for a minute."

"Sure, sure. Go ahead." Dev waved his hand as if he was shooing Sam away. "You go on and I'll see what I kin see."

As Dev walked around the main house, he smiled at the memory of the first time he met Sam. It was the barn fire at Doc Morrison's place. He had seen the smoke and the reflection of the fire on the bottoms of the evening cloud cover, called Marti in a panic to come and stay with Mandy, and then raced out to join the crew at the scene.

He had found the volunteers struggling to get the hoses and the new-to-them pumper hooked up.

"Ye were a brazen, arrogant sot, Dev O'Brien. Weren't ye?" he half said, and half chuckled at himself, remembering how he had jumped in and started hooking up hoses and pointing first to one man and then to another, directing them to take the hoses to the front corners of the barn. "Ye never even asked if they wanted yer help," he continued to himself.

He had taken the nozzle on the third hose and led two other men around to the side door near the back. Once inside, it had only taken ten minutes to stop the fire's advance, and in another half an hour, with the three teams fighting it from both fronts, they had it knocked down completely. That was when Sam had met them coming out of the side door, demanding to know "Who in the devil are you?"

Dev had smiled and extended his hand. "You must be the chief. I'm Devlin O'Brien—Dev to me friends. I was with a ladder company in north Dearborn for eight years and an EMT trained in post-fire trauma. Moved here about a year and a half ago. Saw the fire t'night and thought ya might could use a little help."

Sam had smiled at him and shaken his hand. "Aye, I know who you are. I've seen you around town and at Jeff's Grocery. Just didn't know you had training in fighting fires."

Dev had nodded and walked back to the pumper with Sam.

"What brought you to our little mountain town?" Sam had asked, and Dev remembered how vivid the memories crashed through his mind. How much trouble he had trying to stay focused and doing his job after his wife had died. He and Mandy had not been handling it very well, and he thought about the conversations they had, finally deciding they needed to make a new start. She had been six at the time.

"Sad story actually," he had told Sam, sidestepping all of the details. "We came after me wife and Mandy's mother died a few years ago. Roosevelt seemed like a nice place to be. Quiet. Someplace where we could breathe again."

"I know what you mean. And for whatever the reasons, welcome, Dev," Sam had said, and clouted Dev's shoulder. "Think ya might like helping on a regular basis? I need a battalion leader. Someone that knows what to do when the calls come in. Would ya be interested?"

Dev had nodded. "I think I might be."

That night, Dev and Mandy had become "official" residents of Roosevelt and begun settling into their new life, no longer seen by the town as a couple of transients, hanging around until something better came along.

Dev finished his inspection of the area around Dale's house, gave Sam an all-clear, and then headed back into town. He was going to be a little late for work at the grocery store, but Bob Jeff knew what had happened and would be understanding.

Dev thought about his first week after they had arrived, staying at Betty's Bed and Breakfast. He had scoped out a couple of houses to look at, but they had stopped at Jeff's Grocery for a few dinner items before they went looking. Bob had asked the usual battery of questions one asks new folks in town, and he had told Dev about elderly Mrs. Wilberson and her need to move out of her place. It was not listed and was not one Dev had in his plans to look at, but the moment Mandy saw it, the last of the two houses at the top of Lincoln Street, backed up against the national forest, she made her mind up. Nothing else would do. To Mandy, that was their new home.

By the end of the week, Bob had offered Dev a job in the grocery, stocking shelves, cleaning, and helping the older school kids with the cashiering and assisting the customers with carrying their groceries to their car. Mrs. Wilberson had accepted his offer on the house, and within two more weeks they had closed and quickly moved in. In the years since, Dev had bought the three lots across the street and the one east of them, and after removing the house on the corner to the east, Mandy essentially had the entire block on both sides of the dead end street for her private playground.

Before school started that first year, Dev had gotten to know the townsfolk and arranged a babysitter for Mandy so he could have an occasional night out, and for some after-school support in those cases when his schedule needed him to be away from home. Mandy had settled into school and made friends quicker than he had expected. Laughing, he chalked that up to the resiliency kids seemed to have.

¤-¤-¤-¤-¤

Mary watched from the front porch of her new house in Roosevelt, Colorado. Ms. White, the navy-blue-suited agent the witness protection agency had assigned to her, disappeared around the corner onto Tenth Street. The movers in the small cube van had already gone and now she felt very much like an unwanted plant, plucked from a flowering bed, shoved into a new pot and told to "get over it and grow new roots."

"Damn you, God! Why didn't you just let me die?"

She stomped back in through the front door, one part of her wanting to slam the door behind her in frustration, but another part questioning the why; there was nothing to actually gain by it— no one was there to hear it and she really did not have the energy necessary.

Mary stopped and looked into the large room on her right, through the door between her and the foot of the long staircase up to the second floor. She stepped in and noted it was a bedroom. Absently her gaze took in the details, besides the obvious furnishings, that belied its original purpose as a sitting room: the trimming details of the ceiling, the crown molding, and the closet door with different trim set in the room's back wall near the outside.

Across the hall from the stairs was the living room, with a wide, arched opening in the hallway wall facing the oversized stone fireplace on the west wall, a sashed window set on either side, and a bay window at the front with a view onto the porch and the front yard.

A full bathroom had been configured under the stairs where

a half bath had once been, and Mary barely noticed the style or character as she entered the dining room again, remembering her recent conversation with Ms. White. The kitchen and laundry were to her right as she faced the back door that opened onto a small porch with steps down to the yard.

"Why is it important that he doesn't know where I am?" she asked out loud, as if God or someone would honestly answer her. "Sooner or later he'll find me and I'll be dead. There's no reason for all of this! It's just postponing the inevitable."

Mary turned and looked through the various cabinets, assessing the dry goods in the pantry, the dishware and an odd assortment of glasses, the cooking and baking utensils, and the meager food supplies in the refrigerator and freezer. She did not like Ms. White's idea of going outside or into town to shop, but it was obvious she had not wanted to make Mary overly comfortable; she would have to purchase some things if she were to fix any sort of a decent meal. At least, she admitted with a sigh, she did have a microwave, a coffee maker, and a tea pot to boil water in.

She shook her head and closed the cupboard. Eating and preparing meals were not things she thought much about; usually eating just did not seem worth the effort.

After an hour of aimlessly wandering around her house, acquainting herself with its nooks and crannies, and unpacking the four boxes of new-to-her clothes (most of them bought in Denver the night before), and the one box of her "personals" (her toothbrush, soaps, lotions, and ointments), she acquiesced. She threw her light jacket on and prepared for a slow walk into the downtown area.

She stepped onto her wide porch, pulling the two-wheeled wire grocery cart behind her. Carefully holding the railing with her right hand, she glanced down Lincoln Street and wondered if they had a liquor store. "Meds be damned, I need a liquor store. I really, really need a liquor store."

Locking the door behind her, she inhaled. Then, dragging the cart by its handle, she started down Lincoln toward the town she was forced to live in.

Mary had barely noticed her surroundings that morning when Ms. White had brought her to Roosevelt, driving up Main to let her get a feel for the town's layout. Now, reluctantly, she wished she had paid a little more attention. Not that she really wanted to get to know the town or even care about it, but there was the immediate need to know which way she needed to go. At least she remembered they came uphill to her new-to-her house, so town had to be downhill from it.

She turned right four blocks from her house, just after crossing a small creek she would later learn was called Bear Cub Creek. She should have enjoyed the fresh scent of the tall pines, the fall sounds of the birds and ground squirrels, the gentle burble of the creek, but Mary was too deep in her depressed funk to enjoy or notice much of anything. The only thing she did actually take note of was the effects of the thin mountain air and the effort it took to walk and breathe at the same time, even when walking downhill into town. At nearly nine thousand feet, Roosevelt was the highest Mary had ever been while still on the ground.

A block down on the corner of Hayes, she saw a liquor store on the southeast corner and made a stop.

"Thanks for the small favor," she muttered softly with a sigh, and forced herself to breathe somewhat normally.

She collected two large bottles of white wine and stopped when she saw the aisle with a number of her dad's favorites. She studied the choices, chose one, and was quickly on her way with her bounty wrapped in paper bags and a knitted tote bag she had found in the laundry room, the memories of her late father tightly pushed to the back of her mind where she would not lose them.

Another block farther, she stopped and leaned against the corner of a building, holding her chest and softly gasping for air. Slowly she caught her breath and looked around, realizing she was on the corner of Sixth Street facing Main. The building on her right that she was leaning against was the side of Stumpy's High Country Café and Saloon. Diagonally cross the intersection and to her left was City Hall.

Mary pushed herself upright, steadied herself for a moment, and then crossed the street to her left; going downhill seemed better than the inevitable alternative.

Near the end of the second block, not too sure she was pleased at being forced to accomplish this short yet arduous trek, Mary stepped into Jeff's Grocery Store.

She took her time and wandered around the store, first to calm her pounding heart and to get her deep breathing under control, then to understand the layout and organization of the store, and lastly to decide what choices she wanted to make. Looking for familiar brands and reading the labels as she checked the breads, the basic vegetables and other perishables, condiments and prepackaged sandwich meats and cheeses, she slowly made her selections and dropped the items into her cart.

When she stopped to glance at the meat counter, a tall, very nicely built man with a pleasant smile and wearing a long apron with the store logo embroidered on it stopped beside her and casually greeted her. "Good mornin," he said softly and gestured to the counter. "May I show ya somethin' from our cold meat and cheese counter? I'd be happy to slice any of them to yer likin'. We also have beef, pork, venison, and buffalo cuts available individually or packaged in small quantities."

She froze and stared blankly at him, unable to utter a sound.

Oh, damn! This can't be happening.

Unlike his pleasant, clean-shaven look under wavy red hair and his deep, expressive green eyes and gentle smile, his accent triggered a terror filled image. Her chest tightened and she shook—not a good shake.

No, no. God! What the hell is someone like him doing here? she asked herself in disbelief.

When he asked her if he could help her with any of the other products in the cold section, she stepped back, her steps unsteady. She backed into the cart and quickly spun around and retreated down the nearest aisle. All logical thought ceased and she could only think of getting away from him! She needed to put as much distance as she could between them!

Oh, God, did you put him here to spy on me? To tell him where I am?

Mary stopped at the cashier and quickly paid for her items, constantly glancing around the store to see if that man was watching her. She certainly did not want someone, especially not someone like him, following her back to her house.

Three

Dev looked up from straightening the cans on the display endcap when he saw the golden brunette stop in front of the meat counter. Considerably shorter than he was and wearing a rather shapeless dress with a skirt that nearly reached the floor, she had a beautifully proportioned face under bright golden highlights that made her shoulder-length brown hair shimmer. He felt the image of her all the way down to his knees, thinking they might fail him if he was not careful. He took a deep breath and stepped closer, softly asking her if he could get her anything from the counter. He quickly added the selections he had available and that he would gladly package anything she needed. When he finished, he was surprised he was able to speak clearly at all.

But the woman looked up at him and stared. Dev saw the fear in her eyes and it tore at his heart. Surprised, he realized she was instantly afraid of him.

She stepped back and turned, her beautiful mouth moving with unsaid words, and hurried to the front of the store. Dev just stared after her. He did not know what to do except to give her the space she needed. No one had ever been afraid of him—no one he ever knew of, anyway. He had seen fear many times in his firefighting days, but never fear directed at him.

He slowly stepped back to the endcap, making certain to stay out of her sight. The way she had reacted bothered him. It bothered him a lot, and he wanted to understand what was wrong. He knew he had not done anything, having never seen her before, but he did not want to add to her worry.

Ye'll just have to wait and see if ye can find anything out, he told himself, his mind still lingering on her beautiful, deep blue eyes, the shape of her mouth, and her shimmering golden brown hair.

Dev was not sure why her appearance had affected him so much, but something had stirred in him. Maybe it was just a concern for her fears, he thought, and worry that he had caused her discomfort. "Don't know what ye did, Dev, ol' man," he said softly to himself, "but ye sure got her attention. And not in a good way, I think. I guess the first thing ya need ta do is find out who she is and see if there's a way to apologize to her."

Through the Winter

The weeks dragged slowly by for Mary. On a subsequent walk into town she found the library and stopped at Stumpy's for lunch. Then, on another walk, she tried the Tall Pines Café.

She kept her conversations with the waitstaff or the librarian or the occasional shop owner brief, intentionally not wanting to mix with or grow friends, keeping a low profile and keeping to herself as much as possible. Her random trips to the grocery store went without a repeat encounter with the redheaded man. On one visit she asked a clerk about the man's schedule and found that he never came in before nine; so she made sure her subsequent trips were before he was there.

She made connections with Sheriff Martin like she was instructed to do, and promptly on the middle and last Saturday of each month, navy-suited Ms. White paid her a morning visit.

Winter set in, and having to accept that she was going to be there into the cold season, she let Bob Jeff make arrangements with someone local to supply her with firewood for her fireplace and to service her propane tank, keeping it full for heat and hot water. If she did not need food or liquid tranquillizers, she kept to herself, grieving and mourning the nearly unbearable loneliness she was enduring. There were days when it was not worth getting out of bed, and there were some when she simply sat in front of the fireplace until the fire had died and the ashes had turned cold.

"What am I going to do?" she asked out loud, unable to speak his name. "I can only remember the lunches we had together, but the nights are disappearing. I can't recall them. Where was your warmth when I needed you so very much?"

She sat cross-legged on her sofa, staring at the fireplace in the dark room. Night had fallen and deepened, yet she had not noticed. She was lost and so deep in her despair that she could only question her memories. She only ate occasionally; her routine, or lack of it, continued. As the holidays approached, Mary's depression deepened as she tried to remember one when she and her husband had been happy.

That year would be her first Thanksgiving and Christmas without him, and all she could remember was the loneliness, both then and now. But now, she felt complete abandonment. She had no one and, except for Ms. White and her visits, the world around her seemed to barely notice that she existed.

On the Monday before Thanksgiving, she was crying again. She had cubed potatoes, some smoked meat, and was dicing onions for a light stew. As she finished with the onions, she stopped and studied the knife. "If I just fall against the point. It couldn't hurt too long. Then all of this heartache would be gone."

Experimentally, she positioned the handle against the edge of the cabinet beside the stove so the point was just at the bottom of her breastbone, and she gently leaned in against it. As the point pinned her blouse tight against her chest, the onions began to make her eyes water and sting. She tried to ignore the onions' effect and began to shake as she glanced down and leaned a little harder.

"Just a little more..."

The stinging in her eyes intensified, and without thinking she tried to wipe the tears away. The juice on her fingers suddenly made her eyes burn and her whole body flinched. The knife pierced the blouse and she gasped as her knees buckled.

The knife clattered to the floor and she crumpled into a crying, wailing heap, ashamed for trying to kill herself and ashamed for failing. She did not know how long she lay on the floor, hugging her knees, upset because she could not even do the simplest thing, like killing herself. But when she finally sat up, she saw the excessive puddle of blood. She looked at her bloodstained blouse and suddenly the images of other splotches of blood filled her mind. Panicked, she stripped her shirt off to inspect the long gash; when she had flinched, the knife had penetrated deeper than she thought, leaving a deep, two-inch slit. She held her wadded shirt against the bloody wound and climbed her stairs in disgust to take care of it.

-¤-

Christmas was an even worse time for her, but trying to overdose on sedatives on Christmas Eve simply made her sleep through Christmas, the next day, and most of the third day. The rest of the week she lay around her house and cried, lamenting her situation .

Spring

Mary's days and nights blurred together and winter finally turned to spring. Determined to try again, she made one of her somewhat routine trips to the grocery store and the liquor store and realized she was walking and breathing better, becoming more acclimated to the altitude. On her way home, she studied the mountain ridge rising up behind her house and began to form a plan. If she could not fall on a knife or poison herself, maybe there was another way to kill herself and stop the dark memories that followed her—or, in many cases, to stop worrying about the good memories that refused to come to her anymore.

The next morning she ate a meager breakfast and dressed.

"Today, it's hiking boots and a small backpack," she told herself, and headed into town to Bill's Outdoor Wear. After lunch she hiked up the trail behind her house onto the first ridge above. After a half hour of climbing the steep trail, she realized she was not making very good progress, and by the time she actually made it onto the ridge, the afternoon clouds had settled and obscured her surroundings in fog and mist, keeping her from exploring the area further. Dejected, she slowly made her way back down, a dog with her tail between her legs. It was nearly dark when she finally reached her house, entered, and locked the door behind her. She wandered through each room, checking the windows around the ground floor to be sure they were locked and secure.

After showering to wash some of her depression away, and dressed in her pajamas and a robe, Mary descended the stairs and made her way to the kitchen. She switched the vent hood light on. The house was deathly quiet as she opened the cabinet by the sink. At least she had a plan, and the chances were better that she could succeed where her previous attempts had failed.

She took a short goblet from the upper cabinet to the right of the sink, added one ice cube, and filled it from a bottle of aged Irish whiskey. She switched the vent light off and sat down at her dining room table, raising the goblet high to the dark room.

"Here's to you, Da. At least I remember yer teachin' me the easiest way to quiet the clamoring voices in me head. God, I miss you and Mum and the happy times growin' up in yer house, and bein' loved by the both of ya."

She lowered her glass, wiped the tears from her eyes, and took a long sip, inhaling sharply like she always did when the first drink seared her throat, bringing more tears to her eyes and stealing her breath away.

She smiled, nodded, and coughed. "Aye, a couple of these and maybe I kin fergit and stop thinkin' for a few hours."

¤-¤-¤-¤-¤

Two weeks later, the weather cooperated, the trails were dry, and Mary climbed up to the ridge again, explored, and discovered the terrain was much too gentle for her purposes. "There has to be suitable cliffs around here somewhere."

She tried some other trails, or what looked like trails to her, only to be further disappointed. When she got back to her house, she changed and walked into town to Bill's and bought a set of topographical hiking trail maps for their area.

A week later, the weather cleared and she tried again. She had mapped out a track that would take her to a pair of cliffs she had noticed, and after a couple of hours of climbing, she stood on the first precipice, looking down at the town of Roosevelt, snuggled in the narrow bowl-shaped valley amongst the unbroken forest of pine trees. "This looks better. One step or a slip and it's out of my control."

She shook her head and forced herself to not look at or think about the beauty of everything around her. She had a mission, a plan, and she was determined to follow it. "This time it has to work." She wasn't going to be lonely anymore; she had to stop the demanding, dark memories.

Mary stepped closer and peered over the edge, trying to decide whether she would fall straight to the rocks below, or bounce off the rugged wall on her way down. It was steep, and she thought it would probably work; she would not feel much after the first bounce.

She waited, listening to the soft wind, wondering why the banshee did not wail. The banshee always announced an impending death. She did for her dad and for her mom and when... She stopped thinking and listened.

Something swooshed by very close and screeched behind her. Startled, she spun to look. Her foot slipped and she fell! One leg and arm dangled precariously over the edge, her other hand clutching for anything but grabbing air, gravel, and grass instead. Panic filled her! Her heart raced! Then suddenly she was lying flopped on her back, her chest heaving in ragged, deep breaths. She stared at the white puffs of clouds floating in the serene blue sea of the sky, trying to coax herself to calmer, slower gasps. When she finally blinked, or realized she had, she saw the eagle circling her like she was his next "roadkill" meal.

She had failed again, but this time she remembered the panic when she slipped. Maybe she really was not ready to kill herself. Maybe.... She did not have the courage to just do it, and now she had messed up the simple act of falling off a cliff. The banshee had not come and she was still alive. She stared at the clouds again, and for a brief moment wondered if someone was trying to tell her something...

Defiantly, she slapped the ground beside her and pushed herself up, deciding that if she had fallen, it would probably be her luck that she would have just injured and maimed herself, forcing her to live in physical agony instead of the peaceful sleep had hoped for. She was angry again and the tears came. "Shit! I guess I just have to wait for him to find me and kill me instead."

Summer

Spring turned to summer, and accepting that she was not going to kill herself, Mary became lethargic, uninspired, unmotivated to do anything. She ignored the upkeep of her house and yard, not even realizing how deplorable it had become. Outwardly, it was a sign to the whole town of her inward desolation.

On a Wednesday in July, not long after her twenty-seventh birthday, almost eleven months after Mary came to Roosevelt, Mrs. Nancy Arnold from the elementary school stopped by to visit with her. Surprised, Mary, standing in a soiled, holey T-shirt and similar matching sweatpants, hair disheveled and unbrushed, invited her in but stood in the foyer, not thinking clearly enough to offer her guest a place to sit, or to have coffee or tea.

"Mary, I'm Nancy Arnold, principal of the local elementary school. A Ms. Gray called me and suggested I consider you for a position."

"A position?" Mary asked, surprised anyone wanted anything to do with her.

"Ms. Gray started the process to have your teaching certificates transferred to Colorado," Nancy said, "and to finish the process, the state needs a school to stand up and offer you a position. I told Ms. Gray that I would talk to you and see if you'd consider teaching again."

"Why would I want to do that?" Mary asked, and stared out of a window.

"A job, doing something you once liked. It would get you out of this house and back doing something useful again with your life," Nancy said with a sigh. "I understand how hard this situation is for you. Ms. Gray has told me the details of what happened and why you're here. I guess I'm part of your secret now and I want to help you get your feet under you and move forward."

"How do I do that? All I can think about is what went wrong and why I'm here. I'm scared to step outside for more than a trip to the store. Every breath of wind makes me nervous and I hide in here so I don't hear it, so no one can see me or know where I am."

"Mary," Nancy said, and touched her arm.

Mary did not look away from the window.

"We are a small town and are very protective of what we have. No one can come into this town without everyone knowing. Take a deep breath, clean yourself up, put on some nice clothes, and come to the school to see what we have. See if you can think about teaching again. We have a fourth-grade class that needs to be split into two classes this year. You'd be helping Debbie Cotton a lot. She's our fourth-grade teacher. Please come and see."

Mary thought about the offer and the meeting for a couple of days, and finally, the following week, telling herself it was no different from going to the store, she walked down to the school to see Mrs. Arnold. A week later, Mary's teaching certificate arrived in her post

27

office box and she had a fall semester job.

¤-¤-¤-¤-¤

"Da?" Mandy asked as they passed Mary's house. It was about nine in the evening the week before school was scheduled to start, and they were passing Mary's house after finishing the prepping at the grocery store for the Friday deliveries.

"Yes, love?"

"Why doesn't Miss Gorden take care of her yard? Isn't it dangerous to have the grass so tall and all of those weeds, bushes, and shrubs growing wild around her house?"

He shook his head and looked at the unruly, ignored yard and the vines, barely visible in the darkness, climbing and clinging to the porch posts and spreading across the roof. He knew she was remembering the wildfire that had nearly destroyed the Osborne place twelve miles down where the spur highway from Roosevelt joined the valley road from State Highway 24. Everyone in town knew they had been lucky to stop that one before the house and barn turned into soot and ash.

"Aye. It is dangerous, love," he told her. "But Mary doesn't seem interested in doing anything about it."

"But Da, it's dangerous for the Jacksons and the Palmers too," she said. "They live right beside her, and if anything happened—"

"I know," he interrupted. "But it is her place and how she keeps it is up to her."

Mandy stomped as they walked on. "There ought to be a law and the town ought to make her clean it up."

That had started him thinking; *maybe there is something I could do to help her.*

¤-¤-¤-¤-¤

At the end of her first week of teaching again, Mary had an unusually difficult Friday night. She finished her wine and went to bed, yearning for her past life, their happy, optimistic times and

28

intimacy. But the memories of how their togetherness changed flooded her senses. As his work crept in and slowly stole his sensitivity and attention, she was left without his comforting warmth. The chill of the night and of her dreams made her toss and turn and she sought the happy, sunny mornings. But she remembered their arguments and his apologies, his attempts to make her feel good again. Then she remembered the falling lunch basket, the exploding windshield, and the red splotches. She screamed, hearing the gun *pop, pop—*

She abruptly sat bolt upright in her bed, her scream cut short. She was breathing heavily, her heart pounding with each *pop, pop, pop...* She shook her head. She was awake. It was daylight and she was in her room. But the pops kept popping. Popping against the humming, purring background and—*a lawnmower?*

She threw the covers off, swung her legs out, and ran to her west bedroom window and looked out. Below she saw a man in a ball cap pushing a rebellious power mower up her side yard.

She yelled at him to stop, but he did not hear her over the mower or through the closed window. She tried to lift the sash as she yelled again, but the sash was too heavy and she turned and ran down the stairs and out onto the front porch, yelling, "STOP! Leave my yard alone!"

She kept screaming and yelling at him, and finally he came down the side yard into view and saw her wildly waving and screaming, "Get away! Leave my yard alone! Go away!"

The mower stopped and the man stood there staring at her as she repeated her demands. Finally, he nodded and said he would just pick his stuff up and... He stopped explaining and kept looking at her.

When she looked down at herself in her skimpy pajamas, she shrieked and ran back into the house, slamming the door behind her, ranting and yelling at him through the walls. She stormed upstairs and watched him from one of her front bedrooms as he loaded his equipment into his trailer, glanced back at the house, and scratched his head before he got into his truck and drove away.

"Ugh! Of all the stupid, dumb things to do," she said heatedly as she stomped back to her bedroom and did a faceplant on the bed. Slowly, she remembered him as the man at the grocery store. "Damn! Why would you do such a thing?" she muttered into the sheets.

¤-¤-¤-¤-¤

When Mary walked home after school on the following Monday evening, she stopped at the foot of the walk up to her house and stared, shouting out loud, "DAMN! *Damn you!* I told you to leave my yard alone!"

The lawn was completely mowed and all of the loose trimmings were gone. The vines that had nearly overtaken her front porch and reached for her upstairs bedroom windows were cut away and all of the debris removed. Even the shrubbery was neatly reshaped and the trimmings removed, leaving the house beautifully set behind the shrubs and the spotty yet neat lawn.

Mary shook her head and walked up to the house, unlocked the door, and went in. Once she had secured the lock and checked the windows, she dropped her satchel on her dining room table and went to the refrigerator. With a wine bottle in one hand and a water glass in the other, she sat down to think about this. She filled her glass and took a long sip, wondering what in hell this man was thinking.

Three weeks later the scene repeated itself, and Mary shrieked to the sky and anyone close by, *"Why do you keep doing this?"*

She turned on her heel and marched back into town and stormed into Jeff's Grocery. Seeing Bob at the back of the store, she shouted, "Make that stock boy—man—stop mowing my yard! I keep telling him to stop, but he won't! Make him stop!"

"I can't make him stop," Bob replied loudly with a shrug. "Go to his house and tell him again."

"I'm *not* going to go near *his* house!" Mary glared at Bob for even suggesting such a thing, spun around and marched out of the store.

Winter Again

Mary's second round of winter holidays was a little easier than the first one; teaching helped fill her days and she actually found herself enjoying the children. But it was the nights. The active days made the nights stark and cold in comparison.

Then, on one of her trips to Jeff's Grocery, Bob had stopped her before she checked out.

"Miss Gorden," he had begun formally. "Please don't take this the wrong way, but I know you don't have any family here and I don't suppose you have planned anything for Christmas dinner."

Mary was surprised at his comment but had simply shaken her head slowly. "No, I usually don't celebrate the holidays."

Bob had nodded. "I was wondering if you knew that Stumpy does a Christmas dinner on Christmas day, three 'til nine, for all of us that don't have family here anymore."

"No, I didn't know about it," she admitted. She glanced away and then back at him. "I didn't know you were alone too."

Bob nodded. "Six years ago. Stumpy, myself, and twelve others here in town have lost our spouses. Well, a couple haven't actually been married but they don't have family here either. Stumpy puts on the feed bag and the price is a donation to Pastor Emlich's church mission fund. You should think about coming if you're of a mind to."

"I'll think about it," Mary had said.

On this her second Christmas morning in Roosevelt, Mary watched the fire in her fireplace and wrestled with her memories, but this time the increasingly recurring thoughts and questions about the man that insisted on mowing her yard during the spring, summer, and fall crept back into her mind. She had begun to wonder what his and his daughter Mandy's life was really like. She had found out through the other teachers—well, from Debbie Cotton, at least— about his loss and what he'd done since he came to Roosevelt. She had also told her that when Mandy was not in school, the two of them were seldom more than a few feet apart, or so it seemed.

She slowly smiled. At least they had someone—each other—for comfort.

At three o'clock, Mary slipped her boots and heavy coat on and casually walked down to Stumpy's, actually feeling somewhat curious to see who the other familyless "singles" were.

Four

Tuesday, August 22
Eight Months Later

"I know ya know what ya think ya know," Devlin O'Brien said. He kept his tone soft and civil as he looked down and studied the expression on the stern face of the petite, five-foot, maybe five-foot-one-inch brunette woman. Her golden brown hair was mesmerizing, pulled back and clasped into a wide waterfall look that fell to the middle of her back. He could barely concentrate on her words as he beheld her beautiful face, her deep blue eyes, and her determined countenance as she stood rigidly in front of him, fingers clasped together and firmly held, palms against her waist.

He had thought about coming today, knowing it was the first time he would speak directly to her, in an actual conversation. He had worried about her reaction, remembering the two encounters they had already had, feeling there was something about him that offended her.

Maybe, he hoped, that might have changed. Those incidents were a while past.

Before he reached the school, he had intentionally decided to try to see what she really thought about him. He wondered if his speech or accent implied a lack of education to her. But she had been frightened, and now he still was not sure.

"'Tis still pronounced O'Bry-an, not O'Bree-an," he said firmly, forcing himself to remember what he wanted to say. "Dunna matter how it's spelt."

"Yes, yes," Mary Gorden, Mandy O'Brien's fifth-grade teacher rebutted without looking away; her tone and posture respectful yet not apologetic. "Your daughter Amanda, I mean Mandy, repeatedly explained that. I am terribly sorry that our discussion upset her."

"Discussion?" Dev asked softly, surprised at her distinction. He

33

had privately called it something else after sitting on the edge of his ten-year-old's bed the night before, listening to her down-hearted concerns when he finally got her to talk about them. "From what Mandy said, I wouldna call singlin' her out and makin' an example of her in front of the class on the first day a 'discussion.'"

"Well, Mr. O'Bry-an," Mary snapped, shoulders back, emphasizing the pronunciation of his surname, making it sound like she was forcing herself to say the name out loud. "I wasn't making an example of *her*. We were discussing the different ways words are spelled and still have the same sound. I assure you I was not singling her out for any reason. The way your name is spelled is somewhat unique, maybe...maybe unexpected is a better way to say it. The example was intended to be of the difference in the spelling and the pronunciation and not of your daughter."

Dev ran his hand through his still bright red wavy hair, trying to think of a suitable retort. But he just sighed and looked back at Miss Gorden, captivated, holding her large blue eyes for a moment longer than he should have. Then he let his gaze drop to the floor, absently taking in the look of her straight, loose fitting, shapeless dress with a slight flare in the skirt, belted loosely at her waist. He noted her lightly scuffed boot toes peeking out from under the long skirt's hem.

Dev knew she had to be a few years younger than he was—probably not yet thirty. Her look was the same overly conservative look she had worn each time she had been out in public since she had arrived in Roosevelt two years past; except once... He kept his expression under tight control, remembering the fascinatingly fetching image that he had seen of her on her porch.

He looked up, catching her eyes again as he softly continued. "All I kin ask is that ye think a little more before ya say somethin' that makes someone feel like there's somethin' wrong with 'em, like they're a freak or somethin'. Mandy's had it hard and there're thin's that upset her, maybe some more than they should." He sighed again and absently looked across the school hallway at the row of lockers and bins behind Miss Gorden, more to break the effect her beautiful eyes and hair were having on him than anything else. Then he looked back, took a breath, and glanced at her perfectly formed nose and lips instead. "So, I thank ye for takin' the time ta speak with me."

"You're welcome, Mr. O'Bry-an," she said, again stressing the pronunciation, and nodded. "Now I must get back to my class. If you will excuse me?"

"Sure, sure," Dev said, nodding. "Mandy was just upset and I tol' her she shouldna be. Thanks fer giving me a piece of yer lunch break and lettin' me hear yer side."

He held his hand out to shake hers, a simple gesture to show that he was not taking any offense, but Miss Gorden simply glanced at it and then smiled sweetly. "Everyone's had it hard at one time or another, Mr. O'Bry-an. I will speak with Mandy and assure her I was not trying to be cruel or unfeeling."

"Thank ya. May the rest of yer day be better'n the first." Dev let a slight smile cross his face as he nodded and turned to leave. "I've gotta git ta work m'self."

¤-¤-¤-¤-¤

Dev made a quick walk through the grocery store, checking the aisles of shelves as he went, half-heartedly looking for gaps or arrangements that needed refilling or straightening. His mind really was not on it.

"Hey, Bob," Dev said, catching Bob Jeff in his office. "I'll be back midafternoon to restock and realign the shelves."

"Take your time, Dev," Bob said as he glanced up from his paperwork with a smile.

"Thanks," Dev said, and smiled, remembering how much of a blessing Bob had been for them when he and Mandy came to Roosevelt four years before.

"Shouldn't be too long," Dev said as he straightened a display shelf beside Bob's office door. "The Coopers asked me to mow and stack a load of firewood they had delivered. Me and Mandy will be back after supper to get ready for tomorrow's incoming deliveries."

"Thanks, Dev," Bob said, and turned back to his papers. "See you then."

-¤-

Dev walked back east, past the combined elementary and high school complex to get his truck from Zeke's service station. He had Zeke do an oil change and put new snow tires on it while he was at the school, in anticipation of the coming winter weather.

He drove out of town on Harrison Street to the Cooper's place, thinking about how surprised he was that his accent did not seem to faze Miss Gorden. Their conversation was not like the few encounters had been in the past, and that let him hope he was pleasant and civil enough to not put her off any more than he had already.

He was honestly concerned over Mandy's reaction to the name thing, and was pleased to find out Miss Gorden had not been purposefully mean. She seemed troubled, attested to by her manner of living—secluded, withdrawn, and reclusive—but she did not seem to be mean. *Maybe angry was a better word*, he thought. Whatever it was, there was something else bothering Miss Gorden, keeping her fearful and unwilling to engage with others. He had not figured out what it was; not yet.

Dev remembered when Mary had first shown up in Roosevelt. It was sudden, unexpected, like a spring snowstorm. She had just arrived, and in less than an hour, the vans and all the people that had helped her were gone. Her coming was very unlike how people usually "came" to somewhere—unpacking and meeting their neighbors, wandering around a town to see what was there, what might fit with their likes, and greeting people they met along the way, sometimes explaining they were new and asking questions about this and that. Even he and Mandy fell into that normal manner of coming to a new town. But not Miss Gorden; she just appeared, and barely gave anyone the merest glimpse of her after that.

She did not go out of her way to meet or greet anyone. She kept to herself, securely out of sight behind the shade-covered windows of her home. He could not understand it; she was a beautiful woman, even if she did dress deplorably—at least in his opinion.

He remembered the first time he had seen her, and their one-sided confrontation in the grocery store. He remembered what she had in her cart, what she bought. But Mary Gorden, as he later learned was her name, saw him and looked up, her beautiful, enchanting blue eyes holding his a long moment. He remembered seeing a deep sadness and a sudden fear in them, and his heart had suddenly felt for her. Then she had abruptly turned and walked away; no "hello" or "thank you" or "goodbye."

One afternoon months later, as he was walking Mandy home from the library, they saw her sweeping the porch of her home, the old Davis house, two blocks east of their home on Lincoln. Mandy waved and he nodded, touching the bill of his ball cap when she glanced their way, but she literally turned her back to them and continued her chore. He and Mandy shrugged, looked at each other, and continued on their way, both of them simply accepting that she did not want to be sociable.

Dev had watched Mary's quiet solemnness through the winter and into the next spring. When she first came to Roosevelt, it had been just over two years since he and Mandy had lost his wife and her mother and Dev was still not looking for female companionship. His grieving was over, replaced with the nearly aimless melancholy of routine; except that he had Mandy and she had him, and together they were coping, sometimes even happily losing themselves in each other and the life they still had.

But something in Mary's manner kept beckoning to him, calling to an inner feeling he had. He knew she was afraid of him, of the people, yet there seemed to be a longing for some kind of contact. He had wondered, feeling like she was trying to find her way back from somewhere, much like he and Mandy had been doing. He had tried to dismiss the feeling, telling himself he was most likely wrong. He sometimes was. But he had to admit there was something about Mary Gorden, and he realized he wanted to know more. Her sadness bothered him more than he wanted to admit.

That following summer, Mary had surprised both him and Mandy, and probably most of the town. Over the winter, he had joined one of the school board's subcommittees for fund-raising to support the kid's holiday programs. During one of the summer meetings, the elementary school's principal announced that Mary Gorden was a qualified and accredited elementary school teacher before she came to Roosevelt, and had just gotten her state certificate granted. Mary would be their second fourth-grade teacher that fall.

Talk about being knocked over, completely blindsided; Dev was beyond surprised. He was happy for her, but admitted he would never have guessed that quiet, reclusive Mary was a schoolteacher—especially not an elementary school teacher.

The memories of Mary after her first week of teaching that fall suddenly filled his mind and he smiled. He could not help himself.

It was the Saturday morning after the first week of school, and he had set out to mow Mary's yard for her. He sincerely wanted to help her, and not cause the trouble that he apparently did. The sun had been up and Mandy was getting around, said she would fix a brunch for them when he got back. So he had left, taking his lawn mower and debris trailer down to Mary's place where he had started "harvesting" the grass; it gave his mower so much trouble, he later told himself he should have started with a scythe. He had the grass in the front done and side yards nearly done before he heard her screaming from her front porch.

"Get away! Leave my yard alone!" she was shouting when he casually walked out of the side yard, taking off his gloves as he came into the view of her, ranting and shaking her fist at him from the end of the wide front porch. "What do you think you're doing? Get out of here!"

"Yes, ma'am," Dev had said casually as he stopped and looked at her. "I'm almost finished with the grass. Just need to rake it up and pile...it...into..." He wanted to say "the trailer," but her genuine, fully feminine appearance in the cropped-topped, bikini-bottomed pajamas had startled him speechless. She sure did not look like the prim, figureless woman he had seen around town. No sir, she was anything but figureless and her pajamas did not leave much to his imagination.

When she had realized he was staring and glanced down at herself, she had shrieked and darted back inside the house, slamming the door behind her.

Dev had gathered his tools, loaded everything onto the trailer, and returned home. Mandy had called him in for brunch as he got out of his truck, still chuckling at the morning's surprise.

To keep some peace in the neighborhood after he went back and finished trimming over his lunch break the following Monday, he had left an unsigned note explaining that he was simply keeping her from receiving a city fine for an unkempt yard, citing the new fire hazard ordinance. Well, he corrected himself, the city council had not actually passed it yet, but he knew they would at the next monthly meeting after he introduced it.

Only once had he tried to speak with her again when she came to the grocery store, but she had glared at him, turned abruptly, and left the store, leaving her groceries behind.

Dev sighed and wondered why it mattered to him what she thought or wanted or even needed as he finished laying the Cooper's cut firewood into appropriate one-cord stacks. That was the past fall, and what she thought or felt should not matter, but he admitted as he laid the last of it in the racks, that for some reason, it did; he had been thinking more about Mary in the last six months than he ought to have been. He admitted that seeing her in her pajamas that Saturday morning had awoken something in him that he had not felt in a very long time.

He double-checked his stacking of the wood, pleased that Seth Mayer had given Harry Cooper almost an extra half rick. Then Dev loaded the mower into his trailer and took the cuttings to the town landfill on his way home. He smiled. Another hour at the store and he would meet Mandy. They would have dinner together and then go back to the store to prepare for the arrival of tomorrow's supply truck. He sighed in anticipation; he did not know what he would have done if he did not have Mandy—if she had not survived...

Five

Mary Gorden—shoulders back , posture straight and rigid—stepped back to her classroom door. She glanced at Devlin O'Brien's six-foot-plus, broad-shouldered, narrow-waisted back as he walked away, surprised that he had not been upset over his daughter's reaction to the session yesterday.

She had glimpsed him when he entered the school's foyer and stopped at the reception desk. It had been a moment of truth for her, anticipating the face-to-face with the redheaded man she had first seen in the grocery store her first day in Roosevelt, an almost overly friendly clerk or stock boy or something behind the scenes.

She was thankful that school policy required someone from the school staff come and get her instead of letting visitors interrupt classes. The moments between her glimpse and the coming for her had given her time to settle herself and shift her posture to be as ready as she could be to meet him. He was the man she had spoken fewer than a half dozen words to in her two years in Roosevelt, except for the day he had first mown her yard...

She was not certain what to make of him as she turned back to the children, rubbing the soreness across the nape of her neck, the ache from holding her head back so far to look up at him. Seeing Mandy's name yesterday had thrown her a horrible curve, and she had tried to cover her own reactions to seeing the name O'Brien, both the spelling and the pronunciation. She honestly had not meant to make it an issue, but the shock had nearly driven her to fits, to the brink of losing her self-control. It was no wonder that Mandy felt picked on and her father would come with questions.

His manner was what Debbie Cotton had described, but it still surprised her. He was polite yet concerned, and very interested in her side of the story. Not the type of parental encounters she had faced before; those were simply ego-driven, uninformed, preconceived notions of the truth, made up to *defend* their little "Johnny" or "Jane" before they came to hear what really happened with their *precious* child.

She admitted she liked Devlin O'Brien's manner, and from what the other teachers in her new school had told her after yesterday's incident—yes, it was almost an incident—he was always courteous and concerned with the facts, not speculations. Even Nancy Arnold had told her he disliked hearsay as much as he disliked lying.

She remembered asking Debbie Cotton, Mandy's fourth-grade teacher that previous year, about him. "Yeah, he's a courteous one, that one," she had said. "They came to town about four years ago."

"Why?" Mary had asked. "I mean, why here instead of one of the more popular towns or larger cities?"

"Bob at the grocery said after he lost his wife the year before"— Mary had heard the stories around town about him losing his wife— "they were just looking for a quiet place where he and his daughter could recover."

"I see. Where did they come from?"

"From...Gee, now that you ask, I don't think anyone ever said."

Debbie had given her the complete lowdown on Dev, as she called him, at least as far as the things she could remember from the perspective of one of the town's single and always-looking women: he was a widower, hard worker, educated, pleasantly mannered and, in her opinion, very nice looking.

But, Debbie had noted, for being a widower and single dad as long as he had, she was surprised he did not seem interested in pursuing any of the single women in town. Mary did not admit that she could understand why he was not.

-¤-

"Mandy?" Mary asked when the bell rang, announcing the end of the school day. "May I have a moment, please?"

"Yes, Miss Gor-den," Mandy said, and stopped in front of her desk.

Surprised, Mary looked up and slowly smiled. "I guess I deserve that."

Mandy smiled also.

"I just wanted to apologize for yesterday. I can't say why, but something about your name, the spelling or something, surprised me. Your father came by today to talk to me about making you feel bad, and I wish I hadn't. I didn't mean to make you feel like you were being picked on or anything like that."

"That's okay, Miss Gorden," Mandy said, and smiled. "Da said he was sure you didn't mean for it to come out like that."

"Da?" Mary asked, again surprised, remembering her own use of the term so very many years past.

"Sure. Always, ever since I can remember. Is there something wrong with that?"

Mary smiled, recognizing the mild challenge. "No, dear. There is nothing wrong with that."

"Da called his dad Da also. So do my uncle and aunts."

"Oh," Mary said. "Do they live close by?"

"No, they're back in Brighton," Mandy said. "We haven't been back to see them in a long time, but Da lets me talk with everyone when we call them once a month. It's almost as good."

Mary inhaled and thought about the only Brighton she knew, but decided to not ask for too much detail. There might be another time—a better time—to ask.

"Well, that's nice, Mandy. I just wanted to be sure you're okay after yesterday and that you know I'm sorry for making you feel like there was something wrong."

"Thank you, Miss Gorden."

"One more question, if I may?" Mary asked as Mandy started to turn.

She stopped and looked back, her head cocked in question.

"Your dad's accent? Does he turn it on and off to intimidate people? When I've heard him in the grocery store, he's always well spoken, but today..."

Mandy smiled and looked away a moment. "Today he was concerned," Mandy said with a twinkle in her eye. "I might've been a wee bit tipped up last night and he probably wanted to see if you held any unspoken biases."

"So..." Mary hesitated and looked at her. "...he was testing me?"

"May...be a bit," Mandy said, and then let her accent loose a little.

"He oft' wonders why ya don' talk to him when he's seen ya at the grocery or elsewhere. And since ya dunna know us vera well, he mighta just wanted ta to see if 'twas just us, or somethin' we mighta dun ta tip ya a bit."

Mary giggled. "I see. I wonder if I passed?"

"Probably. Da is very fair-minded," Mandy said with a wide smile. "May I go now? I have to help with dinner and we have work to do at the grocery store."

"You have work to do?"

"Not me, really. I just keep Da company while he works, so it's like we're doing it together."

"I see," Mary said, and smiled. "Well, don't 'work' too hard. See you in the morning."

Mandy nodded and smiled again. "Thank you, Miss Gorden. May the angels watch over you until a brighter day comes."

Mandy turned and hurried out of the room, leaving Mary astonished that she would give her a simple yet heartfelt (and unknowingly appropriate) blessing for the evening.

¤-¤-¤-¤-¤

The daylight had disappeared behind the mountains by the time Mary closed her files and locked them in the cabinet in her classroom. She glanced out through the windows at the night, again not looking forward to the loneliness of another night tucked away in her dark house with only her black thoughts for company. She had finally gotten past most of the terror she felt when she was alone, but she still wondered if the "authorities" were ever going to find her husband's killer; would there ever be a time when she did not have to think about him finding her, a time when she could feel like she could breathe again, without fear.

At least now she had the routine of grading class papers and planning to help fill her evenings, reducing the amount of time available for her madness to creep in and hold her hostage. She may not have liked coming to Roosevelt, but she had to admit the town had become a place where she felt relatively safe.

When she stepped out onto the walk in front of the school, her thoughts returned to her meeting with Mandy's father. She realized she had been thinking about him before today when he came to the school. Actually, she had been thinking about him a lot; it was hard to keep ignoring Devlin—Dev, as Debbie called him—and his continuing courtesy and generosity. Her common sense told her she had to keep her distance, but being alone, with no one to talk to, even about the sunsets or the wind in the beautiful trees, was becoming hard to take. But after this eventful day, finally being forced to speak directly with this man, Dev, she wondered what he might be like to talk to when he was not testing her. She chuckled and then somberly remembered her late husband and how much she missed the days when she was able to talk to him, before their relationship had become one-sided. He was gone, and she took a deep breath and forced her thoughts away from him.

Mary knew she had been in Roosevelt long enough that by now she should know every single soul in town and the details of their lives. But she could only remember the children's names and occasionally one or two parents if they happened to come to the children's conferences or programs regularly. She was adrift, blown about by winds that she could not control, and she hated it. The teaching job was a godsend, helping to keep her from going crazy during the long days, but she was still alone—very alone—and the long, empty nights still threatened her sanity.

Crossing Fourth as she walked along Main, Mary glanced through the front window of Jeff's Grocery Store and saw Dev moving boxes of goods out of the back room. Mandy sat atop a tall wooden crate, swinging her feet and laughing over something her "da" was saying. The serenity and the sincere, unpretentious warmth of them together pulled hard at Mary's heart and her mind jumped back to her husband and the man that had killed him. *Damn!* Because of *him*, her own serenity and warmth were gone; everything normal was gone, everything special was gone. *Damn! Damn!*

Her arm twitched as she turned away and continued along Main. She rubbed it, remembering how long it had taken to heal.

Stumpy's High Country Café and Saloon, better known as simply Stumpy's, was open, and seeing it, Mary quickly decided she did not want to cook for herself tonight in a lonely house. She stepped in and took a seat at a side table in a dim part of the dining area near the back. A girl she remembered that had graduated that past year,

Connie, stopped and asked what she would like. Mary asked for a pilsner and took the menu the girl proffered.

Being a Tuesday, business in the café was light, and Connie returned quickly with her draft and asked if she saw anything that looked good to her. Mary scanned the menu once more and asked what she would suggest, and it not be something fried.

"I think you might like the grilled meat loaf," Connie said, and leaned closer to look at the menu with her. "It's a baked meat loaf, Stumpy's mother's recipe. Stumpy throws it on the grill to get a little smoke flavor mixed in, and with the okra—fried, I know—mashed, and a salad, it makes a nicely filling meal, Miss Gorden."

Mary smiled and looked up, surprised Connie even knew who she was, much less remembered her name.

"That sounds very good, Connie," Mary said. "I haven't had anything substantial to eat all day." *Actually,* she admitted privately, *with me doing the cooking, I haven't had anything substantial to eat in months.*

When Connie left to turn in her order, Mary took a notebook out of her purse and began reviewing the entries she had made. After a few minutes, she realized someone had stopped across the table from her. She looked up to see the fiery redhead, Mandy, politely waiting for her to see she was there. "Hey, Mandy," Mary greeted.

"Miss Gorden," Mandy started matter-of-factly. "It isn't proper for you to be sitting alone in the dark to eat your dinner." Mandy looked down, pausing as if she needed to remember something. Then she whispered, "Oh yeah," and continued in a normal voice. "My father and I would like you to join us. You may converse…yeah, talk to us if you like, or not if you don't. But please join us and not eat in the dark. Aaah, or alone."

Mary stared at Mandy for a moment and then slowly smiled. "Did your father put you up to this?"

"No, it was my idea but," Mandy said with a huge smile, "we always work together. We saw you when we came in and thought you shouldn't be eating alone in the dark. Please come and join us."

Mary looked across the room to the table near the front window where Dev was quietly watching, holding his expression in check, pleasant but nothing more. He was a nice-looking man, she admitted to herself—well built, muscular, young (about her age, maybe a little older), clean-shaven with red hair, though not as fiery and bright as Mandy's. "And why would you want me to join you, Mandy?"

"Just being neighborly, Miss Gorden," Mandy replied quickly. "People shouldn't be alone if they don't have to be."

"That's a nice thing to say," Mary admitted, again thinking how much she really missed simple company.

"Good then," Mandy said, and spun on her heels, taking Mary's comment as an agreement. "Connie," she hollered, not quite a full yell as she hurried to the kitchen door past the end of the bar.

Oh shit! Mary thought, realizing how Mandy had taken her answer. *I guess I'm going to find out how you are to talk to when you're not testing me.*

Mandy quickly returned. "Connie will bring your order to our table when it's ready. May I help you carry anything?"

"Thank you, but I think I have everything," Mary said, placing the notebook back in her bag and the strap over her shoulder. She stood up and picked up her beer in one hand and her jacket in the other and followed Mandy between the tables and across the room.

Dev stood as she approached and gestured to a chair with its back to the front window. "Would this one be okay?" he asked.

She nodded and he pulled it out for her like a gentleman and helped her slide up to the table once she was seated.

"Thank you," she said as Mandy slipped into her previous seat on Dev's opposite side. Mary refrained from making any remarks about manners, thinking anything she said would most likely be taken incorrectly. She looked at Mandy and scrunched her eyebrows. "I thought you told me you were going home to help with dinner, not go out for dinner."

"Oh, we've already eaten dinner," Mandy said.

"She was such a good helper tonight at the store," Dev said softly, "that I told her we could stop for dessert if she wanted. And of course, she wanted." He chuckled and Mary felt a warmth in the way he sounded and in how he looked at his daughter. "So she's having..."

"A banana split with hot fudge, cherries, and raspberries," Mandy happily finished for him.

"And I'm just going to enjoy a pint while she eats."

Mary smiled. "Thank you for inviting me to sit with you. I hadn't actually planned on eating out, but when I passed out front, it sounded so much better than going home and fixing something. I don't even know what I have to fix, come to think about it." She suddenly felt like she was gushing.

"Have you thought about calling Bob with a list?" Dev asked in a casual tone and the barest of a smile on his lips. "He can have it packaged up and ready for you to pick up. Or if the order is too large to carry, he can have it delivered."

"You make that sound tempting, Mr. O'Brien," Mary said without stammering over his surname. She inhaled at her success.

"It's Dev, please. Actually Devlin, but everyone calls me Dev," he said, and smiled as Connie brought Mandy's banana split and a glass of water.

"I'll be right back with your Guinness, Dev," Connie said, and then saw Mary's nearly empty glass. "Would you like another, Miss Gorden?"

"Sure. One more, then water please, Connie."

"Yes, ma'am. Coming right up." Connie turned and walked quickly back to the bar.

"It's just a thought," he continued after Connie left. "You've lived here long enough that I'm sure you already have everything figured out."

"Thank you, but not everything," Mary said, and took another sip.

Connie returned and set the dark stout in front of Dev and another pilsner in front of Mary. "How's the split?" Connie asked Mandy and got an ice-cream-filled smile and a thumbs-up in answer.

"Mr...sorry. Dev?" Mary began. "I have to ask what happened to your brogue. And did I pass?"

Dev smiled and cocked his head at Mandy.

"Yes, she explained you might have been testing me," Mary said with the barest of a smile.

"Actually, yes," Dev said, and sipped his stout. "I don't mean to sound like I'm pryin', but I've wondered for a while why you wouldn't talk to me in public. I wondered—"

"If it was me or something you might've done?" Mary finished for him, smiling as she glanced at Mandy. "I have to say it's the way I am. And that brings up another question. Without meaning to sound ungrateful or unappreciative, may I ask why you insist on mowing and trimming my yard, especially when I—"

"It's just a kind gesture, Miss Gorden. May I call you Mary?"

She nodded and he continued.

"Since you hadn't tended to your yard, I figured that either you don't like to do yard work or just don't want to do it. The why isn't important, but there is a hazard to yourself and your neighbors if it isn't cared for—"

"Da's a fireman," Mandy interrupted between mouthfuls. "He worries about fires and what they can do."

Dev smiled. "As Mandy says, I do worry about fires. But really, I thought that you might want it cleaned up and didn't know who to ask. So I did it for you."

"But I screamed and yelled at you to go away so many times," Mary said, and stared at her glass. "I was mean to you the way I acted. I...I—"

"'Tis not to worry, lass," Dev said, and took a sip of his stout. He caught Mandy's surprised expression, but did not make a comment. "I had the time and I figured I had just surprised you. I obviously needed to work on it when it would not wake you or offend you, so I've come by during the day on my lunch hour."

"I guess I should say thank you, but I'm not supposed—" She stopped her explanation. "I'll just say I should be taking care of it myself and not putting the task to you, or anyone else, for that matter."

"I don't mind," Dev said, smiling. "It gives me something to—"

"Okay, Dev. I don't want to talk about it anymore. Can we change the subject? Please," she said, and glanced away from him. "I'm sorry I brought it up. I thank you for your kind help." Mary turned to Mandy as Connie brought her plate of meatloaf and sides. "And what do you do in your free time, when you aren't at school or on weekends?"

◻-◻-◻-◻-◻

"Da?" Mandy asked as he sat down on the edge of her bed for their nightly ritual of goodnight blessings and kisses.

"Yes, love?" he asked as he tucked her covers around her.

"Why does Miss Gorden stay by herself so much?" Mandy asked. "I mean, she doesn't talk to other folks like people normally do."

"How do you mean?"

"Like other teachers," Mandy explained. "She talks to Mrs. Arnold and Miss Cotton, but no one else really. I don't think she's very happy, Da."

"No," Dev said softly, and squeezed Mandy's hand. "I don't think she is either. I think tonight was hard for her to even talk to us as long as she did."

"Did something bad happen to her? I don't think she's just one of those kinds of people—sad and always disliking folks."

"I don't know, and I don't think she's one of those either, love. Now, let's get you to sleep. School tomorrow," he said, and leaned over and kissed her cheek. "Love you, scamp. May yer tomorrows be filled with God's sunshine, love."

"Thanks, Da. I love you too," Mandy said, and rolled onto her side. She stopped before she pulled the covers up over her shoulder. "Pray for Miss Gorden with me, Da?"

"Sure."

Mandy took his hands and held them between hers. "Dear God in Heaven, please watch over Miss Gorden and help her to understand we want to be her friends. Help her find her happy again and help us to show her we want her to be happy too."

"Amen," they said together.

"Lovely, lass," Dev said, and kissed her again. "'Night, love. We'll try to help make Miss Gorden feel at home and to be happy."

"'Night, Da," Mandy said, and snuggled under her covers.

She watched as Dev turned out the light and started down the stairs, thinking about his remark at dinner. *I know you want her to be happy too, Da. Ye did call her "lass."*

Six

Saturday, August 26

"Get up, sleepyhead," Dev said loudly as he made his way from his bedroom to the bath between his and Mandy's room, squarely at the top of the stairs. Anyone coming into the house had an unobstructed view of the bathroom door.

"Ahead of ya, Da," Mandy chirped from downstairs. "Yer the slowpoke. Not me."

He chuckled and closed the door behind him. As he took care of the morning necessities, washed, shaved, and combed his hair, the memories of the past week came back to him.

He had not seen Mary since Tuesday night, and Mandy had mentioned that she had seemed sad at school. Her guarded nature during their dinner together—well, her dinner and his and Mandy's desserts—bothered him.

He shook his head and went downstairs to help with breakfast, unable to think of anything he might do to help Mary out of her sadness.

"Hey ya, scamp," he said, and ruffled her unkempt hair. "Yer up early. What's up for you today?"

"Maybe hiking," Mandy said, and flipped the shredded potato patties in the black iron skillet. She turned to the counter and began stirring the egg-and-milk mixture in a measuring cup. The smell of bacon filled the house.

"What can I do?" he asked. "Hiking with who? The Martin kids?"

"Ya kin get the toast goin," she answered, and began pouring the mixture into another iron skillet. "Mary. Maybe."

"Mary?" He was surprised, but tried to keep it to himself as he took two slices of bread from the wrapper and dropped them into the toaster.

"She has a meeting this mornin," Mandy said as he pushed the lever down. "She said it was important, but if she felt okay after, we could do the hike to Doe Basin and the pond there."

"I didn't know she hiked," Dev said, suddenly conflicted. He knew Mary had a different schedule this year, and was away from her house most Saturdays, and though he had not seen her around town at those times, it had never occurred to him that she might be hiking. Then he remembered the days during the summer when she was away from home and he had not seen her around town then either. At the time, he had just figured she wanted to be away when he mowed and trimmed. But now he realized Mandy had been talking with her at school and he smiled, figuring it would make sense that Mary would enjoy Mandy's company.

"Yeah, couple of days a week during the summer. She says now that school has started she only goes when the weather's good and only on weekends when she doesn't have to go over school papers. Usually she goes alone." Mandy deftly flipped the vegetable-and-cheese-filled egg omelet and plated the potato patties.

"Juice?" he asked.

"Sure, sure." She nodded and set the plate of bacon on the table. Dev poured.

Mandy cut the omelet in uneven halves and added them to the plates with the potato patties, added the bacon slices and set the plates on the table; she put the plate with the larger omelet half at her place and sat down. She glanced over her shoulder to be sure the stove was turned off as the toaster snapped and Dev collected the slices.

"Are ya tryin' to put me on a diet?" Dev asked, looking at their plates.

"No, Da," Mandy giggled. "I'm a growin' lass and need the extra nourishment for the growin.'"

He chuckled and smiled, lightly ruffling her fiery tresses. "Aye, ye are. And my favorite lass, fer sure. When you're back from your hike, we'll call your aunts and uncle. 'Tis the last Saturday, ya know. Maybe Gran will feel up to talking with you a bit."

¤-¤-¤-¤-¤

"Do you have any word?" Mary asked as she paced her living room, back and forth in front of the oval coffee table. She dodged the modern stuffed chairs with polished wood arms setting across from the sofa where her guest, Ms. White, sat. "Anything to help?"

"I wish I did," the woman in navy blue pants, white blouse, and a navy jacket said. "Every time the police get close to him, he disappears."

"So I'm no better off than the day—"

"Don't," Ms. White said sharply. "It isn't that simple. He still thinks Cali is dead and he does not know who or where Mary Gorden is. We know more about what he's doing than we did then, and we know there is nothing happening that will threaten your safety. So long as you're here."

"But I'm still stuck! Until you can find him, I'm stuck. He stole our lives!" Mary's voice was becoming shriller by the moment. "It's been over two and a half years since he—!"

"Mary! Stop!" Ms. White said sharper yet, then continued in a more conversational tone. "Control yourself. You've made some great headway. This is the start of your second year teaching. That was something you liked very much, and you've met some of the townsfolk, made some friends—"

"Not real friends! Not like I had before. Friends I grew up with," Mary said, her temper cooling some as she turned to face the woman. "I'm lost here. I can't get a grip on anything! Can't you understand that?" She turned and began pacing again. "I'm lost in a strange place! And I need—"

"Mary, I know how you feel—"

"How can you?" Mary snapped loudly. "You're not the one trapped in an alternate existence with no connections between who you were and who you've become. You're not the one that heard the banshee scream and saw him die—snatched away in a heartbeat, your whole life with it! You're not the one that was shuttled from place to place for months and then dropped in a nondescript mountain town and told you had to stay out of sight! You're not the one that has no

53

one to calm the nightmares, to tell you everything is going to be all right! I have no one! And everything is *not* going to be all right! How? How can you possibly know how I feel?" Mary was screaming and had to stop, doubled over, panting to get her breath.

"Yes, you're right about those things," Ms. White said. "But you can't go back—not ever. You have to stay out of sight. You have to, Mary. He doesn't know you're alive or where you are. That's the key point. And we have to keep it that way."

"I...know..." she said softly through ragged breaths. "But I don't have to like it. I just wish I could—"

Mary looked up, startled. Her words were cut short by the heavy knocking on her front door.

"Expecting someone?" Ms. White asked.

Mary shook her head and slowly pushed herself upright. She turned, went to the door, and peeked around the window curtain.

Surprised, she wiped her face with her hands and slowly opened the door.

"Dev? Mandy?"

"Sorry to be botherin' you, Miss Gorden," Dev said, pleasantly impersonal, yet with a tone that told Mary he could help if she needed it. "I was just wondering if today might be all right fer mowin' yer yard." He let his accent deepen. "I'm goin' ta be busy on Monday when ya wanted me ta mow, so I wuz wonderin'."

Mary stared up at him a long moment, suddenly happy to see his broad-shouldered, tall figure looming up in front of her. Then she answered slowly. "Sure. Maybe later this morning or afternoon. I'll be away for a while"—she winked at Mandy, then continued—"so that would be a good time."

"Thank ye, ma'am," he said with a smile. "Is there anythin' else yer might be needin'?"

She saw him flick his eyes toward the living room behind her.

"No, I don't think so," Mary said. "Thank you though, uh, for asking. Bye now."

"Good day to ya then, ma'am. May the sun always warm yer face and yer days be happy."

She watched as Dev caught Mandy's shoulder and together they stepped off the porch, walked down the walk to the sidewalk by the street, and turned right.

"Well, it looks like you've made a few friends," Ms. White said as Mary closed the door and turned back inside.

"Not really," Mary said, trying to hide the smile she felt. "He's a handyman around town, stocker at the grocery store, and has a very nice daughter. She's one of my students."

"And he's been mowing your yard?"

Yes. Mowing and trimming," Mary admitted. "Against my wishes, he started taking care of it so I wouldn't get fined for violating a new city ordinance."

"At least someone is interested in helping you," Ms. White said, "one way or another." Ms. White stood up and collected her purse. "I'll be back on the sixteenth. Until then, please just take deep breaths and we'll do the same. He has to slip up, and when he does, the police will get him." She paused. "I'm glad the principal of your school was understanding and could work with us to get your certificate transferred and sealed."

"I am too," Mary admitted. "Teaching has helped, a lot. I know you're trying, but it's very frustrating being isolated and not knowing what's going on."

Ms. White nodded and shook Mary's hand. Mary opened the door and stood on the wide porch as the navy-suited woman got into her car and backed out. She watched the car turn on Tenth Street heading back to Main, and then turned to watch Dev and Mandy walking up Lincoln, back toward their home two blocks farther on. She wondered why they had chosen that particular moment to knock on her door.

¤-¤-¤-¤-¤

"What was going on, Da?" Mandy asked as they crossed Twelfth on their way back to their house. "Was someone shouting?"

"Screaming was more like it, love," Dev said, and slipped his arm around her shoulders. "Mary was definitely screaming."

"She seemed okay when she answered the door."

55

"Aye. Seems odd she can switch so quickly from being upset to being so pleasant," Dev said, puzzling over what they saw. "But I wouldn't mention that we heard any of that when you're with Mary. We shouldn't have been eavesdropping on their argument."

Mandy giggled. "She was so loud, how could we not eavesdrop?"

"But she doesn't have to know we did," he said, and squeezed her shoulders again. "I wouldn't want to embarrass her by telling her we heard."

"Da? Who died? Who was she talking about?"

"Dunno. Must've been someone very close to her," Dev said.

"And she said she has to stay out of sight. I don't understand why, Da."

"Me either, love," Dev said. "But if we pay attention, watching carefully, maybe we can help her by seeing anything unusual."

"How will we know what's unusual?"

"I guess you and I will have to figure that out." Dev chuckled. "Which means we'll have to get to know Miss Gorden well enough so we know what's usual."

"You'll like doing that, I think," Mandy giggled, and hip-checked him.

"And you won't?"

"Of course I will, but it isn't the same, Da, and you know it." Mandy giggled again. "I know you like Mary—at least a little, or you wouldn't've called her 'lass.'"

"Well smarty, what's not to like? You like her too," Dev said with a chuckle, but he did not tell her about the image of Mary that flitted through his mind—the one of her standing on her porch in her barely there, bikini-bottomed pajamas, ranting and shouting for him to go away. He smiled. *Yes sir, it will be a cold day in Hell before I forget that one.*

"Yeah, Da, I like her too."

Seven

"Hey there, Dev," Henry, his brother, the third oldest of the siblings, said when he answered the phone. "Hold on a sec." Then he announced loudly to his mother's house: "Dev's on the line. Pick up, everyone. Grab a phone."

Suddenly Brenna the oldest, Derry the second, and Moira Anne the fourth oldest's voices all said "hello" and Dev, the youngest, stammered a "hello" in return, still overwhelmed after four years by the avalanche of curious concerns from his family; their simple greetings conveyed mountains of love and happiness for him and Mandy.

"Yer late, brother," Henry said with a laugh. "We expected you to call over an hour ago."

"Mandy was hiking with a friend," Dev said to them all. "She'll be on the line in a minute. Just got back and needed the loo."

The sisters giggled.

"How's mum?" Dev asked, his voice soft with concern.

"Reasonable," Henry replied. "She stays to herself mostly. I make sure she eats."

"That he does," his sister Moira Ann said. "And a good job of it too. The doctor says she's gettin' on much better."

"Good, good. And how're the Frasiers?" Dev asked Moira Ann, his youngest married sister, his happy tone returning. "And the boys?"

"Everyone's fine, Dev," Moira said. "Carl has them at soccer, practice. They dropped me off on the way so I could talk. They should be back soon. How're you doin' with work and all?"

"Good, good," Dev said. "I still get a lot of extra jobs and the store is always busy. Mandy helps me once a week."

"Do ya have any new pictures?" Derry asked before anyone else could monopolize the line.

"No, though I do need to take some," Dev admitted. "Mandy's tall, like Da. Well, maybe not as tall as me, yet. How're Will and the girls?"

"What's wrong with bein' tall?" Brenna interrupted sharply. "Especially if everythin' of importance stays in proportion?"

"Nothin', nothin' at all, sis." Dev chuckled.

"They're all fine, Dev," Derry continued to answer. "Will's workin' this mornin' and Kiera and Keena are downstairs in front of the telly. How's Mandy?"

"Ah, here's the girl now. She can tell you all about what's happening," he said as Mandy grabbed Dev's wireless bedroom phone and said "Hey."

"Hey, girl," Henry said first, and was promptly lost in the *hellos* from his sisters.

Their conversation went as usual, with each of them asking Mandy questions about her school, friends, and anything else they could think of. Dev let Mandy dominate the conversation, pleased with how well she got on with her aunts and uncle, but Mandy caught him by surprise before she said her goodbyes. "...and we had dinner with my teacher on Tuesday. Da does her yard every week and I think he likes her—"

"What?" Moira's voice rose above the others, followed quickly by the other three. "Dev's seein' a girl?"

"No," Dev said a little louder than he intended, looking up to where Mandy sat, smiling from the top of the stairs. He gave her *the eye.* "No, she just seems to be havin' some hard times and I'm helpin' out. No datin', no goin' out, no—"

"Ye like 'er. Don' ya?" Henry asked with a chuckle.

Dev did not answer.

"Don't take it out on Mandy, now, brother," Brenna said softly over Mandy's giggles. "Obviously she sees somethin' you don't. And it's probably good that yer talkin' to a woman now and again."

"Well, I don't see what she's talkin' about, sis," Dev said firmly, then changed the subject. "I need to talk to Henry for a minute before we get off. Is that all right with all of you?"

"Sure, Dev," Moira said playfully, "as long as you don't talk about your girl behind our backs."

One by one the sounds of the three phones clicked off and he waited until he heard Mandy drop off last. "Thanks, love," he said with a smile as Mandy came down the stairs, glanced at him, and then went out and sat on the front porch.

"I think they're off, Dev. What's up?"

"Just wonderin'," Dev said. "I don't want to get everyone worked up, but I saw on the news that there has been some riotin' back there and was wonderin'—"

"Wonderin' if it was Einri's doin's?" Henry asked firmly. "It was, at least some of it. He has a bit of a gang now, and has been stirring up trouble all around the docks and industrial areas."

"Are ya still having trouble with the name thing?"

"Yeah," Henry admitted. "Last week the precinct chief hauled me in for questioning. Again. You'd think that after nearly sixteen years they'd be able to keep us straight."

"I suspect the problem is they can find you and can't find Einri." Dev hesitated. "What does his da say about his whereabouts?"

"Nothin'," Henry said, disappointment in his voice. "He says he doesn't know where he is and doesn't want to know."

Dev hesitated again. "And you? How are you holding up?"

Henry took a moment and inhaled deeply. "He came by last week. Near midnight. They'd been chasing him all evening, from just after five. He said he'd lost them and came to see if he could hide out..."

When Henry hesitated, Dev asked the obvious. "Did ya?"

"Course not," Henry said softly. "I knew the cops wuz just minutes away and I tol' him they'd be here hassling me as to whether I'd seen him or not." Henry took a deep breath. "I tol' him I wouldn't lie for him and that I wouldn't hide him in me mother's house either—nor anywhere else, for that matter. What he's done, I—we—can't condone. I tol' him I wuz sorry, but he'd made his deal with the Devil and I couldn't help him." Henry hesitated again. "He asked if I wuz goin' to turn him in and I tol' him I wouldn't lie if they asked about him being here. But if he kept comin' back, I'd have to call the precinct and tell them he keeps comin' 'round."

"What about the girls? Do they know?"

"Brenna knows. She was here with Mum that night and heard me telling him what I said," Henry continued. "So far, Einri has not

59

come back around and hasn't tried anything with the family. We've been keeping together just in case. Why the questions? What's on yer mind, Dev?"

"I'm not sure yet," Dev admitted. "I went to the library while Mandy was hikin' and I looked up some history on Einri. I have a couple of suspicions that I have to work on, but I want to be sure you and the girls and Mum are all right before I dig too much farther."

"Whatcha diggin' into, Dev? How's it affectin' the family?"

"I'm not sure yet, Henry," Dev said. "I'll let you know if I find anythin' of importance."

"Okay," Henry said softly. "Don't do anythin' stupid where Einri is concerned."

"Not plannin' on it, brother," Dev chuckled. "You tell me if he comes around the house again, or if he does anything you think I might want to know. I'll call next month unless I have somethin' to tell you before then. Bye for now. May the road rise up to meet you and your days be sunny."

"Bye, Dev. Give Mandy our love."

-¤-

Dev stepped out onto the porch and sat down on the steps beside Mandy.

"Uncle Henry sends their love," he said as he put his arm around her shoulders. He pulled her tight against him.

"What's the matter, Da?"

"Nothin' serious, love."

"Come on, Da. Give," Mandy pushed, and nudged his ribs.

He inhaled deeply. "You know of me cousin Einri, by me da's brother. He's been getting deeper and deeper inta trouble back home. Uncle Henry has been keepin' watch so he doesn't start anythin' ta implicate the family in his misdeeds, but I'm a little worried."

"I know he's been worse than a pain in the—"

Dev slapped his hand over her mouth and stared at her. "No cursin' or bad language is necessary."

"I was just goin' to say 'in the behind,' Da." She giggled and he chuckled.

"Good, good, love," Dev said with a brighter smile. "So tell me

60

how your hike went. Spare no details, since I wasn't invited."

"In a minute," Mandy said, and looked up at him. "Did you find anythin' out about Mary in your searchin'?"

"What makes you think I would be checkin' up on her?"

"Just a hunch, Da." Mandy giggled again, her face filled with a wide smile. "Why don' ya want the aunts and Uncle Henry to know you like Mary?"

"Because it isn't whether I like Mary that counts. It's whether she likes us that's important." He looked at her and cocked his head. "Understand?"

Mandy slowly shook her head. "Not really, Da." Then she snuggled under his arm, slipping her arm around his waist, and then she straightened up and began. "First we went up the trail off Main Street to the meadows by Little Moon Lake. There were a few wildflowers, but they were almost all gone. Too late in the fall. Then we took the switchback trail up to Doe Basin and saw a small herd of deer. Then..."

Mandy continued her nonstop description of her wonderful midday hike with Mary, including all the details she could remember and highlighting everything about Mary that she thought her father would like to know.

¤-¤-¤-¤-¤

When Mandy left her, anxiously talking about a phone call with her uncle and aunts, Mary stepped inside and closed her front door behind her. She absently thumbed the deadbolt and dropped her small backpack on the floor. In the kitchen, she poured herself a glass of tea, added a couple of ice cubes, and slowly dropped into a chair at her kitchen table. The heady thoughts of her hike, the remembered details of her afternoon with Mandy raced around in her mind.

Mandy was a surprise on all levels, she admitted. A very knowledgeable child, quiet some of the time and bursting with energy and information at others. She smiled, recounting the many things Mandy had said concerning the other children she had met when they moved to Roosevelt. She even had interesting things to say about each of their families.

But Mary sipped her tea and thought of the things Mandy had mentioned regarding herself and her father. She already knew Mandy had lost her mother in an accident, but she was surprised by the intensity of her connection with her "da"—the term made her smile—and how close they were, neither doing anything without the other or without the other knowing what they were doing or going to do. It was heartwarming to see and experience that closeness, that commitment. She thought about her years growing up and realized she had not experienced that kind of closeness—not even with her own folks.

Mary finished her tea and climbed the stairs to her bedroom with the lure of a warm soak in the tub to soothe her tired muscles pulling her on. She set the temperature of the water, first having to wait for the hot water to reach the bath and then, when it felt right, for the tub to fill. She slipped out of her capri jogging pants and her three-quarter-sleeved top and dropped them into her clothes hamper. Then with a sigh, she unwrapped the long strip of cloth from around her chest and torso, freeing herself from the form-changing constriction. She straightened, arching her back in a stretch. When she finished undressing, she grabbed a washcloth, began rubbing the long scar on her upper left arm, and slipped into the inviting tub of bubbles and warm water.

Eight

"Maarryy."

The distant sound of someone calling her name drowsily pulled her out of a very sweet dream. She wanted to linger and not leave his arms, but the voice persisted.

"Maarryy. Can you hear me?"

She opened her eyes, recognizing Mandy's voice, and abruptly realized Mandy and Dev had been in her dream.

"Maarryy. I know you're in there," Mandy's voice continued.

Mary slowly shook the sleep from her mind and realized her bathroom was nearly dark and the water had cooled considerably. "In a minute," she hollered, and fumbled to stand up and find a towel. She stepped out of the tub, patted herself dry, and wrapped the towel tight around herself. At the windows over the front porch, she looked down and saw Mandy and Dev standing in her front yard.

"What?" she hollered through the partially open window, resisting the urge to push the curtains aside to see them.

"It's fish night," Mandy yelled back. "You said you'd come with."

"I did, didn't I?" Mary replied in a softer voice. "Give me a minute or two. I fell asleep."

"'Kay," Mandy said, and turned to speak to her father.

Mary hurried back to her bedroom and quickly found a clean and pressed blouse, pants, and socks. It took her more than a few minutes, but she appeared on her dimly lit porch as quickly as she could, stopped instantly by Dev's wide smile and cheerful eyes.

"What?" she asked, and glanced around and down at herself.

"Nothing," Dev said. "Other than you do look very fetching, Miss Gorden. Very fetching, fer sure. Doncha think, Mandy?"

"Yup." Mandy smiled. "I agree, Da. I do, fer sure."

Dev stepped forward and offered his elbow, but Mary chose to walk with Mandy and not cling on his arm.

"Sorry," Mary said softly as they reached the sidewalk. "I don't want anyone to get the wrong idea, Mr. O'Brien."

"Not to worry, lass," Dev said, and smiled his wide smile. "I'll just keep hopin' there might come a time."

Mary studied his pleasant expression for a long moment as they walked from streetlight to streetlight down Tenth Street with Mandy between them, wondering if Dev was actually serious in what he was saying.

-¤-

"More?" Mandy asked as she stood up and stepped over the bench seat to leave the picnic table. "I'm going for more. More, Da? Mar—er Miss Gorden?"

"No thanks, Mandy," Mary replied, smiling at Mandy's attempt to stay formal in front of the gathering of townspeople, all seated under the firehouse's driveway lights. There were numerous picnic tables scattered about, with oilcloth spread over them for the monthly fish night. "I've had three pieces already. I think that's enough for one go."

"Okay. You, Da?"

"Nope. Just yerself, love," Dev said with a wide smile. "I've had me limit, but you go right ahead. Catfish is good fer ya."

"Oh, can I get our picture first?"

"Picture?" Dev and Mary asked at the same time.

"Yeah." Mandy smiled.

"No, Mandy," Mary said, resisting in wide-eyed concern. "No, please. No pictures. I...I don't like my picture taken. No."

"Maybe not this time, love," Dev said to Mandy as she turned to face Mary.

Mandy hugged Mary, making her even more uncomfortable. "Please, Mary, please. I just want it fer my night table, beside me bed."

Mary's expression pleaded with Dev, and Mandy squeezed her shoulders again.

"Mandy, if Mary doesn't want her picture taken—"

Mary reached out and touched his arm, and her eyes looked down at Mandy still hugging her. Mary had not embraced Mandy, but she shook her head slowly, and with great apprehension, reluctantly gave in. "Okay...okay, Mandy. Just for you."

"Thank you, thank you," Mandy said, and held her hand out to Dev. "May I use your phone? Please, Da."

Phone in hand, Mandy turned quickly and caught the hand of the elderly lady at the next table.

"Mrs. Bowers. Would you take our picture? Please."

Mrs. Bowers agreed, and Mandy took Dev's phone and showed her how to hold it and take a picture with it. Then Mandy went around their table and snuggled into the space between her father and Mary, each turning to face Mrs. Bowers.

"Okay, Mandy. One. Two. Three," Mrs. Bowers said, and the phone made a camera shutter sound.

"Thanks, Mrs. Bowers, Da, and you too, Mary," Mandy said as she jumped up, took the phone from the elderly woman, and passed it to her father. "Print that out for me tomorrow, Da. Please."

Mandy grabbed her plate and hurried off to the table where Chief Delany and one of the other firemen were laying the fillets out on paper towels to collect the deep fryer's oil.

"Are you sure you're okay with this?" Dev asked as Mandy left.

"No, Dev," Mary said with a tight smile, not looking at him. "But I think I need to be." She hesitated and then continued. "I'll be okay with it. I just have to accept that I'm among friends and..."

Dev caught her hand and squeezed it. "That ye are, lass," he said softly, and watched her until she looked at him. "That ye are."

-¤-

Mandy held her plate out, waiting for Chief Delany to realize she was there.

"Well, well, Miss O'Brien. Back for seconds—or is this thirds?" Chief Delany asked with a chuckle.

"Fourths," Mandy said. "I wait all month for this day to come around, and I want to make the most of it."

Chief Delany slid two more fillets onto her plate. "You know you can fix catfish at home and not have to wait all month."

"I know." Mandy smiled. "But we don't have a deep fryer and they don't come out the same in a skillet. Thanks, Chief. Do you have any more coleslaw left?"

Chief Delany pointed to the large tub on the next table. "Help yourself, missy. Just don't eat so much you can't sleep tonight."

"I won't," Mandy said, and giggled. "Went for a long hike today to work up an appetite just for tonight. Thanks, Chief." And Mandy turned to the side table, the coleslaw, and another cup of punch. She saw some friends from her class and went by their table to visit on her way back to her father and Mary.

-¤-

"Where does she put it all, Dev?" Mary asked. Her concerns over the picture seemed to have disappeared, at least for the moment, as she watched Mandy hurry to the table where the chief was laying out the fish fillets. "That's her fourth time and she hasn't an ounce of fat on her anywhere."

"She's a lot like her mother in that way," Dev said, and smiled at a thought. "A very high metabolism. I think she burns energy off just thinkin'." He chuckled. "She seldom stops unless she's asleep or extremely tired, but when she does run out, it's like a light switch."

"She is a wonderful girl," Mary said, and smiled in Mandy's direction. "I was concerned about taking her on our hike today, but she convinced me she could handle it." Mary giggled softly. "And she did, sometimes hurrying me along behind her."

"Thanks. I think so too," Dev said, his smile fading slightly. "I almost lost her too, ya know."

Mary shook her head. "No, I didn't know."

Dev looked at Mary and held her eyes, forcing himself to not feel sad. "I know you've heard that we lost my wife, Mandy's mum, in an accident. Everyone in town knows and has talked about it, so I know ya know. She was with her mum, that day," Dev said softly, glancing across the crowded driveway to be sure he knew where Mandy was. "Anne was taking her folks to a doctor's appointment just after lunch, and Mandy was in the back with her gran. On a highway overpass, one of those undivided ones, a big truck—a tractor-trailer rig— veered across the center markers into their lane. Anne's was the first of nine cars to collide with the rig."

"Oh, Dev," Mary said, and covered his hand with hers before she realized she had. "How awful."

Dev nodded. "That it was, lass. My brigade—remember Mandy tol' ya I was a fireman—well, we had just finished knockin' down a small house fire in Southfield, a few miles away, when we received the call to assist with an accident in Royal Oaks."

Mary looked at his distant expression, suddenly remembering that Mandy had mentioned they were from Brighton. They were nearly neighbors.

"I had a strange feelin' but didn't know what had happened until after we got on site and started pullin' the mess of cars apart. We found Anne's car under the nine-car pile, wedged partway under the rig's overturned tractor. I didn't remember hearin' the banshee's wail until that moment, and I'm still not sure if it was just me rememberin' or if she was wailin' with me after that." He took a deep breath. "They were all dead except for Mandy, and she spent more than a month in the hospital findin' her way back to me."

"I'm so sorry, Dev," Mary said softly. "I don't know what to say."

"It was tough, Mary," Dev continued, keeping an eye on Mandy, comforted by knowing where she was. "As you can imagine. Once she was home, we tried to make things right, but it wasn't. Never would be again. My three older sisters doted over her so much that she became confused as to who she was supposed to listen to, who was to guide her, and I felt I was losing what little I'd gotten back."

"How old was she?"

"Five when the accident happened," Dev said. "She was going to start the first grade, but with the accident, her hospital stay and lengthy rehab, I started her late. I homeschooled her the best I could. But the following summer, things hadn't gotten any better and I decided we had to have some space, separation from my family. They meant the best for us, but it was us—we weren't handling it very well. I was still havin' trouble doin' my day job and worryin' about her, so Mandy and I talked it over, decided, and I packed us up, gathered all that mattered to us, and came here, where we could start new, grow, and learn to love and support each other." He sighed. "I think maybe her brush with death might be the reason she looks at everything in life the way she does. She wants to taste everything and touch and feel everything. If it's good, she wants all she can get."

"Like catfish?" Mary asked softly with a smile in her eyes.

"Yeah, like catfish." He looked up and held Mary's eyes for a very long moment, and finally Mary withdrew her hand, still looking back at him.

"My dad used to say," Mary said with a sigh, "we should drink in every moment because we don't know how many we have been given. I can't discuss it, Dev, but I know some of what you've been through."

"Aye," Dev said softly, and looked down at her withdrawn hand.

She watched as he took it again and held it between his hands and smiled.

"I can see it in yer eyes and in yer manner, lass," he said, and she started to say something but he held up one hand before she did. "You don't need to defend yourself or explain anythin' that you don't want to or shouldn't. I'm here if you ever do want to. I can keep secrets, though you don't know that. And I am a loyal friend, but you don't know that either. You can trust me, if and when you feel like you want to. Take your time, lass. Let the sun shine on your face and show you the happinesses and kindnesses you deserve. Then, if you want, you can tell me anythin' you want to."

He held her eyes, seeing her emotions flicker through them, but he knew she wasn't nearly ready to explain herself. She was still watching when he smiled and gently placed her hand on the table, taking his back. He turned to see Mandy still talking with a girlfriend from school, her plate nearly empty, again. He smiled and gestured so Mary could follow his gaze.

"She'll sleep tonight, that's fer sure," he said with a chuckle. "Good thin' it isn't a school night, 'cause I think she might miss church in the mornin'."

Mary giggled with him as he stood up and collected their paper plates, plasticware, and cups.

"Would you like somethin' more to drink?"

"No. I think I'm fine, Dev." She smiled and he disposed of the trash.

Mandy was back and dropped her trash in the barrel before he got back to the table and Mary. Mandy yawned a huge yawn and quickly covered her mouth. "Sorry, Da. I think I'm done."

"So I see, lass," he said, and offered Mary his hand to help her up. He looked at her and said, "Looks like this one's about reached the end of her today. I need to get her back home before the lights go out. Interested in company walkin' back to yer place?"

Mary stood up, taking his hand, and the three of them walked back west along Main; Dev walked in the middle.

Nine

Mary went inside and around the downstairs rooms of her house after Dev and a very tired Mandy said goodnight at the foot of her front walk. Like she had every night since she arrived in Roosevelt, she checked the windows and doors, making certain they were closed and locked.

Mary opened her refrigerator, took out a bottle of chardonnay, and filled a water glass from the cabinet beside the kitchen window. With the bottle back in the refrigerator, Mary switched the lights off and took her glass up to her bedroom.

She laughed softly as she picked up the thrown towel and hung her unused choices of clothes in her closet. She realized as she changed into her skimpy pajamas that in her rush, she had forgotten to wrap her chest and torso when she dressed. Glancing at herself in her mirror, she knew why Dev had looked at her like he did. Her smile widened as her cheeks warmed; he obviously liked how she really looked.

Mary settled into the cushioned chair beside her nightstand and slowly looked around the room, wondering what Dev and Mandy's home was like. She remembered he said they had brought what they needed from their previous home in...in...she faltered and slowly remembered he had mentioned a fire in Southfield and the accident that killed his wife and her parents was in...Royal Oaks. She blinked and stared at her glass; the only Southfield and Royal Oaks she knew of were in the northwest Detroit area.

She had lived in Ann Arbor and he said he had worked near Southfield or Royal Oaks. He had confirmed that they came from nearly the same part of the country; they had been neighbors in her previous life. *How odd*, she thought, but quickly reminded herself that she could not tell him she was from there. *Damn!* She slapped the arm of the chair, and its strangeness again caught her attention.

It was new to her, not hers from her previous life. She couldn't bring their furniture or any of their personal possessions when she was whisked up and away. She understood that he was dead and would never be coming back, but tears still filled her eyes when she looked around at the strange things in her "home." Nothing except a few clothes from before; everything else was new or used so she would have the presence and the appearance of some past personal history. Even the clothes she wore to school were new-to-her and tailored differently than she liked, to give her a more authoritative, less feminine appearance.

At least the furnishings were modern—more to her liking than the furniture she saw in most of the older available Roosevelt homes. She thought of the pictures she had seen when the "program" was searching for the right property.

But she wasn't certain she liked any of it. Without her husband's criticisms—veiled in witty comments—on her choices and thoughts, she could not tell if she was choosing right. She had let him be her compass in almost everything, and now, in the years he had been gone, she had to accept her own ideas as good enough. Sometimes that was as frightening as the thoughts of being discovered.

She had people skills, not creative skills. But she was not allowed to use either of them, told to keep a low profile; get to know her surroundings, the people she would have to deal with, but do not get too close.

Damn! she thought again. *I'm being treated like this is someone's mission. But this is not a mission! It is my horrible, stinking LIFE!*

She caught herself and refrained from throwing her glass of wine. She took another long sip and remembered Ms. White, the woman that visited twice every month. The woman that kept reminding her that she could never go back.

Suddenly an urge replaced the morbid concerns, and she got up to use the bathroom, absently trying to remember what Dev had called it.

Afterwards, she made the trip downstairs, refilled her glass, and returned to the security of her bedroom. She tried to remember more of the details of the day she had just had—a great day by all standards—but her mind would not settle down, and she flitted from one thought to another like a moth from flame to flame. *Can I get burned?* she absently wondered, forgetting her memories of the day and thinking about herself as the moth.

Mary finished her wine, feeling its buzz, and was happy to stop thinking. She switched the nightstand light off and slipped under the covers. She pulled her extra pillow up in front of her and wondered if there really could be happiness after so much sorrow. Was Dev someone she could trust and be happy with? She fell asleep pondering that thought.

Saturday, September 2

"Hey, how are the hikers?" Dev greeted. He was loading the last of the trimmings into his old trailer when Mandy and Mary came around the house from the trail down the hillside.

"Doin' good, Da," Mandy hollered back, and waved. Mary waved with a smile as she led Mandy into the house through the front door.

Dev straightened and inhaled the sight of the girls. He smiled and combed his hair back with his fingers, certain that Mary looked better today than she had in the past. At least she was smiling when he was around, and he figured he would count that as a bit of a win.

When he had finished loading his trailer, he stepped up on the porch and knocked.

"Hey, Dev," Mary said when she opened the door. "You could've just come in."

He smiled but knew he wasn't on that level of familiarity with her yet. "I noticed you're back early, and I—"

"Yes, a little," she said. "A rain shower is blowing in from the southwest. Shale up there gets slick with the rain, so we headed back."

"Aah, I see. I was wonderin' if I could take you out for a bite of lunch," he said, slowly taking in the beautiful look of her standing there in her hiking gear. "Since you're back early."

"No. Can't, Dev," Mary said, wiping her hand on the towel she held before she looked up at him again.

Dev knew his disappointment must have shown.

"Sorry. I didn't mean it to sound that way. I have class planning that I have to work on this weekend, and I have to turn my syllabus plans in on Tuesday."

"I see," he said, and took a step back.

"Could we, maybe, do a light dinner tonight instead?" Mary asked. "I'll need a bit of a break by then."

"Sure, sure," Dev said, and his smile slowly grew. "I'd like that. Say six thirty? We could go down to the Pines, if you'd rather not go to Stumpy's again."

"That would be nice, Dev," Mary said, and smiled.

"Thank you." He looked back at her as he stepped down off the porch. "I'll run the trash out to the dump and you can send Mandy home whenever you're tired of her company. I'll be back to the house in half, three quarters of an hour. Just so she knows."

Mary waved to him and closed the door.

-¤-

"Your father says he's going out to the dump," Mary said as she closed the door. She pushed the curtain aside and watched him as he checked the ropes on the trailer, stopped at the hitch, and then got into the cab and closed the door.

She snapped back and dropped the curtain when he started to pull away and glanced back at the front door. She turned and walked back to the kitchen, where Mandy was nibbling on a cookie from the plate she had set on the table.

"Your father seems like a very determined person," Mary said absently as she took the chair next to Mandy.

"How so?" Mandy asked, and sipped the glass of milk Mary had poured for her.

"Like him doing my yard," Mary said softly, and smiled, "even when I told him not to, that I didn't want him to." Mary studied the front door from their end of the long hall.

"And?" Mandy asked as she watched Mary's detachment.

"And he asked me to join you two to eat again," she said. "I don't know why, but I think I'm glad he asked."

"When?" Mandy asked softly.

"Tonight," Mary said, and remembered she was talking to Mandy. She returned from her thoughts and smiled at her. "He asked me to join you for lunch, but I can't. I have to do my classroom planning today and over the weekend."

"Classroom planning?"

"Yes," Mary said, and took a bite of her cookie. "I have to write down what I'm going to teach you and the rest of the class in the next nine weeks. Then nine weeks from now, I get to plan the next nine weeks."

"Sounds like work." Mandy giggled and finished her cookie. "So, did you accept? Are you going to go out with us again?"

"Six thirty tonight," Mary said with a smile. "We're going to grab something at the Pines and then I'll have to get back to my planning."

"Good," Mandy said, and picked up another cookie.

Ten

"Brenna," Henry called from the front foyer of his mother's home. "Come look. We have a letter from little Mandy," he continued as Brenna, their oldest sister, came down the stairs from their mother's room.

"A letter?" Brenna asked, and turned the envelope so she could see the front. "Well? Are ye goin' to open it or frame it?"

Henry smiled and tore the top open. He pulled the folded sheets out and realized there was a picture slipped in the fold.

"Well, well," Brenna said softly as she looked at the image of a smiling Mandy between Dev and the bright, smiling face of a pretty woman who had brunette hair with golden highlights. "I see Mandy was right."

"Yes, you could tell Dev was a little put off by Mandy spillin' the beans," Henry chuckled.

"Suppose it's serious?"

"Now, now, Brenna," Henry said, still smiling. "Let's see what Mandy has to say."

Henry unfolded the sheets, and together they read the handwritten message explaining what had been happening since Dev had met Mary at school. "...and her name is Mary Gorden. I'm not supposed to give anyone Mary's picture since she only let me take it just so I can have it by my bed."

Henry raised his eyebrows and looked at Brenna. "She wanted this Mary's picture to keep by her bed? Must be serious to someone."

He turned back to the letter. "So please don't tell anyone you have this, but I wanted you to see how pretty she is. I like her a lot and Da seems to too. Mary's very nice and..."

Henry and Brenna read on as Mandy explained that Mary was her teacher at school, that she had invited Mandy to go hiking with

77

her a number of times, and that the picture was taken on catfish night, last Saturday of the month at the volunteer firehouse.

"Is Dev volunteerin' as a fireman?" Brenna asked Henry, obviously not expecting an answer. "I thought he said never again."

Henry nodded. "Two years ago I think—spring of their second year there. He said the risks were low and he has a sitter available if he gets called at the odd hours. Seems to be helping keep him grounded."

"Will wonders never cease," Brenna said. "Do the others know?"

"Nah. He wanted to keep it quiet, sayin' it wasn't a big deal," Henry chuckled. "And he likes his job at the grocery, stocking shelves and makin' deliveries. He says it lets him have time when Mandy is out of school."

"Bless the man for his concern for Mandy and his takin' care of her. I know it hasn't been easy for him," Brenna said as she walked into the living room and took a small picture frame from the mantel. "Here, see if it's the right size."

Henry held the picture in front of the frame and smiled. "I guess old Aunt Julia will have to go," he said as Brenna unfastened the back.

"We have the larger one upstairs," Brenna said, and slipped Mandy's picture in front of the ancient picture of their grandmother's sister, "so no one can say she isn't properly represented in the family pictures." She set the frame back on the mantel. "Now we'll see how long it takes for the others to notice."

"Aye," Henry chuckled. "That way we're not tellin' anyone we have it."

Monday, September 4
Labor Day

"Mum? What're ya doin'?" Derry asked as she turned at the sound of her mother coming down the stairs.

"What's it look like I'm doin'?" her mother, Maeve, asked in reply. "'Tis time I come down and help with the fixin's."

"Are ye sure?" Derry asked as Moira and Brenna came in from the dining room.

"Mum?" Moira repeated in surprise.

"Don't fuss so," Maeve said. "I've let m'self worry too long and so it's time. Everythin's fine." Then she looked at Brenna. "Did ya get the fresh green beans like I asked ya?"

"Sure," Brenna said, still trying to accept that her mum was up and getting around, after being so ill and staying sequestered in her room for most of the summer. "Nearly three quarters of a bushel from the farmer's market this mornin.'"

"Where's Henry?" she asked, looking around the staircase toward the dining room and kitchen.

"Here, Mum," he said loudly as he hurried from the family room behind the living room. "I'm here."

"Out in the shed, out back," Maeve said. "Get the girls the two big colanders that're hangin' on the back wall. They'll need them fer washin' the beans and potatoes."

"Yes'm. I'm on my way," he said, and headed for the back door.

Maeve turned to the living room and slowly walked around the room, as if inspecting it before company.

"We've tried to keep it clean fer ya, Mum," Derry said as she followed her around the room.

"You've done very well," Maeve said, and smiled at her daughter. "You've all done very well, keepin' me place nice with me forsakin' my duties."

"You've not been forsakin' anything," Moira said sharply. "You've been ailing and we've just watched over you."

"Thank you, dear, but I should've been back to the doin' long before now," Maeve said, catching Moira's chin with the curl of her finger.

Absently, Maeve started straightening the pictures on the mantle, stopping suddenly at the new one in the back row.

"What's this?" she asked, and held the picture and frame up for them to see. "This one of Devlin and Mandy in me aunt's picture frame? Who's the woman with them?"

"Mandy says that's her schoolteacher," Brenna said quietly. "She also said she thinks Dev's a little sweet on her, but won't admit it."

Maeve studied the picture closely. "She seems to be happy in the moment, and both Devlin and Mandy look very happy." Then Maeve looked at Brenna with her head cocked to one side.

"Mandy says she wasn't supposed to tell anyone and we're not supposed to tell anyone we have the picture," Brenna explained. "She coaxed them into having it taken at a fish fry they have at the firehouse there, and said it was supposed to just be so she could have it beside her bed."

"Beside her bed?" Maeve asked, as if she had not heard her right.

Brenna nodded. "That's what her letter said. But she wanted us to see her, even though we haven't met her yet. Her name's Mary Gorden—been there over two years now, according to Mandy."

"Maybe them movin' was a good thing," Maeve said, and looked at the girls. "I never saw Devlin look this happy in all of his years he was livin' here. I dare say, forgive me for sayin' it, but not even when he was married and Anne was alive."

-◻-

Henry stepped out onto the back porch and skipped down the steps, very pleased to see his mum up and willing to come down and be a part of the day. It was a good time, with the girls there and later their families coming: Moira's husband Carl and their two boys, Carlin and Ferris, Derry's husband Will and their two twin girls, Kiera and Keena, and Brenna's husband Merril and their boys Oran, Quinn, and Riley. He smiled as he crossed the yard, feeling it would be a good day, even if Dev and Mandy weren't there.

He was hoping they were having a good day also when he reached the shed at the back of the yard and pulled the keys from his pocket. He grabbed the padlock and froze; the hasp was cut, rendering the lock useless and the door unlockable.

He inhaled and studied the door for a minute, noting that it was closed and the hasp aligned so its nature would not be noticed from the yard or from any distance. He braced himself for what he might see, stood to the side of the door, and pushed it open.

Suddenly he was both relieved and angry. The shed was unoccupied, the stored items rearranged but generally unharmed. The center of the floor had been cleared and a rumpled sleeping bag spread over the cleared area. He clenched his fist, certain he knew who had been hiding there.

Henry collected the colanders, picked up the sleeping bag, and stepped back outside, closing the door behind him. He would get Carl, Will, or Merril to help him secure the door later. And with that, he turned back to the house and decided he would call the sergeant down at the precinct and let them confirm his suspicion of who's been sleepin' in his shed.

Tuesday, September 5

"Thanks for calling, Henry," the Brighton police detective said as he took the sleeping bag from Henry and a patrolman held a large plastic bag for him to deposit it into. When the patrolman folded the top of the plastic bag and attached the seal, the detective turned back to Henry. He held out a business card and Henry took it.

"My suspicion," Henry said, "like I told the sergeant when I called, is that my cousin Einri has been hiding out here. As I explained over the phone, he came around here a few weeks ago looking for a place, and I told him I would not hide him and neither would my mum."

"You talked to him face to face?" the detective asked, surprised.

"That's right, Detective, aaah"—Henry looked at the card again—"Williams. Right, Detective Williams. And I told him if he came around again, I'd call the precinct, you guys."

"I'm surprised he was civil with you," Detective Williams said.

"His da, Gallagher, was me da, Finnian's, brother," Henry said. "I was a little surprised too, but I suspected he was somewhere nearby layin' low."

"Okay. Have you looked to see if anything is missing?" the detective asked.

Henry shook his head. "Some, but we had family here yesterday and I didn't take the time to look closely. Derry's husband helped me replace the hasp and lock, and that's the only time we spent out here."

Henry took the key out of his pocket when they got to the shed. He unlocked the hasp and pushed the door open for the detective and his men to look inside.

"It's only ten by twelve, but it would be better if the door faced the house," Henry said as the detective stepped back to let his two patrolmen look around inside.

After a few minutes, one of the patrolmen picked up a small wooden keepsake box about the size of a cigar box.

"Is this yours?" the patrolman asked as he extended his arm and held the box for Henry to see.

"Could be Mum's," Henry said, "but I don't recognize it."

The patrolman carefully opened the box as they all watched; it was filled with old photographs of people, most with a black ink X over the person or people in the picture.

"Strange," the detective said as the patrolman sifted deeper into the box, "being marked with an X."

"Looks like someone was checking them off of a list or something," Henry said absently. "May help if you can identify a few of them."

The detective nodded. "I think we'll do just that. If your hunch is right and Einri has been staying here, maybe he left this by mistake. Maybe he heard something and had to leave quickly, leaving it behind. We'll see what we can. When the lab boys have finished with these, I'll get back with you. Maybe there's someone in here that you'll recognize."

"I doubt it, but sure, sure. I'll be here."

The patrolmen and the detective spent nearly two hours checking the shed, looking for fingerprints or anything that might help them identify the transient occupant. Finally they exhausted their efforts and stopped, bid Henry a good day, and told him they would let him know what they found when the lab tests came back.

"Thanks, Detective," Henry said, and went back inside to explain to his mum, Brenna, and Derry what they had found and told him.

Eleven
Thursday, September 7

It was the beginning of the morning recess and Mandy followed Miss Gorden out of the classroom. She was heading for the playground and Mary was going to pick up some colored paper in the office, but as they reached the door, the principal, Mrs. Arnold, called, "Cali, er sorry, Mary. California's what I was thinking about, and I was wondering if you'd ever been there."

Mary froze in place and Mandy bumped her from behind as she stopped unexpectedly.

"Sorry," Mrs. Arnold said. "I was thinking about something and was wondering if I may see you for a minute?"

"Sure, sure," Mary said, and turned to see who had bumped her. "Oh, Mandy. Would you be a sweetheart and get these colored papers from Mrs. Pruit in the supply room? I need to speak with Mrs. Arnold."

"Yes ma'am," Mandy said brightly and took the list from Mary. She followed Mary and Mrs. Arnold until they stopped in the school office. Mandy noticed Mrs. Arnold placed the folder she had been carrying into the secretary's in-basket, and then the two of them went into Mrs. Arnold's office and closed the door.

Filled with curiosity by Mrs. Arnold's comment in the hallway, Mandy looked over the half wall at the folder in the basket, on top of all of the others. The name *Mary Gorden* was typed on the label on the tab, but there was a pink and a yellow sticky note on the front. On the pink one someone had written "Refile" and on the yellow one, "Cali Marrow."

Mandy stared at the note for a long minute, then glanced around the room, wondering if she dared peek inside. But voices coming from the hallway, flowing into the office through the open door, were getting louder and she quickly went on to find Mrs. Pruit and get the colored paper she had been asked to get.

Saturday, September 9

The thunder clap woke Mandy with a start and her heart instantly sank; she was supposed to go hiking with Mary again, but they couldn't if it was raining. The trails would be too slick and many of the washes would be flowing streams. She rolled over and pulled her covers over her head.

"Get up, sleepyhead," her father said as he left the bathroom and started down the stairs.

"But Da! It's raining!"

"Come on anyway," he said from the bottom of the stairs. "I'm goin' ta fix chocolate and strawberry pancakes. I need me sous chef."

"Bacon or sausage?" she asked through the covers.

"Bacon."

She threw the covers off and sprinted to the bathroom.

-¤-

"Tell ya what, love," Dev said softly as Mandy finished her third and fourth plate-sized pancakes, stacked with butter between and their own special-to-them homemade maple-raspberry syrup over the top. "Since it's a rainy day and I know you had your heart set on spendin' some time with Mary, why don't we put on a roast—ya know, boiled potatoes, gravy, carrots, onions and the likes—and you go and invite her for dinner?"

"'Round five?"

"'Round five would be gran'," Dev said with a wide smile. "And be sure she knows we'll not be takin' a 'no' fer an answer. Maybe she's a card player and she can beat ya at rummy."

"Hah! No way, Da," Mandy said, accepting the challenge as she stuffed the last strip of bacon into her mouth.

¤-¤-¤-¤-¤

"That meal was unbelievably good, Dev, Mandy," Mary said as

she finished the last of her roast and cleaned her plate, a quick swipe with her biscuit to catch the last of the gravy. "Thank you."

"I'm very glad you liked it," Dev said, and smiled at Mandy. "This one worked hard on the vegetables and the biscuits."

Mary smiled at Mandy. "I knew she must have had a hand in it somewhere. Too good to just be a man's cooking."

"Now wait a minute—" Dev started, but Mary and Mandy's giggles interrupted him.

"Thank you, Dev," Mary said, and smiled at him sincerely. "Now I know you have a little pride and some spirit in you somewhere. Nice to know."

"And why would ya think I haven't any pride?" Dev asked, and cocked his head. "I'm very proud of my daughter, the home we have fixed for each other, and for puttin' in an honest day's effort for an honest day's wages."

"Those things are good and basic," Mary said softly. A cloud somewhere behind her eyes hid the previous moment's gleam, but only for a second. "A man should be proud of who he is, what he stands for, not just what he has." She looked at him and smiled again. "It's called integrity, Mr. O'Brien, and I think your heart is full of it and your pockets have caught all that spills over. Your daughter has a fine example to learn from."

"Thank you, lass," he said, and smiled at Mandy. "That's a very nice thing to say to an old feller barely able to keep up with his precocious ten-year-old daughter."

"Whatcha mean old, Da?" she said, and winked at Mary. "Actually, he is. He'll be *thirty*-two end of the month." She stressed the "thirty."

Mary feigned dismay, covering her mouth at Mandy's disclosure. "Oh my! No! That's really old."

She and Mandy giggled again.

"Okay, okay, you two," he said, and began gathering plates. "Who's in the mood for a slice of Gran's famous peach pie?"

"Peach?" Mary asked in surprise. "Canned?"

"Now, now, lass," he smiled. "I'll not be givin' away me secrets 'til after ya try some. If it's not to yer likin', I'll give ya double yer money back."

Mary giggled again; double nothing was still nothing. "Can I help?"

"I've got it, but thanks," he said, and carried the stack of plates into the kitchen.

Mary took the moment to slowly look around the living room, clearly visible past the front door and the stairs. "I'm surprised your furniture isn't more modern," Mary said absently as she looked at the style and wall colors.

"I don't remember much of before," Mandy said, following Mary's gaze. "But I do remember some of our conversations when we decided to move. Da didn't want to be a fireman anymore and we both felt something was wrong. He's told me since that he had a hard time leaving me when he had to work, and especially when they had a bad fire."

Mary sobered at Mandy's tone and turned to watch her.

"Da said we talked about bringing our things, but he said I was the one that thought we should buy new, different, since our lives were going to be different."

"Sorry, Mandy," Mary said, and covered Mandy's nearest hand with hers. "I didn't mean—"

"It's okay, Mary," Mandy said, and smiled up at her. "I don't remember Mum except in pictures. We kept one large album for the future and we decided to start and make a new one once we got here." Mandy nodded and glanced at the table. "Da's taken so many pictures we'll soon have to start a second album."

"I'm glad," Mary said. "Something I should think about doing too."

"Do you have pictures of your family?" Mandy asked, instantly contrite when Mary's expression faded and turned somber. "Sorry, Mary. I shouldn't have asked."

"No, Mandy. It's all right. I don't have any pictures. Everything's gone. I'm all that's left, and I need to follow your example and make the best of what I do have." She smiled at Mandy and squeezed her hand as Dev returned with two plates, each with a slice of warm peach pie and a scoop of vanilla ice cream on the side.

"Looks good, Da," Mandy said, and Mary was certain Mandy was trying to change the subject and lighten the mood. Dev went back to the kitchen to get the third plate.

-¤-

"Mandy told me you accepted her challenge at cards," Dev said when they were finished eating.

Mandy collected the pie plates and took them to the kitchen, rinsed them, and stacked them in the dishwasher before she returned.

"She asked if I would play with her, implying that she held some sort of a record in rummy wins," Mary said, and cocked her head at him.

"She has been on a bit of a winning streak lately. 'Tis true," Dev said, and nodded.

"Oh really?" Mary asked, and glanced at Mandy as she finished clearing the table, carrying the last items to the kitchen, putting the butter dish, the condiments, and the biscuit basket away. "How many wins in a row?"

"I've lost count," Dev said, and smiled a wicked smile. "It took her a couple of years to get the game down, but..."

Mary smiled at him and glanced over her shoulder at the kitchen doorway. "And I suppose she's been winning for a long time."

Dev nodded. "Started July before last..."

Mary's eyes widened. "July...before last..."

Dev nodded again.

"You don't play very often?"

"About three nights a week, unless she has too much homework," he said. "And weekends. Most nights in the summer."

"I think you're embellishing just a bit," she said as Mandy sat down at the table again. She looked at Mandy and asked, "When was the last time you lost at rummy?"

Mandy shrugged. "Last summer sometime."

"I see. Do you play with just your dad?"

"No. I play with him and the men at the firehouse, including Chief Delany."

"Are they any good?"

"Mmm, yeah. But not good enough," Mandy said matter-of-factly. "I don't like to sound boastful. Da says it isn't right to boast about how good you are because there'll always be someone better down the road, sometime."

"Very good advice," Mary said.

"Are you still game?" Mandy asked.

"I'll give it a try, young lady," Mary said, and looked at Dev as Mandy took the cards from the bureau drawer behind her.

She handed them to Mary. "Please be sure they are all there, including the jokers."

Mary looked at Dev with her eyes wide and a thin smile in an "I don't believe it" expression. "Are you playing, Dev?"

He shook his head. "Not tonight, lass. I'd rather not expose me poor wits to the superior and beguilin' ways of a fine and educated woman."

"Beguiling?" Mary asked with eyebrows raised again.

"Aye, lass," he smiled. "'Tis true. I'd not be keepin' me eyes on me cards, definitely givin' you the upper hand."

Mandy giggled as Mary tried to count the cards.

"Well, I'm not a fine woman and only educated enough to do what I need to do. Does Mandy beguile you also?" Mary asked, her expression sober as she concentrated.

"More often than not," he admitted, smiling as he thought about how differently Mary affected him. He winked at Mandy. "She surely does. Mostly every day."

Twelve

"Boy, she does have a switch," Mary said as Dev picked a limp Mandy up from her chair and cradled her in his arms. "One minute she playing cards like there's no tomorrow, then a huge yawn and she's out."

"Yup," Dev said as he started up the stairs. "'Tis the way it happens."

"Mind if I follow?"

"Nope. She won't mind either," he said as they climbed the narrow staircase. "She keeps an unusually clean and orderly room."

Dev turned to open her bedroom door, but Mary reached under his arm and turned the knob.

"Thanks, lass."

Dev carried Mandy to her bed and Mary pulled the sheet and light blanket back for her. He laid her in place and started undoing her shoelaces.

"May I help with her shirt?" Mary asked and began unfastening the buttons when he nodded.

"I'll let her sleep in her undershirt," he said as he set her shoes next to the closet door a short distance from her bed. Then he turned and slipped her jeans off and Mary spread the covers over her.

"I put her pajamas here on the foot," he said as he did. "That way if she gets cold or needs the loo in the night, she'll know where they are if she wants them."

He bent and kissed her cheek and noticed Mary had picked up the picture of the three of them. She was looking at it as he stood.

"It's a very nice one, if you ask me," he said with a nod.

Mary set the picture back on the nightstand. "It came out very nice, I agree."

Dev reached for the nightstand light, but Mandy rolled over, eyes barely open. "Mary?"

"Yes, dear," Mary said, and leaned close.

"Thank you for coming tonight. It was nice having you here," Mandy whispered. "May the angels watch over you the rest of the night and your morn be bright and sunny."

Mary leaned down and kissed Mandy's cheek. "Thank you. Sleep tight."

Mary crossed around the foot of the bed, and when she reached the door, Dev switched the nightstand light off and followed her out.

At the bottom of the stairs, Dev asked, "Would you like a wine or something and sit out on the porch a little bit?"

Mary looked at her watch, and seeing that it wasn't very late, agreed.

"I have a nice white, a chardonnay I believe, a couple of reds, and I do have an ale or two," he said as he opened the front screen door.

The soft patter of the light rain added to the hush of the evening, the normal gentle noises muted in the lulling sound of the rain in the trees. Dev gestured to one of the two rocking chairs that flanked the small round table between them.

"The chardonnay sounds nice, Dev," she said, and took the rocker on the side away from the door.

"Are you warm enough? I can bring a shawl when I come back," he said.

"Sure. That'd be nice."

Dev went to the kitchen, found a wine glass, and poured the chardonnay. He got himself a Smithwick, picked up a shawl off the living room sofa, and was back out on the porch in a matter of minutes.

He handed Mary the wine and set his bottle on the table. She leaned forward and he spread the shawl over her shoulders and tucked it behind her.

"Thank you. Does Mandy sit out here with you much?" Mary asked, and sipped her wine as he sat down in the other rocker.

"Sometimes," he said, and opened his bottle. "Usually it's just me after she goes to bed. Thanks for helping with that. I'm sure it meant a lot to her."

Mary smiled. "I've never put a child to bed before."

"As you can see, it doesn't really take much."

"Was she always an easy child to put to bed? I've heard so many mothers talk about how their kids want to stay up and stay up, screaming and hollering if they can't."

"Mandy was an odd one," he admitted, and sipped his ale. "When she was very young, up to about a year, maybe a little more, her days and nights were mixed up. It took a lot to get that straightened out, but once we did—probably more Anne than me gettin' her there— she settled down and into the routine. She was always an early riser, unless it was like today: rain. She feels the rain keeps her from doing things."

"How about the winters?" Mary asked, then continued carefully. "From what you said the other night, I gather you've lived where winters can be cold and snowy."

"She handles that fine," Dev said, and shook his head. "The cold, the snow, the wind. I haven't figured out what it is about the rain that makes it different."

"Could be all of your Irish blessings," Mary said, "talking about always having the sun in your face and your days being sunny and bright."

"You could have something there, lass. I'll study on that a bit."

Mary giggled. "I'm sure you will. You don't seem to take anything lightly when it comes to Mandy."

"'Tis true. If anythin' happened to her—"

"It won't, Dev," Mary said, sharper than she meant to sound. Then softly, she continued. "Nothing's going to happen to her. She has you watching out for her, a whole town that watches out for her, and now, maybe I can help watch out for her too. I know you worry, you have to, but others care too, and can help."

"Thanks, lass. That's very nice of you." He took another sip and smiled at her.

"You're welcome, Dev. I mean it." She smiled in return and sipped her wine again. She watched the quiet street for a moment longer. "So you think I have beguiling ways? Is there something there you want to talk about?"

"I only said that because it's true, lass," he said, and looked at the street also. "It's me own feelin's that are at work here, not yours, and nothin' for you to worry about. I don't want to make you feel uncomfortable in any way but for you to know you're welcome anytime with no obligations or favors to return."

"Why do you say it's just your feelings?"

"Mary," he said, and turned slightly in his chair, rocking slowly. "I know it's obvious that Mandy and I like your company, and I hope it won't cause any troubles with you at the school, visitin' the parent of one of your students often. But I know you have things going on in your world that are none of mine nor Mandy's business, and I don't want you to feel like I'm—we're—intruding on your privacy or space. I've wanted to get to know you and to help you since the day you first came to town, but I don't want to make you feel uncomfortable. But fer my feelin's, I just have no choice, ya see. You have beguiled me with your ways, lass. I can't get ye outta me head."

"I see..."

"Maybe ya do"—he smiled—"and maybe ya don't. Time will tell, Mary, but I do not want you to feel like I'm pressurin' you one way or another in anythin'. You have to live your life the way you see appropriate. But please know that I'm here, willin' to help if you need me for any reason, at any time—even in the wee hours if you have a need. I'm certain Mandy feels the same way."

"That's nice to know." She turned in her seat, a little more toward him. "I think you've beguiled me a little also. Probably not the right word; 'beguile' is thought of as what a woman does to a man, and often implies that there is an ulterior motive in there somewhere."

"Well...I'll not perjure m'self by sayin' I haven't had thoughts about you, Mary Gorden." He smiled and held her eyes. "Though my motives are not ulterior. They are as honest and genuine as they can be, but I will admit that seeing you that morning last August—you in your pajamas, yelling at me the way you were—well that started me thinkin' of things I hadn't thought of in many, many years—"

"Dev! Really," Mary said loudly. "I'd forgotten about that. Oh dear! What you must've thought—"

"I thought I'd died and gone to heaven, lass," he said softly, and looked back at the street. "You weren't like you were when I saw you in the store or when you were walkin' along the streets. You weren't afraid. You were full of fire and determination! You were alive! And it caught me by surprise."

"Yeah, and that I was almost naked!"

"Nah," he said softly. "You were covered and not inappropriate under the circumstances, but I saw yer spirit and I liked that very much. After that, I knew it was there and just needed a little friendly coaxing. And all right, I admit the pajamas made me think some things I have no right to talk about. I've told no one 'ceptin' yerself just now. Was my private secret. But I liked seein' you like that too, lass."

"Are you always so direct, Dev O'Brien?" Mary asked, looking at him.

"Probably too direct," he admitted. "After the accident, I realized how short life can be, and I feel it's important to tell people the important things when the opportunity comes. If we wait, there might not be another chance."

Mary studied her glass for a few minutes and then finished her wine in a couple of long sips.

"Dev, I think I need to go home and think about what you've said. There are so many things about you that I like as well, but I don't know if I can...even think about giving you anything like I'm sure you want. I don't even know how to say what I'm trying to say. You've shown me kindnesses beyond what I could have possibly expected— more than I can possibly deserve after the way I've treated you since I came here, hiding in my house, hoping the world would go away and forget me. What can I possibly say or do that makes any of that right? I—"

"There's nothin' for you to say or do, lass. That's all behind you and behind me. It doesn't count anymore unless there's a reason lingering in the past. Of course, I've come bumbling in like a bull in me mum's dinin' room, and I know I don't say the thin's most women want to hear—at least not the way I say them—so I understand. And don't ye be worryin' about it. Frettin' will get ya nowhere, so don't be makin' it more difficult than it is. I'm just your friend, unless you decide you don't want me to be. I like your company, but if you wish to not spend your time with me, that's okay. That's your choice."

"Thanks, Dev," she said, and stood up, handing him the shawl. "Would you get my jacket? Please."

He stepped inside and paused as he picked up her jacket. He wiped his face with the palm of his hand, wishing he could wring his own neck for being too honest, too pushy, and definitely for doing everything too soon. He knew from overhearing her screaming at her company that her life was already in turmoil, and here he was stoking the fire. *Ya can be such a stupid and ungrateful ass sometimes, Mr. Devlin O'Brien,* he said to himself, and inhaled as he turned and pushed the door open.

"Can I walk you home?" he asked.

"No, silly. I don't want you to leave Mandy alone."

He helped her slip her arms into the jacket sleeves and then wrapped the shawl around her shoulders. "The shawl will help keep the chill off yer shoulders while you're walkin'. Sorry about me big mouth—"

"Hush, Dev. And thank you. I just need some time to think." She turned at the edge of the porch as he handed her her umbrella.

She looked up at him and he smiled, realizing how close she was and how nicely she fit, her beautiful upturned face at just the right height. He chided himself when he wondered how her curves would feel if she were—

"It was a very nice evening. The dinner was wonderful and makes me wish I knew how to cook better. Maybe you and Mandy will teach me. Tell Mandy I really enjoyed playing cards, even if she did win every hand. You really were telling me the truth! She does know the game rather well." Mary giggled. "Don't 'I told you so' me. I had to see it to believe it."

Then she rose up on her toes and kissed him, slipping her arms around his waist, pulling herself tight against him for a couple of seconds. She slowly relaxed and set herself back down on her heels, smiling and holding his surprised gaze. "I wanted to see how that would feel and how we would feel together. Next time you'll have to participate so I can get the whole experience." She stepped off the porch onto the step. "Goodnight, Dev. Thank you for being honest with me."

"Goodnight, Mary," Dev said, hardly believing she had kissed him. He waved as she walked quickly to the sidewalk and turned down Lincoln. She waved back.

Thirteen

Sunday, September 10

Mary finally forced her sleep-deprived body out of bed when the morning's sun persistently filled her room. She had tossed and turned all night, the recounted memory of her actions with Dev bouncing around in her head, denying her any form of meaningful sleep.

What were you thinking? she asked herself, and then replied with a girlish giggle that she knew exactly what she was thinking. *How do you think this will actually work out?* she argued, and then the same girl giggled that she did not know.

She rubbed her head and tried to run her fingers through her matted hair as she sat up on the edge of her bed. *You stupid, stupid girl. You have only known the man three weeks,* she told herself. But she smiled and giggled again. *That's not entirely true.*

He has tried to talk to me. Almost every time he's seen me since I first got here. Even when I wouldn't let him, he smiled and was pleasant if I think about it objectively. Even after I yelled and hollered at him for mowing and trimming my yard.

She giggled again; he was persistent—or maybe just a wee bit stubborn.

She pushed herself up and went to her bathroom, took care of the necessities, brushed her teeth, washed her face, turned the shower on, and tried to comb her tangled hair. She absently wondered how tossing and turning at night could tangle her hair as much as it always did. Then she looked closer at her hair and saw the blond roots were beginning to show.

She absently looked in the cabinet beside her sink, but knew she had used the last of the rinse she kept there. She swore and closed the cabinet door, thought about it, and reminded herself it was Sunday and Dev was not working the grocery this morning. Maybe she could get another rinse without running into him. Maybe she ought to get a couple. Then, as she turned to the shower, she smiled; the thought of "running into him" in a different context crossed her mind.

As she bathed, she wondered if he would understand her need to color her hair dark, and as she rinsed the suds off her scarred arm, she wondered if he would still look at her the same way after he saw the long, snaky scar, or the spidery ones on her back. She leaned her head against the shower wall and let the hot water run down her back, warning herself that she could not explain how she came by such hideous disfigurements. She suddenly started to cry.

She had to live in her new life, but she could not tell anyone about her past because she did not have one. She could not tell Dev why she was the way she was, because without a past—the how she got to be this way—she did not exist. She sighed. But if she did not exist, why did it hurt so much to remember, to know the possibility of a new future was just out of reach?

Tears mixed with the shower water and she knew she did not have any answers. Her heart had awakened to forgotten feelings and she wanted more, and like Mandy, she wanted all she could get. But the probabilities of that happening did not look very good.

She forced herself out of the shower, turned the water off, and dried herself, lingering over the thoughts of Dev and what it might have been like to be together.

Monday, September 11

"Have you decided?" Dev asked Mandy as he rinsed their dinner dishes and set them in the dishwasher.

"I don't need a sitter, Da! I'm ten! Nearly ten and a half," Mandy retorted from the dining room.

Dev stepped back into the doorway between the two rooms and looked at Mandy. "I know how you feel, love," he said as gently as he could, "but 'tis me worryin' about you when we're not together and me not bein' there for you."

"I'll be fine, Da," Mandy said, her irritation cooling some. "I have your number and can call if I need anything. Mary's just down the street. I just don't feel like sitting and listening to your meeting tonight." She looked at him and added, "It isn't that I don't like to go with you, but..."

"I know, love," Dev said, and pulled a chair up beside her. He sat down and slipped his arm around her shoulders. "So tell me how ye think we can fix this."

"Would you consider lettin' me go to the library?" Mandy asked. "I can spend my time lookin' for books I might want to read and maybe play on their computer some."

"Hmm," Dev muttered, and rubbed his chin, feigning deep thought. "I don't see why not, love. I just don't want you to be alone or with help too far away. I think the library would be a suitable alternative."

Mandy turned and threw her arms around his waist and hugged him. "Thanks, Da."

"Welcome, love. Now let me finish rinsin' the dishes and we'll be off."

¤-¤-¤-¤-¤

When Mandy reached the library, she went straight to the computer niche and the library's four terminals. Mandy selected one and quickly logged into her school account, thinking specifically about the name she had seen on Mary's folder at school.

She accessed the internet and ran a general search for the name Marrow. As she had expected, there were hundreds and hundreds, and she tried again, looking for Cali Marrow. This time the search results were much smaller, and of those, many were near matches with first names that simply started with the letter C. But there were only two Calis.

Mandy selected the first one and got an obituary of a woman that had died many years before in her late eighties—obviously not the right one.

She tried the second and got a details page on a Cali (Hughes) Marrow, wife of a Robert A. Marrow of Ann Arbor, Michigan.

Mandy smiled, not knowing if this could be the one on Mary's folder, but it was a real person. And it was from near her gran's home. She selected a printout.

Then, following her curiosity, she searched for Cali Hughes and was surprised when she found two again. One was a Georgia Cali Hughes and the second was a Cali Eilís Hughes. Mandy instantly recognized the Irish middle name, absently saying "I-lish" out loud. With a hopeful smile and a heart full of giddy curiosity, she selected that one first.

A details page popped up giving basic information, date of birth, general description, parents' names and limited details, but both parents were listed as deceased. Farther down the page, a checked marriage status box confirmed her marriage to Robert A. Marrow when she was 21 and he was 22. By her date of birth, and confirmed by her marriage date, Mandy figured she would be 28 now. Then Mandy smiled and looked back at the date of birth. She and Cali had the same birthday: June 20.

Mandy selected another printout and then checked the other Cali, seeing by the ages that she could possibly be the mother of the first. She printed it out as well.

She collected her printouts, folded them neatly, and slipped them into her school bag, then began perusing the light reading section of books for children her age, though she tended to drift to the books for older kids. She was scanning a new mystery book the library had just received when her dad stopped beside her, leaned down, and looked over her shoulder at the book.

Mandy looked up and, seeing him, turned and gave him a quick hug. "Hey, Da."

"Hey, yerself, love." He smiled and nodded to the book. "Find anythin' you like?"

"Not really, but this one could be interesting," she said, and slipped it back onto the shelf, careful to put it into the spot she had taken it from. "Just not tonight. You must be finished with your meeting."

"Yes. And you were right. It would've bored you to tears."

He straightened up and together they left the library and headed west up Main.

"Can I tell you something, Da?" she asked as the two of them walked past Stumpy's. "It has to be kept secret."

"Sure, love," he said, wondering about the sudden sense of concern in her voice. "What is it?"

"I'm truly not sure, Da." She studied the dark sidewalk. "Last Thursday, our principal, Mrs. Arnold, caught Mary in the hallway at recess and asked her to come into her office to talk with her."

"Yes, seems like somethin' she might do," he said softly, knowing that was not Mandy's point. "Go on."

"The trouble is..." She looked up and held his eyes. "Da? What if Mary has a different name?"

"What do ya mean, love?" He stopped and squatted down in front of her, catching her hands.

"Mrs. Arnold called her 'Cali' and then corrected herself, making up an excuse that she was thinking about California. Mary froze and I ran into her when she stopped." Mandy wiped a tear from her eye. "Da, I'm sure it's something that concerned Mary, a lot. Maybe even scared her some."

"Aye, and you can't just ask her about it," he said, "can you?"

Mandy shook her head. "That's why I wanted to go to the library." She pulled the sheets out of her school bag. "I looked at the folder Mrs. Arnold had with her when she asked Mary to come and talk with her. Mary sent me to do the errand she was on and I saw Mrs. Arnold put the folder in the basket on the secretary's desk when they went into her office. So I looked over the wall at it and there was a sticky note with the name Cali Marrow on it. So tonight—"

"Tonight you went lookin' for this Cali Marrow."

"Yeah," she said softly, and handed him the folded sheets "This is what I found. This Cali Marrow is married and was a Cali Eilís Hughes before. I know I shouldn't be so nosy, but I'm wondering if you could help me search a little more."

"Now, why would ya be wantin' that, love?"

"If it is Mary, I need to know why she has a different name now," she explained softly.

"Are you feeling guilty for lookin'?" He knew she was and figured he knew why.

"Could she be hiding from her husband, Da?" She stared at him, her eyes filling with unshed tears.

"Meaning she could only be a friend, and nothin' more?"

Mandy stepped forward and hugged him tight, nearly pushing him over backwards. She nodded silently against his neck and he slowly set her back on her feet.

"Mandy, love," he began. "I know you're very fond of Mary, but there is no guarantee that she and I will become partners in that sense. She doesn't belong to us until she decides she wants to, if she decides or even if she has the opportunity to decide. We have no claims or rights where she is concerned."

"You don't love her?" Mandy asked, and looked at him in surprise.

"What would you say if I did?" he asked, and waited, watching her expression.

"I think I do, Da," she said slowly. "It's okay if you do."

"Thank you, love, but it isn't what you and I feel that matters at this moment," he said heavily. "It is important that I like Mary a lot, enough to want the very best for her in all she does or faces, but Mandy, it's her feelin's and what she decides that matters. Not mine. Not yours." He hugged her again and held her for a very long moment. "And aye, love. I think I've been in love with Mary, in one way or another, for some time now. But that's our secret."

Mandy shook her head without releasing his hug. "I think she knows how you feel, Da. And I know she's kissed you, at least once."

Tuesday, September 12

"Miss Gorden?" Mandy asked softly, stopping in front of Mary's desk as the rest of the children hurried to the playground for the afternoon recess. "Mary?" she whispered when Mary did not look up at her first call.

"Oh, hey Mandy," Mary said as she looked up from the test

papers in front of her. "Sorry. What can I do for you?"

"Are you mad at me? Us?" Mandy asked, her brow furrowed with concern.

"No," Mary answered in surprise. "No, I'm not mad at you—either of you. Why do you ask?"

"I don't know," Mandy said. "You just seem so different yesterday and today. Different than you were Saturday. It's like you have something you don't like on your mind, and I figured it has to be something me or Da have done."

"I'm sorry, Mandy." Mary smiled. "You've done nothing wrong. Neither of you have. But you're right, I do have a lot on my mind, and I'll just have to work it out."

"We can help if you want us to."

"Thanks, but this is something I need to work out by myself," Mary said. "I'll try to not look like I'm angry with anyone."

"Okay." Mandy smiled. "I'm glad it's nothing we did. I'd hate to think we've upset you."

"You haven't. Tell you what, just so you'll know you haven't, come hike with me again on Saturday?"

Mandy's smile stretched across her face. "Sure, sure, I'd love to. I'll tell Da what's happenin'."

Mandy hurried after the other children and Mary watched her.

Sure you'll work it out on your own. How can you possibly fix what you've started, Mary Gorden?

Mary shook her head and slowly returned her attention to the papers on her desk.

Maybe Ms. White will have an idea.

Fourteen
Saturday, September 16

Mary poured Ms. White another cup of coffee and sat down in the cushioned chair across the coffee table from her.

"Same story," Mary said, and sipped her own cup. "But I have to ask what I'm supposed—no, what I'm *allowed* to do while I wait. At this rate, this Henry O'Brien could be on the loose for the rest of my life—" She giggled at the thought. "Either way, he finds me and my life is over or I live in fear and hiding the rest of my life. Either way, night and day, I'll have no life, biding my time, waiting for the banshee to come wailing."

"What do you mean? The banshee?"

"It's an Irish thing, a guardian spirit—*bean sídhe* in the Irish tongue. When someone is going to die, she comes and wails to announce the impending death," Mary said, and sighed. "Some say the banshee is imaginary, not real, while others say they have heard her..."

"Are you saying you have?"

Mary cocked her head and shrugged one shoulder. "Not really. Maybe. I heard something the night my dad passed away, and again when my mom went, but nothing before the attack...before...I didn't hear her...until the shooting started." Mary shook her head vigorously and forced a smile. "For many people, it's just a saying, but I heard... something...

"There was too much happening, but the next time I'm sure I'll hear her, because she'll be wailing for me."

"Well, I don't know anything about banshees and things like that, but you seem to be handling the situation here better than you were the last time I was here," Ms. White encouraged.

"You mean by not yelling and screaming in frustration?" Mary asked, her smile more genuine. "Things are not better but they are different. Back to my question though: what am I allowed to do in this new life of mine? Do I get to start over, make new friends, new lovers, new anything?"

Ms. White raised her eyebrows. "The yard-mower guy?"

Mary smiled and shook her head. "Probably, if things went his way, but I don't have a past that I can talk about, which really sucks, using my students' phrase. I cry myself to sleep because I don't know how to look forward to a new future. It feels worse than suffering the loss of my past. How can I get close to anyone when I can't relate normal things, like how I grew up, who I knew, where or when? But it seems that I can move forward, I'm allowed, but what does that look like? I've come to grips with my loss, but there's a hole that needs filling and I can't figure out how to do that and not share something, something about me and what makes me tick."

"How much can you trust him?"

Mary studied the woman for a long moment, wondering if... "Maybe more than anyone I've ever met."

"Tell me about him."

So Mary started slowly at the beginning: the first time she saw him, in the grocery store the day she had arrived in Roosevelt. How pleasant and helpful he had tried to be, but with her just back on her feet from the surgeries, still disoriented by her loss and moving from place to place, she had shunned him and refused to converse with him. He had left her alone, only offering to help when she was in the grocery or when the owner, Bob Jeff, asked him to get something for her.

She explained how the first year had gone, seeing him more and more around town with his daughter, and how she had actually asked a few people what they knew about this kind and helpful man called Dev. Then she had discovered that he was also a volunteer fireman under Chief Delany at their only firehouse, and that he was on one of the school board's subcommittees, helping to support the preparations for those elementary school functions like the Thanksgiving play, the Christmas pageant, and other similar activities.

She told her how Mrs. Arnold had called her and told her she had been working with Ms. Gray. She had been able to get her teaching certificates reassigned to her new name, and Mrs. Arnold had asked if she would consider teaching their fourth or fifth grade class. Mary expressed how that gave her something meaningful to fill her days with. But last year had also been the year this man Dev had decided to start mowing and trimming her yard.

She giggled, knowing how bad her yard looked, nearly hiding her beautiful house behind a wall of overgrown weeds, vines reaching up onto her house above her porch roof, the gangly shrubs and unsightly trees. She told Ms. White how she had yelled and screamed at him for waking her and for trimming her yard the first time he did it. She had been so mad she would have physically taken him on, but had realized too late that she was in her skimpiest pajamas yelling at him from her front porch in broad daylight.

Ms. White chuckled at the image Mary evoked.

"But this year I got a very unsettling surprise," Mary continued. "It was my surprise that caused the issue, but Dev's daughter Mandy is in my class this year, fifth grade, and on the first day while I was checking attendance, it was the first time I saw their surname, O'Brien. Spelled just like—"

"Oh no."

"Yeah," Mary said softly, the brightness in her voice suddenly gone.

Mary took a moment and slowly collected her composure.

"I let the surprise cause an issue, realizing later that it was just the coincidence of the spelling that caught me off guard. I had made Mandy feel like I was picking on her, and the next day Dev, her father, came to school to ask about it."

"Was he upset?"

Mary shook her head. "No. I expected him to be, but he was just like everyone said he was. He was courteous and inquisitive. He wanted to hear my side of the story and to understand the issue. We even bantered over the pronunciation-versus-spelling thing." Mary took a moment, inhaling deeply as she remembered. "When I apologized to Mandy later, she told me he had told her the night before that I didn't mean for it to sound that way—almost like he knew I wasn't intentionally being mean."

"So what else do you know about this man Dev—specifically? His background?"

"Specifically, from the searching I did at the library and on the school's computers, I know that Dev lost his wife over five years ago in an accident in Royal Oaks, Michigan. He was a fireman and his brigade was nearby at the time and was asked to assist when it happened. His wife, her parents, and his daughter Mandy were in the first car in the pileup. A semi crossed in front of them and they collided with it, along with the eight cars behind them. Mandy was the only survivor in their car.

"Dev was a sergeant in his ladder company in north Dearborn, where they lived. He was a fireman before he got married and he was twenty when he married his wife Anne. She was nineteen. Mandy was born just over six months after they were married. The dates indicate Anne was pregnant before they got married. Nothing indicates Mandy was a preemie."

"What did he do after she died?"

"I don't have any real details, but I suspect he felt the same way I felt, except worse; he was one of the men that found them. As for what's public, he stayed at his job for about ten months. He told me it was hard for him. Mandy was in and out of the hospital for months with surgeries and therapy, and finally, Mandy told me, he didn't want to be a fireman anymore. He couldn't stand leaving her alone—that is, her with his family and him not being with her. He told me she got a lot of doting from his mom, brother, and sisters, but it became hard for them, and together they decided to move. I'm not sure how they picked Roosevelt, but they sold their stuff, bought new, and he and his daughter came here to mend their lives. 'To learn to love and support each other' is how he described it."

"So?" Ms. White asked. "Can you trust him with your life? That's the question, Mary. The bottom line."

"What?"

"You heard me. If you're not in love with him, you aren't far from it," Ms. White said, smiling for the first time in all of her visits. "I saw that in my last visit, when he knocked and you opened your door. All of your frustrations stepped aside when you saw him. But it isn't that simple and you know it. You really, really have to be able to trust him to keep your secrets if this is more than a fling, a couple of nights of passion, which I would strongly advise against doing in a town this small. You know your life depends on what can be found out about either Cali Marrow or Mary Gorden. Will he protect you if it comes to that? Or at least try?" Ms. White shook her head. "I don't envy you, Mary, and under normal circumstances I'd have to encourage you to stay away from this sort of an entanglement. It's dangerous to say the least. I'd say keep it platonic, treat him like the brother you never had."

Ms. White sighed and looked at Mary with deep concern and conviction.

"But I think you want it to be more than that," Ms. White said. "And if that's true, you have to be absolutely certain you can trust him and you have to be certain he's willing to stand with you, even at the potential cost of losing his or his daughter's life. If you're wrong, it could cost you...everything, with a capital E."

¤-¤-¤-¤-¤

Dev clicked on a second search for the name Robert A. Marrow and waited for the computer to do its hunt. His week had been busy to the point that he couldn't follow up on Mandy's request that he help her search for data on this Cali and Robert Marrow, but today, with her off with Mary on another hike, he decided to see what he could find.

The screen blinked and he chose the Ann Arbor, Michigan Marrow. The screen blinked again and the same details page Mandy had found popped up.

Dev decided to start with the Ann Arbor public records and see if the different direction would give something different. The screen blinked again and three items were listed on the page. The first was a Robert Alan Marrow by name, giving personal details, but what caught his attention was the listing of a Date of Death: three years earlier on the ninth of April. No cause of death was noted. He looked closer and noticed his occupation was listed as a police officer and the marriage status block was checked: married.

He leaned back, straightening as a thought crossed his mind and his heart felt suddenly heavy. He turned to the second listing. It was from the Ann Arbor Department of Law Enforcement and listed Robert A. Marrow as a veteran beat officer assigned to the downtown district. He was a lieutenant at the time of his death. Again, no cause of death listed.

He searched the back pages of the website and found a gallery of pictures of the numerous officers, some with their spouses. After a minute or two, he found Officer Marrow with his arm around a blond "Mary" in short hair.

"Well, lass," he whispered to himself, "now I understand. You've seen the Devil's work too. And like you said, you understand me as well."

He selected a number of pages for printout, went and collected them, and returned to continue. He went back to the search page and selected the third listing. It opened to an obituary with a public notation added at the end.

He read the obituary, seeing all of the normal information one tends to find in such postings, but the lack of surviving family surprised him. There was no one listed. Reading further, he discovered Robert was an only child and his folks had died before him. But his wife, Cali, was also not listed.

Dev sat back and questioned himself, but without any obvious answers he quickly turned to the added public notation.

The notation was a simply worded posting, noting that Officer Marrow, age 26, and his wife, age 25, had been fatally shot on a street near the University of Michigan on Ann Arbor's east side. He was shot nine times, once in the head at close range, and she had been shot four times. The statement said she had died in surgery at St. Joseph's on the same day. No one had been charged with the slayings.

Dev sat back and looked at the printout picture of Robert with his arm around his blond "Mary" and he slowly nodded to himself. "My dear God in Heaven, ye must've seen who did it, lass. I see now why ya've been scared out of yer mind when ya see or meet anyone new. These last two and a half years must've been the most terrifyin' years of yer life."

Dev glanced around him, and seeing that he still had time, he selected the public admissions records at Ann Arbor's St. Joseph's Hospital. After a few dead ends, he finally found where Cali Marrow and been admitted for severe gunshot wounds, and nowhere did he find that she had been released. Then he started a diligent search of the releases, and two months later he found Mary Gorden. The release notes claimed she was treated for a bronchial infection during her stay. He looked closer, but he could not find when she had been admitted.

Dev printed the two pages, collected them, and placed them in the folder in his backpack. He stood up, stretched, and threw the pack on. Then he remembered the government car that always showed up in the middle and at the end of the month, and it made sense now. He sighed and looked at his watch, figuring he might have time for a pint before Mandy got home. He was feeling like he needed one this time.

Fifteen

"What colors are the O'Briens'?" Mary asked as they worked their way down the switchback path toward the south side of town.

"Not sure," Mandy remarked after she negotiated a steep step and turned to follow again. "The clan has a shield—a herald, if ya will—but we haven't found a tartan that's universally accepted, or even that a majority has accepted. Personally, I always think of a green field with blue crossin' stripes, but that's just me."

"So I take it your favorite or preferred color would be green."

"Yup," Mandy said, and jumped down over another switchback. "Bright kelly green—or O'Brien green in our case." She giggled. "But the herald has very little green in it. Da says they're mostly reds and yellows—golds, more likely—with green and yellow ribbon banners off the flagpoles. Swords 'n shields are silver with gold trimmin's."

"Do the kids ever tease you for calling your dad 'Da'? Or your accent?" Mary looked back over her shoulder.

"Sometimes. They aren't clansmen and just don't understand usin' 'da' instead of 'dad' or pop." Mandy smiled. "I know you understand, but many outside the Irish don't. The accent I try to control in public. With friends and family, I let it come as it wants."

"I was told once that I have a little Irish blood," Mary said, and turned on another steep switchback.

Mandy held her tongue, remembering the middle name of Eilís from her list, thinking maybe her inklings were right, or at least close.

"That'd be good," Mandy said. "And you already know, so the terms and accent don' bother you."

"Yes, I do know, and the accent is nice, comforting to my ears," Mary said, and smiled up at Mandy from where she was on the lower section of the trail. "Tell me though."

They turned onto the gentler downward path leading into town.

"Does your father always refer to the women he meets as lasses? It was strange at first, a surprise, but I like the way he says it, the way it makes me feel. Almost special."

"No, he doesn't," Mandy said, and found the trail wide enough that they could walk beside each other. "I thought you knew."

"Oh? Knew what?"

"A lass is a female that is close, family or...or...or a trusted, close friend."

Mary looked at Mandy and wondered at her hesitation and rushed finish. "So I'm a trusted, close friend?"

"Sure."

"And your dad calls his sisters lasses? Since they're family?"

Mandy hesitated again and swallowed noticeably. Mary stopped to look at her.

"Not...really, Mary," Mandy slowly explained. "Closer than that. Gran told me once that he only called Mum and me lass. And now that he's met you, he calls both of us lasses." Mandy watched Mary's expression, fervently hoping it was not making her angry. "Please don't be mad. It's supposed to be a private, endearing term."

"I see," Mary said, and slowly smiled. "I hadn't put it together, but after all you two have told me and the way your father keeps helping me, it makes sense."

"I know you like him," Mandy blurted, and saw Mary's expression stiffen. "And I know he likes you, a lot."

Mary shook her head. "Well, we'll keep that between us and wait to see how things work out. I won't promise you anything, except I'll try to be your friend, when I'm not your teacher."

Mandy nodded and smiled.

"What now?"

"Oh, nothing really." Mandy smiled. "Da told me that's the way it should be unless you decide differently."

Mary tried to playfully swat her shoulder, but Mandy ducked and skipped ahead a step.

"Seems to me you spend a lot of your time talking about other people," Mary said, and started a brisk walk down the trail to the footbridge across Roosevelt Creek.

"Only one," Mandy said, hurrying to keep up.

¤-¤-¤-¤-¤

"Glad to see you decided to join us for supper," Dev said as he stood.

Mary entered Stumpy's and he took her hand to help her into her seat.

"Had a lot of papers to work this afternoon," she said, and smiled at Mandy, "so I wouldn't promise Mandy that I could."

"Understandable," Dev said, and took his seat. "Do you have more to do, or are you finished for the evenin'?"

"Finished," Mary said, and smiled at him. "Sorry I made eating late though. I think I'm crowding Mandy's bedtime."

"I'm fine," Mandy said, and stifled a yawn. "Just worked up an appetite with all of the walking."

"Walking, climbing, and trotting are more like it," Mary said. "We did work a bit today."

Connie stopped at the table and asked what they would like.

"Hey, Connie," Mary said brightly. "Are you here every night? I know I don't come in often, but it seems like you're usually here."

"I work all of the days and nights Stumpy will let me," Connie said softly. "I'm trying to buy a car, so I need the hours."

"Very nice," Dev said, and gestured to Mary and Mandy. "Are you ready to order, or just somethin' to drink right now?"

Mary looked at Mandy. "I think both. A pilsner please and the meatloaf again, for me. Mandy?"

"The junior burger with cheese and chili fries," Mandy said, then looked at Dev. "Da? May I have a float?"

"Sure," he said with a nod.

"Root beer float, please. And water on the side," Mandy finished.

Connie turned to Dev.

"The half portion chicken-fried steak, Connie, and a cup of coffee."

"Thanks, Dev. I'll get these turned in," Connie said, and hurried to the kitchen.

"No pint tonight?" Mary asked, mildly surprised.

"No. I had a pint earlier this afternoon before Mandy got home," Dev explained. "So I don't think I really want another. Mandy said you two worked each other hard today. I hope she wasn't too much of a bother for you."

"No, Dev. She was fine," Mary said, and smiled at Mandy again. "It's nice to have her company."

"I'm glad you're up to it, lass," Dev said as Connie brought their drinks and Mandy's float. "I can hardly keep up m'self."

Dev glanced at Connie and did not see Mary's smile at his calling her "lass," but Mandy did.

"I brought this," Connie said as she sat the float in front of Mandy, "thinking you might want to start on it before your food gets you distracted. Enjoy."

"Thanks," Mandy said, and Dev watched her dig in with fervor.

"Easy, love," he said, and held up his hand. "It isn't goin' ta run away from ya. Slow down and mind yer manners."

"Yes, Da," she said, and smiled, taking the next scoop with more deliberate attention to where it was going.

"How was your quiet afternoon, Dev," Mary asked, "with this one out of your hair for a few hours? Did you get a lot accomplished?"

"Oh, not so much as I should have," he replied. "Checked in some books at the library and stopped by the firehouse for a few minutes. Seth Mayer asked me to look at his hydraulic wood splitter, so I helped him work out a kink in the linkage. Then I took a short nap and came by here for a pint."

Mary looked at Mandy. "We've been working off the calories and he's been lazing around and drinking all afternoon."

"Now that's not what—"

"Gotcha again, Mr. O'Brien," Mary laughed, and Mandy giggled. "You can give it but..." She shrugged her shoulders.

"I can see I'm going to have to get used to bein' ganged up on every now and again." Dev smiled and patted Mary's hand where she had it on the table.

He did not hold her hand, still feeling like he had pushed her some the previous weekend. On the surface, he knew he should be happy that she had taken the advantage and kissed him, but underneath it all, he worried still that he was going too fast for her to really know how she felt about him. He was becoming more and more certain of his own feelings, but after his searching today, he knew he needed to pay attention to the details, the little signs, and not entice feelings from her that she might later regret.

Dinner came and the conversation was light and pleasant. Mandy fought the end of her today, but on their way home she was all but done. Dev carried her like he had when she was little, but soon had to change and cradle her in his arms.

"She is gettin' taller and heavier," he said with a chuckle as he shifted her so she folded into him, one arm behind him and the other dangling in front.

"Here," Mary said, and placed Mandy's dangling arm on her lap. "I don't think I can help much with the other one."

"Thanks, lass," he said, and started walking again. "She does use up all she has in a day, I'll say that much for her."

They walked quietly up Main to Tenth and then turned up the hill to Lincoln. When they passed in front of Mary's house, she asked if he minded if she walked on with him.

"'Course not, lass," he said. "We both like it when you spare the time to join us. Ya know yer always welcome and really don't have ta ask."

Once they had Mandy tucked in, suitably kissed, and her pajamas across the foot of her bed, Dev turned her nightstand light out and followed Mary down to the front porch. He asked if she wanted any wine or something else to drink, and when she shook her head he picked up the shawl and wrapped it around her shoulders before she sat down in the same rocker she had used the previous weekend.

-¤-

"You can't imagine how much I like just sitting here, Dev," Mary said, watching the silent street. She glanced around and noted the placement of his house. "I hadn't noticed until last week that you are the very last house on this street, the entire block, both sides to yourself."

"I'm pleased that you like sitting with me, Mary. I enjoy havin' your company, and bein' back a bit and separated from the noise and commotion of town is nice, I think," Dev admitted. "The house just to the east was vacant, run down, and I bought it and the lots across the street. I had the house dismantled three and a half years ago. With it gone, the lot cleaned up and leveled, and with the national forest behind us, the space has given Mandy a lot to explore without giving either of us any worries over the years. With all that's happened in our lives, we've been truly blessed to be here. I don't think Mandy or I would've made it if we hadn't come. I surely don't."

Mary stared at him, wanting to confirm that she had heard him right about the lots, the property, but she held her questions, not wanting to change the turn the conversation had taken.

"You told me about the accident," she said instead, "but what was your wife like? Was she strict, happy go lucky, in between? I know she was nice by Mandy's personality."

She watched him as he thought about his answer, glancing at her and taking a deep breath. He straightened and leaned back in his rocker.

"Anne was a quiet, kind woman, my first, last, and only serious romance in high school. When she graduated, her folks sent her off to Michigan State in East Lansing to study the performin' arts. She was fairly good at actin' in high school and her parents had high hopes for her."

"Was she into just being an actor or was she a singer too?"

"A little of both." He smiled. "But when she was back the first summer break, she told me she didn't want to do either. She preferred painting and interior design."

"Did she tell her parents she had different ideas? Or was that improper?"

"She planned on telling them, but we sort of got lost in being together again and just after her classes started up that fall, she found out she was pregnant with the young'un." He gestured to Mandy's room upstairs above the porch. "'Twas my fault, but when the families found out, there was no explainin' anything. We were married a little before Christmas and Mandy, sorry, *Amanda,* came in June the following year. Anne's folks hated nicknames."

"Wow. How did Anne handle it? I assume she dropped out of college."

"Anne put on her actin' face and studied to strengthen her interior design talents." He smiled. "She was very good at it, but her parents always put her desires and capabilities down—kept her ashamed of getting' pregnant, havin' to marry a fireman and not aspirin' to bein' a great actress on Broadway or the big screen. That sort of took the bright luster off her pleasure of bein' with me."

"That had to be hard. What about your parents? What did they say?"

"Ah, well that was another matter." He tightened his smile. "Da and Mum had very different, opposin' opinions on the matter, and at first it made all of us kids nervous bein' around them, but finally we realized their banterin' was their way of dealin' with thin's bein' the way they sometimes are. They loved Anne as much as she would allow them to, and were supportive of us as much as they could. Of course they had no issues with their son bein' a fireman and married to an up-and-comin' interior designer. Da was a fireman until he was seventy-two. Worked in the offices after he turned sixty-five, but he was there every day."

Mary was surprised at how relaxed he made her feel and how much she enjoyed rocking comfortably on the porch with him.

"Da passed when Mandy was two, so she doesn't remember him at all," he continued softly, "except for the pictures Mum keeps on her mantle."

"Mandy told me she doesn't remember her mother except from the picture album you kept. She said it was for the future."

"Aye. So she'll be able to look back and know what she had, even if she doesn't remember."

"I wish there was a way to see your mother's house, the place you grew up in," Mary said wistfully.

Dev just nodded and smiled back at her.

"Mum had a bout with somethin' like flu, only worse," he said.

"Had her down since midsummer, but I got a letter from my middle sister, Derry, sayin' Mum was up and around to help with the Labor Day dinner. All of the family except Mandy and I were there, but it was still a houseful—fifteen, countin' Mum."

"A big family."

"Aye." There was a long pause in his reply, and he cocked his head, but when she did not say anything, he continued. "Have your friends at school started talkin' about you and the volunteer fireman yet?"

"Not really," Mary said, thinking about her inquiries about him. "Debbie Cotton, Mandy's teacher last year, talked to me a little about you. I guess she thought I needed to be prepared in case you noticed me." Mary giggled and Dev smiled.

"Debbie is a nice-looking, pleasant girl." He smiled again. "Dresses nice. She would try to warn you about me."

"And why is that?"

"Just her way, I think," he said. "I'm one of five single men under fifty in town, if you haven't noticed. So I guess I'm some kind of threat, though I must admit I've not been out seein' who's available."

"No?"

"Not really." Dev gave her a mischievous grin. "Though I do know there are fifteen eligible, unattached single women under fifty, not countin' yourself. Debbie's one of them."

Mary smiled and shook the table, unable to reach him without leaning up from her comfortable position. "You would."

She watched him as he stretched his legs out, letting his chair rock with the movement of his feet, his heels firmly planted on the boards. "I don't recall," he continued softly, "ever havin' an evenin' this nice before—quiet, weather coolin' towards winter, a soft breeze, Mandy safe and comfortable in her bed, and very pleasant company to share it with."

"I'm sure you and Anne had nights like this."

"Nay, never like this, lass," he said, and closed his eyes.

After a few minutes, she cleared her throat and leaned forward in her rocker. "Are you asleep?"

He turned his head and smiled. "No, lass. I would never be so rude. I was just listenin' to the sounds of the night and the gentle squeak of your rocker. I truly like havin' you here too."

Unable to form a suitable response to his frankness, she proceeded to stand. He quickly stood with her.

"Thank you for the wonderful evening," she said, turning to face him. "But I think I should go. I've had a busy day and should get some rest."

"I understand," he said, but slipped his arms around her, catching her a little higher than her waist as he gently pulled her to him. "But before you go, I believe it's my turn to participate."

-¤-

Before she could say anything, he bent to her, his lips lightly caressing hers before catching them fully. He held his kiss, soft and tenderly; he felt her lips slowly respond to his and he felt her arms wrap slowly around his neck. He pulled her gently up and to him, feeling all of her length against him. Then after a long moment, knowing she felt all of him, his body against hers and how she moved him, he slowly released her lips and sighed softly, kissing the side of her neck as he gently lowered her down onto her feet. "I definitely think you have seriously beguilin' ways about ye, lass. And that's no lie."

-¤-

Mary was still walking in a fog when she entered her house and closed and locked the door behind her. She checked the windows and doors by rote, then made her way up to her room and fell back onto her bed, wondering if what she was feeling was real or just a dream. She touched her lips and knew it was real. Dev was definitely real.

"Wow, double wow. No one's ever done that to you before, girl," she admitted softly to herself. Relishing her warm feelings, her body unwilling to move from where she lay, she closed her eyes, savoring the memory of Dev, his arms wrapped tight around her, their bodies tight against each other, and drifted off to sleep.

Sixteen
Monday, September 18

Detective Williams had the Xed-out pictures from the box they had found in Henry O'Brien's shed spread across the small table in the precinct conference room. There were eighty-seven with Xs over the image and forty-six without. Each day he scanned the pictures and tried to match them with names of missing or deceased people, following the hunch that Henry might have been right, that someone was marking off some sort of a list. If the box and pictures did belong to Einri O'Brien, then the detective figured they were pictures he used to select or verify his targets. But he worried about the ones without Xs; were they future targets?

Handling them carefully by the edges because the fingerprint boys had not announced their conclusions, the detective sighed and held one picture next to another with his vinyl-gloved fingers, looking for similarities. He figured they would know soon.

When one accidently fell off the table, he bent and picked it up, flipping it face up—the image startled him. He picked up his palm-sized magnifying glass and studied the couple. Both were Xed out, but the man, half a head taller than the smiling woman, was a police officer.

"Kenny," he said to the assistant in the next room. "Come look at this."

Kenny pushed himself up from his desk and walked over to where the detective stood in the conference room doorway, studying at the picture. "Whatcha got?"

"Looks like a police officer," the detective said, working his magnifier. "Ann Arbor, and the name kinda looks like it starts with an M, maybe. Then, an A-R-R-O-W. Marrow, maybe. Give the Ann Arbor Police a call and see what you can find out."

"I'm on it," Kenny said, and took the proffered picture. "Anything else?"

The detective shook his head. "Not yet." And he returned to the table to continue studying the other photos.

"Williams?" someone hollered from the hallway that ran through the building, connecting the various departments.

"In here," he shouted back. "Conference room."

A heavy-set lieutenant came in with a sheet of paper. "Lab report's back," he said. "That sleeping bag."

"Yeah, let's see it."

Williams quickly glanced through the list of things found on the bag, and shuddered as he read. "He sure didn't bother to clean that bag," Williams said. "Guess that's a good thing." He slowly reread the description of body hair, skin flakes found, and some dried bodily fluids and mucus.

In the short summary paragraph at the bottom, the DNA from the majority of the analyzable items was identified as belonging to Einri O'Brien; the second significant count was his brother, Scanlon O'Brien; and the third group of nearly insignificant fibers was synthetic hairs and wool.

Detective Williams nodded and looked back at the man that had brought the report. "Have any of our stakeouts reported seeing anyone around the shed?"

"I'll check, but I don't think so," the man said, and started to turn to go.

"Make two copies of this," Williams said, and handed the man the report. "Then give one of the copies to the chief and put the other copy and the original in my in basket."

"Got it," the man said, and hurried back into the hall.

Williams put the magnifying glass on the box that the pictures came from and stepped into Kenny's office just as Kenny hung up his phone and looked up.

"Lieutenant Robert Marrow, a veteran beat cop on the Ann Arbor force. He was assassinated at a park near the university when his wife came to meet him for lunch, three years ago next April ninth. He was shot nine times, once through the head, and she was shot four times. He was dead at the scene and the Ann Arbor report says she died in surgery later that day. Before they took her into surgery, she was coherent and named Einri O'Brien as the assailant. The escorting officer and the doctor witnessed her identification.

"There's a photo gallery on their website," Kenny continued as he looked up the Ann Arbor Police Department's webpage. "Bingo! Looks like Einri printed the gallery shot."

"Any idea why he was targeted?" Williams asked.

"The man I talked to," Kenny continued, "said Marrow had been assigned to the task force looking into the unrest down by Zug Island and the steel works, a few months before he was killed. Einri was a prime suspect for inciting the unrest and vandalism in that area, so there is likely a motive in there someplace. Maybe this guy found something he shouldn't have."

"Most likely," Williams said.

"Too bad about his wife," Kenny said. "She was cute."

"Yeah," Williams said, and turned back to his desk. "Too bad for both of them."

"Yeah," Kenny agreed, and looked at the photo again.

"I need to call Henry, Finnian's son, and tell him about the sleeping bag," Williams said as he dropped into his chair.

"Henry O'Finnian, 'cause he's Finnian's son?" Kenny asked, and chuckled.

"Might be a good way to keep the investigators from confusing Henry and Einri again." Williams smiled. "They just never seem to learn to look at the spelling." He sighed. "We'd have to call the other, Einri O'Gallagher, then."

"Works for me," Kenny said, and turned back to the set of pictures on his desk. "If it would keep him from being dragged into the precinct so much, or questioned every time Einri O'Gallagher did something, I think O'Finnian would go for it."

Williams picked up his phone and dialed Henry's number.

Tuesday, September 19

Dev noticed the morning winds had swung around to the north and that it was cooler than the past week. He had Mandy dress accordingly, leggings under her skirt, long-sleeves, and an extra sweater in her backpack. He also had her take a short-sleeved shirt in case it warmed up by the time school was out.

With an hour for lunch, Dev stepped out onto the sidewalk in front of the grocery store and settled where he could enjoy some of the day's sunshine. He chuckled, remembering Mary's comment about the Irish always wanting sunshine, giving blessings about sunshine in your days and in your faces. Why he remembered that, he did not know, but he did know that Mary had been on his mind more and more each day.

He hadn't spoken with her since Saturday night, and in a way he was glad of that. Kissing her had sent him to a sensual place he did not remember ever being before. And the way she had left him when she walked home, not quite like her normal self, he suspected she had much the same experience and a "cooling off" period was definitely in order. Many more moments like that and their already complicated single lives could become much, much more complicated.

Then he began to think about their relationship more objectively. He had known *of* her for just over two years, and had only begun to converse with her and get to know her, the real her, the animated, spirited, everyday her, for almost yet less than a month. And in that short span of time, he and Mandy had welcomed Mary wholly into their hearts.

Dev worried about the things he had discovered in his computer searching, and how they would work out, but he felt he knew the essence of Mary and that he could trust her with anything. Then he chuckled at himself. He was the one always worried about Mandy and keeping her safe, but when Mary had come on the scene, he knew. He had not once had a concern for Mandy's safety when she was with Mary, and that surprised him.

Dev absently ate the sandwich from the lunch bag he had brought from home, lost in his amazement over how completely Mary had, indeed, beguiled him. He was still chuckling to himself when Bob Jeff came out of the store looking for him.

"What's up, Bob?" Dev asked when Bob motioned for him to come back into the store.

"Delivery," Bob said. "Mae Cooper called with a list of things she needs. She said they were leaving this afternoon for Colorado Springs and wanted to know if I could deliver her things before she has to leave."

"Aye," Dev said, and tossed his empty lunch bag in the trash barrel at the back of the store. "I can get me truck and take them out in just a couple of minutes."

¤-¤-¤-¤-¤

Dev had driven the road out to the Cooper's ranch many times since he had come to Roosevelt and knew to be cautious through the short, narrow canyon five miles down where the Roosevelt and Carter Creeks joined before cutting through the trees and then the wooded Cooper ranch five miles farther on. It was all downhill, though steep in places, but he made it in reasonable time and stopped in front of the long ranch home as usual. He picked up the first two sacks and went to the front door where, not as usual, a note greeted him.

Mae wrote, "Dev, since you've delivered to us many times, please go ahead and put the groceries and other items on the kitchen counter. I'll put them away later. Lock up when you leave. We'll be late getting back. Thanks, Mae."

Dev remembered Bob telling him that Harry and Mae were going to Colorado Springs to pick up their son and his wife. They were coming to spend a week or two at the ranch, which was why Mae wanted the groceries.

He chuckled at the note and opened the door, taking the sacks to the kitchen as Mae had asked. The second trip got the three remaining sacks in and then he set himself to putting the grocery items away. It took him a bit to figure out where Mae kept her pantry items, but once he knew, he put things in order. Finally all of the sacks were empty, and he folded them and slipped them in with other paper sacks in her pantry.

Dev checked the house to be sure the windows were closed so none of the furry, four-legged neighbors could get in. Then he locked the front doorknob and pulled the door closed behind him.

He looked at his watch and smiled. He could be back in time to give Mandy a ride home. But two hundred feet past the start of the first winding uphill grade, a half mile from the house, Dev's truck died.

"Of all the knuckle-headed, forgetful dummies," Dev said, and stared at the gas gauge. He knew his plan to refill the truck on Saturday had been interrupted by the day's full routine, with most of it spent in the library, but he had never before been so addle-brained as to forget to put gas in his truck, or any vehicle of his, for that matter.

With a deep sigh, Dev started walking. *With any kind of luck, ye'll make town in two to two and a half hours, ye dumb twat.* Then he thought he could call Mary and have her look after Mandy until he got there, but when he reached for his phone in his shirt pocket, he realized it was not there. He slapped his forehead. *Twat! That's what ye are!* Then he started chuckling; his single-minded thoughts of Mary were making him completely absentminded. *Not just a little beguilin' are ye, lass. Oh what a dumb twat ye are, Devlin O'Brien!*

⌗-⌗-⌗-⌗-⌗

"How long will ya be?" Billie Ray asked as she stopped her car near a large cedar. It was nearly two in the morning when she turned her car off Grand River Road and wandered through the neighborhoods to reach the midblock shadows.

Scanlon held his small flashlight close to the paper and read his notes. "Mik said I should always write down what I wuz tol' ta do," he said as he read his scribbled hand. "Twenty minutes." He looked up at her. "Is that long?"

"No," she said, and sighed. "I'm not sure I shoulda brought ya here. How will you know when to come back out?"

"If I follow the steps like they're written, then it should be twenty minutes," he said firmly, and he switched the flashlight off and pocketed it. He folded the paper and slipped it into his shirt pocket, smiling back as he opened the passenger side door.

"Whatcha lookin' fer?" Billie Ray asked.

"Just goin' to take a picture. Me cousin said cousin Dev has a girl. Said she was real pretty and I want to see and show it to Mik and Einri. He hasn't had a girl since his wife died."

"To take a picture? Of his girl?"

126

"Yeah. I'll be back out in twenty minutes."

Billie Ray shook her head. "I can't stay and wait fer ya, so if I'm not here when you come back, hide under that tree"—she pointed to the cedar—"and come out when you see me comin'. An' don' wake anyone up while yer in there!"

"Okay, I willna wake anyone," Scanlon said, and slipped out of the car. He closed the door and quickly crossed the street, disappearing into the darkness beside the tall fence.

Billie Ray drove away down the street.

-¤-

Scanlon quietly crept out of the cellar stairwell into the back part of the kitchen. He waited a moment to let his eyes adjust, remembering the many times he had been in this room as a small boy, smelling the aromas of holiday dinners in the making. He started smiling, thinking about his cousins and the fun they had had when he and his brothers came to visit. They played in the backyard when his uncle had shooed them out for being underfoot while his mum and his aunt fixed dinner. Absently he turned to look out into the dark yard, and smacked his forehead on the open door to the cellar. He grabbed the door and held it, reminding himself to not make any noise!

He muttered and realized it was dark, not the middle of the day many years ago. He checked his notes, reading by the light coming from the hood over the stove. Then he slowly walked through the kitchen and dining room, forcing himself to walk quietly and concentrate on the instructions on his paper. In the living room, he stopped and slowly looked around the room, first at the walls and then at the end tables, and finally he focused on the large fireplace mantel.

As he leaned close to the mantel, he pulled his flashlight out but remembered he had to check his notes. In big letters, he saw his warning: "NO FLASHLIGHT!" He nodded absently and put the flashlight away, then leaned close again to look at each picture.

He started at the left end and was almost to the far right end when he saw the small frame on the back of the two rows of pictures. He smiled when he saw Devlin's grinning face and quickly picked up the frame to study it. He reached for his phone to take a picture of Devlin, Mandy, and the woman's smiling faces when a noise from upstairs startled him. He lost his grip on the picture, juggled it frantically as it slid down his pant leg, and finally caught it before it reached his foot.

He looked up and held his breath as someone went into the upstairs hall bath and closed the door.

Scanlon slipped the picture into his jacket pocket and quickly crept back through the dining room and kitchen and down the cellar stairs.

-¤-

When Billie Ray's car slowly turned onto the street a block away, Scanlon crawled out from under the cedar and crouched in the shadow. He stepped out into the street when she was close and hurried around the car and got in when she stopped.

"Finally," she said as he closed his door and she started driving away. "What took so long?"

"Wasn't long," Scanlon disagreed. "I did what was on my list, except I did better. I got the picture instead of taking one."

"You didn't get the picture?"

"No. I took the picture instead."

Billie Ray stared at him for a long moment, then turned onto the main road and started driving back to Dearborn.

Seventeen

"Mary?" Mandy asked softly as she came back into Mary's classroom where she was finishing her after-class paperwork.

"Hey, Mandy," Mary said, and slipped the sheet she was working on into a folder and closed it.

"Sorry to bother you," Mandy said, and Mary looked around, realizing it was quite dark outside.

"What is it?" Mary asked, and turned to face Mandy.

"Da's late," she said softly. "And I tried to call him from the office, but he's not answering his phone."

"Do you know what he was doing today?" Mary asked as she tapped Dev's icon on her mobile phone. "Has he been late before?"

"Just working at the grocery," Mandy said. "He's only been late a couple of times, but he's told me ahead of time and made arrangements. He doesn't like me walking home alone yet, especially after dark."

"I would agree with that," Mary said, and looked at her phone. "That's odd. It just rings and rings." Mary put her phone away and collected the papers and folders on her desk. "I think we'll just head that way, and I'll finish this in the morning." Mary put the papers into her file cabinet and pushed the drawer closed.

Together they walked up Main, chatting about how Mandy felt about the day in school and what she had done with the rest of her weekend. As they passed the grocery, Mary saw the closed sign indicating that Bob was taking a dinner break, and the smaller sign noted that he would be back within the hour. So they walked on. When they stopped in front of Mary's house, Mary suggested they go on to Mandy's house since that was where Dev would most likely be.

"The truck's gone," Mandy said softly as they walked up to the front porch. Mandy got the "hidden" key from the small nail on the trim of the window farthest from the front door and smiled at Mary.

"I know it isn't very well hidden, but it's too obvious for most people to find."

Mandy opened the door and led Mary in, switching on lights as she went.

"Da? Da? Are you home?"

There was no answer and Mandy turned back to Mary, her brow wrinkling in worry, her eyes slowly filling with uncertainty.

Mary hugged Mandy and held her tight. "I'm sure he's all right," Mary said softly, slowly rocking Mandy back and forth. It was the first time Mary had actually held Mandy, and the sensation somehow comforted her as well.

"Can you wait with me?"

"Sure, sure," Mary said, realizing she had unintentionally used Dev's phrase of encouragement again, thinking it was strange how he was affecting her—even her speech. "And look at what I see," she continued when she saw Dev's phone on the dining room table.

Mandy wiped her eyes and giggled. "He lays it there when he gets the truck keys down from the cabinet. I wonder if Mr. Jeff sent him on a delivery."

"Let's see," Mary said, and started to call the grocery when Mandy heard someone coming up the walk.

"Da!" she shouted as he reached the steps.

Mandy was out through the front door and swinging in Dev's arms before the screen door had a chance to slam shut again. Mary was right behind her, but she stopped herself from leaping to hug Dev like Mandy had, startled when she realized that was what she had intended to do.

"What happened to you?" Mary asked, her smile fading as she looked at Dev when he set Mandy down. Dev's jacket and jeans were covered in dirt, weeds, and thistles.

He chuckled. "Did ye know 'tis sorta dark out in the forest under an overcast sky and with no moon or stars to guide ya? Tumbled inta the brush a time or two."

"Where's the truck, Da?" Mandy asked as she started brushing his pant legs off.

"Well, ya see," he began with a wide smile, "I was plannin' on

filling it up on Saturday, but I got busy lazin' 'round and drinkin'"
—he glanced sideways at Mary, reminding her of her comment—
"while you two were off burnin' calories, and then I got completely
distracted by someone over dinner and afterwards, so refillin' the
truck completely slipped me mind." He chuckled and slipped his arm
around both of them and turned toward the house. "So the truck is
about nine miles out on Harrison, waitin' fer me to bring it some fuel."

Then Dev squatted down and pulled Mandy in front of him. "I'm
terribly sorry for worryin' you over this, love. When I knew I was
stuck, I was goin' to call, but guess what?"

"What?" Mandy asked, and held his phone up in front of him.

"That's the what," he said, and hugged Mandy as tight as he dared.
"I am so very sorry, love. Can you forgive me?"

"Sure, sure," Mandy said, and winked at Mary. "But only if you
take us to dinner for all of our worryin', and then we can go feed the
truck."

Dev looked up at Mary, and when she smiled and glanced away,
he said, "Deal. I'll have to wipe a little of this dirt and grime off first."

"Da! Go upstairs! Shower and change your clothes. Then we can
go."

He looked at Mandy then at Mary with a surprised smile. "Yes,
ma'am. I'll be down in a jiff."

⌑-⌑-⌑-⌑-⌑

"I didn't thank you for watchin' over Mandy tonight," Dev said,
and caught Mary's hand where it rested on the table between them.
"But I do thank you, Mary."

"I'm glad she came to me when she needed help, Dev," Mary said,
squeezing his hand and smiling at Mandy across the table and on his
left. "I should be sorry that you think I distracted you, but I can't say
that I am."

Mandy giggled.

Dev leaned back and inhaled deeply. "I think I have to figure out
how to keep me wits about m'self when I'm under the influence of you
two. I also think that's goin' to be hard to do."

131

Mary and Mandy both giggled.

"So, Mary?" he whispered, and leaned to her. "I know you don't have a car, but I'm thinkin' ya probably know how to drive." He cocked his head.

"Yes, I know how," Mary said, "but I don't have a license."

"Aaah, now that's goin' ta make me a very bad example for me young and impressionable dotter," he said with a wicked grin as he flicked his eyes at Mandy. "But maybe, if we stay to the south side of town, Sheriff Martin won't notice us slippin' back home."

"What are you talking about, Mr. O'Brien? Slippin' back home?" Mary asked, and straightened in her chair.

"Just that if you two are finished with your meal," Dev said, and smiled at Mandy, "I think we need to go and feed the truck. And since we will have two vehicles out on the dark road, we'll need two drivers." He winked at Mandy and then looked at Mary. "Mandy hasn't driven in the dark yet, so I'm hopin' I can count on yer help just a wee bit more."

Mary stared at him. "Mandy hasn't..."

"Da sometimes lets me drive when we're out on the back roads," Mandy said matter-of-factly. "But the road to the Coopers' is scary, even in the daylight."

"Well?" Dev asked, and looked at Mary.

"What two vehicles?" she asked.

¤-¤-¤-¤-¤

Dev punched the buttons on the garage door keypad and stepped back as the door slowly rumbled up and out of the way. The double garage sat at the back corner of his and Mandy's house, but was usually closed with the old pickup truck and the trailer sitting in front of it. With the door raised, Mary saw the trailer was sitting in front of the empty side. Dev stepped in and switched on the lights.

"Come on," Dev said to Mary as he opened the passenger door of the red, two-door Jeep with oversized aggressive tires, a cable winch, and high-intensity lamps on the front bumper. "You'll have to fight Mandy for which seat ya get, front or back." Then Dev walked back to

Mary where she stood transfixed.

She had not moved, still staring at the jeep in surprise. "I didn't know you had anything besides the pickup," she stammered. "Or this nice."

"Aye, lass, we do," he said softly, and pulled on her arm. "'Tis our winter vehicle, or sometimes it's our vacationin' vehicle. Come on." He led her in and held the passenger door. "You and Mandy can sort out which seats you're gonna take."

Mary stepped up on the tall running board and got in as Dev searched for, and finally found, the red plastic jerrycan.

Dev drove to the east edge of town and filled the can at Zeke's Conoco on Main, and then they dropped south on Meridian to Harrison and followed Harrison out of town.

"My thought, lass," Dev said, and smiled at Mary in the right front seat, where she had finally settled, "is that you'd drive this one back and I'd follow with the truck. Are ye good with that?"

"Sure, sure," she said softly, smiling at herself. "I haven't driven in over three years, Dev. I..."

"You'll do gran', Mary," Dev said with a wide smile, and patted her leg just above the hem of her skirt, where it revealed her knee and a bit of her toned thigh. He stiffened, trying to conceal how much that touch had moved him, making his mind reel and his heart race. "I know ye will."

"Thanks, Dev," she said, and slowly smiled at him.

After a much quicker drive than the walk, Dev stopped in front of the pickup, letting the headlights shine down the side to help him with the fueling. He set to the task and was soon finished, setting the empty jerrycan in the bed. He walked back to the jeep as Mary got out and stepped down on the passenger side.

"Ye can drive a stick, right?" he said stopping in front of her.

"Oh God, no!" Mary said, and looked up at him in disbelief.

"Nay, lass," he said. "Just checkin' though."

She slapped his chest and he wrapped his arms around her and pulled her tight against him.

"'Tis an automatic, lass. You'll do fine." Then, without releasing his hold on her he looked into the dark interior of the jeep. "Mandy, you ride shotgun with Mary. Keep her company."

Mandy got out and came and hugged both of them, then jumped back in, closing the door behind her.

"There's a wide spot just down the hill and around the bend, lass," he said, and pointed down the slope. "I'll let the truck roll down to it, where it will be level before I try to start it. Then I'll help you turn the jeep around. Are ye ready, lass?"

She looked up and held his eyes for a moment. "Yes, Dev. I'm ready."

He nodded and turned her, led her to the driver's door, and helped her in. He showed her where the seat's controls were and had her adjust the seat to suit her.

"Okay. Follow me down the hill, lass. I'll use your lights to see where I'm goin'." He squeezed her hand and turned to the pickup.

The whole getting the truck down the hill, started, and turned around only took a few minutes, and he followed closely as Mary led the procession back to town. She drove slowly across town, staying on Harrison until she turned north at Twelfth. She turned and stopped in front of Dev and Mandy's house, and Dev parked the truck in the driveway in front of the trailer.

Dev walked back and helped Mary out of the jeep, saying it was good where it was for the night. Then he looked at his watch and then at Mandy.

"Did you have schoolwork tonight? I clean forgot to ask earlier." He smiled and looked at Mary. "See whatcha do to me, lass?"

Mandy giggled. "No, Da. I had a little but I did it while I waited for you after school."

"Good, lass," he said, and smiled. "Go get yerself washed up and ready fer bed, then maybe we can talk Mary into a cup of hot chocolate with us before ya go to bed."

"Okay," she said, and then stepped up to Mary and hugged her tight. "Thank you from me too, Mary." Then Mandy spun on her heels and hurried to the front door, unlocked it, and scampered upstairs.

-¤-

Mandy straightened in her chair and yawned, stretching her arms high over her head. She looked sleepily at Dev and then smiled at Mary. "Da, I think I'll go up now."

Dev caught her as she tried to stand up. Mary caught the chair as it wobbled sideways.

"I think so, love," he said, and scooped her up. Mandy reached out to Mary and closed her eyes.

Mary shook her head and took Mandy's hand, then walked behind as Dev carried Mandy to her room. Mary quickly pulled her bed covers down and Dev stretched her out on the bed. Then, with the covers pulled up around her shoulders, Dev kissed her cheek.

"Night, love. May yer dreams be happy ones."

Mary leaned down and whispered her goodnight to Mandy, and then she went to the door as Dev switched the nightstand light off.

At the bottom of the stairs he stopped and turned to look back up at Mary. "I know it's a school night, but would you like something more to drink before you head home?"

"No thanks, Dev." She smiled and stepped down into the room. She went to the single chair across from his sofa and sat down, looking up at him. "I know how protective you are about Mandy, not wanting her to walk anywhere alone, not being alone after dark, and all of the other times you won't let her out of your sight."

Dev sat down on the edge of the sofa and leaned forward, elbows on his knees, to listen.

"Why is it that you don't worry about her when she's hiking with me, away and off into the hills where you don't know where she is? Well, tonight isn't a good example because I know you were worried that you couldn't let her know what was wrong or where to go. But you don't know me at all, Dev. I'm a virtual stranger, one that you've seen around now and then over the course of the past two years or more. How can you—"

"I know it's hard to understand, lass," Dev interrupted, "and sometimes I wonder m'self. But I've seen you when you come grocery shoppin', checkin' every label, takin' little for granted, particular and conscientious. I've seen how you are with the kids at school and what other parents say about you and how you care for their kids in the classroom and out. I've watched you with Mandy and listened to what she says about you, and I've been touched by your feelin's of carin' and compassion when I've told you about how we got here, how tough our road has been.

135

"When I met you at school over the name thing, I already had feelin's for you, and after I had met you I just knew I could trust you, in anythin', in everythin'."

"But to trust a stranger with the wellbeing of your only daughter?" Mary asked almost as a whisper.

"Mary," he said. "I trust you with me very life and hers too. I know you, Mary. Maybe not the one that was hidin' when she came here, or the one that was afraid to talk to me for so long, but I know you and how you feel and care about people." Dev inhaled, stopping what he wanted to say, knowing his thoughts were getting far too personal. He still felt it was too soon for her to know him well enough. Instead, he said, "And me showin' me trust in you, lass, helps Mandy to grow. She likes you a lot, and her seein' me trustin' you lets her know I support her and her instincts and choices."

Mary wrung her hands and slowly stood up. Dev stood with her, looking down at the top of her head as she studied her hands. He waited, captured in the moment by her long, gently curling locks as they disappeared over her shoulders and down her back. Then she suddenly leaned forward and wrapped her arms around his waist, the side of her head turned and pressed hard against his chest.

"I truly don't deserve a friend like you, Dev," she said softly, "but I'm very glad you're here."

"I am too, lass," Dev said softly. "I am very glad too. Any time you need me or my support, you just ask for it. You will always have it. You have a friend to help you against the darkness that brought you here. To help you through any darkness that comes into your life. You deserve all of the bright happiness you can possibly get. That is my prayer for you, lass, that you will find true happiness and never have to be afraid again."

"Thank you, Dev," she said, and slowly relaxed, letting her arms release him.

She stepped back and looked up at him, then picked up her coat and stepped to the door. Dev opened it and leaned toward her, but she held up her finger, gently pressing it against his lips.

"Not tonight. The last time I let you kiss me I didn't wake up until after ten in the morning." She held his eyes for a long moment. "I have school in the morning, and if we start something, I'm not sure I'll want to stop. Goodnight, Dev."

"Goodnight, Mary," he said, still holding the screen door open.

He watched as she walked down the front walk and then along the street. He sat down in one of the rockers and watched until long after she had disappeared from his view, thinking this was one of those little things he needed to watch out for.

Eighteen
Wednesday, September 20

"Da?" Mandy asked as she dried the hand-washed dishes. Dev washed them and set them in the second sink. "Sunday I forgot to ask and we've been busy the last two nights, but did you do any checking on the information I gave you?"

"Aye, love," Dev said, and took a deep breath, wondering how he was going to explain what he found to a ten-year-old without giving her nightmares. "I checked on a few thin's last Saturday while you two were out hikin'."

Mandy smiled. "What did ya find out? Did ya find out who died? Who she might be hidin' from? Is she—"

"Mandy, stop!" Dev said, and turned to catch her shoulders. "Control your eager questions and let's finish what we're doin'. Then we'll sit and talk about it."

"Okay, Da," she said, eyes wide as she considered his sober response. "Sorry. It isn't good, is it?"

Dev did not answer and Mandy quietly finished drying the items in the sink. Dev put them in the cabinets and drawers. When everything was put away, the counter wiped clean and dry, and the towel hung by the refrigerator, he looked at her.

"Let's go up to your room," he said as he went to the front door and turned the lock. He saw that Mandy noticed and hesitated on the bottom step until he joined her and together they went up to her room. Dev stopped in his bedroom and picked up the folder he'd put away in a dresser drawer.

She had settled cross-legged in the middle of her bed, and when he sat on the edge of her bed facing her, he began softly.

"Mandy, this may be the hardest secret you'll ever have to keep," Dev said, "but we work thin's together, so I'll tell you the basics. There are details that can wait for later, maybe sometime when Mary is willing to share what happened. But for now, you were right that she was called Cali Marrow." Dev slid the picture of blond "Mary" and Robert out of the folder. "Get your picture, love," he said, and pointed to her nightstand.

Mandy lay back and reached for the picture, then sat back up. Dev handed her the one he had printed out.

"She's married? That's her husband? A policeman?" Mandy studied the picture, glancing at Dev a number of times. She compared the image of Mary in both. "Her hair was lighter then."

"I'm sure she dyes it to help her hide."

"Is he bad? Did she do somethin' wrong? Is he looking for her?" Mandy asked, full of questions and curiosity.

"No, love," Dev said, and nearly choked. Tears collected in his eyes, and he wiped them as he answered. "He died. That's part of why Mary's here, hiding."

"Then who's she hiding from, Da?" Mandy asked. "It isn't from him if he died."

"I don't know for sure," Dev said softly, "but I think she might be hiding from the man that shot him, and then shot her."

"Oh no, Da. He was killed and then she was shot too?" Mandy's eyes quickly filled with tears, glistening as they slowly escaped and ran down her cheeks.

Dev pulled her close, hugging her gently. "Yes love, but she did survive. She's very much alive," Dev encouraged, and explained what little he knew from the police department's obituary and the public notification. "I think she was in the hospital two or three months, longer than you were after yer accident, before they started moving her around, looking for a place where she would be safe."

"Oh Da? Who else knows?"

"I don't know, love," Dev admitted. "Here in Roosevelt, I think the sheriff knows and I think your principal, Mrs. Arnold, probably knows. But I don't know who else."

"The woman that comes to see her two times a month," Mandy said with conviction. "I bet she knows."

"Could be so, love," he said, holding her hand as he sat back to see her. "It would make sense."

Dev wiped her cheeks, and suddenly she looked at him and her eyes went wide. "They haven't caught him yet, have they?"

"I think that may be the case, also, love." Dev tried to smile. "We just have to pray to God in Heaven that whoever shot Cali in Ann Arbor doesn't find out she survived. And there's no way he can know she's Mary or that Mary lives here now."

Mandy squeezed his hand, but Dev did not notice her sudden shiver. "Do you know who?"

"Nay, lass," Dev said, shaking his head. "But I'm trying to think of who I can call to get some more information. Maybe I can find out. In the meantime, we,—that is, you and me—will have to help by keeping watch for new strangers."

Mandy giggled, but not a funny giggle. "With hunters coming in from everywhere this time of year, you want to watch for strangers." She smiled. "Maybe we shouldn't be lettin' her walk home alone either."

"Now that's a very good idea, lass," Dev said, smiling for the first time since they had gone upstairs. "I don't think she would think it was too strange if I asked to walk her home at night. No one would even notice."

"No, Da. No one would, except the whole town." Mandy giggled again, this time because he was funny. "I think a lot of people are noticing that we spend a lot of time with Mary, and the other way around. Even a few of the kids at school have mentioned it."

Friday, September 22

"Henry?" Derry asked loudly as she walked through their mother's dining room to find Henry rinsing the last of the breakfast dishes and filling the dishwasher. "There you are. Have you seen Dev and Mary's picture?"

"What?" Henry said, and glanced up, hearing her over the loud hissing of the rinse water. He shut the water off and asked again. "What, sis? I couldn't hear ya over the water."

"Dev's picture, have ya seen it?"

"It's on the mantel." Henry shrugged and turned the water on again.

Derry stepped up beside him and shut the water off. "'Tisn't. I've been dusting"—and Henry noticed the hand-duster in her right hand and the spray cleaner and rag in her other hand—"and just finished the mantel. It isn't there."

"Then I'd check with Mum," Henry said with a shrug. "Maybe she took it upstairs. With him and Mandy gone, ya know, she might've taken it to look at in her room."

"Aye," Derry said, and turned. "She might've at that."

Henry watched her as she left and turned through the dining room into the central hallway. When he heard her start up the stairs, he turned the water back on and continued rinsing.

-¤-

Henry was humming a new tune he had heard on the radio when a tap on his shoulder startled him. The plate he was rinsing clattered in the sink when he jumped and turned to see his mother with Derry just behind her.

"Henry, Derry says Dev's picture is missing," Maeve said.

"So she said," Henry said as he turned back and picked up the plate he'd dropped, and when he had inspected it, he set it in the dishwasher. He straightened and wiped his hands on the dish towel. "I haven't looked at it since the whole family was here, what, Labor Day," Henry said, and walked to the living room as if he would be able to see the picture when his sister could not. "It was right...here." He stared at the vacant spot on the mantel, between a picture of his father and one of another aunt. "Well, hmm. That's where it was."

"Yes, it was," Derry said, and smiled, "but 'tisn't now."

"That's odd," Henry said. "Probably ought to call Brenna and Moira and ask them."

Henry glanced at Derry and saw that she was already on her mobile phone, checking with them. After a moment, she turned to him and their mother, shaking her head.

Without further coaxing, Henry started looking around the room for signs of anything else that might be missing. He checked the living room again, then checked the den and then his dad's office where they routinely managed his mother's books. Maeve, seeing what Henry was doing, sat down at the large desk and began checking the items on the desktop. She checked each of the drawers while Henry confirmed the family safe in the side closet was closed and locked.

"Have you been in the safe recently, Mum?" he asked, and Maeve thought a moment.

"Yes, Monday or Tuesday," she said. "I wrote a check to the missions."

"Aye," Henry said softly, and punched the combination into the keypad. He opened the heavy door and quickly confirmed the ledger, checkbooks, and other valuables seemed to be there. He closed the door, swung the locking handle, and cleared the keypad. "Seems to be in order, Mum."

"Are you thinkin' someone would come into the house and steal just Dev's picture?" Derry asked.

"Not sure about that, sis," Henry said. "But if someone came into the house and took Dev's picture, I'm sure they were looking for something else first—something of value. Dev and Mandy's picture wouldn't be valuable to anyone except us—monetarily valuable, that is."

Henry stepped behind the desk and their mother and checked the window latch, then moved to the next window. Derry followed his example and started checking the other windows around the first floor. When the windows were all found locked, Henry checked the front and back doorjambs and latches for signs of forced entry, but they too seemed to be normal.

"Well, so much for in here," Henry said with a sigh. "I think I'll walk around outside."

"I'm coming too," Derry said, and followed Henry out through the back door and down the back steps. "What are you lookin' for?"

"Don't know yet, sis," Henry said as he looked at the faces of the house within the back fence.

Seeing nothing out of place and no broken cellar windows, he led the way through the gate into the side yard. Near the front of the house, he noticed scratch marks on the old, boarded-up coal chute. It was secure when he tested it, and then a thought hit him. "Come on," he said, and got up.

In the backyard, he went straight to the old, double-doored outside cellar entrance and pulled on one handle and then the other.

When he pulled on the second handle, the door swung up and open.

"I'm thinkin' this is how they got in," he said, looking at the wooden locking pole, sawn in two through the slot between the doors. Slowly, he started down the steps into the cellar. "I still don't know what they were looking for, but I think I need to call that Williams fellow, the detective down at the precinct."

"I think so too," Derry said softly as she followed him down the steps.

¤-¤-¤-¤-¤

Mary's phone dinged in her purse and she stopped reading the students' work papers in front of her. She opened the bottom drawer in her desk and took her phone out, giggling softly as she read Dev's text message.

"Dinner at Stumpy's? Six?"

She looked at the time—five thirty—and typed a question. *"Six thirty?"*

Mary smiled and looked back at the paper, and made a couple of marks before her phone dinged again.

"Six thirty will be fine, lass. We'll be by to walk with you."

Again, Mary smiled. She set a reminder alarm to notify her when it was six fifteen, then she put her phone back in her purse, closed the drawer, and returned to her papers. Time flew, and she had two papers left when her reminder chimed. Reluctant to stop at first, she forced herself to put the papers in the folder and file them away in her cabinet; there would be time over the weekend or Monday morning to finish them.

Mary slipped her arm and head through the shoulder strap of her purse and straightened her chair, then she switched the lights off and closed the classroom door as she stepped out into the hallway. She stopped near the front door to wait for Dev and Mandy, and just as they arrived, Mrs. Arnold saw her and asked her to come into her office for a moment.

Mary stopped at the counter as Dev and Mandy entered, and she motioned to them to wait and where she was going. Dev smiled and gestured for her to go on.

"Hey, Nancy. What can I do for you?" Mary asked as she stepped into the office.

Nancy looked at Mary and glanced past her to where Dev and Mandy took a seat on the chairs in the hallway.

"First, Mary, I want to ask how you are doing? You seem to be doing well in your classes, and I feel like you're feeling better about yourself."

"I am, thank you," Mary said, and smiled. "A few things are looking up, and I'm a little happier than I was for a long time after I got here."

"Because of Dev and Mandy?" she asked straight out.

"Yes, to a large part," Mary said, still smiling. "They've made me feel welcome, even when I didn't want to feel that way."

"I see," Nancy said, her tone still stern.

"You don't like that?" Mary asked. "That I like being with them?"

"No, Mary," Nancy said. "I'm sorry. I'm just concerned, knowing how difficult a time you were having getting settled. No, I think it's nice that you have someone to be with. But the children and some parents are beginning to notice, and some have made comments."

"Comments? About?" Mary asked. "What am I doing that warrants people's concern?"

"It's just a small town," Nancy said, "and people noticed how reserved you were and now, since school started, you're different, dressing nicer, out more, being seen all over town, and mostly with Dev and Mandy."

"So? Are they claiming I am doing something sordid or improper with my time with Dev and Mandy? Or is it because there are fifteen eligible single females that wanted a crack at Dev?"

"I...I don't know," Nancy said.

"Well, we meet in public and we're always with Mandy," Mary said with a tight smile. "Dev almost won't let her out of his sight, so it's pretty hard to do anything improper, or that a ten-year-old should not see or hear. And if it's the other fifteen, daughters of hopeful mothers or whoever, you can just tell them I don't know why, but Dev asked me, not the other way around."

"Okay, Mary," Nancy said, and smiled. "I'm not your mother and you've done nothing wrong as far as the school is concerned, but do be careful. Does he know why you came here?"

"No. I've talked to Ms. White, and she says I should tell him if I'm sure I can trust him."

"Can you?"

"Yes, I'm certain of that." Mary smiled a tight smile, holding her few doubts tightly in check.

Nancy nodded. "I would have to agree with you on that. I just wanted you to know that some folks are talking behind your back. Be careful, but most of all, try to be happy. Whatever it is that's been happening, it looks good on you. I'm sorry if I'm causing you worry. I truly don't mean to be. Now go on. Don't keep them waiting."

Nineteen

"So what's the occasion, Dev?" Mary asked, and slipped her jacket over the chair back.

Dev helped Mandy with her jacket and then sat down in the chair between them, his back to Stumpy's front window.

"Well, it's Friday night, both of you are out of school, and I figure it's time to get thin's started."

Mary's eyes went wide, immediately thinking of her comment the previous Tuesday night, when she would not let him kiss her goodnight.

Mandy just glanced at him and opened her menu.

"What are you planning to—"

"A fire, Mary," Dev said with a knowing smile. "After dinner, I would like to go back to the house and start a big fire in the fireplace, turn the sofa to face it like we do every winter, and then have hot chocolate and marshmallows toasted on the fire for dessert."

"S'mores, Da," Mandy said, and stopped her pointing finger on a menu selection.

"S'mores. What did ya find, love?" Dev asked, and looked at her finger on the menu.

"May I have the half-size chicken-fried steak, Da?" Mandy asked, showing him her choices for sides.

"Looks gran', love," Dev said, and smiled at Mary as Connie came up and asked for their drink orders.

Dinner was leisurely and the conversation bounced from his forgetfulness on Tuesday to hiking in the morning and on to the broader topics of fall programs at school. Finally, when they were finished, he asked Mary if she was game for hot chocolate by a fire, and she agreed.

Dev paid the tab and led their procession up Main to Twelfth, and on to his and Mandy's house. Mandy hurried ahead, unlocked the door, and was in, switching the lights on before they reached the porch.

Mandy hung their jackets on pegs behind the front door as he turned and centered the sofa. Then he started laying in the kindling and the starter logs in the fireplace. When he had everything to his liking, he turned to Mandy.

"You want ta do the honors tonight, love?"

"Sure," Mandy said, and slipped down onto her knees beside him. She took the long match and struck it, waited a second for the flare to die into a flame, and then she set it to the kindling. She turned and smiled at Mary to be sure she had seen her do it.

"Looks lovely," Mary said, and took a place at one end of the sofa.

"Thanks," Mandy said, and hurried to the kitchen. "I'll get the stuff ready for the hot chocolate."

Dev chuckled and pushed himself up from his position on the floor. He looked at Mary and smiled. "Ya know she really enjoys it that you will come and spend time with us."

"I've told you before that I really enjoy it too," Mary said. "What can I do to help?"

"Any good at makin' s'mores?" Dev asked with a wink.

"I've been known to make one or two in my time," Mary said, and got up.

She followed Dev into the kitchen and he pointed her to the pantry closet where he said she should find everything they would need.

Mary was surprised at the orderliness of the pantry and quickly found the graham crackers, the bag of marshmallows, and the chocolate bars.

"Roasting skewers are hanging on the end of the cabinet," Mandy said as she set the pot on the stove and began slowly heating the milk, stirring gently.

"I have them," Mary said, and carried her collection into the dining room and set them on the table.

"We have folding trays beside the fireplace," Dev said as he glanced her way from where he was measuring the ingredients for

Mandy. "They might help."

When Dev helped Mandy carry the cups of hot chocolate into the living room, Mary was patiently waiting, sitting on one end of the sofa with all of the s'mores items arranged on the coffee table in front of her. Equal stacks of crackers and chocolate were arranged beside the open bag of marshmallows in the center of the table. Mary adjusted the stack of paper napkins beside it.

As he bent over, holding the tray so Mandy could set the cups on the coffee table coasters, he smiled at Mary's pleasantly changed appearance: no longer wearing the long, figureless gowns she had worn when he met her, but now in a nicely cut three-quarter-length-sleeved blouse that let her charms show, and her knee-length skirt that showed off her beautiful legs. He inhaled and took the empty tray to the dining room table, hesitating before he turned around, lest he return too soon and melt into a puddle right there beside the sofa. *Damn, but ye do take me breath away, lass.*

Mandy chose him to be the designated marshmallow roaster and she sat with Mary. Together she and Mary stacked the cracker and chocolate, waited for him to announce another marshmallow was ready, and for him to turn the skewer so they could capture it with the second cracker. Dev interrupted his roasting to eat one and then he hurried to keep up with the demand of Mary and Mandy's appetite for chocolate.

"Oh my," Mandy said, smiling hugely as she finished her last s'more. "Those were sooo good!"

"I quite agree," Mary said, and flopped back against the sofa.

Mandy sat down in the middle of the sofa and snuggled against Mary, holding Mary's arm around her shoulder.

Dev smiled and began picking up the discarded wrappers and set the cups on the tray. He collected everything and made it to the kitchen in one trip. He was still chuckling at Mandy's manipulation of the evening so she could spend as much time as she could with Mary; tonight Mandy was in control, and he enjoyed seeing her and Mary together. He put the trash in the bin beside the counter and rinsed the cups and saucers. Finished, he went back and sat down on the other end of the sofa, turning and smiling at Mandy snuggled against Mary's side.

"Hey, Da," Mandy said, and smiled from under Mary's arm.

"Hey, scamp." He smiled and gently rubbed her knee. "Have enough sugar to keep you awake?"

"I don't...think so," Mandy said through a huge yawn and then smiled up at him.

"Then I think you should go up and get ready for bed. Brush your teeth and we'll come up and tuck you in."

"Okay, Da," she said, and stretched as she sat upright.

Dev helped her up and pushed her gently toward he stairs. "Holler when yer ready, love."

"I will," Mandy said, and shuffled up the stairs.

He smiled and listened as she closed the bathroom door and started the shower water. Then he turned to Mary. "I almost feel left out tonight."

"Left out?" Mary asked, laughing. "You were the center ring act tonight. Mandy kept you hopping."

"That she did," Dev said, and leaned back where he sat and smiled at her. "So, where are you two planning to go tomorrow, weather permittin'?"

"Mandy asked if we could go back to Doe Basin, but by way of Stag Hollow," Mary said. "It's a bit of a hike if we do both and take the long way she likes, but shouldn't take more than a couple of hours, maybe three to get there, an hour or so to eat a sandwich and explore, then two or three to get back. Stag's a bit farther up. If the weather looks good enough, we'll need to head up around nine or nine thirty."

"Aye, the forecast sounds like it'll be a clear but cool day," Dev agreed. "For some reason, she seems to like the Hollow and the Basin."

"I think it's the mineral ponds and the wildflowers when they're in bloom," Mary said. "I'm not completely sure, since she seems to be interested in everything, all the time."

"Yes." Dev smiled and then held her eyes. "If it's good, she wants all she can get. And I think she sees her time with you as very good, a very special thing too. Thank you."

She smiled and looked down at her hands, folded in her lap. "I hope it's okay with you, Dev, but I feel much the same way about my time with her. Being with her seems to help me in ways I've never experienced before. A very excited, yet calming, comfortable time in all of the good ways. Both of you have shown me something about life that I realize I've never had and I think I've been looking for. And without the two of you, I'd still be holed up in my house, yelling at people passing by or complaining about my untidy yard."

Dev chuckled. "It was a bit untidy, lass. But I'm happy that you let us invade your life. I think between us, maybe we've blessed each other just a little."

"Thank you, too, Dev."

He reached over and squeezed her hand just as Mandy opened the bathroom door and hollered, "I'm ready, Da, Mary."

"Shall we?" Dev asked, and stood, helping Mary up.

Mandy was already in bed with her sheet and blanket up under her arms when Mary and Dev entered her room. Mary went around to the far side of her bed as usual and sat down on its edge.

Dev leaned over and kissed Mandy on the cheek. "Mary says ye need to be up and around early tomorrow. Ya need to be off by around nine if the weather will let ya."

"Okay, Da. Pancakes in the morning," Mandy said.

"Pancakes it is," Dev agreed, and kissed her again. "Lovely dreams, love. Tomorrow's another new adventure."

"Thanks, Da. Love you too."

Mary leaned down and whispered her goodnight, but Mandy quickly reached up and caught Mary with both arms, pulled her close, and kissed her cheek. "May your dreams be happy ones too, Mary."

Then Mandy released her and rolled onto her side, pulling the covers snuggly around her shoulders.

Dev stood and waited for Mary to reach the door before he switched the nightstand light off. He followed her out and down the stairs. At the bottom, Mary stopped and studied his living room and Dev waited. He knew there was something on her mind.

"Dev?" she asked finally. "Is there any way we can have an hour or two alone together—just the two of us?"

Dev's mind jumped from his own intimate wishes for time alone together to his darker thoughts concerning her situation. He sobered his emotions and listened to her. This was another of those little things he needed to watch for. *Pay attention, Dev.*

"It'll take a little planning, lass," he said softly, trying to not let any of his eagerness slip into his tone. "When would you like me to try and arrange something?"

"Soon, Dev. Very soon," she said, and then slowly turned and looked up at him, holding his eyes as she hugged him. "There are a couple of things I need to tell you about me. But at the same time, I don't want Mandy to feel like I'm avoiding her. In this case though, I need to explain some things and they aren't appropriate for a ten-year-old's ears."

"Come and sit with me for a bit," he said, and guided her to the sofa. He helped her sit and then he sat down beside her, leaned back, and curled his arm around her shoulders, pulling her gently against his side. "Now this is better."

She snuggled against him and took his other hand in hers.

"Now then," he said. "May I ask you if there's any way you can take a 'sick' day off, get a sub or somethin'?" Dev asked. "I don't know how that all works, but that might be better than me gettin' a sitter and takin' you on a delivery or a pickup, say down in Buena Vista or Salida on a weekend."

"That might actually work," Mary said softly. "Mrs. Arnold commented on the change she's seen in me and asked if it was because of you and Mandy. I told her it was."

"Thank you, lass," Dev said, "but I haven't asked ye to change."

"No, but you made me want to change, Dev. You and Mandy want to be with me and I want to be my best for you. I don't want people to think I'm actually the unkempt and discourteous woman that you started mowing yards for. You—"

"You mean the almost naked woman—"

She slapped his chest and he chuckled.

"I want to look nice for you and Mandy," Mary continued. "I want them to think well of you and your choices."

"I appreciate that, lass," Dev said, and smiled at her. "I especially like how nice you look. Even in your hikin' clothes and in your school clothes, ye take me breath away. And that's fer sure. You make me want to be better as well, and to be a man you'd be pleased to be with. And I've seen how much Mandy has changed toward her school work. She wants you to be proud of her too."

Mary squeezed his hand and leaned into him as he tightened his arm around her shoulders. Together they watched the fire until it finally flickered into embers.

Twenty

Wednesday, September 27

"What can I get you, Dev?" Connie asked as he sat down at a table near the front window.

"Hey, Connie," Dev said. "How 'bout a glass of your iced tea and a side of chips—I mean fries. I brought my lunch and I'm lookin' for a warm place to eat. Oh, and put some cheese and chili on them too."

"Got it," Connie said, and turned. "Thanks, Dev."

Dev glanced around the room, seeing a few regulars and a couple of new faces. He focused on the new ones and guessed by their dress that they were hunters in for the week, possibly staying at the Bear Canyon Motel east of town or one of their two B&Bs—the Whispering Creek on Buchannan and Seventh or Betty's on Hayes and Second. No matter why they were in town, Dev was alert to their presence and knew it was his knowing Mary's plight, even though she had not explained it yet. He was becoming wary of strangers, but knew that was silly because no one knew Mary was here or who she had been. He forced himself to relax.

Connie brought him his tea and side of cheesy chili fries and he slowly ate his lunch. Stumpy switched to the noon news on the television at the end of the bar and Dev absently listened to parts of the telecast from Denver. He paid some attention to the weather, noting the possibility of light snow in their area by the weekend, the first for the season. Maybe it would hold off and Friday would be dry.

He continued eating his sandwich and nibbling on his fries until a quick national news flash caught his attention: a tractor-trailer semi rig had overturned on Interstate 75 on the south side of Detroit, causing a fifteen-car pileup. Some fires, and the only fatality known at the time was the truck driver. No count yet on the fatalities or injuries in the affected cars. Then the news jumped back to the local telecast.

Dev stared at the television for a long moment, his thoughts racing back five years past. But that accident was on Interstate 96 in Royal Oaks, north of Dearborn. He shook his head to clear the unwanted memories and slowly began eating again. But the similarities between the two accidents would not leave him alone.

-☒-

When Dev finished lunch and started back to the grocery store, a thought crossed his mind and he entered a number into his mobile phone.

"Hello," he said when a young woman answered, noting that he had reached his old hook and ladder company. "Is Captain O'Malley available?"

"Yes," the woman said. "May I say who's calling?"

"Devlin O'Brien."

"Thank you," she said, and his ear was filled with scratchy hold-music.

"Dev?" a gravelly voice asked suddenly. "I don't believe it. How're things?"

"Doin' pretty well, Mike. Mandy's growin' like a weed and becomin' a regular mountain climber," Dev said. "But why I'm callin' is that I just saw a clip of your area news and a question or two popped into me head. Do you have a few minutes to talk?"

"Certainly, Dev," Mike O'Malley said. "Let me close my door."

Dev heard Mike cross the room, and he envisioned the worn and scuffed flooring in the offices where he used to work. Then Mike was back on the line.

"Shoot."

"I need for you to look at the information on the accident that Anne died in," Dev said slowly.

"Really?" Mike asked. "Do you want to dig that up again?"

"It isn't what you think," Dev said. "I'm okay, but I can't remember what we recorded about the truck or the driver that caused the accident."

"Yeah, you wuz pretty shook up and not much help after you found Anne's car," Mike said absently. "Okay, I have the files pulled up from the historical database. Let's see..." Mike hummed a moment and then said, "Looks like it was a Carlson Transfer truck pulling a load of pig iron for the iron works down by Zug Island. The other EMT worked it because, well, you know..."

"I know, Mike..." Dev admitted softly. "Anything about the driver? Medical condition? Heart attack?"

"Let's see. The driver was dead at the scene. Aaah now here's somethin'. He died of poisoning, the lead kind. He was shot seven times through the driver's door." Mike hesitated. "I'd forgotten that."

Dev sighed, thinking maybe he was on the right track.

"I'm supposin' that accident had somethin' to do with the unrest around the steel mills and smelters," Dev said, "interruptin' the supply of materials. Have you worked any other accidents like that one?"

"Hmm, I think three. The ladder company in east Dearborn has worked a couple, but I'm not sure of the details."

"Can ya look at the three you worked?" Dev asked. "Whose trucks were they and what happened to the drivers?"

Dev heard Mike keying in more entries and then he hummed again. "Let's see. The first one that comes up was also a Carlson Transfer truck down in Wyandotte. No pileup but the truck ran off the road and rolled, blocking traffic on Biddle. Hmm, driver was shot in that one also."

"I think I'm seeing a pattern, Mike," Dev said.

"Yeah," Mike agreed. "The next one was a Richard's Transfer truck. That one just stopped crossways across all northbound lanes when he exited the seventy-five at Schaefer Boulevard. Ran the stoplight, crossed that wide intersection there, and stopped. Yeah. The driver was shot three times and died as he tried to get out of the cab. That one was three years ago. Yer right about a pattern, Dev."

Mike hummed again. "The third one is like Anne's. Carlson's truck. Ten-car pileup and fifteen dead. Driver also shot before the accident in that one. If you want me to look up the ones the Dearborn guys worked, it'll take me a day or so."

"Yeah," Dev admitted. "I think you should and probably ought to ask the Dearborn Police if they've made the same connection. I'm thinkin' all of these can be linked back to me Uncle Gallagher's boy, Einri, and his mob. At least you have an ID on the drivers. That might help. Might get the other precincts and departments to look at them and see what they can."

"Help?" Mike asked. "Dev, me boy? What are ye gettin' yer nose inta?"

"I'm not sure, Mike," Dev said, trying to keep his tone light, "but I'll let ya know when I find it. I just heard they had another one down on the seventy-five. Is Dearborn working that one too?"

"Yeah," Mike sighed. "We heard about that one about fifteen minutes ago. Sounds similar."

"Yeah, it does. I've got to get back to work now, Mike. Good talkin' to ya again." Dev started to switch off, then remembered. "Say Mike, before ya go, do the records indicate if all of the drivers were shot with the same caliber bullet, or were they different?"

"Let's see..." Mike said, and started humming again. Then after a few minutes he continued. "All were the same caliber rounds—nine millimeter."

"Rifle or pistol?"

"It doesn't say, Dev," Mike said. "But since they penetrated the truck doors and were measurable, I suspect they were at least fully jacketed."

"Okay. It was just a thought," Dev said. "One other thing, a bit more of a long shot. There was a Lieutenant Marrow killed in Ann Arbor three years ago—something to do with his assignment diggin' inta that unrest me cousin's been causin'. Can you find out who they think did the killin'?"

"What's that got ta do with the accidents?" Mike asked.

"Just call it a hunch, Mike. It may turn out to be nothin', but it's important that I check. I'd appreciate it if you can let me know what you find out on the Dearborn accidents and the Ann Arbor killin'. I'll talk to you later."

"Is this a good time of day to call ya?" Mike asked.

"Yeah. Mandy's in school and I'm at the end of me lunch break," Dev said. "Thanks."

"Sure thing," Mike said, and the connection broke.

¤-¤-¤-¤-¤

Einri O'Brien walked through the dark warehouse south of

Detroit on a cargo barge dock, situated on the west side of the Detroit River just above Ecorse. It was just past sundown when Einri pushed the door to the small office open and he and his youngest brother Scanlon entered. He sat down heavily in a metal chair near the single table and Scanlon settled on the edge of the rumpled cot, against the wall beside the table.

"Do ya have a beer?" Einri asked, and stared at his other brother, Mikalean, a year younger than him. Scanlon was a year younger again.

"Sure," Mikalean said tersely as he got up, walked to a refrigerator in the corner of the room, and took a can out. He tossed it to Einri. "I saw ya did what ya said you was gonna do," Mikalean continued, watching Einri take a long draw on the can. "Made quite a mess of it."

"No, I did not," Scanlon said. "Einri drove and I made holes from the back seat. Everything went like he said it would."

Mikalean shook his head in disgust and sat down, watching Einri as he finished the beer. Einri crushed the can in his hand and tossed it into the steel oil barrel in the corner, the trash receptacle.

"I hear there's another meeting at the truckers' union hall tonight," Einri said. "Ya need to stop by and listen to what's bein' said, Mik."

"I can do it," Scanlon argued.

"Yes, but I don't want any slip-ups, Scan," Einri said. "This one could be the one I'm waiting for and I don't want ya doin' anythin' that might let them know I'm listenin'. So you stay here and wait for Mik or me to get back."

"Where're ya goin'?" Scanlon asked.

"I need to find me box of pictures," Einri said. "'Tis me list of important people. I misplaced it, but today I remembered where I left it."

"Nora saw one of our cousins last week," Mikalean said. "She and some girls from her office were invited to a brunch that Merril and Brenna were at. Nora said Brenna was talkin' about Devlin gettin' it on with some cute woman out where he and his daughter moved to."

"Sorry for him," Einri said. "Who's the woman?"

"Don't know," Mikalean said, and smiled. "She mentioned gettin' a picture of the three of them, but wouldn't tell Nora who it was 'cause

Devlin was sayin' it isn't serious. Did Scan tell ya?"

Einri shook his head and watched Scanlon dig around in a file cabinet drawer.

"I was tellin' Scan about the picture and he talked Billie Ray inta takin' him out to Uncle Finnian's place. They stopped by one mornin', wee mornin' it was, and Scan snuck in and borrowed it."

Scanlon stood up with a proud, wide smile, turned to Einri, and handed him the framed picture. "She's pretty, but no one I know," Scanlon said.

Einri took it and studied the picture for a long moment. "Dev looks about the same and Amanda has grown a lot. She looks like she recovered okay, but...the woman looks oddly familiar...somehow. She looks like someone I've seen before. Do ya know where she's from?"

"Dunno." Mikalean shook his head. "Nora said Dev met her out west, wherever he's livin' now. Dunno why Scan thought you might like to see it."

"Yeah, well, 'tis good to keep up on the relatives. He's in Colorado," Einri said, and handed the picture back to Scanlon. He looked at Mikalean. "You need to get over to that meetin', and I'm off to Brighton to collect me thin's before our cousin discovers me trove in his toolshed."

Einri stepped out of the warehouse and walked the three blocks to where he hid his car. As he opened the door, he stopped and remembered another car door. It had been midday when he shot that nosy cop and the woman that saw him do it. Einri tapped his cell phone, connected to the internet, and made a quick search. He remembered where he had seen a woman that looked like Dev's picture, only she was dead; he had killed her. The Ann Arbor Police Department webpage popped up on his screen and he searched the gallery.

He smiled at the picture, a look-alike? Maybe, but if there was the slightest chance she had survived—any chance at all... *Well, I'll just have to kill her again.* He had not been able to make his last shot and put a bullet through her head; too many people came out to see what was happening.

I'll kill her this time, fer sure. No matter who she is.

Twenty-One

"Dev," Mary said sternly as they walked up Lincoln toward his house. "You can't keep fixing dinners for me. I should be fixing my own."

"But Mary," Dev explained, "'tis me selfish way fer Mandy and I ta get ta see ya more often."

"Yes, I know," Mary said with a smile. She did not want to hurt his feelings, but three or four nights a week seemed a bit excessive.

"Lass, just tell me if you'd rather be doin' somethin' else," Dev said. "I know you don't want to spend all of yer time with us, so if I'm askin' too much, just tell ye want to spend some time alone."

"It's okay, Dev," she said, and squeezed Mandy's hand. "It isn't that you're asking too much, actually. I just feel like I'm imposing."

Mary was walking between Dev and Mandy, as was becoming her normal place when they were together, unless of course Mandy would change her mind and walk between her and Dev, so she could hold both of their hands.

Dev had fixed a small roast with the usual sides, and Mary questioned the weekend meal in the middle of the week. Dev simply said it was an oven meal and easy for him, since it would cook while everyone was at work and be ready when he got home. He and Mandy had set the table and had everything ready to serve by the time they needed to go and get her from school.

After they ate, they played a card game from a box—not rummy—until it was time for Mandy to get ready for bed. When Mandy went upstairs to shower and get herself ready, Mary told Dev she had things set up.

"Mrs. Arnold was all for it," Mary said, "and I have Mrs. Critcher signed up to sub for me on Friday, all day."

"Then I'll take Mandy to school as usual and come back for you," Dev said, and smiled. "You realize it will be our first time to go someplace, just the two of us?"

"Scary, huh?" she said, and smiled back at him. "I'll be ready. Do you know where you want to go?"

"We'll go down to Buena Vista—half an hour, forty minutes at the most," Dev said. "There's a very nice park there where we can visit, and a nice brewery and café just off the highway on Cottonwood that I think you might like for lunch."

"Okay," Mary said with a shrug. "You know I haven't been anywhere since I've been here. I've only seen what I can from my hikes up into the hills and maps. This will be my first adventure out into the great world around us. I'm nervous and excited, Dev. You'll have to show me what I should be doing."

"Sure, sure. Just be yer beautiful self, lass, and everythin' will be just fine," Dev said. "I'll be right beside you."

The bathroom door opened and Mandy hollered, "I'm ready, Da, Mary."

Dev helped Mary up and together they climbed the stairs to tell Mandy goodnight and to wish her happy dreams. It was becoming a routine, one Mary had to admit she liked very much.

¤-¤-¤-¤-¤

It was near midnight when Einri finally made his way from Dearborn to Brighton. He parked the car he'd stolen a few blocks from his uncle's house and slowly made his way from house to house, using the shadows from the streetlights and the large, aged trees for cover. There was nothing easy anymore when he needed to move from place to place. The police in every village, town, and township were on the lookout for him, his brothers, and many of his close associates. It was that and his need to stay close to the events around Dearborn that had taken him away from his refuge at his uncle's and kept him from making it back.

Einri knew Henry would be very angry if he knew he had been using the storage shed in his backyard, but that had kept him out of sight for nearly a week to let things cool down some before he had to return to Dearborn. *What Henry does not know should not bother him.*

Einri stopped beside a cedar at the street corner, half a block from his uncle's place. He knelt in the shadows of the tree, looked at his surroundings, and tried to make himself small, less of a silhouette. It was not an easy thing for someone his size to do.

He waited and listened. There were only two ways to get into the backyard: the gate beside the house or over one of the three back fences from adjacent yards. The fences were tall and solid, making it hard to see past, but he figured they were his best bet—more shadows and less chance of being seen.

Cautiously, he worked his way along the street to his right and crossed under the shadows of the trees mid-block. Most of the backyard fences in this part of Brighton were wood panels or made-to-look-like-wood panels, so he had to stretch up on his toes to peer into the dark yard between him and his uncle's yard. Then he decided and jumped up on the fence and rolled over the top. It creaked and wobbled, the posts frail with age, but they held and he dropped into the darkness of the first yard.

Skirting the dimly visible lawn furniture, he reached the fence around Henry's yard and again peered over, searching the confines for anything that shouldn't have been there. He waited another long few minutes and then leapt up onto the fence and slowly rolled over and into the yard.

Crouching low, he hurried to the shed and grabbed the lock hanging on the hasp. He pushed, and was jolted when his shoulder hit the door; it did not open. He absently felt the lock and hasp in surprise; it rattled but did not budge. He pulled his phone from his pocket, held it very close to the hasp, and tapped the button, illuminating the screen.

As he realized the hasp and lock were new, a voice shouted, "ON THE GROUND! FACEDOWN ON THE GROUND!"

Einri snapped the phone off and looked up to see shadows hurrying toward him from across the yard!

"Damn!" he muttered, and jumped for the back fence, the closest. He fired a blind shot at the nearest dark silhouette and pistols barked and popped in reply. The fence shuddered under his weight and from the pounding of the bullets. He fired back, blindly, as he fell over the fence. Forcing himself up, he ran; his legs complained painfully. Something was wrong, but he pushed himself toward the darkness beside the house between him and the next street.

-◻-

The Brighton police lieutenant posted near the south side of their loose perimeter spoke softly into his boom mic. "We have a man on foot approaching from the south. He's keeping close to the houses."

"Copy that," the voice of their leader replied in his earpiece. "The squad has been alerted."

A few minutes passed and the lieutenant watched from his position under a cedar just west of the intersection half a block from Henry O'Brien's house.

"He's moving east along the street," the lieutenant whispered. "Crossing to the north mid-block." A moment later: "He's going over, headed for the backyard."

-◻-

"Hold your positions," the leader's voice whispered. "He's coming over the south fence."

The leader and the other officers waited, watching the dark shape as it came over the fence and made straight for the storage shed, like someone that knew precisely where he was going. He heard the thump as the man shouldered the door, then the rattle of the hasp. When the cell phone dimly illuminated, the leader hollered, "ON THE GROUND! FACEDOWN ON THE GROUND!" He and the other officers charged from their hiding places around the yard.

Instantly, the light from the phone went out and the man jumped for the fence, firing a random shot toward the approaching officers.

"FIRE!" the leader shouted, and all four returned fire, focusing on the shadowy blur as it scaled the fence and disappeared over the top. The leader was on top of the shed and the others were vaulting over the fence by the time the man got to his feet and started for the darkness around the house behind Henry's.

As he neared the house, another dark silhouette stepped out to block the way. Both fired.

Twenty-Two
Friday, September 29

"Feels like I'm skipping school, Dev," Mary said as he slowed the jeep, approaching the intersection of the valley highway and Highway 24. "I mean, I guess I am, but...well, you know what I mean."

"Yes, lass," Dev said, and smiled at her, noticing how her hair, gathered and tied behind her neck, reached down her back. It flowed with her movements as she turned her head and looked for traffic with him. "I do know what you mean."

He checked the traffic both ways as trucks, cars, and semis passed the intersection, and then in a suitable gap he swung the jeep onto the highway and headed south with the flow.

"Have you thought about gettin' your driver's license?" Dev asked, making conversation over the roar of the tires and whoosh of oncoming cars as they passed.

"I haven't had a need," Mary said, obviously thinking about something, but she did not say what. "I don't have a car and I have nowhere that I need to go, so it hasn't been a big item on my list of things to do."

"You'll have to tell me sometime what's on that list of yours," Dev said, and glanced at her.

"Now why would I need to be doin' that?" Mary asked and Dev looked at her, surprised at her phrasing of the question and lilted words.

He chuckled. "Just to know if ya might be needin' me help with any of 'em."

"So, you think you're a help now?" she bantered in reply, eyebrows raised in emphasis.

"Just hopin', lass," he said, beaming at her feistiness. "Just hopin'."

Mary smiled and turned to watch the open valley slide past her window. Dev watched her, happy for her, hoping that she would enjoy being with him, and not just with the man with the wonderful daughter. It was not that he was jealous of any of the time she spent with Mandy, but he wanted to know that she liked being with *him*.

He wasn't sure when it had happened, but Dev knew that he wanted to be with this woman, to have her as part of his and Mandy's life every moment of every day. The exact moment it happened escaped him, but he knew she had won his heart completely.

Dev shook his head and forced himself back into the now. He felt like he needed to ease any concerns she might be having and he gently slid into the role of tour guide, identifying the various mountain peaks and offering any information he could remember about the villages, the country, or the people they passed along the way.

The drive did not take long before they started seeing the residential areas north of Buena Vista, past the trailer park on the left, the electric association building, and then suddenly they were stopped in traffic in front of the Family Dollar. Dev drove farther south and turned into McPhelamy Park and stopped beside the pond.

"Is this okay?" he asked, and looked at Mary. "It's still a little cool out, but we can walk a bit if you'd like."

"I think I'd like to walk some," Mary said, and unfastened her seat belt.

"Okay. I brought a thermos of coffee in case ya get cold," Dev said. "Whenever you'd like some."

"Later, Dev," Mary said, and looked at him, her expression drawn and concerned, her previous smile gone. "I think I just need to get this over with and see…"

"Aye, lass," Dev said, and gently caught her arm. "Just remember, ye can't tell me anything that will change how I feel about ya. So please don't fret."

Mary smiled and opened her door. Dev got out and hurried around to help her, but she did not wait for him.

Dev felt Mary's concerns, and he worried about her—whether she was warm enough or…he just worried about her and followed.

-ロ-

Mary followed the bank of the pond under the wintery, leaf-bare trees to the wooden bridge over the northern neck of the pond. She walked out onto the bridge a short way and then stopped and leaned back against the rail, glancing up at Dev.

"Where to start...? I guess at the beginning," Mary said, took a deep breath, and looked at the planks in the decking.

Dev stood in front of her, giving her the space she needed. He leaned back against the opposite rail, leaving the width of the bridge between them.

"Many years ago," Mary began, "I was a different person with a different name. I was born in Green Bay, Wisconsin, a blond girl named Cali Hughes of a German-American mother and an Irish father. My childhood was normal by most folk's standards. Nothing eventful happened until I lost my folks when I started college—drunk driver ran a red light. I fell apart and never got used to suddenly being alone. Then two years later, I met Robert—Bobby. I was going to the university in Ann Arbor, getting my teaching degree, and Bobby was a beat patrolman there." Mary continued to stare at the decking, her hands deep in her jacket pockets. "I turned twenty-eight last June. I knew Bobby for seven months and was twenty-one, almost twenty-two when we got married. He was a year older than me.

"I taught in one of the elementary schools there in Ann Arbor, and he worked at being a good cop. He liked the beat work, the getting to know the shop owners, their loves, hates. It was good for him, but I always worried some—more after we got married. The crime in the Detroit area in general was getting worse, spreading, and I worried a lot more."

Mary looked up at Dev, her eyes damp, full of uncomfortable memories, her heart pounding, uncertain of how Dev was accepting her telling, but he kept his expression soft, and she could feel his concern.

"We'd been married two years and we had started arguing, more and more. I was getting scared with the changes I saw in him, mostly because of his job. So Bobby decided to help make things easier for me. We started doing lunch together twice a week at a park near the university where we met. It was his way of helping me see that everything was okay, but it wasn't. Bobby had gotten a promotion of sorts, helping with some investigation work, and I found out that he'd been confronted a few times by one of the local thugs and his gang, group, whatever they called themselves. Bobby would not blur the lines, as they say, in his line of work, and stayed true to himself and the police force, reporting what he found out and so on. During our last six months I knew things were getting worse, and the lunches in the park only helped a little. He became withdrawn, more nervous, restless at night. And anytime he was at home, he resisted anything I tried to do to comfort him. The winter was cold, and our being together seemed colder yet. Only during our lunches out was he somewhat normal, happier and caring.

"Then on April the ninth, on our third anniversary, I drove from school on my lunch break for one of our lunches together. I parked at the curb by the park and he helped get the picnic basket out of the car."

Mary started trembling and Dev quickly stepped to her and wrapped his arms around her. He remained silent, and she kept her hands in her jacket pockets but turned her head, laying her cheek against his chest, savoring his warmth through his shirt, his arms around her.

"The first sign of trouble was when I heard a pop and the windshield of the car shattered. I saw Bobby fall against the car and then backwards. I heard many more pops, louder, closer, shots being fired as he fell. Someone was screaming! Loud, and I almost couldn't hear anything else. Then everything stopped and I was the one still screaming and I looked up as a tall, broad-shouldered, redhaired man pointed his gun into the car but it did not go off. He was angry. Then something dropped out of his gun and he reached into his pocket, and later I figured out that he was reaching for more bullets. Frantically, I pushed my door open and ran, screaming at the top of my lungs. I crossed the street and something jerked my arm, then something hit me in the back, knocked me down. Everything went black. Then I remember people, a lot of hazy, vague people. I was looking at faces and someone was rolling me over, asking me questions I couldn't understand.

"The next thing I remember was being taken out of the ambulance and into a building—the hospital, I suppose. I was frantic but floating…something they had given me. Everything went blurry and then dark. I guess I passed out. They said later that I had told the doctors and the officers who it was that shot Bobby, but I can't remember telling them.

"They told me I had been unconscious for nearly two weeks when I woke up the first time. Then another two weeks passed before I woke up again and stayed awake for a while. I had had five surgeries for my arm, two for my shoulder, and I don't know how many for the body wounds, but they couldn't get all of the bullet fragments out and I'll have to have more surgeries when I'm strong enough. I've been putting them off, not really seeing any reason to add more pain and suffering…" She inhaled and hesitated before she continued. "It took another month before I could walk again, and I was just able to get around somewhat normally without crutches or a cane when I came to Roosevelt, hidden in a witness protection program.

"When I was able to understand what had happened, they told me I had a new name, Mary Gorden, a new birth certificate that has a different birthplace, and a different ethnic background listed. I was surprised they didn't change my birthdate." Mary let out a cynical half laugh. "Of course, DNA is still DNA. It doesn't change, and they'll be able to identify my body and tie it to my old name when they find me dumped in the woods somewhere."

Dev did not move. He did not speak. She appreciated that he just held her gently against him, his arms giving her a security and comfort she had not expected. Slowly she pulled her hands out of her jacket pockets, slipped her arms under his coat, and pulled herself tight against him.

"I'm sorry Dev, but I was hurting and lost when I came to Roosevelt. I was afraid of everything and everyone. I pretty much still am. I was mourning the loss of my husband and his companionship and I was in physical pain, trying to relearn how to exist, walk, and to just do the normal things we all do every day.

"Well, that isn't entirely true. I hated my situation and that made me angry—angry at everything and at everybody. I felt everyone, everything was an unwanted intrusion, a horrible reminder of what I didn't have anymore. I couldn't even go to his funeral and didn't have the chance to say goodbye before he died. I wallowed in grief and self-pity longer than anyone should. I even tried to kill myself—four times, actually—but I couldn't do it. Something always went wrong.

"It took time for me to finally accept my status, to surrender to my situation if you will, and finally, when you mowed my yard and

I came out screaming at you, something changed. I had grieved for my lost life for so long it just seemed like a habit. I had learned how to walk, hike, and do those normal things, but I was still hiding from everything. Teaching last year helped immensely, forcing me to face my new life and reconnect with one thing that I loved doing, but you mowing and me screaming at you unlocked something more. And then I was suddenly confused, lost again.

"It still took some time, but I began to see you, to realize you were part of the fabric of my new life in Roosevelt. You began to stand out, and then Mandy showed up in my class this year." Mary trembled again and instantly felt his arms tighten gently around her. "I knew you by sight but didn't know your last name, and when I saw it, Mandy's name on my seating chart, I nearly freaked out. I know I scared her and probably half the class."

Mary turned her head up and looked at Dev, catching his eyes.

"I kind of lied to you that day at school. The man that shot Bobby and me was an O'Brien, spelled the same way. I know there are a lot of O'Brien's, but when I saw Mandy's name, I almost lost it. I fumbled and tried to make up an excuse for my actions, or reactions, and that's how Mandy and I got into our 'discussion' about spelling and pronunciation. But that man is still loose and I'm still hiding from him. If he finds out where I am, the name change may not be enough and I could still wake up dead. My time is borrowed, and now I've gotten both you and Mandy involved, and maybe into terrible danger yourselves."

"I know, lass," he said softly, and squeezed her gently, "and we'll help ya face it. But now I have some things to tell ya and maybe do a little confessin' m'self."

-¤-

Dev took a deep breath and held her eyes, his thoughts racing around in his head. Finally, he sighed and knew he just had to let the words come out.

"I have ta tell ya what else's been happenin'. Mandy told me she heard Mrs. Arnold call you 'Cali' at school one day, and you sent her to finish an errand you were on," Dev began explaining. "She's a nosy brat at times and she saw a sticky note on the folder Mrs. Arnold put in her secretary's in-basket."

He felt Mary stiffen in his arms, and her expression turned

serious, cautious, but her eyes did not leave his.

"I had been doing some checking on Anne's and Mandy's accident, talkin' with me old ladder company chief 'bout some similarities with more current accidents," Dev continued as gently as he could, "when Mandy told me the name from the sticky note. The next time I was in the library, I did some checkin' on the name. What scared me the most was how much I was able to find out about the woman named Cali with just a few questions and some simple digging." He sighed again. "I will show you what I found, if ya want me to, when we get home. I told Mandy the high-level details, but not everything, lass. She was afraid you were married and for some reason was havin' to hide from your husband."

Mary half-smiled at the irony, but did not say anything. She waited. He could feel her rising tension, her growing fear.

"Once I confirmed that the woman 'Cali' had been married, I found her husband's information from the obituaries and the police department's website. The truth of what you have gone through hit me very hard when I found the picture of the two of them in the photo gallery they kept on their website. That's when I knew you'd seen the Devil's work too, and I finally understood what you meant that day at school, 'bout everyone havin' it hard at one time or another."

Mary pushed herself back and stared at him. "So...you knew? And let me go through all of this torture of figuring out how I was going to tell you what's happ—"

"No! Yes, some." Dev stumbled, his words and thoughts tangling themselves around each other. "I know only what I found on the internet. I tried to make sense of what you have said, but I didn't know what ya know until ya told me—"

"How long?" she asked sharply, her voice getting louder as she continued. "How long, Dev? When did you go looking? Checkin' up on me?"

He held his breath a moment, hoping the time would help her calm down. He still held her loosely, but he knew their contact was tentative at best.

Dev realized he was holding his breath and slowly exhaled. "'Twas two weeks tomorrow, lass." He waited a moment, hoping—

"Two weeks?" she asked in a deep, accusing tone. "You and...and... Mandy have known about Cali for two weeks...and haven't told me.

You've been spying and...and...what did you want? What were you looking for? Something to hold over my hea—""

"No!" he nearly shouted, the closest he could recall to ever losing his temper, feeling his connection with her slipping. He was breathing deeply and Mary stopped, watching him. "No, lass. There's no coercion or cruelty intended. And I only found what I did by followin' the name Cali, not yours. I didn't truly know ya were the same 'til I saw Cali and Robert's picture. I'm just very worried fer ya. I'm here, lass. I'll always do me best to protect ya and keep ya safe, even against another O'Brien. Me and Mandy both will. And that's fer sure."

-¤-

Mary trembled and studied his face, his expression, the deep, darker green of concern in his eyes. "You're scaring me, Dev. Scaring me a lot." She took a deep breath and exhaled slowly. "I trusted you enough to finally tell you things that you could easily use against me. I trusted you and now...now...now my life could really, really be in danger. I trusted you..."

"Ye still can, lass," he said softly. "'Tis you and yer safety that I'm worried about. You know I mean ya no harm, lass. Ya know it as surely as yer standin' here, this very moment."

"Why? Why would you do such a thing? You don't even know—"

"Shh, shh, lass," he shushed her and she studied his eyes. "Because I love ye, lass. I canna spend a day without thinkin' about ya or wantin' to be beside ya. And, yes, sometimes, worryin' about ya. I thought by now that would be obvious to ya."

Mary's mouth fell open. "You love me? But you went looking—"

"Only because Mandy saw a strange name on the file at school and Mrs. Arnold callin' ya by it." He gently squeezed her waist. "It was confusin' to both of us and Mandy was afraid to ask ya straight out. Maybe I was a bit too, not knowin'—"

"Afraid to talk to me? You?"

He nodded. "I've never wanted to push you or say anythin' that might make ye angry—"

"No, you just kept mowing my yard after I repeatedly told you to stop."

"Aye, but it wasn't meant to make ya angry..."

"Not to make me angry..." Mary cocked her head and a smile slowly crept across her face. She squeezed him, pulling herself tight against him. "No. Probably not. I wondered a lot about that."

"Maybe yer thinkin' me sayin' it is too bold, but 'tis true how I feel. I do love ye, lass."

"After Mandy explained about you calling me 'lass,' I thought you might. I am surprised and you still scare me sometimes, but I need to hear it, Dev. Over and over again, I need to have you remind me that you do."

"I'll do me best at that too, lass," Dev said as she tilted her head back to look at him. He kissed her softly and she melted into the touch of his lips. She pressed her body tight, conforming to him. She felt him respond to her, and abruptly she stiffened and pulled her lips away.

"Dev," she said, taking a deep breath.

"Yes, lass?"

"I could use that coffee now, before me legs go completely to jelly and I do somethin' very inappropriate for us bein' out in public."

"Aye, lass," Dev said, and smiled down at her. "I think coffee would be gran' fer now. We can consider the other when we get back home. We'll have a couple of hours before I have to meet Mandy at school."

Mary smiled and let him lead her back to the jeep.

-¤-

"Tell me, Dev," Mary said, and he watched her finish a bite of the chicken-and-Alfredo-sauce pizza and sipped the brewery's signature pilsner. "What do you plan on doing? Your future?"

"Just what I'm doin' now, lass," Dev said, and took another bite of his piece.

"Grocery store helper and volunteer fireman?"

"Unless ye or Mandy decide we might do somethin' different."

"Me? Mandy I can understand, but—"

"Sure. You too. I came here so Mandy and I could start a new life—one we wanted, made the way we wanted it to be. So far we have, and now that includes you."

"And that's all you want to do?"

"What are ye really askin', lass?" Dev stopped eating, lowered the piece of pizza, and held her eyes.

"I know little about these things, but Bobby was—well, men are usually ambitious, always wanting more of this or that. New careers, more status, more...I don't know. I don't really know what I'm trying to say. I just figured you'd be that way too."

"I'm not like that in so many words, Mary. But I do want more of what Mandy and I have. I do want more of you in our lives, but I like what Mandy and I have made. We want changes, sure, but not to redefine what we've become. I'm happy with a simple life. My skills and training have helped some folks, and maybe they'll help a few more as time goes on. Maybe when Mandy is out of school and wants to move on with her life, I may think about changin' or movin', but that depends on who I'm with and what we all decide together."

"And you can't decide until then, what you want that future to be?" Mary asked, and took another bite.

"Aye, I could, but tell ye what, lass," Dev said, and took a sip his ale. "If ye'll promise to marry me, then we can start working on that now, or at least before the time comes."

Mary coughed and covered her mouth with her napkin. "What? What did you say?"

"Ye heard me, lass. If ye'll promise to marry me, we'll—"

"I thought that was what you said."

"Well, all ye have to do is say ye will and we can go look fer a ring. They have a very nice jewelry store just up the street."

"Dev! Are you mad?" Mary challenged, unable to hold her voice down.

"No, lass. I'm not mad, but I am askin' you to marry me, whenever you wish to set a day, but I wish to be your husband and be at your side for as long as the good Lord be willin'. I want to start as soon as ye'll let me. Will ya please marry me?"

Mary sat back in her chair and stared at him in disbelief, and with wide eyes, chomped down on another bite of her pizza.

Twenty-Three

Dev had dropped Mary off at her house and then had taken his jeep and parked it in his garage. He walked back to Mary's, wondering if this was something she really wanted to do, and prepared himself for her to change her mind. It was a lot of planning and not much spontaneity, unlike their feelings when they kissed on his front porch, or even today in Buena Vista.

He knocked. Mary quickly answered the door and let him in.

-¤-

"You must be expectin' someone," he teased, and caught her in a hug before she could close the door.

"I am." She smiled and gave him a quick kiss before she locked the door and led him into the living room. Then she turned and stopped in front of him. "Before we go any further, Dev, I have to show you something."

"Are ye worried about yer scars, lass?" he asked, and reached out to pull her to him, but she stepped back.

"Yes, Dev," Mary said. "They're hideous to me and I want you to know what you'll see every time we're intimate. I want you to know what you're getting if I go through with marrying you. Part of love is what you see, not just what you feel in your heart. You have to live with both."

"Aye, lass," Dev said, and she slowly unbuttoned her blouse, starting at the bottom where she had pulled the tail out of her jeans.

When she reached the top button, she watched him watching her. Finally unbuttoning the last button, she slowly pushed her blouse off her left shoulder and slipped it off her arm, exposing the long, sinuous scar that ran nearly the length of her bicep.

"This one's the worst one," Mary said, and then began to explain clinically. "The bullet entered in the back just below my shoulder joint, shattered my humerus and exited just above the elbow. There's a shorter entry scar on the back of my arm."

Dev reached out, took her arm, and she noticed that he glanced at the rest of her. She saw him force himself to look away from her chest, only partially covered by her low-cut, nearly transparent flesh-colored bra.

He followed the scar with his finger, gently pushing here and there, sending tingles up her arm, across her shoulders, and down her spine.

"Does it still hurt, lass?"

Mary shook her head. "They were able to reposition most of the splinters and the doctors said they wrapped the bone with some kind of carbon fiber cloth to aid bone growth and to keep the splinters from cutting the muscle and blood vessels. The cast kept it the right length and in the right place while it healed. By now, they say my bone is stronger than it was before. I had a lot of bleeding, but the EMTs were able to stop the flow before I bled out on the street. Mostly, the lingering damage is in my ability to feel things correctly. My skin is sensitive in a weird way, changing, like being almost numb some of the time to feeling too much at others." She held his eyes. "Like now."

"How about yer shoulder?" he asked as he pushed her blouse off and felt the exit scar near the base of her throat. "The surgeon did a nice job stitching this one. It should blend out in time." He turned her so he could see the top of her shoulder. "You must've been turning, maybe falling," he said, and studied the angle of the line between the entry and exit scars.

She nodded. "The doctor made a comment that he thought that was the last one to hit me."

Dev nodded and then turned her to face him. He touched the scar in the center of her chest, just below her breasts. "Now this one is different. Not made by a bullet, I think."

Mary shook her head slowly and whispered as she looked away, "No. I did that one."

"Aye, I see," Dev said. "One of the four?"

Reluctantly, Mary nodded and looked at him.

"I can only imagine, lass. If Mandy hadn't survived, I think I might have felt the same way."

He gently ran his thumb over the exit scar next to her throat as he bent and kissed her.

"The scars are too thick and leathery," he continued as he released her lips and straightened up. "Do you have any body lotions or butters to soften it?"

Mary shook her head. "No."

"That's okay, lass," Dev said, and smiled. "I have quite a few we keep on hand for Mandy."

Suddenly Mary remembered Mandy's accident. She had been so involved in her own worry about how Dev would react to her scars, she never gave Mandy's injuries a thought.

"Oh, Dev. I forgot about Mandy. I didn't think about her having scars."

"Yes, lass, she does." Dev smiled. "Luckily part of me trainin' was for takin' care of wounds and scar tissue. We'll go back to my place later and I'll rub some butter into that scar." He smiled and inhaled, and she stiffened as his appraising gaze drifted down her length again. "Now, lass, I see no other wounds on the front of ya, and what I do see looks very, very nice, but turn around for me now and let me see how well the doctors treated your back."

She did, mentally kicking herself for putting herself on display.

His fingers lightly roamed around the spidery scars on her back, sending shivers up and down her body. Suddenly she wanted his fingers—

He caught her shoulder and gently turned her as he leaned toward her and slipped one arm under her legs and the other behind her. Her left arm instinctively caught his neck as he scooped her up like he did Mandy when she had reached the end of her todays.

"Now lass," he said, and kissed her before she could argue, "please show me which room you would like me to take ya to. I think I need to see if there are any other scars ye be hidin' and that might be needin' me attention." He was already climbing the stairs before he released their second kiss.

-¤-

Mary clung tight against Dev, her leg curled over his as he held her to his side in the afterglow of their first lovemaking. Dev smiled as he absently caressed the scar on the left side of her back; the effects and promises her kisses gave him barely hinted at the wonder and passion she brought to their intimacy.

"You okay?" Mary asked, and Dev realized his deep sigh was audible.

"Aye, lass. Much better than okay. Ye've touched me very soul."

Mary sighed and squeezed him. "I'm so glad they don't bother you."

"What, lass? Yer scars?"

She nodded without raising her head from where it lay on his chest.

"I know 'tis a shame the Devil marked ya the way he did," Dev said, and kissed the top of her head, "but God in Heaven kept ya alive."

Mary was silent for a long moment. "I fought with him. God. For a long, long time. I hated what he did to me, for letting it happen to me. All I could think about was how he let my husband die and kept me from dying. I wanted to die too, so very badly."

"I know," Dev said softly, remembering how he had felt after Anne died.

Mary shivered and Dev pulled the fleece sheet over them.

"At least you had Mandy to help you focus on living," Mary whispered. "And a family that tried to help."

"I know you were alone, lass. Ya must've felt completely abandoned, and I wish it coulda been different fer ya."

"I don't know why Bobby had to die," Mary whispered again. "But I'm glad I could mourn and begin to heal. I'm glad that I was here and that you found me and that you were persistent."

"Ya mean stubborn?"

"Yeah, I thought that at first," Mary said, and tickled his ribs, "but you're not. You're persistent once you've made a decision." She turned her head to look at him and then nuzzled his cheek as her hand caressed his chest and stomach.

"Ye keep doin' that, lass, and ye'll see just how persistent I can be."

"Sounds like a promise," she said, and rolled onto her back, pulling him with her.

Saturday, September 30

"Good morning, Mary," Ms. White greeted when Mary opened her front door to let her in. "It's gotten quite a bit cooler since I was here last time."

"That it has," Mary said happily, and took Ms. White's coat. "Come in and take a seat. Tea? Or coffee?"

"Coffee if you have it," Ms. White said as she sat down in her usual place on the sofa.

"I do," Mary said, and turned to the kitchen. She had the cups and saucers already on a tray, so she took the coffee pot from the warmer and picked up the tray, returning quickly to the living room.

She poured them each a cup and took her usual place in the cushioned chair facing Ms. White. "So, how was your drive this morning?"

"Actually it was nice," Ms. White said. "Dawn is coming later and the roads were clear, very little traffic." Ms. White hesitated a moment. "I wish I had some new news to give you, but things are still the same. The police still have not captured the man that killed your husband." Ms. White sipped her coffee. "So, how have things been with you? Last time you were facing a little bit of a dilemma. And this morning you seem very..."

"I told you about Dev and his daughter," Mary said over the rim of her cup, and Ms. White nodded. "And we talked about explaining my situation to him." Mary inhaled and smiled. "And I did."

"Well, well," Ms. White said with a smile. "And how did that go?"

"Better than I expected. A lot better. I asked him if we could find some time for just the two of us so we could talk, and together we decided the best way was for me to take a day off while Mandy was in school and we'd sneak away. He took me down to Buena Vista to a nice park and pizza for lunch. I can't wait to see the park in the spring when the trees start budding out...Oh, sorry," Mary said, bringing herself back to the moment. "I told him my story from birth to now."

"Was he okay with hearing that? Was he surprised, taken aback?"

Mary smiled and slowly shook her head. "He asked me to marry him."

"What?" Ms. White rubbed her face and stared at Mary. "You told him about your plight and the danger and his response was to ask you to marry him?"

"Yes," Mary said, holding her cup in her lap. "He said he'd always be here for me and do his best to protect me." Mary explained how their conversation over lunch had gone and what he had said when she asked what Dev saw his future to be like. "Then he said, if I'd marry him, we'd figure out together what we do when Mandy is out of school and if she decides to live somewhere else. He also made me pick out a ring before he'd bring me home." Mary stifled a giggle, then turned somber. "After I told him about me, he confessed that he already knew a few bits and pieces of what I told him, but not the details. It seems that Mandy overheard Mrs. Arnold call me 'Cali' by mistake one day at school." Mary explained that Mandy had seen the note with her full name on it and did some searching at the library.

"She asked Dev to help her when she finally told him what she heard, and he told me that he'd found out about Bobby's death." She sighed. "I accused him of spying on me, but he assured me he only knew Bobby and I were married when he saw the picture of the two of us together on the Ann Arbor Police website."

"Oh my," Ms. White whispered to herself.

"I was angry, hurt, confused until we talked it through. He was worried by what Mandy said, and her concerns, but then he was worried about me, knowing what I had gone through. He said he understood me better for knowing. He kept telling me he loved me and that he'd be beside me, no matter what happened, him and Mandy both would be here for me."

"And after lunch, you said he asked you to marry him?"

"Yeah."

Ms. White just sat and stared at Mary for a very long moment. "And...and are you going to? Are you sure about this? Getting married at a time like this? To someone you have only known a short time?"

Mary nodded slowly. "I watched him and asked questions about him over and over since I came here and now, yeah, I definitely want to. I think I knew I was falling in love with him before the day he interrupted us, the day I was screaming. And then you said you thought I was. But yesterday I told him I wouldn't answer him until

I had a chance to talk to Mandy alone and then the two of them together. I'll be goin' over there after we're finished today."

"And he's okay with the whole danger issue?"

"I think he's completely aware of the dangers. Especially after we talked yesterday. He even showed me what he found online. He also said he has some connections back in Dearborn that he can use to see what's happening back there. But to answer your question, he wants me to be safe and I am confident he will do everything he can to keep me safe. The truth is, I can't be in any more danger with them than I am without them. I tried to make him understand that I'm more concerned about how being with me would endanger them, but he said that for him and Mandy it was too late for them to simply walk away. He said we'll face whatever I have to face together, the three of us."

"Wow," Ms. White said. "And you think he means it?"

"Sure, sure. You could come to the fish fry tonight and see for yourself. Meet Dev and Mandy, then you tell me. I believe him and trust what he says. My life is in danger but not because of him, but my life may be worth saving because of him.

"Ms. White, I don't know what you have to report when you go back to your office and tell your superiors what you think, but I'm looking forward in my life for the first time because of the love of a very kind and generous man and his daughter. My past life is over and I don't lament it any longer. I'll always miss some of it, and I'll be happy I had the time I had with Bobby, but that isn't me anymore. It's taken me two and a half years of mourning and rehabilitation of one kind or another for me to learn to trust and live again. I'm not going to ignore this chance to be happy.

"I cannot believe God brought me through all of the hell I've experienced and Dev through all of the hell he's experienced to show us an opportunity like this just to tease us. I'm looking forward to me days bein' sunny and the warm sun in me face and soft rains on me fields. I like bein' called his lass and knowin' I matter as much as Mandy does in this man's life." Mary finally stopped, set her cup on the tray, and refilled it. "More?" she asked, and gestured to Ms. White's cup.

Ms. White nodded and began to smile. "Well, Mary I can only wish you the best and all the happiness possible. I will make a report and make note of your desires and opinion. Do you have a date picked out?"

"Not yet," Mary said softly without her soapbox. "But probably sooner than later. I would like for the murderer O'Brien to be caught and have this whole thing behind us before we get married, but the way this has continued to drag on, I don't want to wait."

"Well, you probably won't like that I did it, but I ran a background check on your Devlin O'Brien," Ms. White admitted, and sipped her coffee. "I got an update to my request on my way out here, and I believe this Devlin's everything you said he is. There seem to be some nefarious sorts on his father's brother's side of the family, but the office did not have the details on that when they called me. Shouldn't worry, since there are probably as many different O'Briens as there are Smiths. I'll have more to talk about when I come back in two weeks, but as far as you should be concerned, Devlin's a very fine and honest man on paper, and from what you've said, and what Sheriff Martin and Mrs. Arnold have said, you have fallen for a very good man. Go and be as happy as you can."

"Thank you," Mary said with a wide smile.

"Now, one last thing for today," Ms. White said, and opened her organizer. "What time should we meet on the fourteenth and on the twenty-eighth? Is early still good?"

Twenty-Four

Dev closed the door behind her as Mary came into his living room. He took her coat and gave her a hug.

"Is Mandy about?" Mary asked, her manner guarded as she glanced around the room and through the dining room.

"Upstairs," Dev said, and gestured toward the ceiling. "Why don't you go on up and talk to her. If you'd like, when you two are finished, I can fix sandwiches for a light lunch. I think she'll want room for the fry tonight."

"I'm sure she will." Mary smiled at him. She squeezed Dev's arm and climbed the stairs. At Mandy's open door she knocked softly. "May I talk with you a minute or two?"

"Sure," Mandy said, looking up from her small desk under the front window, overlooking the front yard and the roof over the porch. She closed the book she was reading.

Mary closed the bedroom door and walked over to the foot of Mandy's bed and sat down. "Mandy, I have something I feel is very serious that I need to discuss with you."

"Okay," Mandy said, and turned her chair to face Mary. "What's up?"

"Your father surprised me yesterday," Mary said softly, thinking of all the ways he had surprised her: his attitude after hearing her story, his proposal, their afternoon after they got back to her place, the way he—

"Mary?"

She shook her head and focused on the now, remembering where she was and why she was there. "Sorry Mandy. I was just remembering something. What I was going to say is that I wasn't in school yesterday because your father and I had to talk about me and why I'm here."

"Besides needing to be here to be our teacher, right?"

"Yes, besides that," Mary said, wondering what Mandy was thinking about.

"I was wondering when you two were going to talk."

"You were?" Mary asked, wondering again when Mandy nodded, but she stayed focused. "Anyway, at lunch yesterday he asked me to marry him."

"He did? Finally!" Mandy said, and jumped up and hugged Mary.

"I take it then, you're all right with him asking me," Mary said, surprised.

"Sure, sure," Mandy said enthusiastically, smiling hugely as she sat back down and scooted her chair closer to Mary. "And you'll be me new mum, right?"

"That's why I wanted to talk to you, to be sure that would be okay. I won't be just marrying your father, but I'll be coming into your life too. And you have to be okay with that or want that for it to be okay with me. If it isn't okay with you, then I won't—"

"Mary," Mandy said softly. "Da and I have been in love with you for a long time. We've just been waitin' to see if you could love us too."

"Oh, Mandy." Mary held her arms out wide and Mandy hugged her again. Mary held her tight. "I do love you and your dad very much. I've no experience being a mum, but I can try to be one of your best friends." Mary straightened and looked at Mandy. "I'll still have to be your teacher and I guess I'll have to learn to be a part of a family, but I'll try to make it work if you will too."

"Fer sure, fer sure, Mary," Mandy said, and squeezed her again. "All new mums have to learn how, so don't worry too much. I told you me and Da talk *about* you a lot, and now we can talk *to* you instead. We can make it work."

"Thank you, Mandy," Mary said, and with a deep sigh, released her. "I guess I need to go now and tell your father I'll accept his proposal."

Mandy was up, pulling Mary by the hand, and opening her door before Mary had finished her statement. Mandy sobered and stopped at the top of the stairs, winked at Mary, and then started slowly down, one step at a time. Wondering what Mandy was up to, Mary started down behind her, matching her somber pace.

-¤-

Dev got up from the sofa and turned to see the slow, stoic procession. He stopped beside the front door and looked from one stern, sober face to the other.

"Da. I hate to tell you this," Mandy started slowly, a hint of dejection in her voice, "but Mary doesn't want to—"

"—be single any longer," Mary said in a rush, finishing Mandy's statement for her in case she was going to take her prank further than she should. Both of them jumped forward and hugged Dev tightly.

He looked at Mandy and then at Mary, with his eyes bright and a smile as wide as his face. "Ye will?"

Mary nodded vigorously. "I will, Dev. I will, Mandy."

Dev stood up straighter and dug the small velvet pouch out of his shirt pocket. "I guess we"—he glanced at Mandy and had her hold Mary's hand also as he knelt down in front of her—"should give you this to show our love and our hearts' intent." He slipped the ring she had picked out in Buena Vista onto her finger.

Slowly he stood up and held Mary's face between his palms, and gently kissed her. Her arms wrapped around him and they held each other's kiss for a long moment. Finally Mandy nudged them, and looking up at them when they separated, asked, "Where's mine?"

Dev scooped her up between him and Mary and they both kissed Mandy's cheeks and squeezed her tight. "There's always one for ye, love."

-¤-

Dev had set out sandwich makings: thin-sliced roast leftovers, cheeses, homemade pickle relish, various condiments, home-baked bread, and a side of coleslaw and potato salad. The three of them sat at the dining room table and enjoyed their first meal together as—as Mandy called them—an engaged family.

"Have you settled on a date?" Mandy asked, looking at Mary and then at Dev.

"Not yet," Mary said, "but I'm supposed to think on it."

"Da? Can we get Gran and the rest of the family to come?" Mandy asked, then suddenly looked at Mary. "Sorry, I just supposed you would get married here, at home, instead of somewhere else."

"It's okay," Mary said. "We haven't talked about it, but—"

"You haven't talked about it? Whatcha been doing instead of talkin' about the important things? Honestly..." Mandy continued, oblivious to Dev and Mary's abashed looks at each other over what they had been doing instead.

"As I was going to say," Mary continued, "I think it would be wonderful if we can get married here, with our friends and in the town we are living in."

"We have our monthly family call this afternoon," Dev said, and smiled at Mandy. "So why don't you invite them, love?"

"What time, Da?" Mandy asked. "Mary wants me to run some errands with her after lunch."

"What do you think—four?" he asked.

"Sure," Mandy said, then looked at Mary for confirmation.

"We can be back by then," Mary agreed.

"Okay," Dev said, and finished his sandwich. "I'll text me brother and let them know the time."

"I don't understand. You call them just once a month?" Mary asked.

"Yup," Mandy said. "Da says it gives me time to talk to everyone—well, not the cousins—and keeps me from breakin' the bank on phone costs."

"True, lass. If I'd let you, you'd be callin' two or three times a week," Dev said, and chuckled. Then he looked at Mary. "We use the house phone for our long distance callin'. Sometimes we talk more often than that, dependin' on what needs to be talked about. But it also gives this one somethin' to look forward to. Always the last Saturday of the month."

Dev started putting the food back into the plastic containers and sealable bags as they talked.

"Let me get these," Mary said, and started gathering the plates and utensils. "Can you get the sides as your father covers them?"

Mandy quickly collected the containers and took them to the refrigerator, and Mary set the dishes in the sink and turned the water on.

Dev leaned over Mary's shoulder and kissed her cheek. "I'll wash up, love. You two go about your errands and I'll see you back here about four."

Mary turned and returned his kiss. "So it's 'love' now instead of 'lass'?"

"No, lass. 'Tis both from now until forever."

¤-¤-¤-¤-¤

It was nearly noon when Mary and Mandy left to run Mary's errands and Dev looked around at his and Mandy's modest house. He smiled and stretched out across the sofa, his head resting on one cushioned arm and his feet reaching to the other, and let his thoughts wander from his and Mary's discussion yesterday to their becoming officially engaged today. He knew Mandy wanted them to be a family, but her teasing on the stairs had made him pause a moment and wonder if he really knew his daughter.

Then he smiled again, realizing how much Mandy was changing, how much she had grown since they had come here and started anew—and especially in the past year. But he liked her growing sense of right, of independence, and her natural curiosity in almost all matters. She was displaying many traits that made him pleased with her natural abilities and inquisitiveness.

He stopped his absent remembering and sighed, knowing they both had many years of learning ahead of them. He was just happy they had the days they had and sighed again as he pulled his phone out of his shirt pocket and tapped the keys to tell Henry their call would be at four their time, six his time.

The message was no more than sent when his phone chimed in his hands; Henry was calling him back.

"Hey, Henry."

"Hey, Dev. Are ye where we can talk a minute or two?"

"Sure, sure," Dev said. "Mandy and Mary are off on errands and I'm enjoyin' me sofa on a very pleasant day."

"Good, good," Henry said, and Dev picked up on his tone. "I've been thinking about calling you, so this is good. A few things have been happening that you ought to know about."

"What's goin' on, Henry? Is everyone okay?"

"Sure, sure," Henry said. "Everyone's fine, but we've had a bit of an odd run these past few weeks..." Henry went on to explain about his discovery of the damaged hasp on the tool and storage shed, the sleeping bag, and what the detective at the precinct had found. He explained what the detective had said about the box containing the strange, crossed-out pictures. Then he mentioned Mandy's picture.

"Oh shit!" Dev whispered, suddenly worried about how Mary would take hearing that.

"Now don't be sore at her, Dev," Henry said. "Her letter sounded like she was so very happy and eager to share. Brenna was here and decided to put it with the pictures on the mantel and not tell anyone, especially since Mandy had asked we not tell." Then he explained how their mum had seen it on Labor Day morning and it was the main topic for the day's dinner and that everyone was happy for them.

"This is not goin' to sit well," he said under his breath as he wiped his face with his hand. Dev was glad Mandy was happy for having Mary become close and now planning to join the family, having Mary's picture spread about was not good. *Damn!*

"But Dev, there is a problem."

"What?" *Oh, don't tell me...*

"Yeah. Friday, a week ago, we discovered Mandy's picture, frame and all, was missing—gone. We looked the house over to see if other things were missing, but didn't come up with any. I searched the house and the yard again and discovered someone had breached the locking bar on the back cellar door. Someone came in that way. We don't know if they knew about the picture, or if it caught their attention or what, but we think that whoever came in is the one that took it."

"Any ideas who?"

"Yeah, and you won't like this. I had the precinct come and look at the shed, and the detective from there—a Williams, said he knew you from school—well he came and led a team of officers doin' the inspection. I had them come back after we discovered the picture was missing, and had them look at the house. When they left, Williams said they would stake out the area to see if anyone comes back.

"I know I'm jumping around a lot, but try to stay with me. The tests on the sleeping bag indicate Einri was the primary user, and he was hiding out in our shed after I told him to go away. The precinct has had a stakeout watching since they got the lab reports back. I told you Williams found a box of crossed-out pictures in the shed. Well, the kicker is that Williams went through all of the crossed-out and brought ten of them that were from places near here. He said it was a long shot, but wanted to know if I might recognize any of them. One of them he showed me was a police officer and a woman with him. She looks like your Mary—same face, but as a blonde with shorter hair, not a brunette with long hair. Williams confirmed the woman and the police officer had both been killed."

I've gotta get that picture taken off the website! Dev did not tell Henry he'd already seen that one.

"Anyway, what you're not going to like is that the pictures in the box had Einri's fingerprints all over them—a few of someone else, they think one of the brothers, but mostly they're Einri's." Henry sighed. "I'm sorry, little brother, but your Mary looks a lot like someone that Einri's killed."

"Aye," Dev said very softly to himself. Then to Henry, he asked, "Does anyone on Gallagher's side of the family know where Mandy and me are?"

"Can't tell, Dev," Henry said, displeasure in his voice. "It's never been much of a secret in the family."

"Yeah, I know."

"Well," Henry continued, "the bad thing is we found Scanlon's fingerprints"—*Oh shit, no!*—"on the mantel, and if he's the one that took your picture, he won't keep quiet. They'll know your Mary is with you and Mandy. Based on the resemblance, they might think she's a relative, a sister to the dead one in the picture, maybe."

"Thanks brother," Dev said. "Anything else?" *Dear God in Heaven, I hope not.*

"Yes"—Dev's heart sank—"as if this wasn't enough," Henry said. "Wednesday night the stakeout saw someone around the shed again. We were woke up by gunfire and a lot of men running, but I don't know what the outcome was. At least whoever it was, Einri or one of his brothers, they now know the place is being watched. Maybe now I can sleep better."

"I doubt it," Dev said.

"Yeah. But I have to ask," Henry continued. "Is there something serious going on between you and this schoolteacher Mary?"

"Who knows?" Dev chuckled heavily, suddenly wondering if this would change Mary's mind. "Ask Mandy what she thinks when we call at four. She's the one that seems to know everythin.'"

Henry laughed. "Okay, Dev. I figured we would talk about the serious stuff early and leave the family talk for the group phone-fest. Is your Mary going to join us?"

"I hope so, Henry," Dev said. "Talk to you at four."

"I'll call this time, at four your time. Bye, Dev. Be cautious and watch the shadows."

"Will do, brother. Bye for now."

Twenty-Five

Mary and Mandy were giggling to each other as Mandy opened the front door and led Mary in. Dev got up and turned to greet them. He tried to smile, but after talking with Henry he was having a difficult time feeling anything but dread.

"Did ya have a good time runnin' yer errands?" he asked as he reached for Mary's hand.

"Oh, we had a grand time..." She suddenly hesitated, seeing his forced smile and the pained look in his eyes. "What's wrong, Dev?"

"Da?" Mandy hugged his waist.

"A lot maybe," he said with a deep exhale. "Come and sit down." He looked at Mandy—"Yer uncle called"—then glanced at Mary as she sat down on the sofa, and back at Mandy as she settled between them—"and wanted to thank ya for the picture ya sent."

Mandy's expression went blank and she swallowed hard. "I...I..."

He looked past her to Mary. "I'm sorry, but it seems me over-exuberant daughter shared a copy of our picture with her uncle and aunts."

"What?" Mary whispered, and glanced at Mandy. "Our picture? From the fish fry?"

"I just wanted them to know who you are and how pretty you look..." Mandy stopped when Mary looked back at Dev, concern deep across her furrowed brow.

"Yes, love," he said, slowly shaking his head. "My smart, intelligent daughter made a copy without telling anyone and sent it. She did ask them to not tell anyone she had sent it, but her aunt Brenna put it in a frame and then set it on the mantel, 'so she wouldn't be tellin' anyone it was there.' But of course Mum saw it, and the whole family discussed it over a Sunday dinner a few weeks ago."

Mary inhaled and tried to stop her lips from trembling. "You...

you shouldn't have done that, Mandy. Really, really should not have done that. Oh, God. What am I going to do?" Mary was up and pacing around the end of the sofa.

Dev got up quickly and caught her around the waist. He held her and slowly she turned in his arms, tears running down her cheeks.

Mandy hugged them both. "Da? Mary? What's wrong? I just thought—"

Dev caught her shoulders and squeezed. "You remember me tellin' you about what I found at the library? We talked about this, and that the man that killed Robert might be lookin' for anyone that looked like the woman Cali."

Mandy nodded as she squeezed the two of them.

"Well lass, he is, and that's part of the bad news and why my brother Henry called early—"

"Henry?" Mary's eyes popped opened wide and the name spilled out, loudly in surprise. "Henry? Your *brother* is Henry O'Brien?" Mary instantly pushed herself out of his embrace. *"Henry?"* she shouted in disbelieving question as she paced once in front of him and then bolted, out through the front door. "Oh God, Dev! No!"

"Oh, shit!" Dev muttered, realizing what had happened. "Mandy! Come on!"

Dev leaped over the back of the sofa and followed Mary. He saw her running down Lincoln toward her house and he quickly cut across the yard and the vacant lot. She saw him and turned down Twelfth, and he put his everything into the run, catching her midblock, past the street corner.

"Wait! Stop!" he shouted as he caught her arm.

"Get away! Let me go!" She jerked her arm away, but Dev grabbed her around the middle.

Mary swung at him, her hand smacking his face as they spun in the middle of the street. Mandy caught up as Dev pulled Mary tight against him, making her second swing less effective as it hit the side and back of his head

"Stop! Mary, please!" he demanded as they spun. He held her, reducing her fight to angry squirms. "'Tis not what ya think! Mary! Listen to me!"

"Let me go! Now!" she shouted, and tried to kick him

He let his voice rise to the level of her shouts. "Mary! Stop! Stop! I can explain! I was tryin' to when ya ran."

Slowly, Mary heard him and relented, but he could feel her tight muscles, ready to spring the first chance she got.

"Mary. I'm sorry. I meant to explain, to warn ya," Dev said softly, speaking close and clearly to her ear, lulling her the best he could as his chest heaved to catch his breath. "Yes, my brother is named Henry, the English name Henry. Remember I told you I had asked my old ladder company chief to see what he could find out about Robert's death? He has not called me back with any news, but when my brother called, he told me our picture is missing and my wicked cousin's brother Scanlon took it. That means the one you're fearful of is my cousin Einri, spelled E-I-N-R-I, named in the Irish. My brother is Henry, with the English spellin'."

"Damn, Dev. That's supposed to make me feel better?" Mary swatted his face again and squirmed. "Dammit! Let me go!"

"Love, please. Please listen to me." He tried to pull her closer but she kept squirming. "My brother and my sisters will never wish ye harm, lass. Never. Please listen to me, love. I feel bad that I let this happen—"

"I'm so sorry, Mary," Mandy said, trying to squeeze Mary too. "I didn't think. I didn't think anything like this would happen. I was just...I'm so very sorry Mary."

Unable to break his hold and feeling Mandy's embrace, Mary slowly forced herself to wait, to listen, her eyes full of tears.

"I know, Mandy dear," she finally whispered. "I know you didn't mean for it to happen."

"We'll keep watch, Mary," Mandy said with determination. "We'll get Sheriff Martin to help watch, and you'll be okay. You'll see."

Finally, Mary leaned into Dev's unrelenting embrace and slipped an arm around Mandy's shoulders.

"Mary, love. So you'll know, our father Finnian has a brother Gallagher, our uncle. When his first son and Da's first son were born the same year, they argued over names for them. They both wanted the name Henry, meanin' the ruler of the estate, or first born. Gallagher was headstrong and wanted his son to be named in the Irish, Einri, pronounced EHN-ree. Da finally decided to not argue further and chose Henry, the English name, for his son. The meanin' was the same but Da felt the English name Henry would actually be accepted better in the business world, giving his son a better chance in life. He was right. And in this case, the spellin' and the pronunciation do make a difference.

"But Uncle Gallagher's son Einri turned mean in high school and Gallagher coaxed our father into tryin' to straighten him out, but that didn't work. Einri got worse, and year after year he got into more and more trouble in Detroit."

Mary turned her head and laid her cheek against his chest, wrapping her arms around him. Mandy squeezed them both.

"I'm sorry I didn't think," Dev said. "Everythin' came to a head so quickly this afternoon. When I was lookin' into Anne's accident, I thought about your original reaction to our name, O'Brien. So when I called my old chief, I asked him to do some checkin' for me. I had a hunch, but no proof. But when Henry told me this afternoon the police found Scanlon's fingerprints all over the mantel where our picture had been, I knew it was our mean and criminal cousin Einri, from Gallagher's side of the family, that shot you and killed your husband. Not me brother, love. That's fer sure, love. That's fer sure."

The three of them stood in the middle of the street, gently swaying together for many long minutes, Dev quietly shushing Mary's fears and trying to reinforce his love and concerns for her.

"You mean everything to me, lass, as much as Mandy does and more in a different way. I hope you can get over bein' mad at how poorly I explained all of this, and for causin' you so much pain. I don't know what we have to do, but I think we have some time to figure it out. Maybe, like the scamp says, we can get Lloyd to help us figure somethin' out."

"I'm sorry too, love," Mary said softly. "It was too much of a surprise, but I know you wouldn't intentionally do anything to harm me or upset me or hide something from me that could. I have to learn to trust you before I jump to conclusions. But I'm scared, Dev. Very scared. We're all in a lot of danger, and it scares me to the bone."

"If we work together, we can figure this out, love." He leaned down and kissed her gently. "Will ya come back to the house and talk to the family with us? They'll be callin' soon."

Mary shook her head. "I need to go home and think for a little bit. Then maybe."

"Okay, love," he said, and slowly released his hold on her, hoping she would not bolt again.

"Please, Mary," Mandy said, her chin quivering and tears still on her cheeks. "Please don't leave us. I'm very, very sorry I hurt you and caused you pain. Please..."

Mary squeezed Mandy quickly, released her, and slowly started walking home. Dev watched her as he and Mandy started back to their place, but Mary did not look back at them.

¤-¤-¤-¤-¤

"Happy birthday to ya, ya old man," Henry said loudly through the speaker as Dev and Mandy answered their house phone. A half an hour had passed since Mary went home, and Dev kept watching through the front window hoping to see her coming up the walk.

"Thank ya, ya older man," Dev rebutted with a chuckle. It was not a real chuckle, being filled with concern and worry that Mary might try to protect him and Mandy by slipping away, but it was the best he could do.

Each of his sisters chimed in with the usual birthday banter, each offering ideas for birthday presents as if he were about to crawl into a nursing home.

The conversation slowly turned to the routine exchanging to details from each of their families' activities over the past month, and Dev noticed Henry kept everyone to the safer subjects and did not bring up anything from his and Dev's earlier phone call.

"I haven't heard anything that sounds like your new friend Mary," Henry said, instead of asking his question. "I take it you said somethin' she didn't like and she's not there."

Dev shook his head noncommittally at Henry's comment and glanced at Mandy's sheepish expression. "She's just busy and hasn't been able to get away. Maybe she'll make it before we get finished, and if not, maybe the next time."

-¤-

Mary was not certain she should be going back to Dev and Mandy's place, but she argued with herself that he had faced her as soon as they got back from her errands, and tried to explain the bad news he had received. He did not wait like he had before, when he told her about his research at the library. She inhaled and turned up their front walk.

She was confused by her two-sided feelings. One side said she should be angry and not want to be around him, and the other wanted to make it right and work together to keep them all safe. She still wanted to be with Dev. And, she admitted, Mandy's idea of telling Lloyd Martin what was going on was a good one.

Mandy may have slipped in her exuberance, but she knew Mandy had shared her bedside picture because she was happy about them being together. Mary chuckled; that was even before she knew Dev was serious about her.

Stepping up on the porch, Mary heard Dev make reasonable excuses to his family, that she was busy and might make it later if she could. She stopped and listened as a woman's voice asked, "So what's she like? I think Mandy said she's her teacher."

"Aye, she is," Dev said softly.

Mary waited to knock and listened for him to continue.

"She's the nicest, most carin' person I've ever met and I think the scamp will agree."

"Aye, she is," Mandy added. "She likes to hike and sometimes she lets me come along. Up to the high basins and small lakes. It's really, really pretty up in the high country."

Mary smiled, trying to remember when Mandy had not gone with her. At least since school started, they went together almost every weekend.

"You looked happy in the picture," another woman said.

Mary stepped back at the mention of the picture, but remembered that Dev said they had all talked about it when his mum found it.

"I think she makes both of us very happy, Moira," Dev said softly.

"Sounds serious," the man said, and Mary figured that must be Henry, the brother with the English name.

"Might be just a wee bit," Dev said, "but time will tell. Mandy and I like it when it's the three of us together, doing this or that, or just bein' together."

Mary smiled, feeling the warmth in Dev's tone. She stepped forward and knocked.

-¤-

Mandy quickly jumped at the knock and hurried the few steps to the door. "Hey, Mary. Yer here. Come meet everyone."

Mandy smiled and pulled her in as the voices from the other end filled the living room.

Dev got up and hugged Mary before he led her to the sofa. "Are you okay? Up to this?"

Mary nodded and smiled. "We can talk about the other stuff later, but right now I want to enjoy being with you two. So, introduce me to your family."

"Okay, love," he whispered, and smiled at Mandy. Then he turned to the phone. "Quiet all of you, please. Mary just arrived and I'd like to introduce each of you to her."

"Okay," than man said. "It's just us sibs."

"First is our youngest sister, Moira Ann Frasier. She's married to Carl and has two boys."

"Hello, Mary," Moira greeted.

"I'm Brenna Morgan," another woman said. "My husband is Merril and we have three boys. Carl and Merril have the five boys at soccer practice, and Will Collins—that's Derry's husband—is picking up their girls from dance. They'll be by later. And Mum should be on her way back from her ladies' Twenty-Five group. She should be here any minute now."

"Twenty-five?" Mary asked softly.

"A traditional Irish card game," Mandy whispered. "It's a hoot once ye get to know it. We'll teach it to ya."

"Hey, Mary. I'm Derry," the remaining woman interrupted.

"And the last one is my brother Henry. Unmarried and generally thought to be unsuita—"

"Hey, hey now, little brother," Henry said sharply.

Mary chuckled.

"'Tisn't me that's being unsuitable. I keep a sharp eye out for someone to catch my attention."

Dev grinned, but did not respond. Instead he said, "Okay, Mary is Mary Gorden. One of our excellent schoolteachers and a very dear friend."

Mary said hello and everyone repeated their greetings again, all at once.

Dev looked at her and whispered, "Have you changed her mind since this morning, lass?"

Mary shook her head and glanced at Mandy, who was keeping the conversation with the aunts and uncle going. "No, I haven't changed my mind. I just had to have time to think, and remember all of the reasons why I wanted to in the first place. Then with a shot of Da's favorite Irish whiskey to settle me nerves, I came back. Mandy didn't want me to go away."

"Neither do I, love. I don't know what I would do if you did. May we tell them?"

He squeezed her hand. She nodded and whispered to Mandy, "Is there some news ye be wantin' to tell yer aunts and uncles?"

Mandy nodded her head vigorously and smiled. "Now? May I? May I really?" Her smile filled her face and her eyes danced when Mary grinned and nodded.

"Go for it."

"Okay," Mandy said from her place on the floor in front of Dev and Mary. She turned to the phone and continued, "I have an announcement and a question."

"Sure, sure," the voices said, somewhat at the same time and again on top of each other.

"First I want to announce that Da and me are engaged!"

"Engaged? What? You and Dev?"

"To Mary, ye daft bunch of relatives," Mandy said, laughing at the confusion. "Da asked Mary to marry him and she said yes. So we're engaged and we're gonna have a wedding."

Everyone started talking again, congratulating them all at once.

"Now," Mandy interrupted again, "Mary has not set a date yet, but the weddin' will here in Roosevelt and we expect all of ya to be here when it happens. Gran is required to be here and my cousins are included."

"Aye," Henry said above the other voices. "Give us a couple of weeks to make arrangements, and we'll be there."

"Thanks," Dev said, and smiled at Mary. "We'll let you know as soon as we do."

With that, the group settled back into their normal monthly conversations, asking how the fall to winter weather was starting to change and a few questions to get to know Mary. Mandy mentioned that the first snow was late this year but the weather bureau was expecting it to be a good one when it came.

Mandy, still sitting on the floor, slid close to Mary and wrapped an arm around Mary's legs as she listened and added her points to the conversation. It was obvious to Dev that Mandy wanted Mary to feel comfortable with the new exposure, and especially after their episode before the call. He thought Mary was responding to her nicely.

Mandy talked more about the many hikes she and Mary had gone on, and the many walks, and even had to tell on Dev and his forgetfulness with the truck leading to his long walk home in the dark.

They had spent just over an hour on the phone enjoying the company of distant family when they finally disconnected. Maeve had arrived in the middle of it all and was thrilled at the news, and Dev mentioned she was most likely making travel plans as they talked.

"I like them," Mary said softly, and looked sideways at Dev. "You knew I would." She smiled and squeezed Mandy's red head against her thigh; she was still sitting on the floor beside Mary, her arm still around her legs. Then Mary reached down and pulled Mandy up onto the sofa beside her and squeezed her in a tight hug. "I'm still a bit mad at you, but I am going to love seeing you and being with you every day." She looked up at Dev. "Can we get married tomorrow?"

Dev smiled and cocked his head. "But, love. We just told the family we would give them some notice. They'll need at least a couple of weeks, like Henry said."

Mary pouted at him and then at Mandy. "I guess we'll just have to wait."

"Oh?" Mandy said suddenly. "Where will they stay? With the hunters this time of year, the Bear Canyon Motel will be full, and I'm sure both the Whisperin' Creek and Betty's will be full."

"Well," Mary said, thinking, "I have three extra bedrooms at my house. That's one for each of the sister's families if the children don't mind sleeping on the floor. Henry might have to sleep on my sofa, because I'm thinking your mum will stay here in the spare room you renovated off the kitchen. That ought to do it."

Dev nodded and smiled. "Sounds like we have that covered very nicely. I can cook in either place and you have a large dining room too, so we can feed the horde either place as well."

Mary agreed. "And if they can stay a few days extra, maybe they'll see why we like it here."

"That would really be nice," Mandy said. "Really, really nice, Da. We haven't seen them, face-to-face or hug-to-hug, in four years."

"I'll see if I can talk them into extending," Dev said, "but it'll depend on whether they can get off work long enough."

"Dev?" Mary asked, and he could see she was thinking again. "What would you say to the Saturday after Thanksgiving? They'll have some time for the holiday and maybe it would be easier for them to come Thanksgiving week. Two weekends and five days, with two celebrations to enjoy."

Dev smiled and looked at Mandy's vigorous nodding.

"I think ya have a gran' idea, love," Dev said, and Mandy hugged Mary again.

"And that gives me seven weeks," Mary said happily, "to get a dress made or altered and everything else planned. Are there any good seamstresses around here?"

"I suggest ye get that driver's license we spoke about and ye take the jeep into Buena Vista—or better yet, Salida. Salida has a number of stores that can help with gowns and things ye might want to look at. And on weekends, yer helper here might have an idea or two. And I might even be talked inta followin' ya around and totin' whatcha find." He smiled at Mandy.

"Text Uncle Henry and let them know," Mandy said emphatically. "This will be sooo cool."

Dev chuckled and pulled his phone out of his pocket.

"Henry, make a note and tell everyone the wedding will be on November 25, the Saturday after Thanksgiving. The party will start on Saturday, November 18 and will continue through the 26th. You and

the sisters and their families will stay at the Hotel Gorden where they will have a room for each family and you'll have a fine bunk on the living room sofa. Mum will stay with us at the Hotel O'Brien. Plan on a great reunion and a lot of face time, especially with your niece."

Dev handed the phone to Mary and Mandy. "Is that okay?"

Mary grinned and nodded. When Mandy nodded, he said, "Send it."

Twenty-Six

The wind was stronger and cooler than it had been when Dev, Mary, and Mandy crossed the street to the firehouse. It was dark, and the two firetrucks were outside on the wide driveway under the bright lights.

"The chief is having everyone inside tonight," Mandy said as they walked up between the two trucks. "He mentioned it when we saw him while we were running errands today."

"Aaah," Dev said as they followed her.

Mandy held the door for Mary, and then Dev gestured for Mandy to follow her in. He closed the door behind them and looked around the packed truck bays.

"Is everyone in town here?" he asked Mary as they wandered down an aisle, looking for places to sit.

"Hey, Dev!" Chief Delany said, waving from where he and Bert Mann, another volunteer fireman, were manning the deep fryers just outside the door and stairs to the firehouse kitchen. "Over here."

Sam pointed to a clear spot at the end of a table close to where he stood.

Dev nudged Mary in the general direction, following Mandy as she cut through the room, heading for the proffered spots.

"Thanks," Dev said as he helped Mary with her heavier jacket.

Mandy took a spot across the table from them and laid her jacket beside her. Dev looked at Mary and Mandy and suggested they go and get their plates and drinks. He said he'd watch their places and go when they got back, but Mary grabbed his hand and led him back to the food table.

"You can talk to the chief while we eat," Mary said with a knowing smile, and stopped behind Mandy as Mandy loaded her plate with hushpuppies, coleslaw, an ear of corn, and three fillets of catfish. Mary followed suit, though she did not pile as much on her plate. Dev filled his plate respectfully and picked up a cup of iced tea as he turned to follow them back to their places.

"I haven't seen this big of a turnout since we've started coming to these," Dev said as he sat down beside Mary.

Sam leaned over and asked how Dev and Mandy were tonight and greeted Mary, thanking her for coming back.

"You start puttin' somethin' special in your fish batter?" Dev asked him, making a gesture like he was smoking something. "You sure have gotten the town's interest."

"Just a cheap meal and a cold night," Sam said, and smiled. "The cold always helps the turnout." Sam winked at Mandy, but Dev had turned to be sure Mary had everything she needed.

"Don' t look now, Da," Mandy whispered loudly. "Manark and Quinly comin' on yer right."

Dev turned as two women about his age stopped behind him and Mary.

"Hello, Dev," the first said, placing her hand possessively on his shoulder as if there was no one else in the entire room. "Haven't seen you around much in the last few weeks. The colder weather keeping you in?"

He smiled and winked at Mary. Then he turned his smile on the two women. "Mary, I don't know if you've met Barbara Manark or Susan Quinly. Ladies, I'm pleased to introduce Mary Gorden, in case you haven't met."

Mary smiled and turned to them, but her position on Dev's right forced her to extend her left hand in greeting. "Very nice to meet both of you," she said warmly. "I hope you're enjoying Chief Delany and the firemen's fish fry."

Mary was pleased that in taking her hand in response, the two women had to take notice of her artfully mounted three-quarter carat solitaire.

"Did I mention," Dev asked, "that Mary and I are getting married at the end of November? I hope you'll be able to come to the ceremonies."

Mary and Mandy were giggling when the women smiled and went on their way.

"Two of the fifteen?" Mary asked softly.

"Aye." He smiled. "They'll all know before we leave tonight."

Mary stifled her giggles and made a sober face at Mandy. "Sorry, Dev. I couldn't resist. You're mine now, love."

"Aye, love." His smiled widened. "I certainly am. Yours and Mandy's and no one else's."

Mary finished her fish and asked if Dev was going after more. He shook his head and she smiled at Mandy. "I know you're going for more."

Mandy smiled brightly as she got up and took her plate back to the serving line.

Mary and Dev watched the people in the firehouse, some in casual conversation and a few with their heads close together, speaking softly. Mary poked Dev when she saw Nancy Arnold and her husband coming their way.

"Good evening, Mary," Nancy said as they stopped. "Good to see you again, Dev."

Dev stood and greeted her and her husband.

"Dev, Mary, this is my husband, Jack," she said as Dev took his hand.

"Nice to meet you," Dev said as Mary stood and Jack shook her hand.

"What's this rumor I just heard?" Nancy asked. "Something about a wedding?"

Mary blushed and nodded. "It's not a rumor. Twenty-fifth of November. Right here in Roosevelt, if we can get everything arranged."

"Let me see," Nancy said, and Mary extended her left hand. "My, my. That is a nice one. I like the way the ring is designed to protect the stone. Very artistic." Then she looked up at both of them. "When did this happen?"

Mary chuckled as Mandy returned and sat down at the table. "He asked yesterday and I accepted this morning after we talked with Mandy."

"Congratulations to all three of you," Nancy said, "and all the happiness in the world, Mary." Then she leaned close to Mary. "I will say that if people want to keep talking about you two, you've certainly given them something nice to talk about."

"Thank you," Mary said. "We're going to try and find all of the happinesses we can." She glanced at Mandy. "Right?"

"Right," Mandy agreed, smiling brightly.

Mary sat back down when Nancy and Jack moved on to talk to other friends. Noticing that Mandy had scarfed down her latest helping of fish, Mary was about to ask if she was finished when Mandy picked up her plate and went to the trash barrel.

"You only made three passes tonight. Are you feelin' all right?" Dev asked when Mandy returned.

"Leavin' room for dessert, Da," she said, and looked at Mary with her head cocked.

Mary got up and spoke with Sam and then glanced at Mandy. She nodded and Mandy got up and followed her into a side room. Dev tried to question where they were going, but they smiled and then ignored him.

Sam rattled his tongs on the deep fryer to get everyone's attention.

"Folks, if you'll give me your attention for just a minute. Thank you." He waited a minute as the room quieted. "Thank you. Many of you know we have a little surprise planned for tonight, but I'd like to say a few words before we get started.

"A few years ago, Roosevelt was fortunate enough to have a caring and talented man come to live in our town. He and his daughter have embraced all that is essential about Roosevelt, and three years ago he became one of our volunteer firemen, showing us some things we didn't know about handling fires and the medical aspects sometimes needed after the fact."

Dev felt uneasy, looking around, trying to figure out where Mandy and Mary had gone.

"You know I'm talking about Dev O'Brien and his daughter Mandy. But tonight is special, as I was told with enough forewarning to make some arrangements. Tonight our fish fry just happens to fall on Dev's birthday, and I know many of you came to wish him a happy one and to thank him for coming and being a part of our community. Dev, happy birthday."

Sam gestured to Dev and made him stand up just as Mary, Mandy, and three other women pushed one of the firehouse's large metal roll-around tables into the room. Atop the white tablecloth was the largest sheet cake he ever remembered seeing.

The crowded room broke into reasonably in-tune singing, and Mandy hurried to him and pulled him to the center of the room.

"We helped get things ready this afternoon, Da," Mandy said in a loud whisper. "That was our errand."

When the singing stopped, Sam resumed.

"With Mary and Mandy's help this afternoon, along with a number of other wives and helpers, we have prepared a chocolate and white cake to go with the normal ice cream for dessert. Is there anything you'd like to add, Dev?"

Dev nodded and slowly turned to take in the whole of the room. Then he smiled at Mandy and then at Mary.

"I feel like I'm being set up fer somethin.'"

Someone chuckled.

"I don't really know what to say. I've never been good at speeches and such, but I do thank you all for the thoughts and the kindnesses you have showered on Mandy and m'self since we came here—since we came home.

"And bein' here to stay, I can only hope that we can give back a little of what you've given us. Thanks."

Dev reached for Mandy and Mary, hugging their shoulders as they led him back to his seat.

"We'll start cutting the cake," Sam said, "and as you finish eating, please take a piece or two and get yourself some ice cream to go with it. If you're not finished with your meal, there's plenty more fish and sides and the cake will still be waiting when you get ready. Enjoy yourselves and make your way around to see Dev."

Dev smiled at Mary and squeezed Mandy. "This is very nice, but you shouldn't have done this. I'm no one special, just a store clerk, delivery boy, fireman, and handyman." Then his smile widened. "You two are the special ones."

"Well, we tend to disagree with you, Mr. O'Brien," Mary said, and nodded to Mandy. "We think you are someone special—very special indeed."

"And that's fer sure," Mandy added. "There's a paper sack under your seat with cards from most of the town, Da. Don't forget to take them home with us." Then she smiled at Mary. "May I get some cake and ice cream now?"

Mary glanced at Dev and nodded. "I think you've earned a couple of pieces, lass," she said.

For the next hour and some, Dev greeted and chatted with almost everyone that had come to the dinner. Finally the crowd began to thin, and Dev and Mary led a tired Mandy home. Dev carried her the last few blocks and Mary took the "hidden" key to open the door for them.

"Put that key in your pocket, love," Dev said as Mary closed the door behind them and followed them up the stairs to Mandy's room. "You'll be needin' one soon enough, so ya might as well have it now."

Together, they got Mandy ready and in bed, tucked in securely, and properly kissed and blessed before they came back down to the living room.

"Have a few minutes, or are ye tired and needin' to get home?" Dev asked, and gestured to the living room.

"Both," Mary said, then hugged him and led the way to the sofa.

Dev started a small fire in the fireplace and settled next to her, but as he sat down, she turned and pushed him back against the cushioned arm, stretching his legs down the length of the sofa. She smiled and lay down on top of him, rolling against the back of the sofa so she could see the fire.

Adjusting her position slightly, she kissed him and let herself float on the sensations their contact aroused. When she broke their kiss he sighed and smiled at her, tightening his arm around her.

"Thank you, lass. Tonight certainly was a surprise," he said softly.

"You're welcome, love," Mary said. "After our *discussion* in the middle of the street and when I went home, I wasn't sure tonight was going to work out. But I realized you were trying to tell me what you knew as soon as you could, even if the news was bad news." She sighed and squeezed him gently. "Your girls, Mandy and I, appreciate who you are and all that you've done for us. I know Mandy appreciates you more than I can imagine, but I appreciate you more and more each day I know you. Thank you, love, for wanting me, for showing me a new future, and for being here for me."

She laid her head on his shoulder, slipped her hand inside his shirt, and gently savored the feel of him, his warmth, the comfort she felt just being in his arms. Dev held her eyes, not wanting to take his eyes off of her. She held his gaze in return until he tilted her head back and kissed her gently, softly letting his lips speak for him.

Twenty-Seven
Monday, October 2

Dev sat just inside Stumpy's front window, eating his lunch and watching the light snow, the result of the clear morning turning sullen with moisture-laden clouds that spilled quickly over the ridge to the north and west of them. The afternoon weather predictions were usual for the first snow of the fall—snow and more snow—and he smiled, knowing Mandy would insist on their first snowball fight on their way home after school.

He smiled and sipped his coffee, nodding brightly as Connie stopped and refilled it. Mary and Mandy were safely sequestered in their classes at school and, so far, Bob did not have any deliveries for him to make. He had filled the jeep yesterday in anticipation of the weather and laid in extra logs for his and for Mary's fireplaces. His propane tank had been filled a week before and Mary's a week before that, so he felt pretty good about being ready for winter's onset. He even had a long talk with Lloyd Martin, telling him about Henry's call and the missing picture of Mary, Mandy, and himself. Lloyd agreed to contact the Ann Arbor and the Dearborn Police to keep tabs on Einri's whereabouts, and said he would alert the hometown militia to be on the lookout for, as Mandy put it, another redheaded man about Dev's size, but with a red beard. Until they knew more, they had done about all they could.

He finished the sandwich he had made at home and the small bag of chips he had picked up at the grocery, and had settled back to enjoy his cup of coffee when his phone chimed.

He glanced at the screen, seeing Mike O'Malley's name, and answered it.

"Hey, Mike. Good afternoon."

"Good afternoon to you as well, Dev," Mike said. "I found out a little more on those accidents and the last one. Thought I should call."

"Thanks. What did ya find out?"

"Looks like the Dearborn Police had the same hunch you did that Einri's gang was behind the 'accidents.' My contact said all of the bullets recovered from the truck drivers were from the same gun, so probably the same man did the shooting."

"Well that may narrow it down some," Dev surmised absently. "At least if it isn't one man, one gun is being passed around."

"True, true," Mike said. "I called Ann Arbor about that Marrow fella, and asked if they had compared notes with Dearborn. The fella there said they had, but wondered what I was lookin' for. So I told him we thought there might be a connection between what we, as first responders, were seein' in Dearborn and what they're seein' in Ann Arbor."

"Have they found anything?" Dev asked.

"Some," Mike said. "They know that Marrow was killed with a different gun than the truck drivers, but they did admit they found an empty nine millimeter magazine at the scene. You'll never guess whose fingerprints were on it."

"Einri's," Dev said softly.

"Got that right, Dev, me boy," Mike said. "How'd ya know?"

"Just a bad feelin', Mike. 'Twas the hunch I had when I asked ya to check," Dev said. "And I'm bettin' the gun used on the truck drivers either belongs to Mikalean or Scanlon. Probably Scanlon, knowin' how Einri tries to use his somewhat deficient brother."

"Deficient? Whatcha meanin', Dev?"

"Scanlon has always been what some people call a little slow," Dev explained. "As a kid, he could only handle one task at a time. Tell him one thing and he could do it, but he took some supervision, guiding. Without supervision, he would get distracted and go off on a tangent until he remembered what he was supposed to do. Give him two things to do, and you might get a third of one done."

"So you think he could easily be a trigger man, if he was suitably guided and kept focused? Is that what yer leadin' up to?"

"In a nutshell," Dev said. "If Scanlon thinks he's playin' a game of some sort, he could be guided to do almost anything."

"Includin' killin' people?"

"Yeah. That's what I think, so long as he doesn't know what he's really doin'," Dev admitted. "Mikalean had brains but didn't have the killin' instincts Einri had. He was good at figurin' out how to get somethin' done, but I haven't figured out how Einri got him to go along with his deeds. He never had a mean streak growin' up.

"Einri was the mad bull. He'd charge in anywhere, against anythin', and didn't care if he caused collateral damage or that people would take notice."

"Interestin' family," Mike said.

"Any idea how large his gang is now?" Dev asked. "When I left four years ago, they were estimating only about twelve or fifteen actually causin' trouble."

"I haven't heard, Dev," Mike said, "but I don't think there's all that many. It isn't like they're sweepin' the city with simultaneous incidents. It's just the continuous one-offs—individual attacks timed to be most noticeable."

"Yeah," Dev said, and smiled to himself. "Maybe that's good in a way."

"Yeah. Okay, Dev. That's all I have," Mike said. "I'll let you get back to work and I'll let you know if I hear anything more."

"Thanks, Mike," Dev said. "It's a help. Talk to ya later."

"Later."

¤-¤-¤-¤-¤

Scanlon waited just inside the warehouse door while Mikalean checked the inner rooms and the office space they used for their hideaway. He was nervous, anxious, and danced from one foot to the other until Mikalean re-emerged from the interior darkness.

"Is he there?" Scanlon asked hopefully.

"Must be someplace else," Mikalean said, and rubbed his chin. "We've checked the five places we normally use and I've checked with the others. No one's seen him since last Wednesday."

"He said he was goin' to Brighton," Scanlon said, "when he left us that night. Do ya think somethin' happened while he was there?"

"I don't know," Mikalean said. "If so, he wouldn't be there now.

Not much use in goin' to check."

"So where is he?"

"I don't know," Mikalean said firmly. "But after he left us, he called me and asked me to find out where Devlin went in Colorado."

"Huh? Does Devlin know where he went?"

"Who?"

"Einri."

"No."

"Then why does Einri want you to find out where Devlin is," Scanlon asked, "if he doesn't know where Einri went?"

Mikalean shook his head and pushed Scanlon through the door and back out into the night. "Maybe Nora knows where Devlin went. We'll go ask her."

"Why do you want to know where Devlin is?"

"Scan, think. Einri thinks the girl in Devlin's picture might be the one he shot when he killed that cop in Ann Arbor, the nosy cop that was tellin' what he found out about Einri's plans. If that's her, she knows Einri did the shootin'. He wants to know where she is, so he can pay her a visit."

"Oooh," Scanlon said softly, and then frowned. "Why does he want to visit with her? I thought he killed her."

"Come on, Scan," Mikalean said. "On second thought, don't think about it."

"Oh, okay."

◻-◻-◻-◻-◻

"Hey Dev, Mandy," Mary said when she came out of the school building and saw Dev standing beside his jeep, holding the passenger side door open for her. She noticed the walk was shoveled, but the snow was accumulating again—nearly a foot deep along the edges of the walk. "I didn't expect a chariot and footman."

"Hey, Mary," Mandy said from the back seats as Dev helped Mary up into the jeep. "The sidewalks are getting a little deep and Da didn't want you to have to walk through it all and mess up your dress and

214

boots."

"Well, I appreciate that a lot," Mary said as Dev slid behind the wheel and closed his door.

Mary leaned across the console and kissed Dev, holding their contact longer than was necessary. Then Mary sat back and looked at Mandy. "I'll give you a proper hug and a kiss when we get out and I can reach you."

Mandy giggled. "Okay."

Dev pulled out onto Main and started up the valley toward their places. "We fixed a light supper, if you're hungry."

"Thanks. I am." She smiled and glanced at Mandy. "I worked the children some today and now I have to pay the price, grading test papers tonight."

"Then we'll try to get you fed and back home before it gets much later."

Dev dodged a car just east of Sixth and another at Ninth, parked in violation of the city's winter "No Street Parking" ordinance as he made his way.

He chuckled and gestured to the snow piled over the cars as they passed. "Those'll be buried by mornin' if the owners don't get 'em moved soon," Dev remarked.

He pulled into his drive, parked, and helped Mary and Mandy out and into the house where Mary made good on her promise, hugging Mandy and swinging her around in the living room.

"You know," Mary said as she set Mandy back on her feet, "I'm glad I was your teacher first, lass. Otherwise I wouldn't be able to resist the urge to hug you every time I see you during the day."

"Thanks, Mary," Mandy said, and took her coat off. "I feel the same way."

"Come an' take a seat," Dev said from the kitchen as he carried a covered casserole into the dining room and placed it on the trivet in the center of the table. He took the oven mitts off and pulled a chair out for Mary.

Mandy hurried around the table and took a chair next to Mary.

"You're not eating?" Mary asked as she sat down to the single place setting.

"Mandy said she was starvin' when she got home," Dev said, "and the casserole bein' done, we ate earlier."

"It was those tests ye gave us today," Mandy said with a wide smile. "Made me work up an appetite."

Mary giggled and scooped a spoonful of casserole onto her plate as Dev sat down in the chair on her left, across from Mandy. "Thanks. But I've told you before, I can fix a supper at home when I've worked late. You shouldn't always be doing this."

"Mary, don't fret about it," he said. "An' I've told ya we don't mind. Very soon, it'll be normal for ya to come home and eat with us every night. I figure we're just helping ya get a little head start on it."

Mary ate and spent some time relaxing with the two of them. She helped with the dishes and putting them back in their places and then they walked her back to her house. On her wide front porch, Mandy hugged her and kissed her goodnight.

-¤-

Mandy stepped back and smiled at her dad, watching as he pulled Mary gently to him and kissed her tenderly, holding their contact far longer than necessary. She savored the genuineness and commitment she saw between them and felt good about where they were heading as a family. The warmth between them seemed to completely fill her and she felt good—better than good.

¤-¤-¤-¤-¤

Mary dropped her school satchel on the floor and hung her coat on the peg behind her front door, and checked the doors and windows like she always did. Then she took her satchel to her dining room and prepared for her evening's work.

With a pot of hot water and a few tea bags scattered near her cup and saucer, Mary spent the next hours going over each paper, making comments and marking answers. She made the necessary notes in her grading book, and after the last grade was entered, she sat back and studied her chart pages. She smiled; with only twenty in her class from all the surrounding small towns, she was pleased at how well they each were doing. It was as if a silent competition was at hand, as she noticed the children with the lowest grades at the beginning of the term had quickly responded to the others with the higher grades and the class average had jumped. She had even noticed during study time how Mandy and Seth Mayer's granddaughter, Kate, had started helping those that had trouble understanding.

Mary closed her book and put the papers back into the satchel. She took her dishes back to the kitchen, put the unused tea bags away, and tossed her trash into the bin, deciding a long soak in a hot tub would help before she went to bed.

She settled into the bath and began washing. As she washed her arms, she stopped to feel the long scar on her left arm, remembering the sensations when Dev had administered the butter and rubbed it deep into the old wound. At first she had thought he was being unduly rough, but he worked carefully and relentlessly, and after fifteen minutes or so, she thought it was feeling different. It had only been three days, but she did feel like it bothered her less, and the pulling when she moved seemed less as well.

Then she smiled, remembering Dev's other touches and the sensations he sent through her, savoring those moments, pleased he was slowly pushing the darkness out of her memories.

Twenty-Eight
Tuesday, October 3

Dev and Mandy were waiting in front of the school at the time Mary normally finished and was ready to leave. But tonight Mary was late and had not come out like she usually did. As they chatted, Mandy began to worry that something might be wrong.

"I'm sure she's just doin' somethin' that's takin' longer than she expected," he said. "But if it'll make you feel better, I'll park and we can go in and see."

"It would, Da," Mandy said.

Dev moved the jeep forward and parked in an empty space.

The snow had stopped sometime late morning and the day had gone under clear skies with a bright sun. The town's plows had cleared the streets, and many of the townsmen had cleared the various parking lots, including the school's. It made everyone feel good that the seasons had changed—if not officially by the calendar, at least by the nature of the weather.

Mandy led him inside and they stopped in the hallway outside Mary's dark classroom. The door was closed as it usually was when she left, so he looked around. It only took a moment before he saw her in the office at one of the computer terminals.

Mary looked up as they stepped through the open office door. "Sorry. I'll just be another minute or two," she said, and turned back to the monitor.

After another five, she got up and went to the printer, retrieving a couple of sheets from the hopper.

"Sorry, but I wanted to get this finished and my receipt printed," she said, and stepped up to him, giving him a quick "hello" kiss and Mandy a hug. "I hope you meant it when you offered the use of your jeep."

"My jeep?" Dev asked, and cocked his head.

She smiled and waved the sheets of paper in front of him. "I just took the written test, so now I just need to do the driving part."

"You're going to get your driver's license?" Mandy asked in surprise.

"Yes, I am, love," Mary said, and looked at Dev. "But I have to take a day off again. The closest DMV office for licenses is in Salida, and they're only open on Tuesdays and Thursdays."

"You tell me when, lass"—he smiled and hugged her—"and I'll be more than happy to drive ya down."

"Thanks," she said, and smiled. "Now, can we go and grab a bite? I think I'm famished. Tests always do that to me."

"They do that to me too," Mandy said, and led the way to the door.

-¤-

"Maybe I can get Mrs. Critcher again for this Thursday," Mary mused between bites of Stumpy's chicken-fried steak.

"I like Mrs. Critcher," Mandy said. "She's funny, always tellin' stories about something that happened here in town or nearby."

"Well, she certainly should know about everything that has happened," Mary agreed. "She was born and raised here."

"Wow," Mandy said, and took another bite of her junior burger. "She must be glad."

"Glad?" Dev asked. "About?"

"For being able to live here her whole life, Da," Mandy said expressively. "I mean look around. Where would ya want to go besides here?"

Mary smiled at him and shook her head. "Very good point, Mandy. I can't think of a better place."

"Me either," Dev said. "Of course you two make it impossible to want to be anywhere else."

"Thanks, Da," Mandy giggled. "But you know we're gonna go wherever you go, if we have ta move for some reason."

"True, true, love," Mary said softly. "Wherever you go, I'm going too."

"Well, dunna worry about it, loves," he said. "I'm plannin' to stay right here for a very long time, with the both of ya to make me days as happy as I can imagine."

"So, would Thursday work for you, Dev?" Mary asked, getting back to the original conversation.

"I'll check with Bob," Dev said, and took another bite of his chicken fry. After a moment, he added, "He usually doesn't have any problem if I need to take some time."

"Okay," Mary said. "Unless you tell me otherwise, I'll make arrangements for Thursday."

Thursday, October 5

"Hello, Scan," Nora said as Mikalean led Scanlon into his and Nora's house and she closed the door behind them. "Are ya hungry? I've just finished gettin' supper ready."

"Sure, sure," Scanlon said, holding his cap in his hands as he followed Mikalean through the living room. "I was hopin' ya might spare a little. Lunch was a bit light."

"Busy, were ya?" Nora asked, and set another plate on the table.

"Nah," Scanlon said. "Just nibbled as we checked on thin's."

Nora set the large square casserole bowl on the table and looked at Mikalean's back as he washed his hands in the kitchen sink. When he turned to look at her, she could tell he was troubled—more than usual. "Scan, yer next," she said, and gestured to the sink.

"Sure, sure," he said, and hurried to wash his hands.

"Yer bothered," Nora said softly as Mikalean sat down in his usual chair at the end of the table. "Yer brother been atcha again?"

Mikalean shook his head and looked to see if Scanlon was finished.

"I haven't seen him since yesterday week," Mikalean said softly. "We've been looking for him in all of his regular places, but he's not been seen."

"Well," Nora said as Scanlon dried his hands, standing at the sink behind Mikalean. "I'll take that as a good sign, Mik. Now, maybe you'll stop follerin' him around and cowerin' to his demands and biddin.'"

"Nora. Don't start—"

"What, Mik?" Nora asked sharply. "Don't want me ta start complainin' again 'bout how much trouble he's gettin' ya inta? I don't want someone comin' to me door to tell me I don't have a husband no more because you followed yer dear brother inta one of his fights with the law. I don't wantcha comin' home ta me dead."

Scanlon sat down and looked from Nora to Mikalean and back again.

"Don't say nothin', Scan," Nora warned. "I don't want to hear about or know about anythin' you do for that brother of yers."

Scanlon nodded and scooped some casserole onto his plate.

Nora scooped some casserole onto Mikalean's plate and then onto hers.

"I talked to yer cousin Derry yesterday," Nora began again. "She was reluctant to give me Dev's address until I told her we wanted ta send him a belated birthday card. His birthday was Saturday and I told her we didn't know how to reach him." She slid a folded piece of paper to Mikalean, but kept her hand on top of it, looking him in the eyes. "I hope yer tellin' me the truth and just want to send him a card. He's been a good cousin to ya, even if he's like me and doesn't agree with what yer doin.'"

"I'm sendin' him a card," Mikalean said, and held her eyes. "I want ya to put yer own note in it too."

Nora reluctantly pulled her hand away and Mikalean took the paper and slipped it into his pocket without looking at it.

When they had finished supper, Mikalean told Nora that he was going to get Scanlon settled for the night and that he'd be back in about a half an hour. Scanlon stepped outside to wait and Mikalean lingered with Nora.

"Ya gotta break it off, Mik," Nora said softly, "before he gets you locked in too deep. I need ya here, not sent off somewhere because ya did somethin' for Einri that ya shouldna done." She paused a moment, then looked at him. "Ye've got a wife and now yer gonna have a family, Mik. I found out this mornin' and I need ya here. Not off doin' somethin' ya shouldna be doin.'"

Mikalean kissed her on the cheek and stepped into the darkness.

"I'll be back as soon as I can."

Mary stood in front of the large poster on the wall for her picture, and Dev made faces at her to make her smile. They had dropped Mandy off at school and then come straight down to Salida, getting to the DMV at East First and C Streets about a quarter before ten. Mary showed the clerk the results of her written test and her receipt, and the clerk verified that her test and scores were in the DMV computer system.

When the driving examiner called Mary for her test, she gave Dev her papers to hold and off she went, keys in hand, almost skipping like a little girl. Dev smiled as she went, but it wasn't a little girl he was watching, in the flouncing, knee-length skirt, with long golden brown hair bouncing behind and a figure that made his heart stop. *No ma'am, lass, yer definitely anythin' but a little girl.*

Dev took a seat near the front window, watching as Mary and the examiner got into the jeep. She adjusted the seat, the mirrors, and glanced at him with a smile before she started the jeep and drove away for her driving test. He settled back for the wait and glanced at the forms she had given him. Most were printouts from her written test, but a couple of the papers were her copies of forms she had filled out by hand when they had gotten there. He smiled at her clear and precise penmanship and her pretty cursive signature.

Then one of the entries caught his attention, and he wondered if Mandy knew their birthdays were the same. He chuckled and happily wondered what other surprises Mary would bring them.

It was almost eleven when Mary stopped in front of Dev, smiling and holding her laminated driver's license out for him to see, a smile stretched completely across her face.

"Well, well, lass," Dev said as he stood up and looked at her license. His smile was almost as big as hers. "Ye did it. I knew ya could."

Mary hugged him, almost knocking him off his feet. "Thank you, Dev. Now I feel like I'm someone again. Not just a shadow wandering around, trying to find out where I belong."

"Aye, lass," Dev said, and squeezed her. "You do belong, and ye certainly are a someone, a very special someone—especially to me and Mandy and then to a lot of children that look up to you every day. You are a very special someone. And I'm very proud of you, lass, every day."

"Thank you, Dev." And Mary kissed him, gently at first and then slowly harder, her fingers clutching the back of his shirt until Dev broke their touch.

"We'll have to continue this later, love. Not here in the DMV."

Mary blushed, giggled, and glanced down, but only for a second. "Okay," she whispered sheepishly. "If you insist."

"How about pizza?" Dev asked. "There's a great pizza place just a few blocks away."

"Sounds gran'," Mary said, and turned Dev to the door.

They stepped outside, Dev handed her the papers he had held for her and he opened the jeep door for her. He drove them three blocks west and then two south and found a close parking spot on F Street, near the pizzeria—the Moonlight was on the corner of F and East 3rd Streets. He led her to the entrance beside the large outdoor seating area.

"Is inside okay with you?" Dev asked unnecessarily, and Mary nodded vigorously.

"Definitely inside," she said, clutching her coat closed as she followed, her arm hooked in his as they entered.

A young woman in jeans and nice top showed them a table and gave them menus. They both ordered waters and began studying the choices.

"Dev?" Mary asked. "Do you mind if we get something more traditional than last time?"

"Not at all. Prefer to not repeat a chicken pizza?"

"It was very good," Mary said softly, "but I have to admit, I'm really a traditional meaty pizza and beer kind of gal."

"Good to know, love," he said. "You can have a beer now if you'd like."

"No. Not now." She smiled. "I'm hoping you'll let me drive home.

At least part of the way."

Dev chuckled. "Sure, sure, lass. You can drive as much as you'd like." Then he turned to the menu. "They have a nice, meaty specialty—a carnivore special: Italian sausage, pepperoni, and Canadian bacon. They'll even let you add salami."

"Okay," she said.

Dev ordered when the waitress brought their waters, and he asked Mary if she wanted to look at any of the dress shops while they were there.

"I don't think so, Mr. O'Brien," Mary said. "You're not going to see my dress until I walk down the aisle. Not even what I'm thinking about."

"Really?"

"Yup," Mary said, and smiled. "It's supposed to be a surprise, and I think Debbie will help me look."

"I see," Dev said, smiling back at her, pleased to see her spirit. "I suppose you'll be askin' to use the jeep?"

"Sure, sure," she said. "You offered and I'm going to hold you to it."

"Good for you, lass," Dev said, and squeezed her hand. "You can certainly use it any time you need it."

Their lunch came and they enjoyed their time together. Dev searched for dress shops on his phone, jotted a number of them down on his napkin, and handed it to her.

"I'll do an internet search and see where to start," Mary said, folding the napkin and slipping it into her purse. "Debbie might also have some ideas."

After lunch, Dev enjoyed riding shotgun and watching Mary take her first road trip behind the wheel in many years. She was happy and comfortable, and that made Dev warm through and through. There was a time he had wondered if she would ever be again and he was extremely pleased to be part of it.

Then a somber thought crossed his mind, and he tried to remember if there was anything else he was supposed to be telling Mary. Every time he saw her happy, he worried that there was something bad he was supposed to tell her. He was becoming paranoid.

¤-¤-¤-¤-¤

Mary pulled into Dev's driveway and parked the jeep beside his pickup truck. He got out and hurried around to help her out.

"Didn't tire you out too much, did it?" he asked as they stepped up on the porch.

"No. Not at all," she said, and smiled at him. "I can't explain how wonderful driving back made me feel. It's like I can do something again. Something that I thought I'd lost forever."

"I can see that," he said, and stopped at the door. "Do you want to come in for a bit or do you want to go on to your place?"

"In," she said, and nudged him.

Dev unlocked and opened the door, gesturing for her to enter first. He followed and closed the door, reaching for her coat as he turned to her. She had let it fall to the floor and caught his face between her palms, kissing him firmly. His arms instinctively wrapped around her, holding her tight against him. When she took a breath, she whispered, "Being with you all day and not being able to kiss you and hold you has been driving me crazy."

Dev gave her a quick kiss and scooped her up in his arms. "Aye, love, 'tis how I feel too, and now I think it's time to introduce you to our room." He started up the stairs and she answered him with another long and tender kiss.

Twenty-Nine

Dev carried the dinner dishes into the kitchen and set them in the sink. Mary and Mandy finished clearing the table of leftovers, condiments, and other remnants of dinner as he started rinsing and hand-washing.

"I'll dry," Mandy said as she closed the refrigerator door and grabbed the dish towel.

"And what does that leave for me?" Mary asked, and looked sternly at Mandy.

"You can put things away when I dry them," Mandy said matter-of-factly. "I still can't reach the high cabinets."

"Okay then," Mary said, and took the first pan from Mandy.

"Da?" Mandy asked as they worked. "Can we play one of the card games? We haven't shown Mary how to play Twenty-Five yet."

"Maybe," he said softly without turning. "We have something else to do first."

"We do?" Mary and Mandy asked together. Mandy giggled and Mary smiled at her because they had asked at the same time.

"Yup," he said, and finished the hand-washing. He rinsed the sinks, put the dish detergent in the dishwasher, and closed the door.

"What do we have to do?" Mandy asked as she hung the dish towel on the towel rack and Dev set the dishwasher to run.

Mary just waited patiently as he turned and smiled at her. Then he looked at Mandy.

"Would you go up and get a T-shirt from me dresser," Dev asked, "and then bring down that penetratin' lotion we use and your jar of skin butter?"

"Sure, sure," Mandy said, and hurried to the stairs. "Whatcha needin' them for?"

"Just get them, please," he said, and stepped into the living room.

Mary watched as he opened the closet by the front door, unfastened a large plastic case, and took out a smaller blue case. He was just closing the closet when Mandy came bouncing down the stairs with the jar of butter, the tube of lotion, and his shirt.

"Da? I thought you made your bed this morning."

Startled, Dev looked at Mary, realizing they had been so preoccupied with each other that he had not noticed the disorderly state in which they had left his room. Mary was looking back at him, barely hiding her smile.

"I did, love," Dev said. "I...laid down for a bit this afternoon."

"Looks more like you had a fight with someone in it," Mandy said absently, and laid the items she carried on the table.

Dev picked up the T-shirt, still trying to compose himself and keep his voice normal as he gently caught Mary's left arm, his thumb rubbing it just above her elbow. "Please go into the bath off the spare bedroom"—he gestured to the room beside the kitchen—"and take your pretty blouse off and put this T-shirt on. I'd like to start working on that scar of yours."

Mary's expression suddenly went rigid and he saw the uncertainty in her eyes.

"Please," he said softly. "Yer home now, home, with yer family, and we all understand. Your secrets and discomforts are our secrets and discomforts now, but they don't have to be discomforts anymore. We just want to help."

Mary slowly nodded, holding Dev's deep green eyes, accepting his gentle smile. She went through the bedroom, into the bathroom, and changed.

When she came out, he had fluffy towels laid out on the dining room table and an assortment of plastic rubbing and spreading "tools" laid out on them. Dev noticed she was covering the exposed lower part of her scar with her right hand.

"Come and sit between us," he said softly, and she sat down with her left arm closest to him.

Mandy pulled her chair up close on her right as he smiled at Mary, took her hand, and slowly withdrew it. Then he rolled the sleeve up onto her shoulder.

"Oh my," Mandy said softly. "That must've hurt somethin' fierce."

"Yes, love," Mary said, trying to smile. "It did, for a very long time."

"Da told me you had been shot too," Mandy said. "I felt so very bad for you. I'm sorry I sent the picture and...and...and caused all of this trouble for you."

Mary exhaled slowly and looked at Mandy. "I know you didn't know, but in hindsight, you should've told your dad you wanted to. But saying that is like handing out umbrellas after the rain stops."

Mandy tried to not giggle. "It just didn't seem real that someone would be lookin' fer ya and wantin' to do ya harm. Kind of like the story about you gettin' shot wasn't real either, but I know that was true. I'll try really hard to not do anything to make you mad at me anymore."

Mary smiled and winced as Dev moved her arm. "I...I'll try to be more understanding too, love. I'm still too fearful that we won't be able to stop him and...and with you two, I have too much to lose this time."

Dev moved her forearm up and down, flexing her elbow, feeling the bicep as he did. "I see that catch still hurts when you move yer arm this way."

Mary nodded. "The lotion you put on it last week helped a lot, but it still catches, still hurts."

"The scar has had a long time to get a good hold on the muscle," he said, concentrating on the movement of the skin, the scar, and what he felt beneath. "I'm guessin' you didn't have any physical therapy."

"There wasn't time," Mary said as she shook her head, watching him as he took the penetrating lotion and squeezed a bead onto her arm. "The cast came off the week I started walking. Use of it was limited, to say the least." She twitched as he pressed with his thumb, rubbing the gel into the scar and surrounding skin.

"Don't be afraid, Mary," Mandy said softly, watching intently. "Mine were tender and painful at first too. I cried a lot, not understandin' why Da was hurting' me, but Da knows what he's doing. Ya almost can't see mine anymore." And to prove her point, Mandy lifted the front of her shirt and undershirt, showing Mary the three long marks from the incisions along and across her tummy and chest.

She took Mary's right hand and gently pulled it to her, letting Mary feel the faded marks.

"I have two more on my back, and Da says by the time I discover boys you won't even see them, unless I get sunburned or something like that. We're hopin' my front ones won't look too bad when I start fillin' out."

"Your dad told me about your accident and that you had scars," Mary said, "but yours are healing very nicely. They might not look too bad, and they're soft enough they probably won't interfere as you grow. We'll keep our fingers crossed."

"At first, Da worked on them every night, then after we came here he went to three times a week," Mandy explained. "He taught me how to do the ones I can reach, my front ones, but he still does my back. Now it's just twice a week. He can have yours feeling better in no time." Then Mandy looked at the "tools" and asked, "Will the paddles still work? Has it been too long, Da?"

"I hope they will, love," he said.

"Those hurt," Mandy said. "At least while he uses them. He has to make the scar let go of the muscle underneath, but when he stops, it feels better real fast. Then he puts more of that lotion on and it makes the skin relax so the pain will go away."

Mary smiled at her and then looked at Dev. "So I'm to be tortured? Something I did wrong?" Then she looked sideways at him, "Something I didn't do well enough?"

Dev caught her devilish smile and the gleam in her eyes, knowing she was teasing about their afternoon "fighting" in his bed. He chuckled and slipped one hand under the table and gently squeezed her thigh. Mary twitched and tried to move her leg away without being obvious.

"No, love," he smiled. "Ye make me head spin just rememberin'." He saw Mandy's curious look. "But Mandy's right, the paddles do hurt for a little while."

He took two fingers full of a thick cream from a jar in his small case and spread it gently over her scar and forearm.

When he picked up the first plastic paddle, Mandy quickly took Mary's right hand and squeezed it gently. "Hold my hand tight and look at me. Don't think about what Da has to do. Just look at me." And Mandy screwed her face up into a goofy expression, making

Mary laugh.

Mary jerked her arm when Dev started, but he held it firmly and she forced herself to watch Mandy's serious attempts to help. It was an unexpectedly long few minutes, she thought later, but when it was over, she encouraged herself in Mandy's assurance that her arm might actually start feeling better. Maybe not that night, but soon.

Dev finished with the paddles, wiped the remaining cream off her arm, and then rubbed the penetrating lotion into the scar. "We'll let this rest a bit," he said, and smiled at Mary. "Now, love, if I can get you to turn toward Mandy, I'll look at your back. Hold the front of yer shirt; I have to pull the back up pretty high."

Mary crossed her arms in front of her to hold the shirt in place as Dev pulled the back up to her shoulders, catching her long hair in the fold.

"Mandy, please stand up and hold the shirt on Mary's shoulders."

Mandy smiled at Mary as she stood and caught the shirttail. "It'll be okay. You'll see."

"Thanks, love," Mary whispered. "I know you're both helping. Oh!" She turned her head in surprise when Dev unhooked her bra.

"Sorry, love," he said. "I just need to move that out of the way for a few minutes."

He slowly repeated the process he had used on her arm, applying the penetrating lotion and following with the cream and the paddles. Mary gritted her teeth and smiled at Mandy as Dev worked on the five four-inch arms of the larger spidery scar to the left of her spine. Then he moved to the second scar, lower on her right side.

Finally Dev laid the paddles on the towel and began rubbing the butter over the scars, and Mary exhaled, suddenly realizing she had been holding her breath.

"I think that's enough for one night, love," Dev said as he gently rubbed the butter into her skin. "We'll see how your back does, but I don't think we'll use the paddles every time."

Mary took a deep breath. "I think that'll be good. I don't have as much padding on my back."

Dev chuckled. "Ya don' have a lot of paddin' anywhere, love. Except where it's supposed to be."

After the butter soaked in for a few minutes, Dev wiped her back with a dry cloth and fastened her bra strap.

"Thanks, Mandy," he said, and took the shirttail and stretched it down to cover Mary's back. "I'll give you some cream you can put on your arm and your right shoulder before you go to bed at night. I'd like to start workin' on yer scars at least three times a week—more if you'll let me," Dev said as he rubbed another dab of the penetrating lotion into her arm and waited for it to soak in.

"Sorry for the smell. It's supposed to be odorless, but I don't think the makers have noses." He smiled at her. "Thanks for letting me help," Dev said softly, "and for letting Mandy be a part of this, love. I've tried to not keep things from her, and not have secrets between us." He winked at Mary, knowing she knew there were somethings they should not share with a ten-year-old. "Now, would you mind if Mandy sees your new driver's license?"

"No, no, not at all," Mary said, and gave him a questioning look. "Would you bring me my purse, Mandy?"

Mandy quickly retrieved her purse and Mary took her billfold out and opened it for Mandy to see. Mandy bent to study the card.

"Mandy, love," Dev said. "Do you notice anything interesting?"

"Hmm. Name and address, that'll change in another month," Mandy said softly to herself. "Aaah, I forgot! You and I have the same birthday!"

"We do?" Mary asked in surprise.

"Yup!" Mandy said, and turned the license as if Mary had not seen it before. "June twenty! Wow!"

"What a nice coincidence," Mary said. "Wait? You forgot. Right, you already knew. From the library searching."

Dev squeezed her arm gently and sat back in his chair. "Aah yes. I forgot she had seen those sheets when she did her first lookin'. But it's nice that you both share the same day, almost like sayin' ye two belong together."

Mary looked at him and then at Mandy's wide smile.

Dev smiled and rubbed more of the skin butter on Mary's arm.

Then Mary looked at Dev and softly asked, "So what do we do now?"

"The one thing that's gonna be hard ta do. Obviously, we wait," he said. "I know it isn't a good answer, but Mandy has asked a number of her friends to help watch for any strangers they see in town—especially redheaded ones about my size."

Mary could not help but giggle.

"I've talked to Lloyd a couple of times but he has nothin' more than I've given him. So in the meantime, we'll continue livin' and lovin' each other as much as we can," Dev said, and slipped his arms around Mary's shoulders. "And watchin'."

"You know this scares the crap out of me?" Mary turned to look at him.

"I know, love. It scares all of us," he admitted.

"You said you talked to your old chief. Did you find out about Mum's accident, Da?" Mandy asked. "You said you had a hunch."

"Aaah, yes," Dev said, and looked at the two of them. "I called my old chief a couple of times. As I've said before, we talked about the numerous accidents that have the same appearance as the one that you and yer mum were in. He checked on any similarities they might have seen at their level, especially concernin' the truck drivers. And they had."

Dev explained his latest conversations with Mike O'Malley and that the police had recorded that each driver in the accidents had been shot while they were driving, thus causing the accidents, killing many innocent people collaterally.

"Seein' that all of the trucks involved were carryin' supplies for the various steel mills, I wondered if me cousin and his mob were behind it. O'Malley confirmed that all of the truck drivers were killed with bullets from the same gun." Dev inhaled deeply and looked at Mary. "Like I told ya in Buena Vista, on a hunch I asked O'Malley if he could find out if your husband was killed by the same gun, but he confirmed a week or so later what you already knew. Einri had done that one. It was a different gun and they have his fingerprints from the magazine he dropped." He paused again. "My personal feelin' is that Scanlon's the one that's been shootin' the truck drivers, with Einri tellin' him it's some sort of a game so he wouldn't know he was hurtin' anyone. But I haven't confirmed that yet."

Mandy got up and came around Mary to hug Dev, and Mary wrapped her arms around them both.

"Our own cousin caused the accident?" Mandy asked softly in

disbelief. "Me mum and gran's?"

"Aye, lass," Dev said heavily, and Mary squeezed them both. "I hate to admit it, but it looks like one or both of me criminal cousins caused it, love."

"How could they, Da?" Mandy cried softly as she pulled an arm away from him and reached around Mary. "And they took Mary's Robert too."

Thirty
Saturday, October 7

"Hey, Scan," Mikalean said, and shook his sleeping brother.

The morning was still dark and cast no usable light into the small room above the dry cleaners off Fort where Delray was squeezed between the 75 and the Detroit River. The splashes from the streetlight were all the light they had.

"Wake up. I brought ye some breakfast."

Scanlon stirred but did not try to get up.

"Scan," Mikalean said again, his voice irritated. "Come on. Ya need ta get up. We need to meet with the others and see where we go from here."

"Shite and onions, Mik. You go." Scanlon mumbled the popular old country curse softly. "Let me sleep."

Mikalean leaned over and shook him again, abruptly standing back. "What'n 'ell did ya do last night? Ya smell like a sewer."

"Lois's," Scanlon mumbled. "Billie Ray took me to Lois's."

"And then where? Were ya too drunk or stoned to find the loo? I sure canna see what that girl see in ya."

"Don' 'member."

"Well, ya need to get up and go clean up."

"Shite, Mik! I don' wanna," Scanlon said, and turned over, his back to Mikalean. "Leave me 'lone."

Mikalean grabbed his blanket and jerked it onto the floor. "Go and wash off. I know the shower works. Go! Before I puke!"

Scanlon cursed and muttered something Mikalean could not make out, but slowly forced himself upright on the edge of the small cot. He rubbed his face and pushed himself onto his feet as Mikalean watched in disgust. Scanlon wobbled to the bathroom, catching the doorjamb just to stay upright.

When he heard the shower running and the toilet flush, Mikalean kicked the soiled blanket into a pile near the door, telling himself he would not take it or Scanlon's clothes home for him or Nora to clean; Scanlon would have to do this one himself.

He opened the blinds on the front window to let more of the streetlight in, and jumped with a start at a noise in the hallway.

"Einri?" he asked in disbelief as his older brother hobbled through the doorway on crutches, one leg and foot in a facsimile of a walking cast. He hurried to help him in. "What happened? Where ya been?"

"Leonard's," Einri said as he slowly lowered himself onto the chair just inside the door, wrinkling his nose at the blanket piled beside him.

"What happened? We looked and looked fer ya."

"Ambushed," Einri said. "Brighton's finest had our uncle Finnian's house staked out. Leonard took four slugs outta me legs and hip and one outta me side. Took some time 'fore I could get back on me feet and start walkin'." Einri took a deep breath. "I think I killed one of 'em gettin' away. Henry must've tol' 'em I'd been comin' 'round."

"Ya said he said he would if ya kept comin' back."

"He didn't have ta."

"What was he gonna do—just ignore you bein' there?"

"Yeah. Would've been nice if he'd waited."

"Waited? Waited for what? He tol' ya not to come 'round and you ignored him! What'd ya think he was gonna do?"

"Mik! We're family and he shouldna called the cops."

"And he's been honest with ya, Einri. He gave you fair warnin' all the while he tries to take care of his mum and sisters. Besides, knowin' yer related, the cops coulda been watchin' without Henry callin'."

"Bah! I wasn't botherin' him. I was just usin' his shed, the one out back. He never saw me or me being 'round, but he changed the lock on me. I'll get even with him fer it."

"Whatcha gonna do—shoot him too? Maybe his sisters also? His mum?"

"Watch yer mouth, Mik."

"No, Einri. You can't just go 'round shootin' everyone that doesn't cower to ya."

"That's enough, Mik."

"Einri! Listen to yerself. He owes ya nothin' yet he's always civil to ya. He doesn't want to be one of yer accomplices. He tells ya what's on his mind and he gives ya as much of yer space as he can."

"Until now."

"Yeah, now. When ya decide he's just bluffin' after he tol' ya what was gonna happen."

"He shouldna called them."

"Shite! Maybe he did and maybe he didn't, but ya gave him no choice if he did. Ya don't use yer head. Ya coulda waited or found someone else's shed, but no, you prod and push 'im and make 'im do somethin' ya don't like."

"I'm warnin' ya, Mik. Shut up. I'll take care of me cousin in me own way."

"He's me cousin too, dammit. Ya gonna kill him too? Ya shoot and kill everyone that ya feel is against ya, or has a different opinion, or if ya just want them outta yer way. Just like ya do with the truckers. Insteada stoppin' the trucks, ya kill the drivers and many more people just because they wuz there, too close to be missin' the carnage. And then there's the cop killin's. Ya don' use—"

"I warned ya, Mik. Stop it!"

"And now ya got yer youngest brother killin' fer ya. He doesn't even know 'makin' holes' kills people. And you keep makin' him do it."

"I said stop it!" Einri growled, and wobbled as he pulled himself up on his crutches.

"Whatcha gonna do—kill me fer tryin' to talk some sense into ya? Yer too stubborn fer yer own—"

"Enough!" Einri shouted, and jerked his pistol from his pocket. He squeezed the trigger just as Scanlon opened the bathroom door.

-¤-

"Einri?" Scanlon asked in surprise as he saw Mikalean fall to the floor. "What'd ya do?"

"Scan, get dressed. Yer comin' with me."

"Why, Einri?" He looked down at Mikalean's still form lying beside the cot. "We gotta help Mik. Why'd ya shoot him? He's yer brother, Einri. Why'd ya shoot him?"

"He was talkin' too much," Einri said. "Now get dressed before you talk too much."

"Where we goin'?" Scanlon asked as he stepped back into the bathroom. "Ya need to call someone. Mik needs help."

"Don't worry about him, Scan," Einri said, and turned to the hallway door. "We gotta go visit a couple of our cousins and make s'more holes."

¤-¤-¤-¤-¤

"Where's Mandy?" Connie asked as Dev took a seat near Stumpy's front window and she stopped to take his order.

"Salida," he said, and smiled. "Saturday's hikin' got preempted by weather and dress shoppin'."

"She's in Salida and you're here?" Connie looked at him curiously. "I could understand it if she were hiking. Doesn't she often go with Miss Gorden?"

"She does, usually. But today's different," he said, and looked at the menu. "They both have just seven weekends to find the right dresses. Debbie Cotton went with them to help with the pickin' out. Give me a bison burger with all the trimmin's, and fries with cheese and chili. Oh, and a Guinness."

"Got it," Connie said, and stopped to look at him. "Then maybe what I heard is true?" She raised her eyebrows at him. "Are you and Miss Gorden really getting married?"

"I'm happy to say so." Dev nodded and smiled at Connie. "I didn't think it would happen again, but we are. Mandy's excited beyond words and it's been a very long time since I felt the way I do now."

"Well, congratulations, Dev," Connie said as she turned. "I'm sure that has upset a few women around town."

"Wouldn't know about that, Connie." Dev smiled again. "I barely have time to try keepin' up with me two girls these days."

Connie chuckled and hurried to the kitchen to turn in his order.

Dev pulled his phone from his shirt pocket and entered a text string: *"How's the hunting going?"*

Connie brought his Guinness and he was about to take a sip when his phone dinged.

"Good, but I have not found what I want yet. Just left the third dress shop. Getting a quick bite of lunch and then off again. Five more to check out."

"Please watch your daylight. It gets dark early and you haven't driven at night," Dev answered.

"I will, love, but it probably will be after dark when we get home."

"Then be careful driving, lass. I need both of you home in one piece."

"We will be careful. I am looking forward to some private time with you later."

Dev smiled and replied, *"I'm game. Let me know when you start back."*

"I will."

Dev tried to relax as he sipped his stout and chatted with Connie briefly when she brought his lunch, but he knew he was worrying. This was the first time since the accident that Mandy was so far away from him. He knew Mary would not do anything intentionally to endanger either of them, Debbie either, but he was still full of concerns. He had two girls to take care of now, and he knew he was not handling them being gone very well.

Thirty-One

Mikalean stared at the ceiling, a dirty yellowish color in the gray morning light seeping past the shabby blinds covering the single window. He tried to remember where he was. Wondering why he was on the floor, he tried to roll over and get up, but the searing pain in his side stopped him; he tried to move his left leg but the pain in his hip took his breath away. Gingerly, he tried to move his arm, but could only bend it at the elbow without triggering the excruciating spasms.

Slowly, accompanied by his deep inhales, he remembered Einri coming into the room, Scanlon's room, and them arguing. Then he remembered Einri had pulled his gun from his pocket! He inhaled again and slid his phone out of his right pants pocket and focused on the screen as he touched the icons with his thumb to get to his phone book. He touched a speed dial icon.

"Hello," the woman's voice said.

"Nora. It's Mik. I need yer help," he said softly, trying to keep his voice level and not sound strained, or show the panic that gripped him. "I need ya to call our cousin Henry, Devlin's brother, and tell him Einri is pissed at him fer callin' the cops on him. Tell him Einri's on his way to see him. Got that?"

"Yeah," Nora said. "I'll call right now."

"Good, good, lass," Mikalean said. "Call him and then call me right back. I need ta know Henry knows and can be ready."

"Okay. I'll call," she said, and disconnected.

-¤-

Nora looked at her phone for a long minute, trying to piece together why Mikalean's call was bothering her. *Why didn't he call Cousin Henry himself?* she wondered, but she forced herself to stop thinking and made the call. She told Henry everything Mikalean had asked her to, and Henry thanked her and said he knew what he needed to do. Then he disconnected.

Nora inhaled, knowing Einri was not going to Henry's for a social call, but she worried about Mik—his whole manner was different and she knew that something was wrong. Mikalean was always with Einri, or so it seemed, and now it seemed he was not.

Then she remembered Mikalean had not called her "lass" in more than three years, and it both surprised and bothered her. Something was definitely wrong—or at least very different, she added hopefully. She tapped his icon and waited as the phone rang. It rang again with no answer and then a third time. She was getting very nervous when he finally answered on the fifth ring.

"'Lo," Mikalean's weak voice said.

"Mik, it's me, Nora," she said, and waited. "Mik?"

"Yeah, yeah. I hear ya," he said, his voice almost a whisper. "I need ya to do me another favor."

"Sure, sure."

"Ya remember where Scanlon hangs out, that dirty room over the old laundry near West Fort and Junction? I need fer ya to come there and get me."

"Yeah, I remember. What's wrong, Mik? Where's your car?"

"Me and Einri had words," he said.

"I can barely hear you, Mik. Speak up."

"I'll try," he said, sounding a little louder but out of breath. "I need ya to come quick, lass. I think I'm needin' a hospital."

"I'm comin' now," Nora said louder than normal as she ran out of the house to her car. "Stay on the phone, Mik. I'm comin'."

¤-¤-¤-¤-¤

After lunch, Dev walked the three blocks down Main to the post office, checked his box, and was surprised to find a letter from his mother, a card from his sister Moira Anne, and a second card; he stared at the return address: Nora and Mikalean O'Brien. He opened their card first as he stepped back out onto the street and began retracing his steps back toward Stumpy's.

He was surprised to see it was a belated birthday card with

a pleasant message inside. He paused to read the hand written messages, one from Nora and one from Mikalean.

Nora's said, "Sorry to be late in wishing you a happy day, but I did not have your address until I ran into Derry at a woman's luncheon. She said you are seeing someone, and I wish it is all you'd like it to be."

He smiled at the unexpected note and then read Mikalean's. "Happy belated birthday, cousin. Sorry I've been such a pain in the ass all these years. I want to say I'm sorry for all of that and I hope to change it in the future. Give Amanda our best and I hope she is doing well. Good luck to you, Amanda and your new lady. You've been a good cousin. Thanks."

Dev stared at the card. At first he thought it was just nice, but then he thought about how Mikalean had always seemed to follow Einri around everywhere, mindlessly doing whatever Einri said to do. He wondered if Mikalean was really ready to change.

Then he chuckled; one thing was for certain: by sending him a card, Mikalean had let him know that he and Einri knew where he was. And both Nora and him had let him know they knew about Mary. Just the fact that Mikalean had warned him was enough for him to know something was changing in Mikalean's life. Something for the better, he hoped.

¤-¤-¤-¤-¤

Dev was pacing around and around in his living room, getting more and more worried by the minute. He wanted to text Mary and see where they were, but he did not want to make her look at her phone if she was driving. He glanced at the clock on the mantel: seven. It had been dark for two hours and he knew they should have started back before now. It was obvious she had forgotten about telling him when they were leaving Salida, but he also knew she had to be excited, getting out on her own for the first time in a very long while.

His phone chimed and he jumped. He grabbed it out of his shirt pocket, almost dropping it.

"Dev," Mary's voice said when he answered.

"Hey, love," Dev said, suddenly relieved, hearing her calm voice.

"I'm so sorry I didn't call earlier. The three of us got to talking about everything and I forgot. Please don't be mad. Mandy's doing great and had a lot of good ideas and comments. We're just leaving Buena Vista. I had to let Debbie drive the rest of the way. You were right about not being ready to drive a lot at night yet."

"Are you doin' okay, otherwise?"

"Sure, sure," she said, and he smiled at her use of his and Mandy's phrase again. "I told Debbie I'd buy her dinner when we got back. Can you meet us at Stumpy's in about forty-five minutes?"

"Of course, lass," Dev said, slowly letting himself relax. "I'll be there. How's your gas doin'?"

"One minute," Mary said, and he could hear her moving around as she checked. "Half a tank. Should we stop and fill it up?"

"You should be fine," Dev said, and smiled. "You've got enough to make it home. Be careful comin' up the valley road, especially on Hunter's Pass. Roads will be refreezin' by now. I love you, lass. Be safe."

"I love you too, Dev," Mary said softly. "We will."

-¤-

They were ten minutes early when Debbie parked the jeep in front of Stumpy's and Dev stepped through Stumpy's front door. He hugged Mary as she got out and then Mandy, helping her down from the high doorsill.

"How was yer huntin'?" Dev asked as he followed the three girls into the café and bar.

"Very good actually," Mary said, and went to their favorite table near the front window. "We went to all of the shops and then had to go back."

"She found one," Debbie said, and Mandy nodded.

"But we can't tell you anything about it, Da, 'cept it's a dress and we think you'll like it."

Dev smiled and ruffled Mandy's fiery tresses. "I guess this is just one more reason to add to why I'm havin' a hard time waitin' for Thanksgivin' to get here." He looked back at Mandy. "Yer hair's gettin' long. Do I need to make ya an appointment?"

"No, Da." Mandy smiled back at him. "I want to let it grow long like Mary's. Is that okay?"

"Sure, sure." He smiled and ruffled her hair again. "I think it will look very nice bein' long." He looked at Mary. "I like Mary's long hair very much."

Connie met them and congratulated Mary and Mandy when she took their orders. When she went back to the kitchen to turn them in, Dev took a folded paper out of his pocket and looked at Mary and then at Mandy.

"Got a letter from Mum today," he said, and handed the paper to Mary. "She already has travel plans made for all of them. Flyin' into Denver and then she's rented a couple of four-wheel-drive vans for the drive over." He smiled at Mandy as Mary began reading the letter. "Here's a card from yer Aunt Moira for me birthday." He handed the card to Mandy.

"Yep," Debbie said, "you're both as ready as you can be." She shook her head and smiled at Mary. "I don't know why you're going to all of the trouble of a big ceremony—it's obvious you're already a family."

"We're not that bad," Mary said with a wide smile and a glance at Debbie. "Besides, we need to set a good example." She nodded toward Mandy. Then she folded the letter and handed it to Mandy. "Want to read what your Gran' has to say?"

"Sure," Mandy said softly, and handed the card to Mary as she took the letter. "I can't wait to see them again."

¤-¤-¤-¤-¤

They dropped Debbie off at her place, a small house on Garfield just south of the school complex, and Dev stopped at Zeke's to fill the jeep.

"Ya know," Mandy said softly to Mary while Dev was tending to the fueling, "we've been hidin' too. Not wantin' to go back to Brighton to see them. That's part of why we only call them once a month."

"I got that feeling, love," Mary said, "but I don't understand why."

"Silly, I guess." Mandy stared down at her hands in her lap. "But we've been so worried about us, gettin' everything worked out, encouragin' each other, and I think we didn't want anything to distract us. At least neither of us gave it much thought. We just lived our lives day to day, being happy with each other and what we've made." Mandy looked up and smiled, a tight, slowly growing grin. "Then we found you and we haven't thought of much else. I mean, we still do what we've been doin', but you made us remember there's more to life than we had been livin'. Does that make sense?"

"Yes, love," Mary said, and smiled. "It makes perfect sense. The same thing happened when I finally opened my eyes and saw you and your dad."

Mandy reached up for Mary's hand and said, "Thanks for letting them bring you here to mend. We need you."

Mary smiled and squeezed her hand. "Are ye sure yer only ten?"

Mandy giggled.

"I'm glad too, Mandy. I need both of you, too."

Thirty-Two
Sunday, October 8

Mikalean looked at the dim ceiling a long time, like he was trying to place a forgotten face in his mind. It was unfamiliar, a clean whitish and not a dirty yellowish color. The light was wrong, and slowly he began to see the things around him: the whiteboard on the wall past his feet, the slightly ajar door to a bathroom, the large window with blinds drawn against the night's darkness, and Nora sleeping, curled up sideways in the chair beside him.

He coughed and cleared his sore throat and Nora stirred. Her eyes held his and she slowly smiled and gently caught his hand. He tried to speak but his voice was just a coarse rumble.

"Don't try to talk yet," Nora said, and leaned closer. "'Tis the tube they had to put down yer throat makin' it sore. The doctor said you're lucky in a way, and not in others. Ye'll recover, but healin' will be slow. You have a lot of intestinal damage and somethin' broken in yer hip."

Mikalean nodded and looked around the room. His gaze stopped when he saw a uniformed policeman outside his door, standing in the hallway.

"Ye asked me to call the Brighton Police to tell 'em about Einri," Nora explained. "And they said they'd get in touch with Cousin Henry. The detective there said he would call the closest Dearborn precinct and have someone come and stand guard here if'n Einri decided to come lookin' fer ya." Nora smiled and looked at the officer. "The detective I talked to wants me to call him when you can talk so you can tell him what's happened."

Mikalean nodded. Then he squeezed her hand and held it as he slowly closed his eyes. He felt worn out, and gratefully fell back to sleep.

¤-¤-¤-¤-¤

Mandy was already in bed with the sheet and blanket tucked under her arms when Mary and Dev came up the stairs and into her room to give her their "goodnights." Mary went around and sat down on the far side of Mandy's bed, as was their nightly routine. Dev sat down on his side, nearest the door.

"Mandy, I want to ask you and Dev about something," Mary said, instead of going straight to the kisses and blessings.

"Sure." Mandy smiled and winked at her. "Are ye goin' to elope?"

Mary smiled and looked at Dev. "That isn't what I was going to ask, but I'll admit that has also been on my mind lately."

"So, love"—Dev smiled—"what's yer question?"

Mary held his eyes for a moment. "It's not as good of an idea as eloping, but your mum said they would be here late in the day the Friday before Thanksgiving, and that she was expectin' us to be ready to start the celebration first thing once they got here."

"I saw that," Mandy said.

"Well, I wouldn't ask you to elope and keep your family from being part of the joys, but I was wondering what you might think about changing the wedding, moving it up from the Saturday after Thanksgiving to late morning or early afternoon the Sunday before, the nineteenth." Mary waited for Dev's response, seeing Mandy's eyes light up. "The children's Thanksgiving program is Sunday night, there's no school that week, and I'd like to have that and the whole Thanksgiving week as part of our first week of life together as a family."

Dev slowly let his grin grow into a wide smile. "You wouldn't let us marry ya last week, and ya won't let me marry ya tomorrow, so I guess the Sunday before will have ta do. I think it's a wonderful idea, Mary. What do you think, scamp?" He playfully jostled Mandy's shoulder.

"I'm like you, Da," Mandy said through a wide smile as she grabbed Mary's hand. "I think the sooner, the better. And I think you said our dresses will be ready in plenty of time."

"Your dresses?" Dev asked in surprise.

"Yes, Da," Mandy said emphatically. "Debbie and I are going to have matching dresses to complement Mary's. Hers will be the prettiest, of course."

Dev shook his head. "I have an appointment with Pastor Emlich Monday mornin', so I'll set up the time and day. What about a place? Do you two have a preference? I really doubt the parish church will hold the whole town."

"The school?" Mandy asked. "The auditorium or the field house."

"Those are probably the largest rooms in the whole town," Dev said. "We plan for about two hundred for programs in the auditorium, but the field house with foldin' chairs on the floor and the bleachers pulled out can manage close to eight hundred. Maybe more."

"Would that be too tacky?" Mary asked.

He looked at Mandy. "Would you be okay with being married in the school field house?"

"I don't think I'm as worried about the place," Mandy said, "as I am about somethin' keeping us from marrying Mary. I love the both of you and I want us to be together as a family as soon as we can get it done."

"Mary, love," Dev said, and reached for her hand. "I think you have our answer. Do you want me to talk with Mrs. Arnold tomorrow? Before I meet the pastor?"

"I'll talk with Nancy first thing tomorrow when I go in," Mary said. "Then I'll text you." She saw Mandy's surprised expression. "Before class starts and the cell phones have to be put away." Mary stuck her tongue out at Mandy and then smiled. "I do remember my own classroom rules."

"Just checkin'," Mandy said, and reached up for Mary.

Mary hugged Mandy and gave her a big kiss on the cheek. "You've come to mean so very much to me, Mandy. Thank you. I love you very much."

"Ditto, Mary," Mandy said, and squeezed her once more before she lay back down. "I can't see our tomorrows without you in them anymore, either."

Dev leaned over and hugged Mandy, kissing her on the cheek also. "Only happy dreams are allowed from now on, lass," Dev said softly. "May they all make yer heart sing and yer steps as light as walkin' on air. Sleep happy, love."

"I love you too, Da, Mary."

Monday, October 9

"Good mornin', sleepyhead," Nora said brightly when Mikalean blinked and slowly opened his eyes. "Are ya hungry? Ya slept through breakfast and nearly through lunch."

"Yeah," he said hoarsely.

"Here," she said, and held a cup with a straw to his lips. "Drink a little juice to wet yer throat. It'll help ya when ya want to say somethin'."

Mikalean inhaled a long sip and smiled at the gentle, soothing sensation as it trickled down. "Thanks, lass. Ya been here all night?"

She smiled and nodded as she pushed the nurse's call button. "Aye. I'm not goin' anywhere till ya can come home." She looked down at her rumpled clothes. "Except maybe to freshen up and come right back."

When the nurse came in, Nora helped Mikalean pick something to eat within the restrictions given by the doctors. The nurse said she was pleased he was awake and feeling better, and then she left to call for his food.

"How bad off am I?" Mikalean finally asked when the nurse had gone.

"Lucky, I'd say," Nora said, and scooted her chair closer so she could hold his hand. "They had to go in from four directions to mend the intestines and clean the poisons out. By this morning, the doctors were satisfied they had gotten everything they could and your body was not reacting to any left behind." She glanced down a minute and Mikalean knew she was thinking hard. "They said the bullet put a large hole and a crack in your left pelvic blade. I think he called it the ilium, which is the bone that connects the hip joint with the spine. They reinforced it with some kind of special cloth—a fabric to help the bone regrow and strengthen."

"Me leg doesn't feel right," he said, and held her eyes.

"They are afraid there might be some nerve damage," she

admitted, "but they think that if there is, it should only affect your feelin' and not yer use of the leg. They said you can start moving yer knee if you want, but your hip is in a cast for at least six weeks."

"Six weeks?" he said, and rolled his head back against his pillow. "By then Einri will have—"

"We'll let the police handle Einri," Nora said firmly. "I called the detective earlier and told him ya should be able to talk this afternoon. After ya eat, I'll call him and tell him to come over. Then you can tell him everythin' ya know so they can deal with Einri."

Slowly Mikalean nodded and lifted his head. "'Tisn't like I have a lot of choice, do I?"

Nora shook her head and smiled. "Not this time, Mik."

He noticed the subtle change in Nora's countenance and was going to ask her what she was thinking when she turned and looked up as an orderly brought a tray of gelatins and juices for him. The orderly set the tray on the bed table and swung it around in front of him.

"I can't raise your bed yet," the orderly said, "but maybe your wife can help you eat. If the afternoon goes well, the nurse says you can have broths and light soups this evening. They usually do liquids first to be sure your bowels work okay, then they can start you on solid foods."

"Thanks," Nora said, and the orderly left them.

Nora helped Mikalean with his light lunch and then called Detective Williams in Brighton. An hour after she called, Detective Williams came into the room and introduced himself to Mikalean. He pulled an unused chair up beside Mikalean's bed, opposite Nora's chair, and sat down.

"So," Mikalean said softly as he looked at the detective, "I hear ya want ta know about how I come ta be in this predicament."

Detective Williams chuckled and nodded. "Of course, Mikalean. We've been trying to find your older brother for many years, and I have to admit, I nearly fell off of my chair when your wife called yesterday. So as you say, I'm very curious about the details leading up to yesterday and you being here."

Nora let go of his hand and got up to leave. She had made it to the foot of his bed when Mikalean realized what she was doing.

"No, lass," he said sharply, then continued in a softer tone. "You need to hear everything I tell the detective." Then he looked at Williams to see if he was going to object.

When he did not, Nora sat back down in her chair and took Mikalean's hand again.

"This affects us all," Mikalean said, looking at Williams, and then he looked at Nora and smiled. "We'll let the cards fall where they may, but this affects you and the wee one too. There'll be no more secrets."

Detective Williams looked from Mikalean to Nora and back, cocking his head.

"We have one on the way, Detective," Nora said with a smile.

"Aaah," Williams said, and smiled at them both. "Congratulations. So can you tell me who shot you and why?"

"I can do better than that, but I'll start at the beginnin'," Mikalean said, "assumin' that if'n I help ya you'll put in a good word fer us, considerin' Nora and the wee one."

"Tell me what you know and I will promise you that I will talk to the judge on your behalf. I'll know more of what I can do after you tell me what you can."

Mikalean looked at Nora and then back at the detective. With a nod, he started telling about his older brother. "'Twas in high school when Einri started having issues with authority in general. He was such a handful that me Da sent him to live with his brother Finnian in Brighton. But that lasted a year at the most, probably a lot less. Einri kept gettin' inta trouble and gettin' hauled in, and finally Uncle Finnian kicked him out. Da wouldn't let him come back home unless he changed his ways, and six months later he was still the same, maybe worse. So Da decided I could try to rein Einri in, and watch over Scanlon too." Mikalean shook his head. "Well, we all know how that turned out. But the sad thing was that Einri learned how to look like he was changin' and not have to. About seven years ago, maybe six—I guess it was just after Nora and I got married—I found out that Einri was teachin' Scanlon how to shoot a gun. Target shootin' and tellin' Scanlon that he was just having fun, 'makin' holes,' he called it.

"I don't know if ya know, Detective, but Scanlon has always had a bit of a learnin' and reasonin' problem. Generally he knows right from wrong, but he's easily misled and if he isn't guided all of the time he can wander off in his own world and ferget what he's been told. Fer a while, I thought I had him on the right track.

"Five years ago, I found out that Scanlon was doin' a lot of Einri's shootin' for him and we had some words. Einri got rough and threatened to visit Nora if I made any waves, or worse." He glanced at Nora. "I was not strong enough to stand up to him, lass. I'm sorry, but I had nightmares over what he might do to ya."

He looked at Williams.

"Sorta cooled the love life, if ya know what I mean. I stayed away from home, tellin' m'self I was keepin' and eye on Einri, but really, I was afraid to go home and have Nora find out that I was a coward."

Nora squeezed his hand but did not say anything.

"As you might know, Detective," Mikalean continued, "Einri started tryin' to extort money from the steel mills and the truckin' companies, sorta like he was sellin' them some kind of protection, but he didn't tell them he would be protectin' them from himself if they didn't pay up.

"Things got rough and a lot of accidents happened, on the roads and off. He'd drive up beside a transfer truck and have Scanlon 'make holes' in the driver's door, then drive away, leaving the carnage behind for someone else to clean up."

"I remember when that started," Williams said. "Don't know if you know, but that first one, up in Royal Oaks, killed your cousin Devlin's wife and her parents. Almost killed his daughter too."

Mikalean's eyes went wide. "Shite! No! Not Devlin's Anne. I never saw a list of names of who died in that wreck."

Williams nodded slowly. "All of the names were initially withheld for the usual reasons. When the names were released, Devlin's family asked that Anne and her parents' names not be included. The obituary just read that they died in a multicar collision. They never explained why."

"Shite! I knew she died in a car wreck, but...Oh, damn m'self fer not standin' up and stoppin' me brother." Mikalean sighed. "Devlin musta had a feelin' 'twas Einri's doin's."

"Knowin' Einri, Mik," Nora said softly, "ya couldna stopped him, no matter what. And ya didna know."

"Was Einri behind all of the other transfer truck accidents?"

Williams asked.

Mikalean nodded. "He caused fourteen countin' the last one here in Dearborn."

"Fourteen? We only have nine on record."

"Five were a ways north of Detroit, west of Port Huron, bringin' pigs inta the mills," Mikalean said, and looked at Nora to be sure she was handling everything all right. "Then three years or so ago, he went after that undercover investigation team that Ann Arbor and Dearborn launched to track him down. I was sent to listen to certain meetings they had with the truckers' unions and the mill staffs, and I gave him parts of what I heard—parts that I thought couldn't hurt fer him knowin'. But I misjudged that one too. He killed five of the seven."

"Why not all of them?" Williams asked.

"The two survivin' paid Einri healthy sums of money to leave them alone and then they gave the police departments false information in return," Mikalean said. "Like me, they couldn't see themselves standin' up to Einri."

"We have reason to believe he's killed about eighty-seven people so far," Williams said. "Does that sound about right?"

"If ya count only the ones he killed personally or had Scanlon kill," Mikalean said softly. "Einri had a box of photos that he kept. They started out as a few pictures of people he didn't like or disagreed with, but it grew. He called it his 'list,' and he would add pictures he collected from various websites or social media sites or that he took himself. Then when he'd killed them, he'd mark them with a big X across the picture, indicating they no longer existed." Mikalean sighed and shook his head. "I never actually counted how many he killed or had killed. Every time I thought about them, I would just feel ill, helpless.

"But that number doesn't count the innocent ones like Devlin's Anne and her parents, and all like them in the other accidents." Mikalean looked at Nora and squeezed her hand, then looked at Williams. "I swear to ya both and with God in Heaven above as my witness, I never shot anyone and I've never killed anyone. I've never shot a gun and would probably shoot m'self if I tried. But now I see that I probably helped Einri kill some of them by not standin' up to him."

"So what happened to put you in the hospital?" Williams asked.

Mikalean chuckled. "I've been tryin' to figure out how I was going to get Scanlon and m'self away from Einri for a number of months now—years, actually—but a week ago we realized we couldn't find Einri anywhere. We looked all 'round, in places we thought he might have gone ta, but nothin'. Then last Thursday, after dinner, Nora and me had some words. Well, Nora had some words with me and then told me we were expectin'. I tried to assure her I was tryin' to find a way out, but I knew she didn't believe me. I mean, why should she? I've screwed up every promise I've made to her and left her nearly abandoned while I lived in this other life and tried to figure out what I was gonna do. I did keep me day job and supported her with honest money, but I was trapped and couldn't support her the way I promised I would.

"I know I'm as stubborn as the mules in Coarha More and I thank me lucky stars that sometimes I do listen. Only me Dingle lass has been able to get me attention when I really need it." He squeezed her hand again. "Then yesterday mornin', before Nora was awake, I went to Scanlon's dirty apartment in Delray to take him breakfast. Bein' a Saturday, I was hopin' to start lookin' fer Einri again, if only so we knew where he was. But Scanlon had a rough night partyin' with his friends and was in no shape for anythin', much less eatin'. I forced him to get up and take a shower, and while he was in washin', who'd'ya think walked in? Einri hobbled in on crutches, sayin' our old friend Doc Leonard pulled five bullets out of him a week and a half ago. He didn't say where he was ta get shot up, but—"

"Your cousin Henry's place," Williams interrupted. "We had the place staked out since we found out he had been hiding in Henry's shed. He was shot trying to escape when the officers tried to surround him. He killed one in his effort."

"He said he killed one gettin' outta some ambush, he called it," Mikalean said, shaking his head. "We got into a heated discussion when he said he was goin' back to teach Cousin Henry a lesson, and when I wouldn't stop tellin' him he was wrong to think of doin' such a thing to his own cousin, he shot me.

"I don't know where he is or where Scanlon is," Mikalean said, and dropped his head back on his pillow. "Nora told ya he was goin' to see his cousin Henry, but he may be headin' for Colorado as well."

"Colorado?" Williams asked, and Nora covered her mouth,

realizing she knew who was in Colorado.

"Aye," Mikalean said. "Me cousin Devlin has a new girlfriend, and Einri thinks she looks like the wife of that Ann Arbor policeman he killed—the one in the investigation team. Scanlon stole a picture of Devlin, Amanda, and his new girl from Henry's house and showed it to Einri. Einri killed the policeman's wife, but he started to wonder if she could still be alive, or a relative, after he saw the woman in Devlin's picture. Obviously, if he thinks the woman in the picture is the one he shot and he thinks she's still alive, he will think she can identify him, firsthand, as the one that killed her husband. I think that has Einri worried. Regardless, if she is or isn't, he'll kill her just to be safe."

"Well, we have your statement now," Williams said. "I will talk to the judge like I said I would. I think I can show him there was enough duress to keep you from coming forward sooner. To help your position, we'll need you to testify when he's brought to trial. Your statement can put him away." Williams looked at Mikalean. "I'm assuming that you will and that's why you called and asked me to come and listen."

"Aye," Mikalean said. "'Tisn't the way I expected to get away from Einri, but it'll have to do." He looked at Nora when she squeezed his hand again. He saw her guarded smile. Then he asked, "What are you going to do for Devlin and the woman in his picture?"

"Do you know where your cousin Devlin is?" Williams asked. "If I know where he is, I can contact the local police there so they can talk to him."

Mikalean looked at Nora and smiled as she pulled a piece of paper from her purse. "I think we can tell you where he is."

Nora handed Williams the paper. "Please copy that down, Detective. The paper is me only copy of his address."

Thirty-Three

"Yes," Pastor Emlich agreed as he reviewed his organizer. He and Dev were sitting in two of the three upholstered chairs in front of the handmade, medium-sized wooden desk in his church office. The office was not ornate, sporting only two small bookcases, a single credenza, and a few religious wall hangings in addition to the desk and four chairs. "I checked and noted November the twenty-fifth, keeping it open after talking with you at the fish fry last week. Morning, afternoon, or evening?" He looked up from his book and over his reading glasses at Dev.

"Late morning," Dev said with a smile, "or early afternoon. But we're changin' it to Sunday the nineteenth instead of Saturday the twenty-fifth. We originally chose the twenty-fifth to allow the family time to make travel arrangements, and we figured Thanksgiving week would be easier for them to get off work."

"That week's a good choice," he said.

"But last night, Mary confided that she would like to have everything happening durin' Thanksgiving week happen to us as a family—her, me, and Mandy. So she asked if we could change our plans by a week, and that way Mandy's school program and Thanksgiving would be part of our first week bein' a married family. Mandy and I agreed with her, so I'm askin' if ya can change as well."

Pastor Emlich checked his organizer and nodded. "You're in luck. I don't seem to have any other weddings planned for the nineteenth." He looked up and smiled. "Even though we have a few hopeful ladies in town, I don't have any other weddings pending anytime in the whole month."

"That's good," Dev said, and smiled.

"Late morning will work. At eleven?"

"Sure, sure. I'll get lunch catered and then we'll have the afternoon to get Mandy ready for her program that night."

"Oh yes, you did mention the school's program. That's good," Pastor Emlich said. "Do you have any idea how many might be attending your wedding?"

"Let's see," Dev said, and thought a minute. "There's fifteen of me family comin' from Michigan, the three of us here, and the rest of the town."

Pastor Emlich stared at him. "You...you invited the town?"

"Sure, sure." Dev smiled. "They're the biggest part of why we want to stay and live here. Wouldn't be right to exclude them, now would it?"

"No. No, it would not," the pastor agreed. "Anyone from Mary's family coming?"

Dev shook his head soberly. "No, Pastor. Mary's the only one left on her side. She doesn't have anyone in her family to invite."

"I'm sorry, Dev. I didn't know. I just need to figure out how to get everyone inside. It's a small church, and we're usually packed with fifty or so."

"We talked about that and Mary checked this morning, and bein' as it's a Sunday, she got permission to rent the field house at the school," Dev said. "It will hold everyone and be out of the cold. And we'll have lunch buffet-style in the school's cafeteria."

"I can work with that," Pastor Emlich said happily. "Church is out at ten, so I'll have time to get there and get my preparations in order. That works very nicely."

"Thanks, Pastor," Dev said as he stood. "I'm hopin' that if I can check off one thing we need done each day, I'll have everything ready before it's time."

"Before you go, Dev," Pastor Emlich said, standing with him, "I want to say I'm very pleased that you and Mandy have come to church a few times, nearly once a month on average. It isn't as often as I would like to see, but I hope you know that you, Mandy, and now Mary are welcome as often as you can make it. May I ask if you and Mary are considering adding a church life to your new one together?"

Dev smiled and shook his head. "I can only say that we are God-fearin' folks. We trust in the Almighty more than you can possibly know, but I have to admit that we haven't discussed the subject yet.

I'm sure we'll still visit some, but I can't say how often or regular we'll be."

"Well, just know it's my hope that you'll make it as often as you can, possibly make it a regular happening in your new life as a family," Pastor Emlich said.

"Thanks. We do intend to be stayin' here, Pastor—livin' in Roosevelt for the foreseeable future. So the chances are pretty good we'll be droppin' by more often."

"Okay, Dev. We'll leave it at that."

Wednesday, October 11

"This is so good," Mary said as she took another spoonful of the stew. "I remember something like this from when I was young. What is it?"

Dev smiled at Mandy.

"It's a traditional Irish coddle," Mandy said. "Normally a way to use up leftovers, but today we made it fresh. As chilly as today started, we decided this morning to have it tonight. We kept our fingers crossed all day, hopin' you'd like it."

"It is truly wonderful, love," Mary said, and smiled at Mandy. "But when did you have time to do it? You and I went to school at the same time."

Mandy laughed. "Da put it together after he dropped us off, before he went to the grocery."

"It's really a very simple dish," Dev explained. "A one-pot meal, as it's called. Usually it's just potatoes, onions, pork sausage, bacon, beef stock, water, and parsley." Then Dev told her that he came home at lunch to put it in the oven to slow bake all afternoon.

"I like it without so much broth," Mandy said, "so Da makes it a little drier than the normal recipe."

"Well, it's very nice. Do I also see thinly sliced corned beef and onions?" Mary asked.

"Yeah." Mandy smiled. "I also add some cream, basil, and a few other spices."

"And the bread rolls?" Mary asked as she buttered her second.

"Mandy made the dough after school," Dev said. "She put them in so they would be ready about the time we brought you home, love."

Mary smiled and continued eating. When she had wiped her bowl clean with the last of her bread roll, she pushed the bowl and plate away and sat up straight. "You know, you're going to have to let me cook some just so I can feel like I'm earning my keep. You're spoiling me with these wonderful meals and no chores."

"We're not tryin' to keep you from cookin', love," Dev said, and caught Mary's hand. "But with you having the more demanding work, we didn't want you to feel like you have to come home and cook too. Ya kin jump in and help anytime ya want, lass."

"Okay," Mary said, and glanced at Mandy. "What would you say if you help me fix something for dinner on Saturday or Sunday?"

"Sounds gran'," Mandy said. "Do ya know what you want to fix?"

"I'll think about it. If I can remember it, there was a dish my mother used to make. Maybe I can find a recipe that's close enough to use for starters." She looked at Dev and then at Mandy. "I'm sorry, but I don't have anything of theirs, and none of my mother's recipes."

"I know, Mary," Mandy said softly. "Let us know when you figure out what you want to fix and maybe we can help you with findin' recipes too."

"Thanks, love. I'll do that." Mary smiled and sighed, a deep, happy sigh. Then she started collecting the plates as she got up. "I'm washin' tonight."

"I'm dryin'," Mandy said, and picked up her plates as she got up. "That leaves the puttin' away fer you, Da."

"Sounds gran'," he said as he got up and helped clear the table.

As he set the dishes in the sink, his phone chimed. He quickly wiped his hands and took the phone from his pocket. Mandy and Mary watched as his expression reflected his surprise. "It's Henry," he said, and then answered the call.

-¤-

"Hey, Dev. It's yer brother, Henry," Henry's voice said in Dev's ear when the connection made.

"I see that, Henry," Dev said. "What's up to get you callin'? All right if I put ya on speaker?"

"Sure, sure," Henry said, and Dev switched the phone and held it between the three of them.

"Okay, Henry. We're ready. Just me, Mandy, and Mary."

"Hey all," Henry greeted, and Mary and Mandy said "hey" in return. "Thought I should share a few bits of new news. Derry saw Nora, Mikalean's wife, at a lady's luncheon about a week ago and she said Nora was askin' fer yer mailin' address. Derry said they wanted to send you a belated birthday card, but Derry was skeptical, and almost didn't—"

"I got their card on Saturday, Henry," Dev said, interrupting Henry. "Both she and Mikalean passed on wishes for happiness and a good future. Apparently she mentioned that I was seeing Mary."

"Oh, well, that's...that was very nice of them," Henry said, surprised. "I didn't know they were card kind of people."

"Seems so," Dev said with a smile at Henry's discomposure. "I'll have to write them back."

"Aaah, that brings me back to the reason for me call," Henry said. "First, Nora called early Saturday morning and told me Mikalean was adamant that she call me immediately to tell me Einri was angry over the 'him-livin'-in-me-shed-when-I-told-him-not-to' thing and was comin' to pay me back for callin' the police and havin' me place staked out when he came back ta get inta the shed again.

"It was surprise enough to hear her call. I don't think we've talked since Anne's funeral. Anyway, I thanked her for the warnin' and then I called your friend Williams, the detective here in Brighton, and they reinforced their surveillance again. But no signs of Einri."

"Well, that's good, in a way," Dev remarked.

"Only means he hasn't come by yet," Henry said, trying to make light of the situation. "Then Monday late, Williams called me and told me Mikalean was in the hospital in Dearborn. Seems Mikalean was tryin' to get a very hungover Scanlon around for the day on Saturday when Einri showed up at Scanlon's apartment. They got into an argument—one-sided debate, actually—over Einri's intentions toward me and the family and Einri shot him—"

"Shot 'im?" all three of them asked at the same time.

"That's what Williams said," Henry said. "Ya coulda pushed me over with yer little finger, ya coulda. Then he told me that Mikalean gave him a full accounting of Einri and his growin' up and what he's been up to since Da kicked him out when he was livin' with us. But he also mentioned a bit of news I was tryin' to not think could be true. I sorta figured, but didn't want to admit it could be..."

"He caused Anne's death," Dev finished for him. "We know."

"Yeah," Henry agreed with a sigh. "How'd you know?"

"Mike O'Malley at the ladder company did some checkin' fer me," Dev explained. "He checked with the Dearborn Police and found out all of the truck drivers involved in the numerous accidents like Anne's were shot just before the accidents. They were all shot with the same gun."

"Yeah, Mikalean told Williams that he tried to get Scanlon away from Einri, but wasn't successful. Einri taught Scanlon how to shoot—target practice, ya know—telling him it was just a game, he was just 'makin' holes.' Mikalean said he wasn't able to get Scanlon to understand that his 'making holes' was hurting people."

"Well, 'tis good Mikalean came clean and now maybe they'll have a better idea of where to look fer Einri," Dev said, and half smiled at Mary as Mandy hugged his waist.

"Williams thought so, but is afraid Einri might have hiding places Mikalean doesn't know about."

"'Tis likely, I suppose," Dev said softly. "But we'll keep hopin' they get lucky."

"Us too, Dev," Henry said. "But so far, none of Williams' men have seen any signs of Einri. Nothing. Mikalean is at a loss too. If you send him a card, better make it a 'get well soon' card. Anyway, hey to you Mandy and you Mary. Sorry to have such unpleasant things to talk about on this call."

"Thanks. Oh, did ya get our card about movin' the wedding up a week?" Dev asked before he forgot again.

"Yes we did. That will just make the partying more meaningful."

"Thank you," Mary and Mandy said together, giggling again because they did.

Then Mary continued, "We're glad you called, no matter why. It's nice to hear from you, and maybe in the future we won't have to limit ourselves to just once a month to talk to the family."

Mandy's eyes went wide, followed by a wide grin.

"I said maybe," she said. "We'll have to talk about it. Maybe, once things are official, your dad will allow it some. I want to talk to Derry occasionally."

"Because she has two girls?" Mandy asked, looking at Mary sideways.

"Aye, scamp, to talk 'bout parentin' girls, if ya must know," Mary said, and looked at Dev and giggled.

"The girls would certainly like that," Henry said. "But for now, I should let you go. I have to be downtown early tomorrow. Think about the happy days ahead. We'll talk to you soon."

"Sounds good, Henry. Happy days to ye too," Dev said, and glanced at Mary and Mandy. "Anything more from you two?"

Mary and Mandy shook their heads. "Nothing from us, Henry. Goodnight."

"Goodnight, all," Henry said, and the connection broke.

Dev put the phone back in his pocket and slipped his arms around them both.

Fearin' the Banshee

Thirty-Four
Saturday, October 14

"Good morning, Ms. White," Mary greeted as she let the protection program officer in and closed her front door behind her. "May I take your coat?"

Ms. White took her coat off and handed it to Mary.

"You're sounding happy this morning," Ms. White said as she turned to the living room like she always did.

"I am," Mary said, and gestured to the hallway. "I thought we'd sit in the dining room today. Table's a better height and the chairs are more comfortable for coffee. Don't know why I didn't think about it sooner. Actually, I do. I think it was Dev waking me up that let me finally accept this as my home."

Ms. White followed the hall and found that Mary had set the dining room table for the two of them with a plate of cinnamon breakfast rolls in between.

"I know it's a lot whiter and colder out today, but I hope you had a good drive," Mary said, and gestured for Ms. White to take a seat. When she sat down, Mary followed suit.

"It was a good drive." Ms. White smiled at the table—the pressed cloth covering and the delicate placemats under the cups and saucers. "Have you recently spruced the place up or has it always been like this and I just hadn't noticed?"

"Recently," Mary said, smiling as she poured their coffee. "I started cleaning it up the week or so before Dev took me to Buena Vista. I think that was about the middle of the month."

"So how are things between you and this man Dev?"

"Wonderful," Mary said, and smiled. "We've moved the wedding up to the Sunday before Thanksgiving. It's the Sunday of the children's Thanksgiving program at school and the Sunday at the beginning of

Thanksgiving week."

"Moved it up?" Ms. White asked, and Mary explained their setting the date so Dev's family could easily get time off from their various jobs, and why she decided she would like it earlier.

"Dev wanted to get married the day I accepted, but he relented, settling on a later date so his family could come." Mary sipped her coffee and then her expression turned more serious. "A few things have happened that you probably ought to know about though. Maybe you already know. There was one confusing issue the afternoon after you were here last. It seems that Dev's brother's name is Henry, the English spelling."

Startled, Ms. White inhaled and covered her mouth in anticipation.

"I freaked out too," Mary said, and nodded her head slowly. "But Dev's brother Henry had called him before their usual end-of-the-month family phone call." Mary explained what Dev had told her about Mandy sending a copy of their picture and that it had been stolen. "Somewhere in his explanation, he mentioned Henry's name and I came apart. I bolted, thinking it was the Henry that shot me and Bobby.

"He realized what had happened, what he said, and chased me down to explain. I fought him as much as I could, terrified by my memories. But he and Mandy held me tight and I couldn't hit him like I wanted to. Finally, I listened to him.

"It seems the name thing has been a bit of confusion for their family as well—even the police back in Brighton have confused Dev's brother with the criminal one from time to time." Mary saw Ms. White's perplexed expression. "The one that shot Bobby and then me is E-I-N-R-I, the Irish for Henry. Dev's dad and Einri's dad are brothers. Finnian is Dev's father's name and Gallagher is Einri's father's name."

Mary explained the argument between Finnian and Gallagher and the final decisions for naming the two sons.

"I was so relieved but still confused when he explained it, and I left them in the street, needing to go home, be alone, and think. I finally settled myself down and realized that Dev was deeply concerned over having to tell me about the picture and what it means. So I got myself under control and went back to his place, and we had a wonderful conversation with his family. I knew then that Dev would not intentionally hide things that could hurt me— my feelings or me physically. Dev asked me if I had changed my mind about getting married, and when I admitted I had not, Mandy announced to their family that Dev, she, and I were engaged and then invited them to the wedding. You know, you are invited to come too, and to Mandy's program that evening."

Ms. White smiled and nodded. "Thank you. No promises, but I'll see if I can attend. I really do want to meet this man and his daughter."

Then Mary sipped her coffee and her expression darkened. She saw that Ms. White noticed.

Mary explained what Dev had told her about Einri hiding in Henry's mother's storage shed without Henry knowing, and how the Brighton Police almost caught him. Then she changed to a happier subject and talked about Dev's family's travel plans and the day she, Debbie, and Mandy went to Salida to shop for wedding dresses.

"You went to Salida? Did Dev drive you?"

Mary reached behind her, pulled her purse off the buffet, and took her billfold out. She opened it and showed Ms. White her new driver's license. "I'm truly a citizen of Roosevelt now, with personal identification to prove it."

"That's wonderful, Mary. I didn't think about getting you a license."

"I don't have a car and didn't need one, but Dev suggested I get one." Then Mary inhaled and began again. "Dev took me to get my license after your last visit." Mary smiled at Ms. White's grin and put her license away. "That shopping day was a double win in my book: girl time with Mandy and time clothes shopping."

Mary continued explaining all that had happened since, from Henry's phone call to Dev to tell them about Einri shooting his brother, to the fact that they thought Einri had seen the picture of her, Mandy, and Dev.

"So where does that leave you? Does Dev think this Einri is coming here?"

"Yes, he thinks so," Mary said softly, her hands trembling against her strained efforts to keep them still; her coffee cup rattled on the saucer. "And it scares me to death. Of course, unless someone from there saw me now, here, no one would make the connection. But in this case, it was Mandy's innocent happiness of knowing me and hoping that Dev would propose that put my picture in the wrong place at the wrong time. And of course, it's that picture that shows I am where Dev is."

Mary took a deep sip of her now tepid coffee. She refilled her cup.

"I'm still trying to come to grips with all of this. But we've told Sheriff Martin and Mrs. Arnold, and Mandy has asked her friends around school to watch for another redheaded man about Dev's size. She hasn't told any of her friends why, but they'll watch with her. Sheriff Martin has alerted the State Police so they'll be on the lookout as well. Dev's been keeping in contact with his brother and his old ladder company chief so he can keep up with what's going on back there, but he was more than surprised when Henry told him Wednesday that the Brighton detective told Henry that Mikalean had given them a statement, the complete story of what Einri has done—everything that Mikalean knows about."

"Wow." Ms. White emptied her cup and gestured for a refill. "It sounds like Dev's trying to look at everything."

Mary nodded and poured the coffee.

"But where does that leave you? We can move you someplace else."

"I really don't want to move. But as for where it leaves me"—Mary smiled—"Mrs. Arnold and the school board would not let me stop teaching, so Lloyd and Dev talked to the school officials and Lloyd says he will be ready if something should start at the school. I don't have all of the details, but he said something about creating a volunteer militia. Dev thinks we should stay here, and with the town's help, we should be able to catch Einri if he comes. But I did finally convince him that if everything we plan fails, we should take his truck or jeep and slip out of town. There are two roads out—the highway and the road down past the Coopers' place; it's a back road that ties into the main highway just above Americus. He reluctantly agreed and put his truck in my garage out back, and since we use the jeep all of the time, it's at his place. We did some looking and picked two places where we could hide and still be close by. Debbie Cotton's dad offered to go with us and give us some protection if we have to leave. And if worse comes to worst and Lloyd can't stop Einri, I have your number and relocating would have to be an option. Dev said that if something happened to him, I would have to take Mandy with me." She forced a smile. "They both want me to adopt Mandy as soon as we can arrange it after the wedding."

Mary took a deep breath and continued. "In the meantime we'll live our new life the best we can, and try to stay alert. I have so many things to be happy about, including Dev's passion, both for me when we're alone together and for my safety, and for Mandy and her safety. He's watching all he can and he shows me how much he loves me the rest of the time. He won't even let me walk anywhere alone, just like he does with Mandy. He simply says he has two girls to take care of now, instead of just one."

Ms. White nodded, looking at the small boxes and tools on the kitchen counter. "Is Dev installing new locks?"

"Yeah. Better dead bolts. He's adding locks and locking bars to the windows, but he says they won't be enough. Einri would just break the glass, so he ordered some security sensors of some kind. Maybe they'll get here this next week."

Ms. White shook her head. "Sounds like you've got your hands full. I am pleased your heart led you to a man that you really can trust completely. And it sounds like he trusts you as well. I'm happy for that, but all of this other worries me more than I can say. Part of the things I was going to talk about today was that our background checks on Devlin identified Einri as the black mark on his uncle's side of the family, the one I mentioned last time I was here.

"I'll talk with Sheriff Martin and then with the program office. I think we, the program, have contingency plans set up just in case the unexpected happens and interferes with the plans you've made." Ms. White sipped her coffee and absently nodded. "Yes, and I'll be sure we have an agent or two work with Lloyd and the State Police."

Mary nodded and gestured to the rolls. "I knew this would worry you. It worries us, and I knew you and the program should know, if you don't already. But I'm glad I'm here and that I'm with Dev and Mandy. I'm still scared to death, but they're more help to me than you can imagine."

Ms. White took a roll and ate slowly. "I have to admit that when you told me you were going to get married, I worried that you were jumping too quickly, but you look like you're happy to be here, in this moment. And after your first year and a half, I think that you being happy is a wonderful change."

"Thanks. I know it seems fast, and maybe it is, but I feel that it's right. They've both been patiently waiting for me to see them, and Mandy says they've both been in love with me for a long time, just waiting to see if I could love them." Mary forked a roll onto her own plate. "She's even been showing me new recipes and how to cook different things—these rolls as an example."

"They're very good," Ms. White admitted. "Maybe someday she can show me how."

Mary giggled and then turned serious again. "I don't know what's going to happen. I'm scared and yet I'm very happy to be here, trusting that Dev and the town can see what I can't see, but I'm keeping my eyes open and looking ahead to Thanksgiving and marrying Dev. If we can get there, maybe the worst will be over and we can focus on the future, with our daughter. And maybe another one or two in time to round out the family.

"When we have to face the reality of my past, I feel lucky to have Dev and a number of our friends here in town to help us watch the shadows. If Einri comes here, at least Dev and I know him and what he looks like. Dev knows Scanlon, so if we stay alert we should be able to stay ahead of them. Maybe we can keep the banshee away."

"Well, Mary," Ms. White said, "I'll get my report in as quickly as I can, and I think I'll talk to Sheriff Martin on my way out of town. There might be some things we can do to help also."

Mary smiled; even the gesture of help was welcome. "Thanks."

Ms. White stood, picked up her cup, saucer, and her plate, and took them to the kitchen. As she placed them in the sink, she glanced out into the backyard.

"Mary? How come all of your trash cans are turned over and scattered around in your yard?"

Mary giggled and came to stand beside Ms. White.

"That's Molly and Patty's doings," she said, and set her dishes in the sink with Ms. White's.

"Molly and Patty?"

"Two black bears that visit every night," Mary said, and giggled again. "Usually just after midnight, sometimes earlier. Once the snows start, Molly leads her cub, Patty, into town to see whose garbage they can get into."

"How long has this been going on?"

"Since before I got here," Mary said, still smiling. "The first winter, Molly scared me to death until I found out this has been her normal routine for nearly eight years now. After the first week, I got some bear-proof cans and now I just have to stand them back up in the mornings. Dev said he'd make something to tie the cans to so she can't scatter them around."

"So this is normal?"

"Yes, it is. Patty showed up this spring," Mary continued. "It was like Molly wanted us to see her new cub. She brought Patty down after dawn and paraded around town, showing her off for an hour or so each day for two weeks, then they went back up into the mountains. They started coming down again with the first snow."

"Don't they have enough to eat, up in the mountains?"

"Sure, sure," Mary said. "It seems like it's more of a ritual for them and not so much as a need anymore. Almost everyone has bear-proof cans, but they come anyway. We give them their space, and they sort of respect ours. Molly seems to like coming and seeing what's going on, and now, bringing her cub with her."

"You see them regularly then?"

"Sure, sure," Mary said again. "On nights when I can't sleep, like after Dev and I have had some private time together, I'll sit up in my room and watch for them to come down. I turn on the back porch light and the one out by the small patio under the trees, and before long, here they come."

Ms. White patted Mary's arm and turned to the hallway. "Sounds nice. But I need to get started back. I'll stop by the sheriff's office and then call my report in on the way back. I'll see you in a couple of weeks. You have my card, so call me if something happens that you think I need to know about."

Mary got Ms. White her coat and watched as she got into her car, backed out of the drive, and headed for town.

◻-◻-◻-◻-◻

Mary, bundled in her heavy coat, gloves, and calf-high boots, slogged through the thigh-deep snow in her backyard, collecting the trash cans Molly and Patty had scattered. She had all three back in the wooden stand beside her back porch when she heard Mandy at some distance. She was talking loudly and occasionally shrieking in laughter. Mary stopped and turned toward her sound, somewhere up slope behind Mandy and Dev's house.

As she listened, she realized there were long pauses in Mandy's shouts. At first they were obviously up on the hillside, and then she would shout from somewhere closer to their house. Another long pause and her voice was again up on the hillside. Mary clipped the chain around the cans and, unable to resist, she went to the street and started walking to see what was going on at Dev's and Mandy's.

Mary walked up Dev's driveway and, seeing no one, she continued on to the backyard. She looked around but saw no one; then, listening, she could hear Dev's voice up the hill and Mandy's infectious laughter. As she stepped into the yard, Mary noticed the wide, flattened trail in the snow leading up onto the hillside. Then she heard Mandy's shrill squeal followed by a rushing sound...like...

Suddenly she saw a bundled figure on a toboggan hurtling down the hill toward her, red hair streaming behind a bright face under a stocking cap, screaming at the top of her lungs. As the toboggan reached the far edge of the yard, Mandy pulled hard on a wooden paddle attached to one side of the sled and snow flew up, engulfing it. The sled slowly turned sideways and came to a stop against the back porch steps. Mandy flopped off the toboggan sideways into the snow, laughing and screeching as she tried to roll over and stand up.

Mary quickly grabbed her arm and helped her to her feet. Then Mandy bent down, grabbed a rope tied to the toboggan, and started back up the hill.

"Come on, Mary," she shouted. "You gotta try this!"

Mary could not help but smile, and hurried after Mandy. She had to admit Mandy made it sound like a lot of fun.

At the top of their improvised sled run, they found Dev working on a metal stand he was securing to a tree.

"What's that?" Mary asked as they stopped beside him, looking at the large-diameter reel and crank affixed to the stand.

"A retrieval system," Dev said, and stood up long enough to catch Mary's arm and pull her close. He kissed her firmly. "Good mornin', lass." Then he turned to the reel and handed the end of the rope wound on it to Mandy. "If it works, I can pull the sled back up for ye and Mandy."

"Me? You knew I was coming?" Mary asked, cocking her head.

"Nay, lass, but I didn't think you could listen to the scamp's screamin' and hollerin' and not be curious."

"You were right about that," Mary said, and smiled. "The way she's been going on, I'm surprised the whole town hasn't shown up to see what's going on."

"A couple of my friends from school will be here before long," Mandy said, and took the rope from Dev. "Kate and Rhonda."

"Hook that onto the ring at the back of the sled," Dev said, and Mandy followed his directions. "When ya get down to the bottom, hook it onto the front rope and I'll winch it back up."

"Okay, Da. It's hooked." Then Mandy waved Mary closer. "Get on behind me. Ya gotta do this."

Mandy scooted up to the front of the toboggan and made room for Mary to slip her legs past her on either side.

"Keep your feet tucked in, Mary," Mandy said, and pulled Mary's legs close against her. "Push, Da!"

"Ready?" Dev asked as he gently caught Mary's shoulders.

Mary nodded and Dev pushed them off the level spot and onto the slope. He laughed heartily as they both screamed and laughed, their shrieks and giggles fading only a little as they reached the bottom of the two-hundred-foot run.

After an interlude of laughter from the backyard, Mandy finally hollered for Dev to pull the sled back up. Dev put his hands to the crank and pulled it back up top. He had the rope switched and the sled ready for them when they reached the level spot.

"Again, Mary," Mandy said, and quickly settled onto the sled again.

Dev helped Mary on for another ride. Then with another gentle push, they were off, and he listened to their repeated shrieks and screams as they tore down the hillside and slid to a stop against the back porch steps.

Dev played ski-lift for the rest of the morning and into the afternoon for Mandy and Mary, and then for Mandy's friends from school. He was pleased with how much fun Mary was having riding, and then helping when the girls arrived. She even helped crank the sled up the hill a time or two. Their day was lost in their time with Mandy, Kate, and Rhonda, and before anyone was ready, Dev noticed the day's light was quickly fading into evening.

When the three younger girls took the sled down for the last time, Dev secured the rope on his homemade winch, wrapped a small tarp over it, and pulled a second sled out from under another snow-covered tarp. He smiled at Mary.

"Care to join me in one last run for the day?"

Mary wrapped her arms around him and hugged him tightly. She kissed him and held it for a long and tender moment.

"I'll join you anywhere," she said softly, and he kissed her again.

He set the sled down and helped Mary onto the front and then settled behind her, wrapping his arms around her as he stretched his legs out beside the sled. "You know how the paddles work for steerin' and brakin', love. So, are ye ready?"

"Ready, love," she said softly, and leaned back against him.

Dev pulled his legs into the sled and pushed them off the level spot.

-¤-

With it getting dark, Dev, Mary, and Mandy drove Kate and Rhonda home, visited with each of their folks briefly, and then started back toward Main Street.

"I don't know about you two," Dev said as they drove across Adams, "but I think I worked up an appetite." He turned and looked back at Mandy in the back seat. "And I happen to know that yesterday Stumpy received a large order of very nice, fresh steaks." He winked at Mary. "Anyone hungry for a really nice, thick steak, and maybe a big baked potato to go with it?"

"Me!" Mandy shouted, and Mary giggled.

"Sounds like it's unanimous, love," Mary said, and reached back to take Mandy's hand.

Thirty-Five
Monday, October 16

With Mikalean pulling on the wheels, Nora—small as she was at only a hundred and fifteen pounds—still struggled backing him and his wheelchair up onto the small porch and then over the step into their house.

"Sorry I'm so blasted heavy," Mikalean said as they reached the level floor and Nora pulled him into their living room.

"Yer not heavy, Mik, just lanky. I'm the one that's a lightweight, and I'm just glad to have ya back home," she said. "I know ya have to be tired of bein' in the hospital, so when they said ya could come home, I said yes."

"Aye, lass." He smiled and turned the wheelchair so he could take in the room. "It was a long week and it's good to be out of there and back home."

"Are ya all right sittin' up a while or are ya ready fer me to make the bed?" Nora sat down on the edge of the sofa beside him.

"I would like to sit together for a bit, lass, maybe talk a little? The new cast makes sittin' a little easier."

"Sure, sure," she said, and smiled. "Ya know, this past week is the first ya have called me 'lass' in many years. I was thinkin' maybe things had changed too much fer us to be the way we were."

"I'm sorry," he said, and sighed, remembering all the things he'd done in the wrong way. "I should've done thin's a lot differently and not stopped."

"I didn't say it at the hospital," Nora said to her hands in her lap, "but thank ya fer includin' me when ya told the detective what's been goin' on. I was fearful of what might've been happenin', but I never understood why ya were doin' what ya were doin'."

Mikalean shook his head. "Me da taught us we should figure thin's out and make our own way, but Einri was a disappointment to him. Why he thought I could change him is beyond me simple brain to figure. But I tried and kept me own counsel, thinkin' that was what a man was supposed to do. But I think now, we should've talked some about it. I shoulda paid more attention to me Dingle lass."

Nora smiled and took a deep breath. "Would've been nice. She woulda liked it, but what're we gonna do now, Mik?" she asked. "Ya can't go back to work for a while—couple or three months at least. I'll keep my job, assumin' I still have one." She looked at him and held his eyes for a long, silent moment. "But after you heal? You probably won't have yours by then."

"Well, dependin' on what the police have to say," Mikalean said, trying to smile, "about me helpin' Einri, I'll either look for another, better one or I won't be needin' to look right away. Either way, I've been thinkin' we need to make a fresh start, if you'll let me try."

"I've been thinkin' about that same thin' this week, Mik," Nora said, and took his hand. "I know the police might bring charges, and if they do, we'll just have to figure out how to deal with that. But I like the idea of goin' somewhere, away from all of this, and tryin' again—especially if we can before the wee one arrives."

"Well, think on it some. So will I," Mikalean said. "We'll talk and figure out what we want to do, dependin' on what opportunities we have. The problem that worries me is what we're gonna do when Einri gets back. No one knows where he might be, but he'll be angry with everyone all over again."

Friday, October 27
Eleven days later

"That baked chicken was wonderful, Dev," Mary said, and laid her napkin on the table beside her empty plate.

"Thanks, lass," Dev said, and pointed to Mandy, "but I didn't prepare the chicken. My tasks were the veggies and rolls."

Mary looked at Mandy in surprise. "Well, love, you certainly did a wonderful job of it. My compliments."

"Thanks." Mandy smiled. "I...I mean, we, wanted to have something nice for you."

Mary glanced at Dev, cocking her head.

"Mandy? I don't understand," Mary said softly. "Everything you've fixed and done since we met has been wonderful—always very nice. Why would you think you needed to do something more special?"

Mandy looked at her plate and then at Dev.

"Go on, love," Dev said. "Tell us what's on yer mind."

She looked at Mary and sighed. "Well. You'll be my new mum and you'll be around us all the time and you'll learn how normal and blah we can be. And that I can mess up sometimes." Mandy sighed again and held Mary's eyes. "I want you to have nice memories to remember when you feel like we're just plain and not so wonderful."

Mary stretched her arms out and Mandy quickly slipped off her chair and came to fill them, hugging Mary tightly. "You'll always be wonderful to me, Mandy. Thank you." Then she looked at Dev. "Tell me she's not really just ten."

Dev and Mary helped Mandy clear the table and put the leftovers away. Dev did the handwashing and the rinsing of the dishes for the dishwasher, Mandy dried the handwashed dishes, and Mary put them away.

"Next time, I'll wash," Mary said as she closed the cabinets on the last of the dishes. "And you, sir, being the taller of us three, can deal with the cabinets."

"Sure," Dev said as he wrung out the dishcloth and spread it on the double sink divider to dry. "If you want."

"I do," Mary said, and hugged Dev. "And that goes for a lot of things."

"Want to start a card game, Scrabble or some other game?" Mandy asked as she joined in, making Mary's hug a group hug.

"Maybe," Mary said softly, and looked at Dev. "But first, since I'm eating so many meals here and coming here straight from school, I'd like to bring a few things from my house and keep them here."

"Sure, sure," Dev said, and squeezed her again. "Whatever you want to have here is fine."

"Good," Mary said, and looked at Mandy. "I still want to set a good example, but I do think a change of casual clothes and a few toiletries would be nice to have."

"Mum—" Mandy clamped her hand over her mouth in surprise at what slipped out, her face slowly turning pink. "I'm sorry, Mary."

Mary giggled. "That's okay, love. Go ahead."

Mandy glanced away and inhaled before she looked back. "I know people live together before they're actually married. And I know everyone doesn't think that's proper, but like Miss Cotton said the other day, I think you two are already married, in here"—she tapped her chest—"even though the pastor hasn't declared it so. I'm okay with you being here, at home, and having your things here with you."

Dev looked down at Mary. "I don't think I could've said it any better, love. Whatcha say we go and get what you want to bring."

Together, clinging to each other in the cold like the family they were quickly becoming, Dev led them back to Mary's house. Once inside, Mandy roamed the downstairs, looking at the things Mary had collected since she had come to Roosevelt while Dev and Mary went upstairs to get her things.

"Do you have an overnight bag?" he asked as she began gathering her toiletries from her bathroom.

"Not really," she said. "I only had boxes when I came, but I do have my backpack and hiking pack. Those'll work."

"Aye, they'll work fine."

"It isn't like I'm moving..." she said, and stopped to look at Dev through the open bathroom door, suddenly hearing herself. "But I will be, won't I."

"I hope so, love."

"What am I going to do with this place?" she asked absently, to no one in particular.

"We'll figure that out as we go," he answered. "I'd hate for you to feel like you have to sell it, but we will only need one house for the three of us. But I'll tell you what."

"What?"

"You can do whatever you want with it, love." He smiled. "This is your house. And yours to keep, sell, or reuse as you see fit."

Mary dropped her toiletries and bathroom items into her small hiking pack and returned to the bedroom where Dev had set out her larger backpack.

"You know," she said softly, "that the one thing I think made a difference for me from the very beginning was how you never tell me what to do. I mean for the real things in life like living, dealing with my things, thinking what I want to think, all of that. Bobby always gave me his opinion when I did something, usually making me feel like I should have done things differently. He was always teasing me over my choices or my thoughts on one thing or another." She smiled and looked at him. "But you always want to know what I want, what I'm thinking, what I want to do. You've always been supportive of me being, well, me."

"Aye, lass," he said, and stepped to her, taking her hands in his. "Thank you. It was you that caught my attention, the you that makes you who you are that I first saw and liked and still like. I don't want a clone of m'self or to make you someone that's afraid to voice her opinions or desires. I like it that you're intelligent, that you can think, and I like your spirit and what they call around here yer pluck—yer courage and determination. I feel so very lucky that you found some little somethin' in me to like and that you have chosen to spend your time, your life, with Mandy and me."

"Well, love," Mary said, and squeezed his hands, "I also feel very fortunate that we have found each other." Mary smiled and took her hands back. "But now I need to choose a couple of outfits for after school."

"And maybe a couple for goin' to school?"

Mary smiled and spent the next few minutes—a half an hour, actually—picking out dresses for work and packing jeans for after. When she had her daily wear—unders and outers—packed, she went to her dresser, opened a drawer, and studied her nightwear.

"Dev," she said absently, "I have nothing suitable to sleep in."

"Well, love, that isn't completely true," he said as he stepped up behind her and slipped his arms around her, again letting his height make him hold her above her waist. "Just wear what's comfortable, but I know fer true, ye don't actually need anythin'. Do ya have a warm robe to use if ya need to use the loo?"

"I do, in fact," she said, and turned in his arms, kissing him gently. "Am I going to be using the spare, guest room?"

"'Tis your choice, love," Dev said, "but after what Mandy said a bit ago, I'm not proposin' it."

"Proposing what, Da?" Mandy asked as she walked into the room to see where they were with the packing.

"Where Mary will sleep if she stays over, lass, if ya really need to know."

Mandy giggled. "That's a silly thin' to be worryin' about, Da," she said, and stopped to look at the things Mary had laid out on her dresser.

"Why's that, love?" Mary asked as she slipped out of Dev's arms.

Mandy rolled her eyes. "Ye belong upstairs with us. Yer not a guest, Mary. Yer family. I'm surprised ya don't know that by now." Mandy looked at the backpack. "Are ya packed?"

¤-¤-¤-¤-¤

"I'm ready, Da, Mary," Mandy hollered from the top of the stairs.

Dev stood and caught Mary's hand, helping her up. He followed Mary as she led the way up the stairs and into Mandy's room, where as usual Mandy was in bed with her covers up under her arms. Mary and Dev sat in their usual places.

"This is starting to feel right," Mandy said, and reached for Mary and her goodnight hug.

Mary hugged her and kissed her cheek. "What's feeling right, love?"

"You being home," Mandy said. "It's feeling better and better each time you're here."

"Thank you," Mary said, and smiled at her and then at Dev. "It feels more and more like home to me too, each time I'm here."

Dev smiled and then leaned down and kissed Mandy on the other cheek. "'Night, love. May the happiest dreams be yet to come."

"'Night, Da. I love you both." Then Mandy rolled over onto her side and pulled her covers up over her shoulders.

Dev waited for Mary to reach the door, turned Mandy's light off, and followed Mary back down stairs.

"Can I get you anything more, lass?"

"No, not really, Dev." Mary slowly went around the living room, nervously straightening the pillows on the sofa, and then took her empty tea cup and saucer to the kitchen. Dev sat down on the sofa and waited for her to come back into the room.

When she did, she settled beside him, sighed, and snuggled with his arm gently holding her shoulders.

"What's the matter, love?" he asked as she settled against him. "Is somethin' botherin' you? Have I—?"

"No," she interrupted. "You haven't done anything except being wonderful and understanding. Things are changing so fast, it sort of takes my breath away."

"I was afraid I might've been moving too fast—"

"You're not," she argued. "I just feel like I'm moving in on you."

"You were invited, love." Dev smiled. "But I can understand if you want to sleep alone."

"Oh, that's not going to happen, Mr. O'Brien," she said, raising her eyebrows and smiling at him. "I'm not going to share your bed and expect to be left alone. I've waited weeks to get some time alone with you, and now we don't have to sneak around and hide. Come on."

Mary stood, took his hand, pulled him up, and then led him to the stairs.

"Besides, with the lotions and all, I need your help getting ready for bed."

Thirty-Six
Saturday, October 28

"Not much has been happening," Mary said as she and Ms. White settled for their morning coffee and cherry tarts, "since you were here two weeks ago. No one seems to know where Dev's cousin is. No sign of him around here, and no one Dev knows has seen him back in Dearborn or Brighton."

"That's a good thing, I guess," Ms. White said, shaking her head. Then she changed the subject, "So it's three weeks from tomorrow?"

"Yes. Some days it seems like the wedding will never come, and others feel like it'll be here before we know it."

"I'm trying to get my schedule rearranged so I can be here."

"Thanks. I'd like that." Mary sighed. "Okay, anything to report from your end?"

"I wish I had some news from the program, but I don't. Just like you said, no one in Ann Arbor, Brighton, or Dearborn has seen anything of this Einri, with the Irish spelling."

"It's hard to believe no one's seen him in three weeks," Mary said, trying to understand what that might mean. Then thinking to herself, she whispered, "Not since he shot Mikalean and said he was going after Henry."

"What was that?" Ms. White asked softly. "Einri shot his brother?"

"Yeah. That's what Mikalean told the police," Mary said, and looked back at Ms. White. "Dev's brother told us the Wednesday before your last visit. I thought I mentioned it."

Mary took a few minutes and explained again what Henry had told them.

"I remember you saying they got into an argument, but I don't remember you saying he shot his brother. With everything else we were talking about, I guess I just missed you telling me."

"Sorry, I figured you guys knew about all of that."

"The program may, but if so, they haven't given me those details," Ms. White said. "This whole thing bothers me more than you know." Ms. White sipped her coffee. "I'll ask back at the office if they have anything new to pass along. They have selected another agent in case he's needed—if this Einri shows up and you need a quick escape."

"That's good." Mary smiled and studied Ms. White a moment longer. "Too bad you didn't wear jeans and have a casual winter coat with you."

Ms. White looked at her, confused. "And why is that?"

"Because Dev, Mandy, and I are going sledding after our meeting," Mary said with a wide smile, "and you should join us. You haven't met my new family yet, and I would like you to."

"But you're right," Ms. White said with a shrug. "I didn't come dressed to be out in the weather."

Mary stood up. "Stand up a minute." She looked at Ms. White's size as she did. "I think I can fix that. So, you can just join us this morning, see my life firsthand for your reports, and have hot chocolate with us afterwards. We had a nice snow on Wednesday so it'll be perfect this morning." Mary nodded as if that was that. "Come on. We can talk while you change," she said as she led the way to the stairs.

Friday, November 17
Twenty days later

"That was Henry," Dev said as he put his phone back in his pocket and walked into the kitchen where Mary and Mandy were fixing a late breakfast: omelets, hash, and German strudel pastries.

"What did he have to say?" Mary asked, stopping to turn and look at him while Mandy continued to work on her newest attempted creation, a fried hash made from drained and diced coddle.

"They're just boarding their flight and"—Dev looked at his watch—"should be in Denver around half twelve our time. Then I'd give 'em forty-five minutes or so to get their bags and the vans, and it's a two-hour drive to get here." He gave Mary a hug. "Henry will call when they leave the airport and start this way, but I'd expect them here between three and half three."

Dev looked over Mandy's shoulder as she studied her challenge. "How's it goin'?"

"Not as well as I hoped, Da," Mandy said, still staring at the hash patties. "I know it's been done, but it seems like I need to figure a way to get more of the moisture out of the coddle before I start."

"That and a hotter fire under the pan," he said, and smiled.

"Aye. That would help." Mandy smiled up at him.

"What can I do, lass?" he asked, and gave Mary a quick kiss.

"You can set the table, love," she replied, and went back to stirring her egg mixture. "You said we can sit, what, twelve at your table?"

"Aye," Dev said as he got three plates from the cabinet beside the sink. "There will be ten adults and eight kids, countin' Mandy. I'm thinkin' I can set up the two card tables in the livin' room for the young'uns."

"That will work," Mary said, checking on the strudel in the oven and then Mandy's hash. "I think we're ready to put the eggs on. Five-minute warning."

"We'll plan on the roasts and sides bein' ready so we can eat dinner around five," Mandy added, and turned her patties.

¤-¤-¤-¤-¤

It was three twenty when Dev stepped outside and put his phone away after giving Henry the directions he needed. The two vans stopped in front of his house, and Mary and Mandy went out with him, each holding one of his hands as the van doors popped opened. Smiling faces appeared and hands waved at them as the family piled out and clustered happily around the trio. Dev introduced Mary, starting with his mum and then down the line of siblings, husbands, and children, saving Henry for last.

Mary was surprised that Henry was more slender than Dev, about the same height with the definite family look, but he did not have Dev's broad shoulders, narrow waist, and muscular build.

"I got the brains and Dev got the brawn," Henry chuckled, seeing Mary's appraising gaze. "And as it should be, the sisters got the beauty.

I'm very pleased to finally meet you, Mary," he said, and held out his hand.

"That's not goin' ta work in this family," Mary said with a giggle, shook her head, and threw her arms around Henry. "Welcome, Henry with the English spelling."

Henry smiled and returned the hug as Mandy stopped beside him, grinned deviously, and punched his arm. "Where's mine, Uncle?"

-¤-

"Mum," Dev said as he slipped around Henry and Mandy. "Let's bring your stuff inside and then I can take everyone else down to Mary's to get them settled."

With Merril's help, Dev got Maeve's bags inside and into his downstairs guest room. Finished, Dev rounded up his sisters and their husbands and drove back to Mary's place. Will, Carl, and Merril each grabbed a couple of their bags and Dev carried two others up to the house where Carl had stopped to look at the front of the house.

"Very pretty place," Carl said, and smiled. "Moira said you had a devil of a time gettin' Mary to let you clean the place up."

"Nah," Dev said. "I just showed her me lovable and generous nature and she—"

"Stubborn tenacity is probably more like it," Carl said as Dev pushed the door open. "Wouldn't take no for an answer? Sorta like yer sisters?"

Dev chuckled, stepped in, and stopped at the bottom of the stairs.

"Okay. The plan is for Henry to use the sofa in the living room. Mary has one bedroom down here and two up fer you with families. Mary's room is up and across the back of the house. There's a hall bath down here and one upstairs. So who wants which?"

Derry looked at Will and chose the downstairs bedroom.

"Oh Dev, this is adorable," Derry said as she turned and took in the look of the room.

"Mary will be pleased you like it," he said, and gestured back to the hallway. "The bath is under the stairs and you'll have to share with Henry." He chuckled as the twin girls hurried into the room and looked around. "Or Henry will have to share with you."

Derry and Will chuckled.

"I have sleeping bags for the children," he continued, and turned back to the others. "Moira and Brenna, follow me." Dev started up the stairs. At the top, he gestured to the two front bedrooms with the bath between them and let them decide. Moira and Carl picked the west room and Brenna asked Merril to put their bags in the east one.

"We've set up a spirits press in the kitchen so you can have a nightcap, but for now," Dev said as he led them back downstairs to join Henry, Derry, Will, and the girls, "I have most of the celebratory refreshments down at my place, so gather anything you'd like to take back and we'll go and get the party started. Dinner will be ready in about an hour, according to Mandy."

Saturday, November 18

"Mandy," Dev called from his place on the raised, circular platform in the middle of the field house floor, encircled with curved rows of chairs facing the platform. The sea of chairs was broken into pie-shaped sections by regularly spaced aisles radiating outward into the large room.

Mandy turned from her conversation with her cousins, having all gathered to one side to watch the wedding rehearsal.

"Please come up here and join us. This will only take a couple of minutes, and then you can go back and show yer cousins around."

"Sure, Da," Mandy said, and excused herself from her cousins.

Dev gestured to the spot in front of Debbie. "You'll be standin' here with Debbie, to wait for Mary to come up the aisle," Dev said as Mandy took her place. He glanced up as Henry hurried up the aisle, half running to get into his place as Dev's best man.

Pastor Emlich verbalized what the sequence would be and motioned for Mary to come forward. She hooked her arm in Lloyd Martin's arm, having asked him, as one of her oldest friends in Roosevelt, to stand in for her parents and walk her down the aisle. When she stepped up onto the stage, Pastor Emlich had her turn to face Dev, then had Mandy move to face him, standing beside both Dev and Mary. Then he went through the description for the rest of the ceremony, ending when he gestured for them to turn and face the room. He said he would then introduce them to everyone in attendance.

When the rehearsal was finished, Henry stepped up to Dev. "Sorry I was late gettin' here, Dev. Moira and Carl were having a little trouble getting the boys movin.'"

"You made it, though." Dev smiled. "That's what counts."

Dev noticed Debbie standing behind Mary with a funny, almost shy expression on her face.

"Debbie," he said, and smiled, holding his hand out to her. "I'd like you to meet my brother, Henry. As you know, he's goin' to stand up fer me as my best man." Then he looked at Henry. "Henry, this is Debbie Cotton. Debbie's Mary's maid of honor and another of our wonderful and gifted schoolteachers."

Henry stepped forward with a wide smile and gently shook Debbie's hand.

"My pleasure," Henry said, and Debbie smiled.

"Nice to meet you, Henry," she replied. "Mary has talked a lot about you and the rest of the family, based on your phone calls."

"We're having the rehearsal dinner this evening at Stumpy's, Henry. Have her there in time," Mary said softly with a wink as she turned to follow Dev and Mandy off the small stage.

"Oh, uh, sure, sure," Henry said, snapping his head to see Mary as she walked away, smiling at him. He turned back to Debbie. "I was actually going to ask if you'd like to have a cup of coffee, or something. That is if you wouldn't mind showing me where in town we could get one."

Debbie smiled. "Sure. I can show you. There's some here in the cafeteria, or Stumpy's is the closest if you want to walk a little."

"I think I'd like the walk," Henry said, "if you're up to it."

"Come on," she said, and led Henry to the coatrack and the side door.

-¤-

Mary smiled as she watched Henry and Debbie leave.

"Aye, lass," Dev said over her shoulder.

She turned and saw his smile.

"Henry has always had an eye for the pretty ones."

"So has Debbie. Why is it he never settled down with one?" Mary asked, knowing she actually knew the answer.

"Obviously, there was never the right chemistry, love. Back in Brighton, the girls seem to always look at a man and analyze his specifications—ya know, job, worth, whether he rents or owns, lives alone or with his mom or parents, his stability. They very seldom look at a man with their eyes or heart."

"Aaah, but ya know, now that ya bring it up," Mary said, casually copying his accent as she turned to look him in the eye, "it makes me ask how yer plannin' on feedin' and supportin' another mouth around the house. Or are ya expectin' me ta support ya?"

Dev chuckled and shook his head. "I can support ye just fine, lass. I make very good wages at the grocery, at me odd jobs, and with what I make as a volunteer fireman." He smiled at her disbelieving expression.

"You don' make anythin' as a volunteer, love," Mary said with her hands on her hips. "Teasin's fine, but it was really an honest question."

Dev sobered his smile. "I know, love. Mandy and I are relatively well off. Due to the very unfortunate accident, Mandy and I became the sole beneficiaries, heirs, of Anne's parents' estate, and I was released from the ladder company with a disabilities/hardship pension because I was suddenly a widowed, single father, havin' difficulty workin' and carin' fer a child alone, and we were both havin' a rough time adjustin'. In addition, Da fortuitously changed the investments that he set up for us kids' inheritances when Mandy was born and arranged my inheritance to provide a monthly dividend for me and Mandy before he died. I reinvested as much of it as I could, bankin' it on our future. Everyone else will get their inheritance when Mum passes."

Mary stared at him, not knowing whether to feel happy for him or sad with Dev's explanation of how his ability to manage came about.

"'Tis okay, love," he said, and curled her into his arms. "It's obvious you have means of yer own, love, but—"

"I do. The program was able to reassign and seal the origins of the trust my parents left me and a little from Bobby's death benefit. I was just wonderin' if ye were expectin' me ta have me a 'dowry.'"

He chuckled and squeezed her. "Nay, lass. A dowry 'tis not required. 'Tis unfortunate the way everything has happened, but maybe it's the way it is supposed to work out. I don't know. Maybe Anne, her folks, and Da will be proud of how Mandy is turnin' out and that she has a good and loved life. That, and that you have one too, is all I can ask for."

"I'm sure they are proud. I am," Mary said as he squeezed her shoulders and she, his waist.

"I love you, lass, and tomorrow I'll start supportin' ya like I should. I hope ye'll think it's enough."

Thirty-Seven

"Are ya feelin' better today?" Scanlon asked as he ate his burger and watched the traffic on the highway speed past.

"Yeah, some," Einri said, and looked up from his lunch. "Why?"

They were eating lunch in the corner booth of a hamburger and pizza place attached to a gas station just off of I-70. Einri had finished fueling the white half-ton van he had "borrowed" from a "friend" in Dearborn before he led Scanlon inside to get something to eat. Einri was glad they were on their way, but the traveling was hard.

His wounds were mending much slower than he expected—especially his leg. It made it hard for him to arrange everything they needed for the trip: the van, the cash, and the "supplies" they would need when they got there.

And then there was the overwhelmingly wasted, lethargic feeling that plagued him, robbing him of endurance and energy. The unfamiliar condition bothered him. Without his usual stamina, Einri had to make adjustments, forcing everything to happen slower, taking longer than he wanted. And it seemed the closer they got to where his cousin was, the more intense his exhaustion got.

Einri stared at the van through the restaurant window. He thought about how he had almost been discovered in St. Louis when he had switched plates with the other white van. That was three days before, at their overnight stop, and he worried that he should make another exchange before they settled and he started looking for Devlin and his woman.

"Just wonderin'," Scanlon said, and sucked on the straw in his drink. "Tuesday we got up and then stopped about lunchtime. That was in Indianapolis, and you slept all afternoon and all night. Then Wednesday we stopped in Saint Louis and then you slept again the rest of the day and all night. Thursday you stopped outside of that place you called Lee's Summit. And yesterday you drove to Colby and stopped."

"So?" Einri asked. "We're making time. I just need to lay down a lot. It hurts sitting and driving for a long time. Me wounds are not cooperatin.'"

"You should show me how to drive," Scanlon said, smiling at his solution. "Then I could take us farther while you rest."

"Wish I could, Scan, but I can't do that. Driving takes a lot of concentration."

"I can concentrate," Scan said, defiantly objecting to his brother's implication.

"I know, but you have to concentrate for long periods of time. Hours at a time."

"Oh. I can't do that very well." Scanlon looked back at his burger and took another bite, the heated feelings of the moment before gone as quickly as they had come.

"We're on the west side of Denver now, Scan, so it'll only be a couple more hours before we stop for the day," Einri said, and took another drink. "A fellow I know has a cabin south of Copper Mountain. He said we can use it. We'll stop and get some groceries and then settle in for a few days."

"Is that where cousin Devlin is?"

"No," Einri said. "But it's close enough that we can drive to his town and see if we can find where he lives. Maybe tomorrow or Monday."

"Okay," Scanlon said, and took another bite of his burger. "It will be nice to see Devlin again. I like him. He was always nice to me, even when I was little."

Einri stared at him, but did not say anything.

¤-¤-¤-¤-¤

Mary, Mandy, and Dev got out of his jeep and stepped up to Stumpy's front door. Mary asked him to wait a moment as she turned to look at him with a grin on her face.

"Da, Mary?" Mandy asked when she saw that Mary wanted to talk.

They smiled at her and cocked their heads.

"May I go on in while you talk?"

"Sure, sure," they both answered in unison.

Mary smiled and motioned for Mandy to go on. "Save us a good seat," she added, and Mandy just shook her head and went in.

"What's up, love?" Dev asked.

"I forgot to tell you that I talked to Lloyd earlier in the week and let him know what we're thinking about for my house."

"I was going to ask him," Dev remarked softly, "if he would have any objections."

"Well, he told me he thought it could be a good thing to do," Mary said, "but he had one or two stipulations."

Dev smiled and waited.

"One, he'll hold you responsible if anything goes wrong, and two, that he expects to help with any fixing up we feel is necessary."

Dev smiled and hugged Mary. "I think I can live with that. Can you, love?"

"Knowing you," Mary said, and kissed him, "yes. Now it's time for us to make an entrance." Mary took his hand and led him into Stumpy's, where the customary rehearsal dinner and celebration was about to start.

Sunday, November 19

At eleven o'clock sharp, a recorded piper began playing a bright Irish tune as Henry led Debbie Cotton in her new pink blush dress with white belting and trimmings up the aisle, her right hand resting gently on top of his left as they walked. Henry took Debbie to her maid of honor's spot and then took his place behind Dev's empty groom's spot. Nate Bucklin followed Henry and Debbie, leading Mrs. Arnold in a matching pink dress to their spaces as second bride's and groom's attendants. Bob Jeff led Connie Morrison behind Nate to their places as the third attendants.

As they took their places on the small, raised, circular platform in the center of the school's field house floor surrounded by the crowded room, they turned and faced the main aisle. The main floor was covered with people in folding chairs, and the fan seating bleachers on either side were extended and nearly half full of happy, supporting townsfolk.

Debbie smiled, winked at Henry, and in a loud whisper, said, "I don't think we've ever had this many people in this building—not even for a championship game."

With the beginning of the second tune on the recording, Dev escorted Mandy—also wearing a pink blush dress matching Debbie's, Mrs. Arnold's, and Connie's—up the aisle carrying the bride's bouquet of fall flowers. Mandy took her place beside Debbie and handed her the bouquet, then glanced at her dad with a wide smile as he took his spot. Then they turned to wait for Mary to come forward.

Pastor Emlich came from behind the stage and took his place centered behind Dev and Mary's empty spot. The music changed from the recorded melodies to the church pianist, and with the start of the wedding march, Lloyd Martin led Mary up the aisle.

Dev's heart skipped when he saw Mary in her long, cream-colored dress with a conservative neckline, white belting, and embroidered white accents around the full skirt and down the three-quarter-length sleeves. He knew Mary would choose a dress that would be beautiful and still hide her scars, but that was where her conservatism ended.

He was completely captivated as he focused on the style and trim of Mary's dress, fit to her in ways he could never have anticipated. Her bright smile just for him and her beautiful, long, golden-brown hair, neatly clasped to fall down her back, gently swaying behind her as she walked, made his heart pound and his legs weak. Later he would realize that he would not have noticed if the building had fallen down around him at that moment.

The pastor's message, the exchanging of the vows (in which Mandy participated by adding her own promises), and the giving of the rings passed quickly. Suddenly Dev was happily kissing his bride—a long, deeply appreciative kiss that was broken when Mandy turned and hip-checked him; those in the front rows chuckled. Abashed, Dev released Mary and turned her to face their many friends, gathered to share this day with them. The pastor introduced Mr. and Mrs. O'Brien, and Mandy, as the recorded piper began playing another Irish love song. Henry and Nate stepped down, inserted two short wooden poles into pockets in the raised platform, and as the music played, they walked around the platform, slowly spinning it so everyone in the audience could see the new Mr. and Mrs. O'Brien.

When Henry and Nate stopped the platform, Dev and Mary, with Mandy immediately behind, stepped down and walked to the foot of the main aisle. Mandy stepped to one side, handed Mary the bouquet, and the fifteen eligible and single women clustered in the aisle behind them. Mary turned and tossed the bouquet back over her head. She quickly turned to the squeals and cheers; Debbie sheepishly stepped out of the crowd with the bouquet in her hands.

Dev smiled and clouted Henry's shoulder, chuckling as he whispered, "Looks like ye might have some serious thinkin' to do, brother. It wasn't yer bank account that got her attention."

Once the gaggle of women ushered Debbie away, Dev looked adoringly at Mary and Mandy. "Anyone fer cuttin' a cake?"

-¤-

After the cake was cut, the pictures taken, and Dev had his first dance with Mary as his new bride, he and Mary took a few minutes to change into something more suitable for the lunch and visiting with their friends and townsfolk.

Ms. White stopped and took Mary's hand with both of hers. She smiled and gently shook it. "You look absolutely radiant, Mary. Doesn't she, Dev?"

"Yes, she does," Dev said with a wide smile. "I'm extremely lucky to be a small part of making her happy. Mandy is probably a bigger part of it."

"I doubt that, Dev," Ms. White said. "I think it's wonderful that you two found each other."

"Thank you, for the kind and happy thoughts," Dev said.

"You're welcome, Dev, Mary," Ms. White said. "Congratulations. What time should I come to the auditorium tonight?"

"About half six, to get a good seat," Mary said. "Thank you for staying and attending. Mandy will be so happy that you did," Mary said.

"How can I not attend? I have to support my tobogganing coach," Ms. White said with a wide smile. "I can't get that Saturday out of my mind. What a day."

"I'm so glad you liked it," Mary said, and winked at Dev. "Please get yourself something to eat and we'll see you later and then tonight."

"Thanks, Mary. I will." And Ms. White turned toward the buffet.

During lunch, Mandy sat beside Mary, snuggling happily between bites with Dev opposite her on Mary's other side.

"Well, Mandy," Mary said softly, leaning close. "What do you think of the day so far?"

Mandy wiped her mouth with her napkin as she looked up and smiled. "I think it's the best, Mum, absolutely the best."

"I think so too," Mary said, and squeezed Mandy's hand.

Dev smiled and gave Mandy a wink.

"Now that we've gotten through this morning," Mary said, changing the subject, "are you ready for tonight?"

Mandy nodded. "Yes, I'm ready. May I get another piece of cake?"

"Okay, love," Mary said, and watched as Mandy slid out of her chair and headed for the cake table. She turned to Dev. "Has she told you what her presentation is?"

Dev shook his head. "Only that everyone in your class had to answer some essay questions for a contest of some kind. She said she couldn't tell me the subject or what she wrote."

"I was surprised when Nancy made the assignment and collected the papers herself."

"So you don't know either?"

Mary shook her head and smiled. "Not until tonight when she announces the 'winners' and they present their essays as part of the program."

"Well"—Dev sighed and squeezed Mary's shoulders—"I guess we'll all find out together."

¤-¤-¤-¤-¤

Einri, leaning heavily on one of his forearm crutches, led Scanlon along Second Street to Adams, where they could parallel Main Street without attracting undue attention. Einri hoped their heavy coats and wool stocking caps would be enough to disguise them as they made a round of the town; Einri wanted to understand the town's layout.

He shook his head and took another deep breath, forcing himself to be patient and take the time to look around.

They had walked three blocks from the gas station where he had parked the van at the edge of town, but he felt like they had walked a mile or two. He blamed it on his wounds—four in his legs, one in his hip, and one in his side. His mending, fractured leg was still tender and painful to stand on.

"Why are we walking?" Scanlon asked as he walked close on Einri's left. "It's cold here and you do not walk good."

"I told you, Scan," Einri said, trying to control his irritation. "I forgot the van doesn't have snow tires. I'll have them changed tomorrow."

"Ooh," Scanlon said softly, almost to himself. "Snow tires because there's snow on the streets?"

"Yeah, Scan, because there's snow on the streets. The snow makes the streets slippery."

"Yeah," Scanlon chuckled. "I almost fell back there by the school. It's just like back home—icy spots." Then Scanlon looked back down the street. "Why are there so many cars at the school? Isn't today Sunday? I didn't know they had school on Sundays. Is that something different they do out here?"

Einri shook his head. "I don't know. Just come on. I want to look around and see where things are."

"Like the firehouse we just passed?"

"Yeah, like that, the school, and others."

"We should go back up on the main street," Scanlon said. "We can see more from there."

Einri considered Scanlon's comment and then decided to risk it; no one would know them or why they were there. He turned on Fourth.

A block up, they stopped on Main, and Einri looked down the street back toward the gas station where he had left the van and then up the street as it rose up and disappeared beyond the town, into the trees and the reach of the valley. He gestured to the near side of the street and led the way past the grocery store on the other side of the street and the hardware store on their left. At the next corner, across from the police department, Einri forced himself to look casual and continue.

Past City Hall, Einri noted Stumpy's on the north side of the street, and in the next block, the Tall Pines Café on the south. Beyond, he could only make out residential houses as the street steepened.

Einri stopped on the bridge over Bear Cub Creek and tried to catch his breath. He looked back down Main Street and realized the amount of climb they had made coming the seven blocks from the gas station. With his legs and hip aching with every step, Einri cursed his weakness and shortness of breath. He blamed it on his wounded and recovering condition and realized he did not have the strength to follow the plan he had originally formed. He'd have to find another way to interrogate Devlin's woman and her background.

"Okay, Scan," Einri said, and turned around. "Let's start back to the van."

"Are we going to eat lunch while we're here?"

Einri shook his head as he started to walk. "Too risky. We'll eat on our way back to the cabin or when we get there."

Thirty-Eight

"Hey, Lloyd," Deputy Nate Bucklin said as Sheriff Lloyd Martin followed him into the police department's office. The wedding was over and they were making a quick stop by the office to check on things before they went back for lunch. Nate pointed as he glanced out of the department's wide front window. "Looks like we have a couple of new visitors in town."

Lloyd crossed the room from the doorway and joined Nate to look at what he saw.

"Dev ask us to keep a lookout for one or two new guys. You suppose they could be them?" Nate asked.

"Yeah, he did. One about Dev's size, red hair and a red beard," Lloyd said, and studied the man with the crutch. "About the big one's size, I'd say. He has the red beard, though it's trimmed shorter than I was expecting."

Nate chuckled. "You were thinking more like our mountain man look?"

"Yeah, I guess I was," Lloyd said. "Did we get that Wanted poster from Dearborn?"

"Not yet," Nate said. "I thought they might've sent it last night, but there was nothing on the fax this morning. Who's that with him?"

"Dev said he has two brothers, and the middle one's been in the hospital and is recovering. Since that guy Einri shot him in an argument sometime last month, that one there is most likely his youngest brother. Dev called him Scanlon."

"He shot his own brother?"

"That's what Dev said." Lloyd nodded. "Afterwards, it seems the brother he shot spilled his guts to the Brighton Police and then called Dev's brother to let him know that Einri was thinking about coming to look for Dev."

"A real benevolent soul," Nate whispered.

"Yeah. I got a call from a detective in Brighton," Lloyd said. "He confirmed what Dev said."

Lloyd watched the two of them walk along the south side of the street, acting like normal visitors checking out a few store fronts, most of them sporting Thanksgiving-themed offerings for the casual shopper. But Lloyd was thinking of the other reason Einri O'Brien was in town, and it was not to visit with his cousin Dev.

Lloyd took his phone out of his shirt pocket, but hesitated. He was about to select Dev's name from his contacts list, but he smiled and put the phone back into his pocket.

"You're not going to call him?"

"Nah. They're not a problem yet and I don't want to ruin Dev and Mary's day." Lloyd turned to his desk. "I'll talk to him in the morning. We'll just watch where those two go." He sighed. "Then we'll go back and enjoy some of Dev and Mary's catered lunch."

¤-¤-¤-¤-¤

"…and that's why we celebrate Thanksgiving," Kate, Seth Mayer's granddaughter, finished.

"Thank you, Kate, for your beautiful essay on the meaning of Thanksgiving," Mrs. Arnold said, clapping along with the rest of those attending the school's annual Thanksgiving Program. "I want to thank all of the fifth-grade class for participating in my essay contest this year. As most of you probably don't know, I sprung this on Miss Gorden's class last month and would not tell her what it was about, other than it was about Thanksgiving. I provided five essay topics and asked each student to prepare a short essay for each. From those essays, I chose a winner from each topic. And so far, you have heard the first four winners.

"Again, thank you to Kate Mayer and her essay on why we celebrate Thanksgiving."

Everyone clapped again.

"Now," Mrs. Arnold continued, "I want to introduce my choice for the best essay in the personal subject of 'What I Am Thankful For,' Miss Mandy O'Brien."

Everyone clapped as Mandy stood up from her seat beside Mary. She smiled at Mary and at Dev, and then at Henry and Debbie on their far side and the rest of her family behind them as she turned and then stepped up on the stage.

Mary grabbed Dev's hand and squeezed it in anticipation. "I don't know what's wrong with me, Dev. I'm suddenly nervous," Mary whispered. "How can Mandy's presentation be making me so anxious?"

"Because ye care, love. Ye care about how well she'll do," Dev whispered in her ear. "Otherwise, ye'd never have agreed to be her new mum."

-¤-

Mandy slowly looked out at the dimly lit auditorium.

"Good evening. Most of you know me or of me. I am Amanda O'Brien," she said clearly, with barely a trace of her accent slipping through. "My friends know me as Mandy, in honor of my father's and my love of nicknames."

"'What I Am Thankful For' was the subject for an essay we were assigned to write. I was asked to share my essay with all of you tonight. So here goes.

"For me, I am thankful for many things: God, sunshine, snow, spring rains, gentle winds, people, and so very much more. It isn't an easy question to answer." She glanced down at her notes and took a deep breath.

"First, I have to say I am thankful for being alive, for being able to stand here today and try to answer this question for you. Most of you don't know that five years ago, I almost died in an accident that took my mother and two of my grandparents from both me and my father. But somehow, God in Heaven was looking over me and I survived. I had already lost one grandfather that I barely knew and don't recall anymore, except for his pictures on my grandmother's fireplace mantel. So all I had left was my father, one grandmother, one uncle, and three aunts. And the cousins, of course.

"Second, I am thankful for my father and for him being my father. It was his love and understanding of what we needed to do after my mother died that brought us here. Actually, that and a throw of the darts."

A few chuckled.

"When we decided we were going to move, my father pinned a map of the country up beside the dartboard on my grandmother's wall, and I was told to throw a dart and wherever it landed, we would go there and learn to love and support each other again—just us and what we found when we got there. With God's clear and knowing hand guiding it, the dart landed on Roosevelt. Well, more like the Coopers' ranch, but we checked their place and the dent wasn't too big."

Another chuckle.

"Third, I'm thankful for my family—those back in Michigan that traveled to be here today and tonight, and for those here, and all of the love they have given us. My feeling of family also includes all of you, friends who have let us come and live with you and be a part of your lives and you a part of ours. It has been a blessing to have your support and encouragements in our dark days, our trials, and our recent joys.

"And maybe the most important thing I'm thankful for is that a special person was brought to this place, to us, almost three years ago. She has also been blessed by all of you and became a part of your lives as a valuable schoolteacher and friend, and it is her friendship that I cherish the most.

"This next part was not in my essay, but I have to slip in that she is also very special to us as you all know, because this morning, Mary married us and is now my new mother, and Dad's new wife." Mandy turned her head, and with a wide grin sought Mary's look in return. Then she looked back at the audience. "Each and every one of you have become near and dear to us, personally. I am truly thankful for God in our lives and for him leading us and Mary to this place. I love you all."

The room was completely silent until Mandy had stepped down off the risers and had taken her seat beside a smiling, tearful Mary on the front row. Then the audience began to clap.

-¤-

Dev noticed that Mary, still clinging to his hand, had tears running down her cheeks when Mandy looked at her from the stage. She sagged against Dev, smiling hugely at Mandy and then at the audience's response.

"Oh my, Dev," Mary whispered. "She's so poised and confident, and like you said before, what she feels is very profound. Truly not what one expects from a ten-year-old."

¤-¤-¤-¤-¤

"I'm surprised you're still walking," Mary said to Mandy as they turned and started up their front walk.

"I'm tired, but I'm too excited to go to sleep," Mandy said, hanging on Mary's arm.

Dev was holding Mary, each with an arm around the other's waist, until they stepped up on the porch and he released her so he could unlock the door.

"Be quiet, Da," Mandy said, "Gran may be asleep already."

"I will, love," Dev said as he pushed the door open and guided Mary in first.

"There ye are," Maeve said from the dining room as they stepped in. "Wow, Mandy! Come here, young lady, and let me give you a hug. You were splendid tonight."

Mandy handed Dev her coat and hurried to the dining room to comply with her grandmother's demands.

"That she was, Mum," Dev said as he hung their coats on the pegs behind the door. "Ya havin' tea before bed?"

"Sure, sure," Maeve said, looking up from squeezing a very happy Mandy. "Always a tea and biscuit before bed. I just helped m'self after Henry brought me by after the program. He wasn't very keen on helpin' his mum home until he realized it would be a longer drive to take Miss Debbie home if he did. I think that one has his interest."

"Debbie is a good one, Maeve," Mary said, and Maeve abruptly stared at her. Suddenly feeling the change in the room, Mary looked at Dev and then back at Maeve. "Did I say something wrong?"

"Mary, dear, it's Mum now. Not Maeve," Maeve said, and slowly smiled. "I thought Devlin would've told you. Even the girls' husbands had to learn."

Mary hurried to the dining room and took Maeve's hands. "I'm sorry. I didn't know if it would be proper. I'm still spinning over

Mandy wanting to call me 'Mum.' I didn't think."

Maeve smiled and squeezed her hands. "You're me new daughter now, Mary. Welcome to the family—and if Dev ever makes you unhappy, you just come and talk to me."

Mary giggled. "I doubt that will happen, but I'll remember that."

Mandy giggled and suddenly yawned.

"Aaah, I see that ye've about used up yer today, love," Dev said softly, leaning down to whisper in her ear. "Tell yer gran goodnight and go up and get ready for bed."

"Okay, Da," Mandy said, and hugged Maeve again. "Goodnight, Gran. We'll do omelets and bacon in the morning"—then she turned to look at Dev and Mary —"when they decide to get up."

"Off with ya, ya scamp," Dev said, and patted Mandy on the rear as he turned her to the stairs. "Let us know when yer ready, love." Then he looked at Maeve. "And you let me know if you need anythin', Mum."

"Take yer own advice, son"—Maeve smiled as she picked up her cup and plate—"and be off with yer bride. Ye shouldn't be makin' her wait while you visit with yer mum."

Dev hugged Maeve and kissed her cheek, and when she stood up, Mary hugged and kissed her too.

"Thank you for coming and being here for us, Mum," Mary said. "I've wanted to meet you and the rest of the family for a long time, and it really means a lot to have you here—especially for today and for the week to come. Let us know if you need anything."

Maeve smiled and gently turned Mary to Dev. "Go. Go you two. Start yer new life." Then Maeve took her dishes to the kitchen sink and rinsed them. "I'll see you two in the mornin'."

Dev took Mary's arm and led her up the stairs and to their bedroom.

"Dev, we can't get ready until Mandy is…" Mary was saying until Dev gently pushed her into their bedroom and closed the door behind them. "What's that?" she asked, seeing the lighted doorway where the window had been that morning.

"What d'ya think it is, love?" Dev said, stepping behind her and wrapping his arms around her waist. "'Tis your new bath, dressing room, and our new closet."

"How'd you ever get it finished?"

"Not just me, love," Dev said, his cheek pressing gently against the side of her head. "Some of the local tradesmen—John, Stewart, Nick, Max, Tim, and Ted—wanted to help finish it for us. They said they wanted you to consider it a wedding gift. Why do ya think we ushered ya outta the house so early this mornin'?"

Mary caught his hand and pulled him with her, stepping eagerly into the bath to see. "It looks like it's right out of one of those home-decorating magazines. It's so beautiful, Dev."

"Yer welcome, love," Dev said, and watched her as she checked out each feature of the room, from the large double shower to a large jetted tub for two, double vanity, and a counter and sitting space for her personal area. He smiled when she noticed the dressing area with two full-length mirrors, angled so she could see both her front and back at the same time. Between them was a full-height, drape-covered panel. Mary pulled the drape aside and revealed the full-height window overlooking the dark backyard.

"Dev. This is breathtaking," she said as she quickly peeked inside the large walk-in closet. "I can't think of the words to describe it or to say thank you." She turned and kissed him.

"I think you've found a way," Dev said, holding her tight until the soft knock on their door caught their attention.

"Da, Mum? I'm ready now," Mandy said through the door.

"Come in, love," Mary said, and greeted Mandy with a hug when she entered. "Did you know your dad was doing all of this?"

"Sure, sure," Mandy said. "We wanted—well, everyone wanted to surprise you."

"Well, you, and they, certainly did. It's so beautiful," Mary said as she turned Mandy toward her room. "Now let's get you to bed so we can go too."

Mandy hurried into her room and slid into bed, pulling her covers up under her arms as she stretched out. Dev took his usual place on the door side and sat down while Mary settled on her opposite side.

"Da? Are you goin' to redo my bath now?" Mandy asked with a huge smile.

Dev winked at Mary. "Now why would I be wantin' to do that,

lass? 'Tis fully functional the way it 'tis."

"'Cause, it isn't pretty like Gran's and yers," Mandy said, still smiling. "That's why."

"Well," Dev said, and kissed her check, "we'll see what we can do, but probably not right away. Only happy dreams from now on," Dev said, and kissed her cheek again.

"The same wish from me too, Mandy," Mary said as she kissed Mandy's cheek. "Only happy dreams, love."

"Thanks, Da, Mum," Mandy said with a bright smile. "The best one has already started. Thanks, Mary, for being my new mum." Mandy pushed herself up and hugged Mary as tight as she could.

Thirty-Nine
Monday, November 20

Mandy collected the breakfast plates and stacked them on the edge of the table as Mary went for the coffee pot and the hot water for more tea.

"That was wonderful," Maeve said as Dev put the lids on the jam jars and the cover on the butter dish. "And I don't think I've ever had a hash like that, Mandy. What was it, dear?"

Mandy smiled and glanced at Dev's nod. "I call it Mandy's Coddle Hash Patties, Gran. Da and Mum have helped me perfect it. I'm glad you liked it."

"Coddle? My, my," Maeve said softly. "I've never thought of using leftover coddle to make breakfast patties before." Then she smiled at Mandy. "Would you mind sharin' yer recipe? Tellin' me what you learned to not do in the perfectin' you did?"

"Sure, sure," Mandy said as she carried the plates and used silver into the kitchen. "But sometimes there are not enough leftovers to make hash, so we have to make new coddle with less broth so we'll have enough."

Mary had set the hot water kettle beside Maeve and was pouring herself and Dev more coffee when Dev's phone rang. He checked the screen and then answered as he got up and went into the living room.

"Hey, Lloyd. What can I do fer ya? No, it isn't too early for a call."

-¤-

Dev's body went rigid as Lloyd explained why he was calling and apologized for being the bearer of bad news.

"Sorry, Dev," Lloyd said. "I would've mentioned it last night, but I figured it could wait. I didn't want to throw cold water on yours and Mary's wonderful day. I presume you survived your first night together."

"Aye, we survived fine, Lloyd," Dev said, trying to keep his tone light. "Thank you."

"Tell Mandy I think she was wonderful in the program last night. Certainly not what I expected."

"I'll definitely tell her, Lloyd. We think so too."

"That's all I have, Dev. Give Mary my best." Then Lloyd broke the connection and Dev stared at his phone.

Mary came into the living room and stopped beside him, hesitant over Dev's suddenly changed manner as he put his phone away.

He took Mary's arm and nodded toward the stairs. "Mum, we'll be back in a minute," he said, and guided Mary up to their bedroom.

He closed the door behind them and pulled her to him, wrapping his arm tight around her shoulders.

"What is it, love? What's the matter?"

Dev inhaled and began to explain. "That was Lloyd Martin."

She nodded, her cheek against his chest, having heard him when he answered his phone.

"He said Einri and Scanlon were here yesterday—"

"No! Nononono. Dear God, no! No, Dev. Not now," she said softly, squeezing Dev, trembling, shaking her head against him. Dev knew Mary wanted to scream and find someplace to hide, but he knew she knew she could not just hide. He felt her frustration; there was more at stake now than just her. "Not now...not now...Dev."

"He and Nate saw them when they broke at lunch and checked in at the office. They were walking east on Main, lookin' inta the stores. Nate followed them as they walked down Main and finally back to Zeke's, where they had parked a white half-ton van. Lloyd said he ran a check on the license plates after they had lunch with us, figurin' they were stolen. The plates are supposed to be on a brown truck in the Denver area.

"He said they got the State Troopers involved so maybe they can follow them back to wherever they're stayin'." Dev sighed. "He figures they were casing the town, obviously lookin' for somethin', and will most likely come back in the night sometime soon." Dev rested his chin on the top of her head. "I'm sure they were lookin' fer us, but so far it doesn't look like they know where we live. Probably just my mailin' address.""

"And that's a post office box like mine," Mary said, still clinging to him.

"Aye. So we'll keep watch for a white van driving around town in the next few days."

"Can't they just pick them up for what they've done?"

"I thought so, but Lloyd says they're waitin' on a warrant. I guess it's somethin' they need before they can officially arrest someone that hasn't done anythin' wrong here—well, besides stealin' someone's license plates."

Mary squeezed him tighter. "I'm scared, Dev. Very, very scared," she whispered. "What if they hurt you or Mandy?"

"We'll not worry about that, love," Dev said softly, gently rubbing her back with one hand while he held her firmly with his other arm. "Our job is to take care of you and to keep them from doin' anythin' to you."

¤-¤-¤-¤-¤

Einri paced nervously as he waited for the gas station mechanic to tighten the lug nuts on the last tire on the van. For Einri, the hour's wait was grueling. He watched the street in both directions, expecting the attendant to figure something was wrong at some time during the tire change. Einri was listening for the sounds of Leadville's finest to come and investigate the white van and the redheaded driver hobbling on canes.

When the attendant lowered the van and backed it outside, he motioned to Einri where he was standing beside the soft drink vending machine. Einri went to the counter and paid for the tires with cash. The attendant did not bat an eye, giving no indication that he thought anything was wrong or amiss; he took the bills, counted them, and placed them in the till. Then he handed Einri his change and a copy of the receipt.

"There ya are," the mechanic said with a smile. "Those'll make gettin' around a whole lot easier."

"Thanks," Einri said, and pocketed the change and the receipt.

He walked out and got into the van and watched the mechanic through the station's front window as he backed out of the north side Conoco; the mechanic put his receipt copies away and then returned to the lift bay. Einri sighed, relieved the mechanic had not hurried to the phone as soon as Einri walked outside.

He pulled out and drove the short distance to the True Value hardware store. Inside, he had a stock boy put four cartons of gloss black spray-can paint, a package of five rolls of blue painter's tape, and a package of plastic drop cloths in the cart. He suffered the clerk's trite comments about him having a big painting project as he paid and smiled, agreeing that he did, and then left to find a car wash.

The whole trip into town cost him a couple of hours. He was hungry and tired by the time he got back to the cabin where he had left Scanlon. He was happy that he had finally graduated to using only one forearm crutch—some of the time. It was still a chore to get around. He hobbled in and found Scanlon looking at an old car magazine he had discovered somewhere in the cabin.

"Are ya hungry?" Einri asked as he closed the door behind him.

"Sure, sure," Scanlon said, and came to show him an article in the magazine.

Einri got the sandwich makings out of the small refrigerator and the paper plates from a sack on the counter. After they ate, Einri led Scanlon into the double-car garage beside the cabin.

"What're we doin'?" Scanlon asked as they stacked the last of the boxes and old tools on one side of the garage.

"We're goin' to repaint the van," Einri said, trying to catch his breath, "and we need the space...to put the van in while the paint dries. Sun's out...this afternoon and...the temperature's just above... freezin'. That'll help keep the garage...a bit warmer than outside." Einri straightened and held onto the van's fender, wondering why he suddenly seemed to always be out of breath. "I...I found an electric space heater...in one of the bedrooms. I'll...put it out here to take the chill off."

Once they had cleared a space large enough for the van, Einri opened the garage door and parked the van inside. He closed the door and got the bag of tape and drop cloths out.

Einri took his time and ran the tape around the windows, covered the door handles and anything else he did not want painted black. Scanlon helped him hold and trim the cut pieces of drop cloth to cover the windows inside the tape outlines. He wiped the expanse of the van with towels and then started painting.

He did the roof first, as far as he could reach. Scanlon tried to steady him against the van while he stood on a makeshift bench—the bench wobbled as much as he did. Einri painted his way down onto the sides, and down off the bench. Scanlon moved to the double doors on the back.

After an hour and a half, Einri was exhausted. He could not believe how often he had to steady himself, breathing deeply each time as he stopped. He used the breaks to shake the numbness out of his fingers and assess their progress. Scanlon's work needed some touching up, but in the end, too tired to spray any more paint, he decided the van was transformed enough for their purposes. It looked like a spray-can paint job with its random twisted streaks of matte over a gloss base, but he figured it would have to do. Scanlon was excited, like a kid a third his age, when they finally started removing the masking materials.

"Einri?" Scanlon asked when he took an armload of wadded drop cloths to the trash. "Why do the trash bins have tops with locks on them?"

"Don't know, Scan," Einri said as he studied the hinged top and the hasp with a spring clip through it. "It really isn't a lock—more like a quick-release kind of clip."

"Looks like a bother when you need to put stuff in it," Scanlon said as he stuffed the drop cloths and the wadded tape in it.

Einri slapped Scanlon's shoulder and smiled. "Scan, me brother," he said, gesturing to the van, "ya did a fine job. We'll worry about...the trash later. But now, why don't ya go...in and get a couple of beers out. I'll be in to join ya...in just a few minutes so I can sit down, catch...me breath, and rest me aches."

"Thanks," Scanlon said with a smile. "I can do that." And Scanlon went back into the cabin as Einri checked for any overlooked pieces of masking tape.

Dev's house had never felt small to him when it was just him and Mandy. Not even when Mary, before the wedding, had started coming and becoming a part of their family. But now, with his mum, his brother, and his sisters and their families, it felt *small*.

The two card tables for the children seemed to crowd the living room more than Dev had thought they would, but he had to laugh at himself; he'd never had guests, much less the entire family horde, descend upon him and Mandy, so he really did not know what he was expecting. He smiled at the extended dining room table with an extra place set; Henry had "informed" him that he had invited Debbie. Dev chuckled at Henry's announcement, as if he should have known Debbie would be coming.

That was another thing that made Dev smile: Henry's sudden interest in Debbie Cotton. Mary had asked him about Henry's nearly obsessive attention to Debbie, and Dev answered her, reminding her of their conversation after their rehearsal.

"Henry's had dates off and on since early high school, but none of those dates went past one or two times out," Dev explained, "and I teased him early on that he might be hitting for the other team. Henry usually responded with a well-placed clout on me shoulder, but I just took it in stride. Henry's me only brother, older, and I figured he would figure it out sooner or later.

"It was obvious that Henry was interested in finding the right one, even though she never seemed to come along. But I don't ever remember seeing him giddy over a woman.

"Henry settled into his career, working for a local Brighton dry goods store as their bookkeeper, and generally stopped looking. Da told me once that Henry was just bein' patient, something that would help him when the right woman did come along. I didn't understand at the time, since that happened about the time I fell for Anne in my senior high school year and me own roller-coaster ride began."

"One hour," Mandy announced from the kitchen. "Potatoes and veggies are needin' ta go in."

Dev chuckled as his sisters scurried anew at Mandy's reminder—
she was definitely in charge of the kitchen today. Then he wondered
how patient Mandy would be when it came her turn to accept a beau.

"Hey Dev," Henry said softly as he stopped beside Dev,
straightening his shirt and buttoning his top button. Mary patted
Dev's arm and turned to the kitchen.

"Whatcha doin'?" Dev asked, cocking his head in curious
question. "Ya look like yer getting ready to put on a tie."

"Think I should?"

"No," Dev said, and stopped to look at Henry. "Unbutton that.
You look nervous. What's goin' on?"

"I am. Do I look okay?"

Dev turned and squared himself in front of Henry, clasping
Henry's shoulders firmly in his hands. "What's goin' on, brother? I've
never seen you like this." Then he raised his eyebrows at a thought.
"Has this somethin' to do with Debbie?"

Henry looked away and smiled. "Maybe."

"I see," Dev said, and smiled. "She's become special, has she?"

Henry's ears turned pink. "I think so, Dev. I felt somethin'
different at the rehearsal, first time I saw her. I've tried to be a
gentleman and be polite and courteous and...and...Am I doin' it
right?"

"I don' know," Dev said with a smile. "What does she say?"

Henry looked down a second and then back at Dev. "I've asked
her out every day since I met her, and she's accepted each time. She
kissed me last night—kinda sudden and quick. We were talkin' about
how surprised I was that I liked your town and the mountains here,
and how nice Mary is and all, and she...she..."

Dev smiled. "They'll do that to ya. She's letting ya know she's
interested too."

"I feel so different, Dev, like I'm a schoolboy again. It's only been
five days, and all I can think about is being with her and..."

"I know," Dev said softly, and turned serious. "I felt the same way
when I first saw Mary, and especially after I got her to talk to me. But
you have to keep yer head. I don't know Debbie in any way other than
Mary's friend, but be completely honest with yerself and with her.

Obviously, you've caught her interest too, so talk about that. Yer both adults, Henry. Treat her like one and yerself like one. Learn all ya can about her and what she likes. Accept her for what she is, not what ya think she could be. And above all, let her know if she makes ya happy. Straight up. No hemmin' 'n hawin.'"

"Thanks," Henry said. "I asked her if I could pick her up today, but she wanted to drive herself. Is that normal, for her to be so independent?"

"Henry." Dev shook his head. "She's been taking care of herself since she left home as a grown woman. Why would she need for you to pick her up? I know she probably liked the offer, but like you said, it's only been five days and she may not be sure how ya feel after she kissed ya." Dev held his eyes for a minute. "Okay, I'm getting long-winded, but I will say one more thin' and then I'll stop. Let her show ya who she is and try to accept that with understanding. If ya like her, then it's her ya like, not someone else, not someone she could be, not someone ya imagine her ta be. And give her someone honest and reliable to depend on. No lies, no games, just you being the man she deserves."

"But what if I'm not as good as she deserves?"

"Ya know the answer to that, Henry." Dev smiled and shook his head again. "But if yer not, or can't learn to be, don't force yerself on her. Show her what she means to ya, but let her decide. Give her time. This is the first thing the two of ya will have to agree on."

Henry started to say something more, but the knock on the front door interrupted him.

"I'm thinkin' ya should answer the door, brother," Dev said, and pushed Henry toward the repeated knock.

Forty

Sunday, November 26
Early Morning

It was still full dark when Henry finished loading Maeve's luggage and Dev, Mary, and Mandy helped her into the van.

"I wish you'd reconsider stayin', Mum," Dev said again as she settled into the seat and slid to the other side to make room. "Christmas is less than a month away and we'd love to have you."

"Thank you, all three of you, but I have some shopping to do before then," Maeve said, and reached out to Mary. "Thank you for the hospitality and for coming into our family," she said when Mary took her hand. "May yer time together be nothin' but happy times."

"Thanks, Mum," Mary said.

"Are we ready?" Henry asked as he stopped beside the side door.

"I think so," Dev said, and slapped Henry's back. "Drive the van and we'll walk down to Mary's house."

-¤-

Carl, Will, and Merril had the second van loaded when Henry parked behind it. He got out and left the van running to keep the inside warm for their mum. Henry was helping load the last of the luggage when Dev, Mary, and Mandy walked up.

They were giving Dev, Mary, and Mandy their goodbye hugs when a gunmetal gray and black jeep turned the corner and slid to a stop across the street from the vans. Debbie jumped out and hurried across the street to say goodbye to everyone, waving to Maeve in the van, hugging the sisters, the kids, and the husbands in turn. Then, as everyone started getting into the vans, Debbie turned to Henry and pulled him aside.

Mary saw them hug, her head against his chest. They held each other for a very long moment before she clenched her fist and struck his chest without releasing her hold on him. Mary could hear her saying something, but not clearly enough to understand her words. Then Henry stopped her, kissing her long and tenderly. The family watched in deep interest as Debbie melted into Henry and he tightened his hold on her.

-¤-

Debbie stood beside Mary, and the four of them waved to the two-van caravan as it turned the corner and headed down Tenth. Mary saw the tears streaking Debbie's cheeks.

"Are you okay?" Mary asked softly as Dev and Mandy went up to the house and went in.

"Yes," Debbie said, and turned to look at Mary. "No."

Mary cocked her head as Debbie took a tissue from her purse and wiped her eyes.

"He was supposed to call and wake me this morning," Debbie began explaining, "when he got up."

"But that would've been before four," Mary said, not understanding.

"I know, but I told him it would've given us another hour or more." She looked at Mary. "And I could've helped, or at least been with everybody a little longer."

Mary slowly nodded and smiled. "Is it serious?"

"I think so," Debbie said. "At least he makes me feel like it is."

"And how do you feel now?"

"Like my heart's being torn out," Debbie said, and looked down at the street. "I know he's planning on being back for Christmas, but it still..."

"Oh my," Mary said, and caught Debbie's arm. "Come on. I think it's hot chocolate time and you're going to tell me what's happening."

Monday, November 27

It was near the end of the first day of school after the holiday week and the spray-can black van was in the library parking lot, across the street from the Roosevelt elementary school. Einri sat on a pillow atop a wooden box, leaning back against the wall of the van. He was watching the school entrance through the windows in the van's double back doors.

That morning over breakfast and a cup of coffee, Einri remembered Amanda and realized she would be in school during the day. So he decided to see if Devlin picked her up or if she walked home after school. Either way, he figured he could follow them and find out where they lived. If he watched Devlin's place, he further figured, he would see Dev's woman before too much time passed. He still had not figured out a way to get her alone, but he was determined to find one.

Scanlon interrupted his thoughts as he adjusted his position against the opposite wall, reading the same car magazine he had found at the cabin. When Einri looked back at the school, two jeeps and a minivan had stopped in the circle drive in front of the school's front doors.

Einri smiled when a man about his size and build with red hair got out of a red two-door jeep and walked up to the front doors. A girl with bright red hair pushed the doors open and hugged him. Einri now knew Dev drove a red jeep, and he figured it should be easy to find in a town as small as Roosevelt.

Einri got up and moved to the driver's seat. "Scan, watch the red jeep and tell me which way it goes." His legs were stiff, still hurting, and getting into the driver's seat was difficult. After a few minutes of struggling, he managed to maneuver around the engine hump and slide under the steering wheel. "Which way, Scan?"

"It's coming this way," Scanlon said.

"Which way is this way?" Einri asked, his irritation rising.

"Here," Scanlon said as a vehicle parked two spots to their left. "It just parked beside us."

Einri turned and saw Devlin getting out of the jeep; he ducked, turning his back toward the door and its window. He heard Devlin talking to Amanda as they went into the library and the door closed behind them. "Damn! Why didn't you warn me?"

"I did. I told you they were coming this way and that they were here."

"Okay, okay," Einri said, and sat back up in his seat. He started the van and backed out of the parking spot, turned, and pulled out onto the street. He went up to Third and then went around the block to the south, returning to watch the library from Second Street near the school.

"Was that Devlin?" Scanlon asked, and Einri nodded. "Why didn't you say hello?"

"We're not here to visit with Devlin," Einri said through clenched teeth. "We're here to see if the woman that's with him and his daughter looks like the woman in the picture from the police website."

"You said we were coming to pay Devlin a visit," Scanlon said, and sat down on his wooden box with his arms crossed in front of him. "I haven't seen his little girl since she got out of the hospital."

"You'll get to see her soon enough, Scan," Einri said. "Just be patient."

¤-¤-¤-¤-¤

"Hmm. Interestin'," Dev said as they pulled out of the library parking lot a couple of hours later.

"What's interestin', Da?" Mandy asked.

"Did you notice the black van when we parked?"

"The one with the ugly paint job?" Mandy asked. "Yup. It was pretty bad."

"Well it moved across the street after we went in, and now it seems to be following us. Do me a favor, love."

"Sure, Da," Mandy said.

"Jump in the back and get down low and watch which way that van goes," Dev said as he slowed and turned onto Fourth. "I'm going to stop at the grocery and go in for a minute. If the van follows us, I want you to stay back there and watch it."

"Okay, Da. You think it's Cousin Einri?"

"Maybe," Dev said, and parked beside the side door at the back of the grocery. "But Einri was driving a white van. I'm supposin' he might've painted it black to throw us off."

"He went straight."

"Okay. You watch and see if it comes by. I'll just be a minute."

Dev stepped inside and collected the two paper sacks he had packed while he worked during the afternoon. Then he stepped back out and set them on the floor behind the driver's seat.

When he got back in, Mandy said, "I haven't seen the van again, Da. It didn't drive back by."

"Well, we can't hide if it is Einri," Dev said, "and it's time for us to pick up Mary. Are you up for Stumpy's?"

"Sure, sure," Mandy said with a smile. "I got my homework done so I'm good."

"Already? I think I'm goin' to have to talk to yer teacher about not givin' you kids enough homework," Dev said. "She's bein' awfully easy on you."

Mandy giggled as Dev turned east on Main.

Fearin' the Banshee

Forty-One

Einri drove past the intersection at Fourth and turned around two blocks farther up the street. He parked on the south side of the street and waited.

"Why are ya waitin'?" Scanlon asked when they stopped. "Devlin turned back there."

"I know, Scan," Einri said, searching the area around him in case Devlin had continued. "I think I was followin' too close. I dunna want Devlin to think he's bein' followed."

They waited impatiently for Devlin's red jeep to reappear. Finally, he saw it pull out onto Main and turn back toward the school. Einri started to follow, but forced himself to wait a little longer, telling himself it was a small town and he would not lose track of Devlin.

He smiled when the jeep finally came up Main toward them. As it got close, he and Scanlon ducked down, but when he looked again, he was surprised to see the jeep had parked just behind them and across the street. Devlin was leading his daughter and a brunette into the café and bar called Stumpy's.

Einri watched, and when he saw them take a table at the front window he decided to pull out and drive down to the gas station and the small deli there. He and Scanlon would grab a bite to eat and then wait for Devlin to make his next move.

¤-¤-¤-¤-¤

Dev raised his pint of stout to Mary and she responded by raising her pilsner to touch his. He glanced past her to the spot the black van had been parked in, but did not say anything. He smiled at Mary and then at Mandy as she quickly raised her lemonade glass and touched it to both of their glasses.

"To my two wonderful girls," Dev said softly, looking at Mary and then at Mandy. "And my heartfelt thanks and love to my wife, Mrs. Mary O'Brien, and Mandy's new mum."

Mary smiled as a tinge of pink rose to her cheeks. "Thank you for asking, Mr. Devlin O'Brien."

Dev sipped his stout and Mary sipped her pilsner. Mandy gulped her lemonade. Dev chuckled and Mandy looked at him.

"What, Da?"

"Take smaller bites and sips, love," Dev said. "I think I may have forgotten to teach you table manners, lass."

"No, ya didn't, Da," Mandy said, and took a smaller bite of her mashed potatoes. "I'm just excited about everything."

"Everything?" Mary asked, and looked at Mandy.

"Yeah. Our new family; me havin' a new mum; my uncles, aunts, and cousins just bein' here, the first time I've seen them since we came here; the perfect sled run and how much the cousins loved it. It's all so excitin' 'tis hard to not forget me manners." Mandy took another drink of her lemonade, sipping this time. "Sorry, Da. I just can't wait for Christmas when we get to see them again."

Dev chuckled and looked at Mary. Then to Mandy he said, "Well let's not be fergettin' too much while we're out in public, lass. Christmas is comin' and I hope it'll be just as excitin', but we still need to act properly."

Dev sat his pint down and cut a slice off his chicken-fried steak. They ate quietly, enjoying each other's company, talking about the week past and what Mary thought about each of Dev's sisters and Henry.

"Now, except for the little you've told me, I don't know Henry's history with dating or with women in general," Mary said, "but he sure turned Debbie's world upside down."

"Is that what you two were talking about after everyone left Sunday morning?" Dev asked.

Mary nodded as she answered. "Do you know how Henry feels about her? She's seeing their relationship as something that is quickly becoming serious."

Dev nodded. "Aye, lass. I would have to agree with her. Henry hasn't said anything more than what she has done to him, making him feel things he hasn't ever felt from another woman."

"Does that bother him?"

"Very much so," Dev said, and saw Mary's expression suddenly sadden. "No, no, love. Sorry. I think it bothers him in a very good way. Henry always dresses nice for work and even when he's casual, knowin' what looks good an' all, but on Thanksgivin', fer example, he couldn't decide if what he wore looked right, if he should put on a tie. He was concerned again when they went out Friday afternoon, askin' me, of all people, what I thought, if he was doin' things right." Dev shook his head and winked at Mandy. "No, love, I think Henry is thinkin' he might have actually met the woman he's been lookin' for."

Mary's expression had returned to its previous warmth and happiness as Dev explained.

"Did you see them saying goodbye?" Mary asked.

Dev chuckled. "I think they surprised the whole family when she got there."

"Aye, probably, love," Mary said with a wide smile. "It was intense, the way he held her. She looked a lot like I feel when you hold me. And I'm sure there was a lot of talk about it on that ride back to the airport and back home."

Dev chuckled. "I'm sure there was."

Finished, Dev pushed his plate back and watched Mandy wipe the last of her gravy off hers. Then when she finished, he asked, "Dessert?"

Mandy and Mary both shook their heads.

"Hot chocolate instead, after I get ready for bed?" Mandy asked.

Dev looked at Mary and she nodded.

"Sure, sure, loves. Sounds good to me," Dev agreed, and waved to Connie.

¤-¤-¤-¤-¤

Following Dev when the three of them left Stumpy's, Einri slowly drove up Main Street, paralleling Dev's red jeep after it turned on Lincoln off of Fifth Street. Scanlon looked up Sixth as they crossed on Main, telling Einri when he saw the jeep cross on Lincoln. They repeated the routine at each street until the jeep did not cross Eleventh.

"Wait!" Scanlon said sharply as Einri continued across the intersection. "Go Back. They didn't cross."

"Okay, Scan," Einri said. "I'll go around the block at the next street."

Einri turned on Twelfth and then backtracked on Hayes. At Eleventh, he switched his headlights off, turned toward Lincoln, and slowly crept along the verge until he could see through the trees in the open lots on the south side of Lincoln.

"I see them," Scanlon said excitedly. "In front of the middle house." He pointed, as if Einri could not see the jeep.

"Calm down, Scan. I see them too."

Einri waited, and after a few minutes Devlin hurried down the walk from the house and got back into the jeep. When Devlin had driven past Eleventh, Einri backed to the corner behind them and began following Devlin a block south of Lincoln.

He turned on Twelfth and parked at the side of the road, watching the jeep where it parked in the drive to the only house on the block. The three got out and went into the house through the front door.

"Okay, Scan," Einri said, and pointed to his door. "My legs hurt too much, so I'm going to give you a job to do."

"Okay," Scanlon said, and wide grin covered his face.

"Now don't get sidetracked. I want you to go and listen at a window for a minute and see what they are doing. Then come straight back here and tell me what you heard. Got that?"

"Yeah. I can do that," Scanlon said as he opened his door.

"And don't let anyone see you," Einri added sternly.

"Okay. I won't."

¤-¤-¤-¤-¤

"Took ya long enough," Einri said softly, his voice somewhere between scolding and eager curiosity. "Hear anythin' int'restin'?"

"Aye, yeah," Scanlon replied as he got in and closed the passenger side door.

"Well? What did ya hear?"

"They went home and are playin' Twenty-five."

"Twenty-five? Playin' cards? That's int'restin'?

"Yeah. And they were talkin' 'bout somethin' little Amanda had to stand up and say at school. Her mum was all gushy and pleased at how well she did."

"Her mum?" Einri stared at Scanlon. "Mum?"

"Aye. She called her 'mum,' little Amanda did." Scanlon glared at Einri. "I heard her."

Einri nodded and glanced away for a moment, muttering under his breath, "Wonder when Devlin remarried."

"Don' know. I canna tell," Scanlon answered, and absently looked back toward Dev's house. "She sounds nice. I like the way she talks to Amanda and Devlin."

Einri looked at Scanlon and watched as he promptly lost himself in his own thoughts. Einri shook his head, but did not say anything.

¤-¤-¤-¤-¤

After their game of cards was finished and the cards were being sorted, Dev told Mandy she needed to get ready for bed and they would start making the hot chocolate. Mandy got up and put the cards away, then stopped beside them and slowly faced him.

"Da, we need to tell Mum about the van," she said. "Before we forget. No secrets, no matter how bad."

Dev nodded. "Yer right, love. Come sit a minute." He held his arms out for her and she stepped between him and Mary, settling on his lap facing her.

Dev took Mary's hand. "We don't know much, but a black van followed us after I picked up Mandy from school."

"It was an *ugly* black paint job," Mandy said. "Da thinks cousin Einri might have repainted the white van with *spray cans*."

Dev chuckled at Mandy's dramatics and gestures. "The paint job was horrible and easily identifiable from other black vans."

"But you think it's Einri," Mary said, suddenly shivering again.

"I think so, love," Dev said softly. "I don't know of anyone else that might want to follow us." Dev shrugged. "It's possible that it's nothin' and not them, but I'd rather not make that assumption until Lloyd can check it out and tell me it isn't them. We'll keep looking around and watchin' our surroundin's."

"Where did you see it at?"

"First at the library after I picked Mandy up. It was parked like it was watchin' the front of the school," Dev explained.

"And after we went over to the library and parked a little ways away from it," Mandy added, "it moved across the street and followed us up to the grocery when we left the library. But it went on when we stopped."

"When we picked you up and went to Stumpy's," Dev added, "it was across the street in front of City Hall. It left after we sat down at the table."

"We know we don't know anythin' fer sure, Mum," Mandy said, and reached for Mary's hand, "but we'll keep watchin'. We won't let anything happen to you."

Mary smiled. "Thank you both—for telling me what is happening. I like you sharing so we'll all be ready. You don't know how much I appreciate that." She smiled at Dev. "Do we need to do anything more? Double-check anything?"

"We topped off the fuel in the jeep before we picked you up," he said, and nodded to Mandy. "And I made sure the truck was full on Saturday."

"Have you called Lloyd?"

"Yeah. I called him when I put gas in the jeep. Just in case."

"Okay." Mary sighed, then looked at Mandy, forcing a smile. "So how about getting that bath and we'll work on the hot chocolate?"

"Okay, Mum," Mandy said, and slid off Dev's lap. She hugged Dev and then turned around and hugged Mary. "I love you, Mum. We won't let anything happen to you."

"Thank you, love. Now scoot," Mary said, and gently turned Mandy toward the stairs.

Tuesday, November 28

The morning recess bell rang, and Mary smiled and watched the children scamper out of the room. Today, with the snow and the wind, they would recess in the field house. Mary waited, and when the last one left the room she laid her head on her arms atop her desk and closed her eyes.

It only seemed a second later that the classroom door opened and Mary looked up see Nancy Arnold's concerned expression as she entered.

"Are you okay, Mary?"

"Sure, sure," Mary said, smiling at her growing habit of repeating Dev and Mandy's saying. "Just a little tired."

"Tired?"

Mary smiled sheepishly and looked past Nancy to be sure the door was closed and the children were all out of the room. "Yeah," she sighed. "Last night was our second night without Dev's mother sleeping in the room below us. So we kept each other up most of the night again, and now I'm paying for it. Sorry for giving you concern."

"You did," Nancy said. "I've never seen you with your head on your desk, and I was—Do I dare ask if everything is okay with you two?"

Mary smiled again. "Sorry, Nancy, I should've gone to the lounge. But yes, everything's very okay with Dev and me. He has the most wonderful ways of helping me...well, I'll just say to relieve my stresses, to forget my troubles and problems...I get shivers and my toes curl just remembering..."

"I see." Nancy coughed and smiled behind her open hand.

"But the problems are still there," Mary said, and looked back at Nancy.

"The problems?"

Mary nodded as her expression sobered. "He was here last Sunday and Dev thinks he was here again last night, checking the town out, looking for where we live."

"Who? Not—"

"Yup," Mary said, her shoulders slumping. "Yeah, the one that killed Bobby. And like Dev and Lloyd said before, he knows I look like Bobby's wife and he knows that I'm here."

"Oh, Mary," Nancy said softly. "I'll alert Lloyd and the fathers that are volunteering to watch the school, but...What are you going to do?"

Mary smiled. "Wait, I guess. We still have our fallback preparations in place." She nodded absently. "He doesn't know we know he's been here, so we're hoping to use that to our advantage. Dev told Lloyd he thinks they painted their white van black, so Lloyd and Nate are looking out for them. Last week, Lloyd called the State Troopers so they can try to find out where they're hiding."

"Oh my," Nancy said. "I didn't realize you were so actively involved in watching for them."

"I wasn't," Mary admitted. "It was Dev and Mandy that got worried and started watching and cluing me in on what's been happening. I'm a nervous wreck, just trying to hold it together and not do something that scares the kids. Everywhere I look, I think I'm seeing that black van. I'm not, of course, but Dev keeps telling me things will work out. I don't think he really knows, but I like the fact that he's optimistic and confident. I don't know how he does it."

"Dev? Dev's been watching?"

"Mandy overheard you the day you slipped and called me 'Cali,'" Mary said, and smiled. "That started a lot of things, but mostly Dev found out how easily he was able to find information on Bobby and his wife. I think it scared him a little."

"Are you okay at Dev's, way up at the end of town?"

"We hope so," Mary said. "Lloyd's increasing his patrols out our way, and Dev is alert, watching. I think we'll be—"

The recess bell interrupted and Nancy smiled at Mary as she turned to the door. "Okay, but you know to call if you need any help."

"I do, thanks," Mary said as the loud sounds of happy children coming up the hall filled the room.

Nancy opened the door and stepped out.

"Well, Dev, thanks for the call yesterday. We haven't seen them walking around since Sunday week," Lloyd Martin said as he watched the few people walking down Main. "And we haven't seen the white van, so you thinking they painted it is probably right."

"Have the State boys seen anythin'?" Dev asked.

Lloyd shook his head. "They followed a white van up to Leadville last Sunday evening but it turned out to be the wrong van. It was a local going home."

"I'm pretty sure it was followin' us when we left the library, and the occupants were watching us when we stopped at Stumpy's for dinner," Dev said.

Lloyd rubbed his chin. "Nate said something about seein' a spray-can black van late yesterday, before he came in and I told him you had called. He said it was leaving town when he saw it. I guess it's been too quiet and we didn't think about them repainting the van. I'll ask him if he knows any more when he comes on this afternoon." Lloyd rubbed his chin and looked at Dev. "Have you ever thought about getting a gun? For protection?"

Dev shook his head. "Don't need one. Wouldn't know what to do with one if I did." He smiled at Lloyd. "No. I'll leave those to you and Nate. I can bare-knuckle him if I need ta." Dev raised his fists, striking a boxer's pose as if to show that he could.

"All right. I understand." Lloyd smiled and extended his hand.

"Okay," Dev said as he got up and shook Lloyd's hand. "I need to get back to the grocery. Let me know if you hear anythin'."

"Will do," Lloyd said, and Dev stepped out and walked to his jeep.

Forty-Two

Dev and Mandy were waiting when Mary finished and came out through the school's front doors. He opened the jeep door and helped her in.

When Dev stopped in his driveway, he helped Mary and Mandy out and into the house.

"Are ya feelin' okay, love?" Dev asked as he took Mary's coat. "You look a bit tired."

Mary smiled and poked him in the chest, leaning close and then wrapping her arms around him. "Aren't you?" she whispered, looking up into his deep green eyes. "Just a little? Last night was something else."

"A bit, love. Definitely, a bit," he said, and squeezed her tight. "'Twas definitely somethin' else, and the first time I've been kept up all night." He kissed her and held her lips to his longer than he realized, and about to say something very personal, he noticed Mandy's attention.

"Da? Doncha want her to breathe?" Mandy asked from where she watched in the living room.

"Sure, sure," Dev said, and looked sheepishly at Mary's wide smile. "But this is somethin' ya might have ta get used ta seein'."

"I know, Da," Mandy said, and smiled. "I like seein' you two together, lovin' each other. Maybe I should take notes fer when I discover boys."

They both turned their heads and stared at Mandy as she got up, went into the dining room, and began setting the table.

Mary looked at Dev. "She's definitely older than ten, Dev."

-¤-

"Dev?" Mary asked when they finished with the dishes. "Would you mind if I soaked a while in the tub? Then I'll probably want to turn in for the night."

"That's fine, love," Dev said, and kissed her. "I'll come and check on you in a little bit."

"Thanks," Mary said, and slowly climbed the stairs to her and Dev's bedroom.

"Why's she so tired, Da?" Mandy asked as she came into the living room and watched Mary go up. "She was sleepy all day today in school."

Dev chuckled. "We kept each other awake last night, love."

"Talkin' a lot? Or was part of it because you weren't sleepin' alone like you used ta do?"

"Maybe a little of the first and a lot of the second." Dev chuckled and turned to the dining room. "Cards?"

When it came time for Mandy to get ready for bed, she put the cards away and headed up the stairs. At the top, she listened at Dev's bedroom door. "I don't hear her, Da. Maybe she fell asleep."

"Probably," Dev said. "You go ahead and get ready and I'll go check on her."

"Okay," Mandy said, and went to her room to gather her pajamas.

Dev stepped into the bedroom, closed the door, and then went to the bathroom door. He glanced at the closet and was pleased that she had thought to take her robe. He knocked softly. Then he knocked again, and when there was still no response, he slowly pushed the bathroom door open and slipped in. Seeing her sleeping in the wide tub, Dev picked up a thick, soft towel from the rack beside the vanity and sat down on the floor beside her. He watched her for a few minutes and then slowly leaned over the side of the tub and kissed her.

Mary's eye lids fluttered, then opened, blinked, and Dev kissed her again.

"Oh, Dev. Did I fall asleep?"

"Yes, love," he said with a wide smile. "That ye did, lass."

"I'm sorry, Dev," she said, and started to get up.

He stopped her hurry and held the towel for her. Then he reached down by her feet and flipped the stopper lever to let the water drain.

"Yer fine, love." He smiled as she leaned back against the end of the tub and he returned to sit beside her.

She smiled. "And do you always sit and watch naked ladies in your tub?"

"Only you, love. Only me beautiful wife," he said, and leaned to her, kissing her again. Then he rocked up on his knees and gave her the towel, helping her up and out of the tub. He grabbed a second towel and helped her dry and then slipped her robe over her shoulders.

"Be careful," she said as she tied the robe's waist band. "Spoil me too much and I might decide I like it and not let you stop."

At the side of their bed, Mary stopped and dropped her robe across the foot. Dev hung it up in the closet and turned to watch her very feminine curves as she slipped into her pajamas' bikini bottoms and then dropped the crop top over her head.

"My God, woman," Dev said just above a whisper, "you are the most incredibly beautiful thing I've ever seen. 'Beguilin'' doesn't come close to what ye do ta me."

"Thank you, love," Mary replied softly as she turned to smile at him. "I hope we're way beyond beguilin' by now."

"Aye, I know we are, but ye still take me breath away." He nodded, unable to look away as she straightened the top, pulled her hair out, and came to him.

She hugged him tight and whispered, "Thank you, Dev. For everything. For liking me, for wanting me, for watching out for me, and for sharing your beautiful daughter with me." She pushed herself up and kissed him tenderly, and he thought his knees would fail him.

"Help me brush my hair?" she asked as she picked up her hairbrush.

He took the brush from her and sat down on their bed. She sat on the edge of the bed beside him and slowly, ignoring how she moved him, he began running his fingers and the brush down the length of her hair. He gently straightened the tangles so the brush would not pull.

"Dev? I know you know I'm naturally a blonde," Mary said softly as he stroked her hair, "from the pictures you've seen."

"Aye, lass," he admitted. "What's on yer mind?"

"I'm just wondering if you'd want me to go back to being a blonde."

He stopped and wrapped his arms around her, pulling her back against him. "I've never seen you in your natural color, other than one picture. And I know coloring your hair and keepin' it this way is a lot of work, but the beautiful golden brown you chose grabbed me heart the first time I saw you.

"But 'tis you I love, lass. Havin' me arms around ya whenever I can, holdin' ya tight and bein' with ya is what matters the most, love. I like ya best as a golden brunette, and if ye decide to change I'll like ya as a blonde, or maybe even a redhead." He chuckled and squeezed her again. "But please, don't cut it until Mandy gets to wear hers long like yours."

"Thanks, Dev," Mary said, and twisted around to kiss him.

-¤-

Dev had just tucked the covers around Mary when Mandy finished and called him. "I'm ready, Da."

He kissed Mary again, got up, and went out and across the hall to Mandy's room. He sat down on the edge of her bed like he usually did.

"I think ya should go in and kiss Mary goodnight, love," Dev said as he pulled Mandy's covers back. "She's already in bed, but I know she'll like fer ya to."

Mandy got up and quietly went into his and Mary's room. After a few minutes she came back to bed. She sat beside him and hugged him.

"Da, yer goin' to have ta not keep her awake all night anymore," Mandy said matter-of-factly. "She had a lot of trouble in school today. Thanks fer lettin' me say goodnight to her."

"Sure, sure. We'll definitely do better, love," Dev said, and smiled, controlling his chuckle. "We have to get used to each other and not tire each other out. Last night was our second night without Gran downstairs. I'm sorry, but you'll see her again first thing in the mornin'."

"I like that, Da—being able to see her first thing in the mornings," Mandy said, and hugged him again. "Thank you for liking her too."

"Yer welcome, love," Dev said, and squeezed her before he laid her back in her bed. "Omelets and bacon?"

"Omelets and bacon sound good, Da," Mandy said, and pulled her covers up around her shoulders.

Dev leaned over and kissed her cheek. "Love you, scamp. Bunches."

"I love you too, Da. And Mary too. Goodnight."

"Goodnight, love. Only happy dreams now."

"Only happy dreams, Da."

Dev switched Mandy's light off and went downstairs to check on the house and be sure everything was off and locked up. He sat down on the sofa and sat with his hands folded, elbows on his knees, and closed his eyes. He inhaled gently and the words started coming.

"Thank ye, Dear God in Heaven, for all that ye've done fer Mandy and fer keepin' her safe, and fer all ye've done keepin' Mary alive and bringin' her to us. And now, with Einri nosin' about, help me see what I need to do to keep them safe from him. Use me however ya need to, to protect them both. We'll do what we need us ta do if ye'll just show us. Thanks."

Dev pushed himself up and then climbed the stairs. He slipped into his dark room, closed the door, and went into their new bathroom to get ready for bed.

Mary stirred as he slid under the fleece sheet and quilt. He hesitated when she rolled over and faced the wall, her back to him. Then he stretched out behind her, and when she felt him near, she snuggled back against his chest and down against his thighs, curling into his bent form as if it was meant to hold her. Dev slipped his arm under her pillow and then under her head and let his other arm gently drape around her middle. He kissed her neck, and as he lay down against her, she caught his hand and guided it under her pajama top and held it tight against her, cupping her breast.

She sighed and Dev listened as her breathing relaxed. He knew she felt secure and had fallen back asleep.

Thursday, November 30

Dev closed the cabinet doors on the dinner dishes and Mandy hung the damp dish towel on the towel rack as Mary switched the dishwasher on. Mary stood up and caught Dev's waist as they walked through the dining room into the living room.

"Any word from Lloyd or Nate?" she asked.

Dev shook his head. "He checked with some of the folks helping to watch, and no one has seen the black van in a couple of days. I saw Nate's patrol car turn the corner and head down past yer place about a half an hour ago. Are ya doin' okay?"

Mary nodded. "Sure, sure. As long as I'm not too far away from you. I guess we'd hear if Nate saw anything."

"Most likely," he agreed, and squeezed her.

"Well then, I think it's safe enough and we should go down to my place and finish drying the sheets," Mary said as they stopped behind the sofa and looked at the fire in the fireplace. "At least I need to put the folded laundry away and pick up some of my things."

"Sure, sure, lass." Dev smiled. "We can do that. I thought we had most of your personals moved already."

"There are still some shirts and a few sweaters I left behind," Mary said, and smiled at Dev. "Someone built me a beautiful big closet and now I need to fill it up."

Dev feigned a gesture of surprised enlightenment, slapping his hand over his eyes. "Are ye gonna be one of those kinds of women, lass?"

Mary and Mandy giggled. "At least I can bring what I have left and put them in my new closet."

Dev smiled and gave Mary a quick kiss. "I think we should go then. I'll get the jeep keys."

"Let's walk." Mary smiled and ruffled Mandy's hair as they got their coats. She handed Mandy hers as Dev collected hers from the peg.

-¤-

Once they were inside Mary's house, they each hung their coats and scarves on pegs behind the door. Mary went to the laundry area between the kitchen and the downstairs bedroom and pulled the damp sheets out of the washer, dropped them into the dryer, and set the timer controls.

"Those shouldn't take too long," Mary said as she returned and led the way upstairs and to her bedroom.

Mary started removing the last of her things from her dresser drawers and laying them on the bed.

"You do have some pretty things, Mum," Mandy said as she wandered around Mary's bedroom, looking at the items on the dresser and on the nightstands. "Even yer dresser is nice."

"Thanks, love," Mary said as she looked up from the plaid flannel blouses she was folding. "But they really aren't mine."

"Huh?"

"I mean, they're mine," Mary tried to explain. "I do own them, but they were bought so I'd have something when I got here. They aren't things I had before I came here. Do you understand what I'm trying to say?"

"Yeah," Mandy said. "But some of them are still pretty."

"Yes they are," Mary agreed. "Ms. White said—"

"I like Ms. White," Mandy said, without realizing she was interrupting.

"Yes, she is nice. She sure enjoyed her time sledding with you." Mary smiled and glanced at Dev.

"Go on," Mandy said as she picked up the framed generic picture from her nightstand, glanced at it with a shrug, and put it back.

"As I was going to say, Ms. White told me they asked the women in her office for decorating ideas and used them to put my place together so it would look homey when I got here." Mary sighed. "Oh Lord, how I needed help when I came. I didn't appreciate what they did for a while, but now I do, and they did a lot for me in those early days."

"Sorry, Mum," Mandy said, feeling Mary's heavy mood. "I wish we could've helped back then."

Mary smiled as she stacked another blouse on her pile. "Wasn't the right time, love. I needed to work through my troubles before I could see you or your father, before I could understand that you were patiently waiting for me."

Mary opened a second large paper sack, laid it on the bed, and slid the stack of blouses in. She added heavy socks and grabbed her second pair of school boots from her closet.

"I think that's all I need," she said to Dev, and smiled at Mandy. "I'll come and clean and make the beds this weekend and I can get my hanging things then."

"We'll come and clean and make the beds," Mandy said, and nudged Dev. "Right, Da?"

"Right," Dev said. "How about we fold the sheets before we go?"

Forty-Three

An hour after dark, Einri drove the spray-can black van up Eleventh to the spot half a block past Hayes where the trees had kept the snow thin. He switched the van's lights off, turned into the block on the east side of Eleventh, and maneuvered in the scant light between the trees until he could snuggle into the bushes and trees on the south side of Lincoln and not be seen. He parked facing the middle house on the north side of the street. From where he sat in the driver's seat, he could see the middle and the west house, but the east-most house was obscured by the bushes and a thick stand of trees.

Each night that week he had found a place to wait and watch from, but this was the spot he had noticed on the previous night. Each night he hoped to see Devlin repeat his activities, showing some kind of a pattern, but each night had been different. Tonight, they settled again and watched the street to the west in silence. Around seven, Einri suddenly shrunk down into the driver's seat as the police patrol car turned onto Lincoln a block up and slowly drove down the street, passing quietly in front of them, and continued on to the east.

"He didna see us," Scanlon said softly, startling Einri as he handed him a wrapped deli sandwich from the small cooler. "Water?"

Einri did not realize he had been holding his breath until Scanlon broke the heavy silence. He inhaled, nodded, and took the sandwich and a bottle of water.

They ate in continued silence.

He watched to the west and Scanlon watched to the east as best he could. It was almost eight when Einri heard the soft voices and checked his watch. The voices were coming down the street from the west and he listened closely, the cold night air and calm wind letting the words float to them.

"Scan," Einri whispered, and felt the pistol in his pocket. "Someone's walking this way. Stay quiet."

After a minute or two, Einri saw the three figures cross Eleventh Street on the north side of Lincoln, coming toward them, down the plowed street. They were walking slowly, taking their time, and he could hear Devlin's voice, his accent coming through occasionally. He smiled and figured they were coming from the house at the west end of the street where Devlin had taken his daughter and the woman after dinner on Monday, and then on each of the other nights after school.

He heard Amanda, happy and energetic. He was surprised at how grown-up she sounded, but reminded himself that she had only been five when he had last seen and heard her. But it was the soft female voice he was most interested in. He waited as they came closer and then focused on them with the heavy low-light hunter's binoculars he had brought for the occasion. He wanted a closer look, especially the woman; shorter than Devlin, taller than Amanda, and with long, dark hair. She was not screaming so he could not match her happy, giggling voice with his memory.

The woman was wearing a hip-length jacket and earmuffs, and walked on Devlin's far side, holding onto his arm. When they turned up the walk to the middle house, Einri heard Amanda call the woman "Mum" as he put the binoculars down. A frown fleetingly crossed his expression as he watched them go inside, remembering Scanlon telling him the same thing on Monday.

They closed the front door and the lights came on, and Einri tried to ignore the confusion that Amanda stirred in his mind. *Amanda really did call the woman "Mum," just like Scan said she had when they were playing cards. But Devlin's Anne is dead. He shook his head. When did Devlin remarry? When? No one's said anythin' about him remarryin'. Damn!* He shook his head and turned to Scanlon. "Let's get ready fer when they start back."

Scanlon kicked the blankets and the sleeping bag out of his way as he went to the back of the van's nearly empty cavern. He opened the back doors, stepped down off the bumper, and turned around to the wooden box he had sat on earlier. He pulled a rolled rag from inside the box and laid it on the doorsill, removed the pistol from the wrapping, and tucked it into his belt.

Einri struggled to get out of the driver's seat, past the engine hump, and hobbled to the back doors. He sat down heavily on the sill and slid out, catching himself with the forearm cane and the less-painful leg. Propping himself against the open door, he turned, unzipped the canvas rifle bag and removed the 9 mm Carbine, and slipped the ten-round magazine into the underside pocket. It snapped in place.

"Why ya takin' the rifle?" Scanlon asked in a whisper.

"Too far fer the pistol," Einri said as he took a dark gray cloth from Scanlon's box and wiped the barrel and dusted the small scope. "Can't hit much with the pistol when it's that far away."

"Ya said ya wanted to talk to her," Scanlon said, confused. "Ya don' need a rifle to do that."

"Yeah, I wanted to talk to her, but without Devlin knowin'," Einri said. "But Devlin's always with her or she's at school. Too many people watchin'. I needed to see her alone, to see what she knows, so I could make sure. Now I'll make sure another way. I'll make sure she can't talk at all. You got a clip in your pistol?"

"Sure," Scanlon said, absently thumbing the release and slipping the clip out. He looked at the cartridges in the top of the magazine and clicked it back in, then put the pistol back in his belt.

"Now we wait fer them to come back out," Einri said, and grabbed the other empty wooden box. They closed the two back doors as quietly as they could and walked up the slope to the driver's door.

Einri was puffing as he hobbled on the cane, leaning against the van for support, his continued and degenerated condition pushing his frustration to a new level. He opened the driver's door wide, but with the van tilted on the uneven ground, it swung closed when he let go. Einri cursed and set the box down so he could sit and hold the door open in front of him. He needed the door to grab and hold to rest the rifle when he took his shot, but the box wobbled and threatened to turn over when he sat down. He swore, took a deep breath, and tried to calm his rising anger, but could not fill his lungs, could not stop the light-headed spinning. Everything seemed to be going wrong, and Einri defiantly twisted sideways and swallowed a yelp of pain when he braced himself with his leg—the bad one the police bullet had broken.

"When they come out, Scan," Einri growled, glancing sideways at Scanlon where he huddled next to a tree. "When I shoot, I want ya to run across the street and keep anyone left standin' from runnin' away. I'll get m'self across the street behind ya as quick as I can."

Scan stared at Einri. "But that's Devlin and his little girl Amanda.

They're family. Our cousins. Why ya goin' ta shoot at them?"

"I'm goin' ta shoot that woman," Einri said, and glared at Scanlon. "I can't take any chances. She might be the woman from Ann Arbor. If I miss, you'll have to go and shoot her for me."

"Shoot Devlin's woman? Noo, nonono. Ya canna. I canna. Whatcha mean the woman from Ann Arbor? Ya said she was dead a long time ago. This is Amanda's mum."

"Don't argue, Scan," Einri said in a low, mean voice. "I want her dead. A dead girl won't tell them that I did it. Don't say anythin' more. Just do what I tell ya ta do."

-◻-

Dev was helping Mary fold the bedsheets, still warm from the dryer, and Mandy was getting herself a drink from the kitchen faucet when something went *thump* in the backyard, next to the house. Wide-eyed, Mandy dropped the glass in the sink and quickly tried to catch it, thankful it did not break.

"What was that?" she whispered loudly as Dev turned and made his way slowly to the back dining room window. The *thump* came again and Mary snapped the porch light on.

Dev turned to her, smiling, chuckling as he patted his chest. "Molly..." he muttered softly between breaths, "and Patty."

"Oh my," Mary said softly, smiling as she covered her mouth and looked at Mandy, still at the kitchen sink.

"Molly's checkin' yer trash can," he said, still chuckling. "Guess she was checkin' to see if ya left the lid loose."

"Nearly gave us all a heart attack." Mary switched the light off and turned back to the laundry, picking up the dropped sheet as she went.

"Aye. She did at that," Mandy whispered, and filled her glass again. "Sure hope they're not around if we ever need ta get to the truck."

-◻-

Scanlon settled against the tree a short distance away from the van's open door, staring at Einri's dark, shadowy form, nearly invisible in the darkness against the black van. Einri's words worried him. He liked Devlin and his little girl and he could not understand everything Einri said about killing the woman. That bothered him too. He was told he was shooting at targets—things; never at people, and now Einri wanting him to shoot at Devlin worried him more; it scared him.

He knew that the gun Einri used could hurt people, like he did with Mikalean. He remembered Einri saying he shot Mikalean for talking too much. He had heard Mikalean through the bathroom door and knew Mikalean had not sounded angry; it was Einri that was angry that morning, like he was now. Abruptly, the remembered image filled his mind; Einri had shot Mikalean with his pistol and Mikalean had fallen down and did not move after that.

Scanlon looked at Einri, suddenly realizing the pistol in his belt was like Einri's and...and...if he shot Devlin or Amanda or...they would fall down and not move either. He suddenly wanted to shout and argue that Einri was wrong to do this, but just as quickly he knew that Einri would just shoot him too, and that scared him—a lot. He did not want to not move any more after that.

They waited, and Scanlon watched Einri more than he watched the house, continuing to worry, his nervousness growing as time passed.

The voices from the middle house startled Scanlon. He looked at the house and then back at Einri. He saw him as he raised the rifle and held it against the edge of the door, trying to hold it steady. Einri wobbled on the wooden box, the door moved with him, the rifle jiggled.

Einri looked like he was holding his breath and Scanlon looked back at the house. Fear gripped him as Devlin, Amanda, and the woman stepped out onto the dark porch.

-¤-

With one of Mary's paper bags of clothes in one arm, Dev stepped out first with Mandy behind him. Mary switched off the inside lights and the porch light, pulled the door closed and locked the new dead bolt.

"That's odd," he said as he turned and looked up at the treetops. A very loud, moaning sound, sort of like a low-pitched, off-tune screech, drifted over them and settled in the trees across the street. "Hear that? Doesn't sound anything like the owls we had back in Michigan."

"No, it doesn't," Mary agreed softly. "What kind do they have up here?"

"I don't know. Don't remember hearing one like that before," Dev said, and shrugged one shoulder as he followed the screech and studied the wooded area across the street. He saw something moving in the darkness. "Get back inside. Hurry!"

-¤-

When Devlin, Amanda, and the woman stepped out onto the porch and into the dim light cast by the two streetlights, Scanlon shifted his position, unable to simply sit still and watch. He saw Devlin look up and he heard the strange loud screech drift over and then go silent behind them. Scanlon started to get up just as Einri wobbled, startled by the screech; the rifle jiggled again, and then *popped* loudly, twice.

-¤-

"Get behind me!" Dev suddenly demanded, his voice sharp and full of concern. "There's something in the brush—"

Something *whapped* the side of the house above them, and he heard the pop almost at the same time.

Dev was at the edge of the porch and Mary had barely turned toward the door when he shouted. Without thinking, Mary grabbed Mandy and squeezed her between herself and Dev. The second soft *pop* followed immediately and something jerked Dev's leg out from under him.

-¤-

Mary screamed when he fell, pulling her and Mandy down with him; she heard the *pops*—

—Suddenly, she saw the car windshield explode, showering her with shards of glass. A loud *pop* echoed in her ears and she saw Bobby fall away from her, bright red splotches appearing across his chest and torso. A large man stepped up beside the car, the gun in his hand firing at Bobby where he lay on the ground. She was screaming, her arms involuntarily twitching and jerking, pulling on the car door—

-¤-

Scanlon snapped his head around to look back at the house. He saw Devlin collapse against the post beside the steps and then fall behind the picketed railing. Scanlon covered his ears, shaking his head vigorously to block out Amanda's and the woman's screams. The rifle fired again and again.

-¤-

—Mary kept screaming until she slowly realized someone else was also screaming, screaming from between her and the man's arms she was jerking. Startled, she shook her head and heard Dev shouting and Mandy screaming!

"Down! Get down!" Dev shouted, and Mandy and Mary both had screamed his name and clung to him as he fell. "Get down! Get behind me!" he shouted again. Mandy kept screaming and Mary pulled them closer to Dev.

More *pops*; the glass in the dark porch light fixture shattered; the bottom pane in the storm door burst. Shards tinkled down behind them and something slapped the side of the house, barely missing Mary as she lay across Mandy, holding her down against Dev's back.

-¤-

Mandy's screams softened into sobs, calling his name. The sound of Mary's scream reminded Dev of what she must be going through, the memories of Ann Arbor tormenting her mind. He reached back to reassure them both as he felt Mandy's slender arm slip under his. Her hand grabbed his phone from his shirt pocket. Seconds later he heard her distressed, muffled voice, "Sheriff? It's Mandy O'Brien! Da's been shot! We're...we're on Mary's front porch! Hurry!"

"I'm okay, loves," Dev said softly as he looked under the bottom picket rail, searching the darkness of the woods across the street. "Are ya okay?"

"We're not hurt," Mary said, her voice amazingly calm in the moment. "We're just scared—"

"Stay down! Both of ya stay down. One of 'em's comin' from across the road." He studied the tall, lanky figure's furtive approach as he ran toward them with a gun waving in his hand. "Oh shit! Help me up. It's Scanlon! Hurry. Get me to m'feet." Dev pulled on the post and the rail, pulling himself up. "I have to stand up. He *has* to see me stand back up."

"Nooo," Mary objected. "He'll shoot aga—"

"Help me up! And stay behind me!" Dev demanded. "I *have* to stand up! He *has* to see me stand up!"

He took a deep breath, and with Mary reluctantly pushing, he stood up and leaned against the post.

"Can ya get inside and get to the truck?"

"We're not leavin' ya here ta face them alone," Mary said, looking past Dev at the approaching man.

Dev was facing Scanlon as he reached the side of the plowed street, where the snow was covering the near-side sidewalk.

"Stop right there, Scanlon!" Dev shouted. "What d'ya think yer doin'?"

Scanlon stopped and stared at Dev a few seconds before he spoke. "Ya gotta stay there, Devlin," Scanlon said, his gun still waving in uncertainty, pointing at nothing in particular. He glanced behind him and then back to Devlin. "Einri says so."

Dev looked at the darkness behind Scanlon and could see Einri hobbling unsteadily out of the bushes toward the street.

"Shoot...her...Scan," Einri shouted, struggling to hurry with his cane catching on things unseen beneath the snow, his labored breathing interrupting his words. Dev saw that he held a rifle in his free hand. "Shoot...her."

"I...I...can't. It's Devlin's woman and it's Devlin," Scanlon shouted back, his gun waving and pointing to nothing as he looked at Dev.

"Ya gotta stop this, Scanlon," Dev shouted. "Yer not goin' ta have any family left when Einri's finished. Ya've already lost Mikale—"

Dev's words were cut short when Mandy jerked away from Mary.

-¤-

Mandy heard the fear in Mary's screams when they fell and the panic in her words as her dad stood up to face Scanlon. She didn't understand why it was important for him to face Scanlon, but she knew it had something to do with stopping him, maybe surprising him—

Without another thought, except that she had to help, Mandy twisted between them and jerked away from Mary, cutting his words off.

"Mandy! No!" Mary shouted as Mandy darted into the yard.

She heard her dad yell for her to stop, to come back, but she kept running until she was halfway to Scanlon.

"What are ya doin'?" she demanded in the loudest voice she

could muster. "Stop this!"

She absently scooped up a big handful of snow, patted her hands together and in one fluid motion, still shouting, threw the snowball. It hit Scanlon squarely in the chest, and not waiting to see its effect, she scooped up another handful and threw a second snowball.

"We're yer cousins! Family!" Mandy continued, shouting at the top of her lungs. "What do ya think yer doin' anyway? First ya kill me mum and me two grans and now ya shoot me da? Ya gonna shoot me and me new mum too?"

Scanlon ducked, raising his arms to protect himself as a third snowball hit him and showered his head. She screamed at him again, launching a fourth.

-ロ-

Mary was filled with terror when Mandy broke away and ran to confront Scanlon, and before she knew what she was doing, she was in the middle of the yard, grabbing Mandy and pulling her back. Mandy launched the third and then the fourth snowball, ignoring Mary's presence.

"You leave us alone!" Mary shouted as she kept pulling Mandy back towards the porch. "How dare you threaten Mandy? We've done nothing to you! Stop it!"

Scanlon brushed the snow out of his hair and turned to Einri. "Ya killed her mum? Anne?"

"Don't...think about...it, Scan. Just shoot!" Einri shouted between deep, labored breaths as he finally stepped into the plowed street.

Scanlon turned around and stood fast, shouting squarely at Einri as he argued. "No! No, Einri! That's cousin Devlin! And Amanda! Ya canna shoot her and her new mum."

"Scan...for the...last...time. Shoot!" Einri shouted, and raised his rifle.

Scan fired twice in reflex, both shots hitting Einri in the chest, and the rifle popped.

Einri's bullet caught Scanlon's shoulder, spinning him around. Mary jerked Mandy down when Scanlon spun, the bullet zipping over them, slamming into the porch post beside Dev.

Einri fell forward in the middle of the street, his rifle discharging once more, snow and dirt erupting in front of him. Scanlon staggered, looked at Dev with a horror-filled face, then turned and ran for the darkness between the houses. From behind the house a deep animal roar filled the night. Scanlon screamed, his pistol popped, and he screamed again. Then abruptly it was quiet.

-¤-

Dev saw Mary and Mandy fall as Scanlon spun around and the bullet smashed into the post beside him. He watched their unmoving forms on the snow long after Scanlon disappeared around the house. He clung to the porch post, terrified, until Mary and Mandy slowly stirred and finally got up, hurrying back to him; their enthusiastic hugs told him they were all right. Dev looked at where Einri lay in the snowy street and realized there were men running, flooding the expanse of Lincoln from both directions, their footsteps muffled by the snow as they came up Tenth and Eleventh. A moment later Sheriff Martin's police car came up Lincoln and stopped a short distance from where Einri lay in the street.

Dev smiled at Mary and Mandy and squeezed Mandy against him. Mary wrapped her arms around both of them.

"What did ya think ya two were doin'?" he asked. "You two scared the piss right out of me." Then after a moment, he gestured to the steps. "I...think I need ta sit down."

They helped him down onto the top step. Mandy had one arm around him and held Mary's arm with her free hand.

"Da," Mandy said softly, "'twas the banshee's screech we heard. She wailed, screamin' for Cousin Einri—not fer Mary, not fer you, and not fer us..."

One of the men crouching beside the man in the street hollered to Lloyd that the man was dead. Lloyd waved back as he walked across the snow-covered yard to Dev and his girls.

He nodded to Dev and reached out to Mandy. "Thank you very much, young lady. You handled that call very well."

Mandy looked back at the sheriff, a sheepish smile breaking out on her tear stained face. "Thank you, sir."

"Scanlon is out back somewhere," Dev said. "I think he ran into Molly and Patty. He has a gun, but I don't think he's in a fightin' mood. Einri shot him in the shoulder. Someone needs to go and check on him."

Lloyd shouted to a couple of men nearby and pointed them in the right direction, and then he turned and looked at Dev and the girls. "Mary? Mandy? Are you two okay?"

When Mary nodded from where she sat beside Dev with Mandy on the step in front of them, Lloyd squatted down and looked at Dev's thigh.

"I think it went through the muscle," Dev said. "I have a kit at the house."

"That's okay, Dev," Lloyd said, and smiled. "I'll let Nate look at it. After all, you did train him for this sort of thing." He turned as Nate got out of the second patrol car. "Get your trauma kit, Nate. Dev took one in the leg."

Mary looked around at all of the men that filled her yard and the streets around them. "Lloyd? Where did all of these people come from?"

"A mass texting," Lloyd chuckled. "I wrote a number of text messages and left them all unsent in my phone. Each one had a different destination noted. After Dev and Mandy and I talked, we put everyone in town that can receive a text message on alert and I had them all on the addressee list." He smiled at Mandy and then looked back at Mary. "I told Dev and Mandy a couple of weeks ago to call me at the first sign of trouble, so when Mandy called and said where you were, I just selected the right message and sent it. I don't know if everyone came, but looking around, I'd say almost all of them did. No one was going to let this guy get away."

-¤-

Nate smiled down at Dev, shaking his head. "Ladies, can we get the man inside so I can see what I can do for him?" Nate wrapped a cloth around Dev's leg to stop the dripping blood as Mary unlocked the door.

Nate, Mary, and Mandy helped Dev inside and Nate asked Mary to clear a spot on the wood floor. She did and he and Mandy helped stretch Dev out in the cleared space.

"Stop hoverin'," Nate said, and started undoing Dev's boot laces. "He's going to live."

Mary smiled at Mandy and squeezed her hand.

"Do you have any towels I can use, Mary?" Nate asked. "They'll get bloody, but I'll need some under him, for cleaning the wound, and you'll probably want something to cover him with."

"Cover him?" Mary asked, confused.

Nate smiled and glanced at Mandy, "When I get his boots off, his pants come next."

Mary's mouth made an understanding O and she hurried to the downstairs linen closet.

-¤-

"Can I interrupt, Nate?" Lloyd asked as he stepped inside.

"I'm sure Dev will be pleased to wait a bit longer before I start cleaning the hole in his leg." Nate smiled and glanced at Mary and Mandy, one kneeling on each side of Dev.

"Just thought you'd like to know that Einri is dead," Lloyd said as he knelt down, and Mary wilted in relief, her head dropping to Dev's chest. Dev wrapped his arm around her the best he could.

"Thank goodness," she whispered, and then kissed Dev.

"We found the other one, Scanlon, out back," Lloyd continued. "Looks like he did run into Molly and her cub. He'll survive, but he needs a hospital. Chief Delany brought the ambulance and will take Scanlon to the helipad where the State boys are coming to pick him up. I understand he shot Einri?"

Dev nodded. "Einri was goin' to shoot us, but he was havin' difficulty gettin' across the street. So he told Scanlon to shoot us, but Scanlon argued with him, sayin' he wouldn't do it. When Einri raised his gun, Scanlon fired in reflex. Twice, I think."

"I see," Lloyd said, and looked at Nate. "Is Dev going to need a ride to the helipad too?"

Nate shook his head. "Nah. Clean shot through the muscle, missed the artery. When I get it cleaned out, he'll mend okay. I've called Doc Morrison and he's on his way up, but Dev's already got two of the best nurses right here."

"Okay, Dev," Lloyd said, then stood up and turned to the door. "I'll get things moving out here and let the Michigan authorities know what's happened." He looked at Mandy and Mary. "Take him home and make him rest for at least a few days." Lloyd smiled, nodding at the three of them.

"Thank you," Mary said as Lloyd stepped out and closed the door.

"Okay, Dev," Nate said as he wiped Dev's thigh with antiseptic and poised a surgical probe over it. "Get a grip on something, maybe a couple of those rolled-up towels, so you won't break Mandy's or Mary's hand. Even with the local, this is going to hurt like hell."

Forty-Four

It was late when Dev and Mary finally retired at home for the night—what remained of it, anyway. Dev was exhausted after Nate probed and prodded him and then Doc Morrison repeated everything once he got there. Nate and Bob from the grocery store helped Mary and Mandy get Dev home, and Mary happily realized everything of importance to her had shifted as she walked with her shoulders under Dev's arm, the overbearing weight of needing to hide unexpectedly lifted. With Einri dead and Scanlon in custody, Mary had only Dev and Mandy to think of, being with them and what new and happy things her future might bring.

She had come face to face with her worst nightmare, the same face under unruly red hair and surrounded with a narrow red beard that stared at her in the car, pointed a gun at her, and pulled the trigger, but when Mandy jerked out of her hands and ran out into her front yard, she only saw the great danger Mandy was in. She could not remember leaving Dev's side; all she was thinking of was to stop Mandy and bring her back. Then she was beside Mandy in the yard, suddenly terrified for both of them, staring at that red-haired man hobbling across the street behind Scanlon.

She had pulled Mandy halfway back to the porch when Scanlon stood up to Einri and shot him. Mary's legs had collapsed, pulling Mandy down; she saw Einri fall and Scanlon stumble and then run between the houses, and all she could think of was to get herself and Mandy back to Dev.

And now, as they guided Dev up the sidewalk to their front porch, Mary knew she was theirs—not just Dev's new wife, but completely, heart and soul, theirs; she had come home.

Once they had Dev settled in the middle of the sofa, his right foot propped up on the coffee table, watching the fire that Mandy stoked back to life, Mary and Mandy settled on both sides of him.

Dev squeezed Mandy and smiled at her, shaking his head. "I

could just wring yer pretty little neck, lass." Then he smiled at Mary, squeezing her as well. "Both of ya. Scarin' me ta death with yer runnin' out to face Scanlon and Einri. He could've—"

"But he didn't," Mandy said sharply. Then softer: "He didn't, Da. I couldn't just wait..."

Dev squeezed her again. "I understand, love. Truly I do," he said, and smiled at Mary, "but I was very afraid fer ya. Are you two gonna cause me ta worry like this often? I feel old age pilin' on me faster than it should."

"No, Da," Mandy said, and squeezed his waist. "Well, some maybe, but not intentionally."

"I guess I'll have to learn to live with you two," he said, and pulled Mandy to him and kissed her cheek. Then he turned his head, pulled Mary to him and kissed her firmly, hoping his kisses would tell her how thankful he was for her courage and concerns for Mandy.

¤-¤-¤-¤-¤

Once they got to bed, Dev lay flat on his back, lovingly holding Mary against his left side. On his back was the only position he could lie in and be somewhat comfortable, and with Mary in her seductive bikini-bottomed pajamas, snuggled tightly to him, he began to relax, accepting that they had survived his worst fears and Mary was safe.

It had taken hours, it seemed, to finally get Mandy settled enough to go to bed. When she was down, suitably kissed and blessed, Mary helped him back to their room, helped him put his pajamas on, and then they turned in themselves.

"Thank ya, lass," Dev said softly, and gently combed a few strands of her hair with his fingers. "Yer a very courageous and strong-willed lass when ya put yer mind to it."

"I surprise m'self sometimes," she sighed, and kissed his chest through the unbuttoned opening of his shirt. "And sometimes I act before I think."

"Aye, love, those are the moments that define us," Dev said, and kissed the top of her head. "Yer new daughter will never forget what you did for her tonight."

"Thanks. I was so scared for her," Mary sighed, and then a soft chuckle slipped out. "I didn't know what to think when she started throwing snowballs at him."

"He didn't either," Dev chuckled, and gently squeezed Mary. "I love ya, lass. You and Mandy are the best thin's to ever happen to me."

"I love you too, Dev."

Mary let their conversation fade into the comfort of each other's embrace. She toyed with his buttons, her leg gently curled over his left thigh, moving him more than he expected and she noticed. She let her free hand wander down his chest.

"We'll not be doin' any of that," Mary whispered, tilting her head back so her breath caressed his ear as her hand teased. "At least not 'til the bandages're off fer good."

Dev smiled at her mimicry and kissed her. "Aye, lass. 'Tis just that I canna hide what ya do to me, even when I canna do anythin' about it. Just thinkin' about ya makes me want ya."

It was difficult, but Dev tried to relax, comforted with Mary beside him. He was nearly asleep when a soft knock on the bedroom door brought him back.

"Da?" Mandy whispered through the crack of the nearly closed door. "Are ya sleepin' yet?"

"Come in, love," Dev said, and Mary rose up on her elbow as Mandy opened the door and slowly came to the side of the bed. "What's wrong, love? Havin' trouble gettin' ta sleep?"

"Yeah. Too many scary thin's still stirrin' 'round in me head," she said softly. "I can't get them to go away."

"Come around to this side," Mary said, and threw the covers back for her. Mandy hurried around and Mary guided her in between them. "So much has happened tonight, I'm not surprised you can't get to sleep. Maybe this will help."

"Thanks, Mum. I love you," Mandy said, and kissed Mary on the cheek. She flopped over and hugged her dad, kissed him on his cheek, and snuggled down against his side.

"We love you too, love," Dev said as Mary snuggled up behind Mandy and caught Dev's arm. Together, they held Mandy tightly between them, encircled in their embrace. "Think of sleddin' tomorrow and how great it is with Mary being ours and us bein' hers. Only happy dreams, love. From now on, only happy dreams. Fer you too, Mary."

Friday, December 1

"Henry? Good morning," Mary said when the phone connection made. She had settled on the edge of the bed beside Dev, and Mandy was curled up on his other side. "Mum said you'd be home for lunch, so we thought we'd call back so we can talk to you also. I'll put you on the speaker."

"Hey all," Henry said as Mary switched the phone and held it between them.

Dev and Mandy returned the hellos.

"Where are you? Aren't you and Mandy at school? It's what, fifteen after ten out there?"

"That's part of why we're calling," Mary continued. "Mandy and I are playing hooky. Can you put Mum on with you?"

"Sure, sure, She's right here. I'll switch to speaker also." They listened to the sounds of Henry fiddling with his phone. "What's up? Playin' hooky doesn't sound like you two."

"Hello again, Mary," Maeve greeted softly.

"Hey Mum," Dev added, his voice sounding a bit hoarse. He coughed and continued bluntly. "We had a close call last night— Cousins Einri and Scanlon were here."

"Shit!" Henry uttered in surprise before he thought. "Oh, sorry, Mandy. I shouldn't be talking like that."

Mandy giggled. "We all felt that way last night."

"Einri's dead," Dev announced, with mixed emotions. "And Scanlon's wounded. The police flew him to a hospital in Denver."

"Dead? Wounded?" Maeve repeated softly. "Does Gallagher know?"

"I don't know, Mum," Dev said, and squeezed Mary's hand. "Someone from the Brighton Police Department will probably tell him."

"Henry and I will go see him this afternoon," Maeve said. "What happened?"

358

"I'll call Mikalean," Henry said. "He called me after he got out of the hospital, apologizin' for all the pain and sorrows his brother caused, so I have his number. I think he'll want to know the situation."

"Aye, I'm sure. Will ya text me his number?"

"Sure, sure."

"Thanks. Now fer the details," Dev said, and started explaining how their night had gone, with Mary and Mandy adding bits along the way so that very little was missed.

"I wish I could say I'm sorry that Einri died," Mary admitted softly when Dev finished. "But truthfully, it will take me some time to forgive him for what he's done to so many people. Especially to Dev and Mandy." Mary stopped herself from including her own hurts and despairs, remembering that the family did not know the truths of her past like Dev and Mandy did. They had not yet decided if they would ever share those details with them, or anyone, for that matter.

"We certainly understand, Mary," Maeve said. "And maybe ye won't ever really be able to. And now that you three have suffered so badly at his hand, I think it might be hard."

"Thanks, Mum," Mary said, and squeezed Dev's hand again.

"Snowballs, huh?" Henry asked, obviously shifting the conversation to Mandy.

"Sorry, Uncle. Everythin' was happenin' so fast, I really don't remember what I did. I just got so mad at them when Da got shot, I...I—"

"Aye," Mary said. "She hit Scanlon four times before I could get to her."

"*Shot?*" Maeve asked, startled.

"Just a nick in me leg, Mum," Dev admitted, trying to down play the incident as if it were inconsequential.

"Yer okay?" Maeve asked, questioning his manner.

"Yeah, Mum," Dev said with a sigh. "The doc says every thin's fine. Just went through the muscle."

"Well," Henry said softly. "We're all very appreciative fer yer quick thinkin', and we're glad yer all safe and not too bad off fer the wear. Sure yer okay?"

Dev chuckled. "Thanks. Yes. I'm just happy the girls weren't hurt.

And me, I'll be up and around soon. I'd be up now, 'ceptin' me nurses have decide—"

"One day in bed. One day won't hurt him, and maybe we can get some things done without him underfoot."

Mandy giggled and Henry and Maeve laughed.

Saturday, December 2

"You said he was very protective, not letting you walk alone and so on." Ms. White sipped her coffee and then slid a tart onto her plate.

"That he is," Mary said, and smiled. "It isn't like he keeps me from doing the things I need to do or want to do, but he just wouldn't let me be alone in public where one or both of the brothers could see an opportunity."

Ms. White smiled. "I'm sure that's the only reason he went everywhere with you."

Mary blushed.

"And now?"

"Now it's almost like it was before," Mary said, and continued to smile. "Only better."

"I see." Ms. White smiled. "I heard Dev was shot. Is he okay?"

Mary nodded and explained how the night had gone, from when she got home from school to Dev taking a shot in the leg and Scanlon turning against Einri when Einri insisted he shoot them, all of them. "He's walking some without the forearm crutch. Won't be too long before he can get around without it."

"You said Mandy broke away from the two of you and confronted Einri? And you went after Mandy?"

"She confronted Scanlon. Before I realized what I was doing, I was out in the yard with her, pulling her back to Dev and the house," Mary said, shaking her head at the blurred memory. "She was yelling at Scanlon, the most defiant I have ever seen her, and I think it startled him. She was attacking him with snowballs, making him duck. I think she hit him at least three times before I got to her. Einri started yelling at Scanlon to shoot. That's when Scanlon said no and shot Einri. He wouldn't shoot Dev or us, his family."

"I don't remember you ever mentioning that Mandy was defiant and aggressive—not even a little."

"She isn't." Mary smiled. "She told us the banshee's screech wasn't for me or her. I think that may have given her the courage she needed to face them."

"Wasn't for her? The banshee again?" Ms. White stared at Mary. "I don't understand."

"Just before Dev was shot," Mary explained, "we heard a loud moaning, sort of a screeching howl cross over us and drift down into the treetops. From where we were on my porch, it stopped so we were looking across the street where Einri and Scanlon were hiding. Dev mentioned that it sounded a lot different than the screech owls we had back in Michigan. It was more of a moaning, ominous sound, not really a wail like one speaks of, so Mandy figured it wasn't warning us of one of our deaths, but of someone else's."

"And Mandy called it the banshee?"

Mary nodded. "Well, to me it was a familiar sound, and in Mandy's defense, it did warn us. It was even a portent that someone was going to die, so it certainly could've been..."

"Okay, I'll never understand all of this banshee stuff, so maybe we should move on," Ms. White said, shaking her head to change the subject. "You told me last time that you knew Einri shot his own bother, Mikalean."

Mary nodded. "Dev said he thinks that may have been the first time Scanlon ever saw anyone get shot," Mary said. "Knowing how Scanlon is, his inability to process some information, Dev thinks Scanlon did not realize that his shooting at 'things' was actually shooting 'people' and he probably never saw Einri actually shoot anyone other than Mikalean. When Einri told him to shoot Dev and Mandy and me, Dev thinks Scanlon may have suddenly realized, to some degree, what had been happening, what he'd done. Scanlon was certainly surprised when he heard Mandy tell Einri that she knew he'd killed her mum and her grans."

Mary poured Ms. White another cup of coffee while she pondered Mary's explanation.

"Well, I'm glad that part is over," Ms. White said, and changed the subject again. "Have you thought about what you're going to do now, being married and all?"

Mary looked at Ms. White and cocked her head. "About school? I plan on continuing to teach."

"Good, but I was wondering about your place here. Are you and Dev going to stay here?"

"Oh, you have someone else that needs a place?" Mary teased.

Ms. White smiled and shook her head. "No, Mary. This is your place. I was just wondering if you were thinking about selling it or what you might be planning since you won't need two places now."

"Aaah. Well, we've about decided to keep it." Mary smiled and took a bite of her tart. "And yes, we're stayin here. This is our home. And concerning the house, Dev suggested that I might consider using it as a B&B and I'm thinking it over."

"You're thinking about running a B&B? But you just said you're going to continue teaching."

Mary smiled. "Yes, for the hikers in the summer and the hunters in the winter. We still have a few details to work out, but I wouldn't be running it. If I do something like that, we'll hire someone to run it for me and we'll manage it."

"Dev wouldn't run it?"

"Dev said he'd help wherever I need him, but he'd prefer to do the upkeep as his main responsibility and then whatever else I needed after that. He's keeping his job at the grocery. He likes the discounts Bob gives him and the people he gets to see. And he wants to stay with the volunteer fire department. But when it comes to my place, here, he says it's my place and he wants me to do with it as I see fit. He'll support my decisions but not make them for me."

"But he made the suggestion?"

"Sure, sure," Mary said. "I like that he's thinking about my situation, but he didn't push me one way or the other."

Ms. White sipped her coffee and ate another bite of her tart before she continued. "Has anyone talked to you about what will happen now that Einri is dead?"

"No, but I suspected that you'd want to do that when you got here."

"Yes, I think I do," Ms. White said. "And I guess the first thing is that based on Mikalean O'Brien's deposition, and the fact that Einri died trying to kill you, a 'mistaken identity,' it's unlikely you'll need to make any statement about your husband's death."

Mary sobered her expression and nodded. "I suspected that. Maybe even felt relieved that I might not."

"The unfortunate thing is," Ms. White continued, "that you have to remember that Cali Marrow was officially pronounced dead, not recovering from surgery. She was 'buried' beside her husband in Ann Arbor." Ms. White sighed. "You cannot go back and resume being—"

"Ms. White," Mary said, interrupting her. "Cali did die back there in Ann Arbor. I didn't know it at first, but her memory began to disappear in the months of mourning here in Roosevelt. As much as I hated to admit it, she died and Mary Gorden lived. And Mary Gorden, now O'Brien, is married into a wonderful family. The program was able to arrange the assignments of Cali's trust accounts and savings to Mary Gorden, so I'm good financially. I'm Mary now. I have a past that I have shared with Dev and Mandy. Some of it cannot be proven, but Dev and Mandy understand and that's all I care about. And a wonderful man and his daughter are in love with me and me with them. What more can I ask for?"

Ms. White smiled. "Thank you, Mary. That helps me a lot. When the paperwork is filled out and filed away, you will no longer be 'active' in the protection program, but I'll know you're doing okay and are happy. That really helps me a lot."

Mary's expression sobered and she looked at Ms. White. "I never really thought about a time when this would actually be over. And I must apologize to you for the way I acted, the way I treated you when you brought me here. I couldn't see anything except what was behind me, all of the hurt and despair. I know I blamed you as much as I hated the circumstances. I have to tell you how very sorry I am for how I was and how I acted towards you."

"The fact that you did come to see the future and regain a life with hopes and dreams made everything worthwhile. Thank you for the apology, but more for you realizing how much your life has changed, seeing that you could recover from the devastating blow you were dealt."

"I doubt I will see you again, will I?"

"Not officially," Ms. White said softly, and smiled. "But I might have to stop by every now and then to see if the toboggans are running or to have coffee or an off-duty drink with a very nice teacher I know."

"I think that teacher would really appreciate those visits."

Forty-Five
Friday, December 8

"Are ya sure she's okay with this?" Mandy asked as Dev pulled into the circle drive in front of the school. The streetlights, the walkway edging lights, and the school's front lights illuminated the drive and walks, making the new, thin layer of snow sparkle.

Dev stopped the jeep and turned to smile at Mandy. "Aye, lass. She's actually the one that thought about it and voiced the idea first. Now, that said, we do have concerns and they have told us they'll do all they can to help make this work."

"I'm glad, Da."

Dev smiled but cocked his head. "Are you havin' second thoughts, yerself?"

"No, Da." Mandy smiled and unbuckled. "I'll just call it guarded expectations."

"Guarded expectations, huh?"

"Yup, that's what I have," she said, and pushed her door open and stepped down. "I'll run in and find Mum."

"Okay, scamp," Dev said, and stepped out on his side. Intentionally leaving the forearm crutch in the jeep, he kept his hand on the fender, just in case, as he slowly walked to the front and waited as Mandy hurried up the snow-covered front walk.

Nate had learned well how to clean and care for the bullet wound and Dev was pleased the physical healing was progressing rapidly. Nate did an excellent job of gluing and stitching the entry and departure openings; the bulky bandages were no longer needed and only small gauze pads taped to his thigh attested to the trauma he had suffered. All in all, the reminders of that night were quickly disappearing.

Dev saw that Mary was waiting for them when Mandy quickly

opened the front door and stopped. Mary stepped out and caught Mandy in a hug. They walked back to the jeep, her arm around Mary's waist and Mary's arm lovingly across her shoulders. They stopped beside the open jeep door and Dev kissed Mary fully, pulling her off balance, captured tightly in his arms.

"I've missed you, love," he said softly, and Mandy giggled.

Mary smiled and ruffled Mandy's knitted cap, making her fiery curls dance. "He says that every night. Should I believe him?"

Mandy smiled and nodded vigorously. "Yes. I think he probably does," she said, and climbed up and into the back seat. "Let's go. I'm hungry."

Dev made sure they were both in and secure, closed Mary's door, and hurried around to get in. Then he pulled out onto Main and started up town, parking in an open spot along the curb, just past Stumpy's.

"Stumpy's?" Mary asked with a smile. "Let me guess—you got busy today and forgot to start anything for dinner? Right?"

"Well, I did get busy and I didn't start anythin' fer dinner," Dev said, and Mandy giggled as she followed Mary out and he closed the door behind them. "But that isn't why we're here."

Mary cocked her head. "Is it steak night?"

"Aye, there is that," Mandy said softly as she caught Mary's hand and began leading them to the door.

"But we have another surprise for ya, love," Dev said as he slipped his arm around her waist and gently pushed her to follow Mandy.

"They're here?" Mary asked, her eyes suddenly wide and dancing.

Mandy and Dev led Mary through the front door and took her coat as they turned to their usual front-window table. Mary instantly saw the redheaded man, about Dev and Henry's height and with Henry's thinner build, and the pretty, redheaded, petite woman standing beside the table.

"Mary," Dev began as they stepped up and stopped in front of the couple. "I'd like you to meet Cousin Mikalean and his beautiful wife Nora."

Mary quickly accepted Mikalean's extended hand and then hugged Nora like a long-lost sister. "Oh, my," Mary said in a rush as

Dev gestured for them to take a seat. "I've been so busy with school I was thinking you wouldn't be here for another couple of weeks."

Mary sat in her usual place to Dev's right and Mandy settled on his left. Nora sat next to Mary and helped Mikalean as he took the place between her and Mandy.

"It is so nice to meet you, Mary," Mikalean said as he nervously fiddled with the edge of the napkin folded in front of him. "I know we've spoken some when Dev and I have talked, but before we go any further, I have to tell you how very, very sorry I am that Einri was responsible for so much hurt to ye and to Dev and Amanda. I sorely wish I coulda been a better man and stopped him."

Mary smiled, forcing her emotions down into a safe place. Mikalean only knew she *looked* like the woman Einri had shot in Ann Arbor. Knowing that that secret would always be something just between her, Dev, and Mandy, she had agreed with Dev to give Mikalean and Nora a chance to find a better life too. After all she had been given, she knew it was the least she could do.

"Thank you. We've talked about it a lot and I understand there wasn't much you could do to stop your brother. My rational side understands, but still, sometimes, I get wound up emotionally, trying to justify things in my head. Even when they can't be justified. Maybe together, I'm hoping, we can build a bridge and get past the troubled waters." Mary inhaled and smiled. "Now, I want to say it is a real surprise that you're here already. I *am* glad you're here."

"We really thought it might be after the first of the year before anything would happen and we'd know if we could leave the state."

Dev smiled and squeezed Mary's hand, nodding for Mikalean to continue.

Mikalean cleared his throat and then looked at Mandy and then at Mary. "The state set my hearing for the Monday after Thanksgivin'. Sooner than we expected, thinking they would wait until they knew something about Einri."

"So you've already had a hearing?" Mary asked.

Mikalean nodded and smiled at Nora. "Could be another one down the road, but fer now I'm on probation with an allowance to come here, and yer Sheriff Martin, I spoke with him this mornin', will watch me and see if I can do things right. He'll help me with the monthly reports I have to make."

"You talked to him this morning?" Mary asked, glancing at Dev. "So you've been here a while and Dev's given you a tour?"

Mikalean nodded. "He said we'd do a real tour when ya got off work."

"He wanted ya to do the real explainin'," Nora added, "about the house and all we'll be doin', so he showed us where it was at and then took us around the rest of the town."

"They allowed you to come here on your probation?" Mary asked, making certain she understood as she glanced at Nora's smile.

"Aye," Mikalean said.

"'Twas yers and Da's letter, Mum," Mandy said, as if it should be obvious.

"It was," Nora agreed. "'Twas yer generous offer to give us a job and a place, with family, that persuaded the courts to let us come. Because of the detective's support and the circumstances, the courts only found Mik guilty of not turnin' Einri in, and with allowances fer the threats Einri made toward me and since Einri was dead, they looked favorably on yer kind letter. They gave Mik probation instead of requirin' him to do time or service."

"And a call to your Sheriff Martin," Mikalean said. "They were pleased ta find that ya had already talked to him and that he was agreeable to the proposed situation."

"Good, good. Any word on Scanlon?" Dev asked. "How's he doin'?"

"Physically, he's doin' okay," Mikalean said softly. "Einri's shot did a lotta damage to his shoulder, but the doctors are encouragin'. They say he'll be back to workin' strength in six months or a little more."

"I think," Nora added with a chuckle, "the bear's swipe scared him more than hurt him. He'd never seen a bear up close like that and his coat took the brunt of the swipe. He's got a good set of marks across his chest, but nothin' life threatenin'."

"I'm glad to hear it," Dev said, and smiled. "Will ya have to go back fer his hearin'?"

Mikalean shook his head. "Scan had his hearin'."

"Really? That's good," Mary said, and both Mikalean and Nora nodded.

Then Mikalean's tone sobered. "The realization of what Einri had been makin' him do about crushed him, Devlin. He can't stop apologizin' fer what he did and he's sorely concerned at what ye think of him. They gave him two months for mental evaluation—"

"To confirm the limitations he has fer understandin'," Nora added.

"Then, if that goes like we think it will," Mikalean continued, "and again thanks to yer letter, he might be released for restricted probation."

Dev cocked his head. "Restricted?"

"Aye," Nora said softly. "Ya know how Scan is, Devlin. A big kid, basically with a good heart, but very easily misled and unable to rationalize his situation..."

"The court will ask ye to take Scan under yer wing, Devlin," Mikalean said bluntly, "to take responsibility fer him, teach him the right way things are, and to see that he stays out of trouble."

Mary looked at Dev and laid her hand on top of his. He looked back at her and then at Mandy. When she nodded, he looked back at Mary and saw her nod as well.

"Aye, we did talk about that and offered it to the courts," Dev said with a thin smile. He looked back at Mikalean. "I have help scheduled to start workin' on a new room fer him right after the Christmas break."

"We've been waiting for the court's response," Mary said, "before we actually committed to building."

"Thanks, Devlin," Mikalean said, and reached across the table, holding his hand out for Dev to shake. "Da says he'll send ya monthly stipends ta help with his support. He thanks ya too, especially fer not holdin' a grudge fer his shortcomin's. Ye've been a good cousin, Devlin—better than we deserved for a long time. Uncle Finnian taught ya well."

Dev took Mikalean's hand and shook it. "Thank you, Mikalean. I've tried, but don't think I'm perfect. I'm just a man—yer cousin and yer friend. We're glad you and Nora have come. But so ye know, everyone calls me 'Dev.' You might as well, too."

"Thanks, Dev," he said. "Nora and our family just call me 'Mik.' I was gonna say our friends too, but we don't have many of those anymore."

Dev was about to reply when Connie stopped beside the table and smiled at Dev, Mary, and Mandy and then looked at Mikalean and Nora.

"Aye, Connie," Dev chuckled. "More redheads. Please meet our cousins, Mik and Nora O'Brien. They're goin' ta be new Roosevelt residents."

"Wonderful," Connie said. "Do you have a place to stay?"

Nora nodded with a bright smile and pointed to Mary. "Mary's house."

"Mik and Nora are going to run my old house as a B&B for us," Mary said happily. "They'll live there, and with some fixing up, maybe we can open next spring. Now that they're here, we can start. Lloyd has some help lined up for the physical work and I'll start setting up advertising and get the registration page on line."

"Planning to stay," Connie said happily. "That's good."

Nora smiled and nudged Mikalean. "We're wantin' to start new. New place and a family."

"Our first is due in June," Mikalean said, and nodded to Connie, then to Dev, Mary, and Mandy.

"Oh, how wonderful," Connie said. "Dad will be pleased to know."

"Your dad?" Nora asked.

"Yeah." Connie smiled. "Dad's the local doctor, Doc Morrison. I'm just supposing you'll be seeing him."

"Aye." Nora nodded again. "We surely will."

"Again, wonderful," Connie said with a wide smile. "Welcome to Roosevelt, one of the most beautiful places on earth." Then she whispered loudly to Nora, "You can't tell I'm a little biased, can you?" Then she straightened. "Now what can I start off a couple of Irish lads and their lasses with? Something to celebrate—a pint for the lads, maybe?"

Saturday, December 9

"You talked to Uncle Henry? Again?" Mandy asked in surprise as she finished a bite of her pork chop. "It isn't the last Saturday."

At Mary's suggestion and since the work on her house had not started, Dev agreed to have Mikalean and Nora join them for dinners on the weekends in an effort to begin some regular family time together—at least until the B&B was fixed up and in operation. And being this was their second night in Roosevelt, Dev was pleased they also thought it was good idea.

"Aye, love," Dev said, smiled, and passed the bowl of mashed potatoes to Nora. "He called with some news."

"News?" Mary asked as she set her glass down and looked up at Dev.

Mikalean and Nora waited quietly for Dev to answer.

"Yup," Dev said, sipped his hot tea, and looked at Mary. "You know the building diagonally across from the police station?"

"The rustic one that needs some TLC, inside and out?" Mary asked.

"That'd be the one." Dev smiled and scooped up a spoonful of peas. After a sip of his tea, he glanced at Mikalean and Nora. "Can we get ya anythin' else?"

"No, Dev," Mikalean said, shaking his head. "This is wonderful. Thanks again for invitin' us."

"Our pleasure. Now, Henry did ask that we don' tell anyone. He doesn't want Debbie findin' out 'til he can tell her himself."

"Get on with it," Mary said, nodding. "Stop keeping us in suspense. We'll keep quiet, especially if he's wantin' to surprise Debbie."

Dev nodded and looked at Mikalean and Nora's confused expressions. "Debbie is our fourth-grade teacher and was Mary's maid of honor. Henry met her at our weddin' rehearsal and spent all of his free time with her while he was here. Anyway, he says he signed the papers on that buildin' and the owner agreed to clean it up and do some renovatin'."

"Renovating?" Mandy and Mary asked, almost together.

Then Mandy asked, "What's he planning on doing, Da?"

"Believe it or not," Dev said with a wide smile, "he's going to move here and start his own bookkeepin' business."

"He's moving? Here?" Mary asked, staring at Dev's nodding

agreement. "And if he doesn't want Debbie to know, does that mean what was going on between them is getting serious?"

"I'm sure of that, lass," Dev said. "He calls her every mornin' and every evenin', and I understand she calls him many times while she's on her breaks."

Mary smiled and looked at Mandy and Nora. "That will certainly be to Debbie's liking." Then she looked back at Dev. "When?"

"He said he's plannin' on openin' the doors after the first of the year, before February. He says he has three clients here in town and one in Buena Vista and he'll hire their present temporary bookkeepers so they won't lose their jobs."

"Wow," Mandy said, and stuffed another bite of potatoes in her mouth.

"He says he's already given notice at his current job," Dev explained between bites of his dinner, "and should be ready to move by the time they come for Christmas."

"Where's he going to live?" Mandy asked, and glanced at Mikalean and Nora.

"In the back of his new office. He said he checked it out while he was here over Thanksgivin' and it has a nice one-bedroom apartment on the back with a private, outside entrance."

"That'll be nice for him," Mary said, and continued eating.

"Oh, and he bought a ring."

"A ring?" Mandy asked, wide-eyed, her face covered with a bright smile.

"A ring?" Mary clarified. "He bought Debbie a ring? He's going to ask her to—"

"Aye, love." Dev nodded and took another bite of his chop. "And ye canna say anythin' before he asks her."

Mary smiled and gently shook her head. "You know that's goin' to be hard."

Dev nodded again and glanced at Mandy and then at Mik and Nora. "That goes fer alla ya."

After a few minutes, still smiling at Dev's news, Mary turned to Nora. "I know I asked how you were doing earlier, but is there anything you need at the house? I tried to be sure there were enough paper goods, towels, bath soaps, lotions, and such."

"Everythin' is gran' Mary," Nora said, and glanced down at her plate. "We're just a bit overwhelmed at ya takin' us in and helpin' us."

"Don't let her fool ya," Dev said, still smiling. "She'll make ya work fer it."

Nora looked up at him, her expression suddenly somber.

"Not to worry, now," Dev quickly added. "I'm meanin' you'll earn yer keep just keepin' that big house clean and livable with all of the remodelin' that'll be goin' on. But if it gets to be too much, ya be sure to ask fer help. We really do want ya to be happy here."

"Thanks, Dev," Nora said, letting out a soft sigh a she spoke. "I thought maybe you expected somethin' more than we talked about."

"Sorry, Nora," Dev said. "Ye'll always know what's expected and ye'll always be part of the decidin' what needs to be done. Please speak up if there's anythin' that ya don't understand, or if there's somethin' ya want ta say."

"Okay. There is one thin' I do want ta say and then one I want ta ask," Nora said, and glanced at Mary and Mandy. "First I want ta say thank you again for all yer doing for us, especially the opportunities. We spent most of the day unpackin' and gettin' to know yer gran' house, Mary, and we went explorin' to get ta know the town a little more. Mr. Jeff at the grocery says he'll help with grocery deliveries and we saw Sheriff Martin again." Nora glanced down at her plate. "Sorry. I guess I just still don' believe we're really here and all of this is really happenin' to us. Thank you, fer remindin' us what family really is."

"You're very welcome, Nora. Both of you," Mary said.

"And I want ta ask how," Nora continued, looking at Mary, "ya did the pork to make it so moist and tender. I've never been able to cook pork steaks or loins so Mik will eat it, and lookin' at his plate, and him devourin' seconds, I think he's found a new favorite. Ye'll have to show me how ye cooked it."

"You'll have to ask our resident chef," Mary said, and gestured to Mandy's bright-eyed, wide smile. "She is turning into a very surprising cook with many hidden talents. Dev did the bread and vegetables and I did the potatoes and dessert. Mandy did the meat and the sauces. Would you care to answer Nora's question, love?"

¤-¤-¤-¤-¤

"I know you explained how Mandy likes to get as much as she can of everything she knows is good," Mary said as they snuggled into bed for the night. Dinner and cards afterwards was a great success and Mary was pleased Nora and Mikalean were settling in nicely. The house was quiet, Mandy was fast asleep in her room across the hall, and Nora and Mikalean had gone back to Mary's house after a light dessert. Mary felt very content and safe for the first time in her life. "And it's so good to see how she lights up when she's with yer family and her cousins. She even accepted Mik and Nora with open arms."

"Aye, lass," Dev said, and pulled her tight, gently letting his fingers drift up and down the depression of her spine.

"You're making me lose my train of thought," she said, curling her leg farther up on his and burying her face harder against his cheek. "What surprises me, love, is how quickly she started liking me. She treats me like she likes me more than her own family." Her hand began to roam over his chest as his strokes crept farther down her spine.

"What can I say, love?" Dev asked softly. "You and Mandy have so very much in common. She feels it. She chose you to be hers, maybe more than she sees you as being mine. I don't know how to describe it, lass, but she fell in love with you very quickly."

"How can she see me...Oh my, Dev," she started to ask, interrupted by Dev's touch. She took a deep breath and forced herself to stay on subject. "The only thing we have in common, besides you, is our birthdays." Mary tried to stay focused as Dev continued his ministrations and fondling.

"You have more in common than that." Dev sighed. "As she said in her presentation, it was the events—the hurts and the despair we felt after losing Anne and the chance throw of a dart that brought us here to Roosevelt. Fer you, it was the similar hurts and despair and the witness program randomly pickin' Roosevelt, over all of the other places they could've picked, that brought you here. A chance move in itself. But it may not have been just chance that brought us together, giving you and us a family again. An 'our' family, one we can make and build on every day.

"Yer her new mum and she showed you how much she cares about you, standin' up against the worst possible danger, protectin' you with snowballs. And you showed her how much she means to you when, riskin' yer own life, you went to bring her back. Those two thin's will be forever in both of yer hearts.

"Then there is the fact that yer both half Irish and..." Dev whispered, "ye both havin' Irish fathers, and...ye both survived the doin's of our terrible cousin Einri...twice..."

"Aye, that we have...I didn't think of those things. Maybe we do have some things in common. What's Mandy's middle name?" she asked at an unexpected thought as his hand followed her curves around to the back of her curled thigh and the other combed through her hair, gently caressing the back of her head.

Dev chuckled and kissed her. "She's me first Eilís, love. Amanda Eilís O'Brien. And yer me second, Mary Eilís O'Brien."

Mary inhaled another deep breath as his caressing continued. She looked at him, barely able to whisper, "Her middle name is Eilís?"

"Aye, lass. Just like yers," Dev said as he rolled her onto her back and began assaulting her with kisses. "Both of ye are 'consecrated to God' and God has brought ya both through yer dire times, like the meanin' of yer names says he would."

"What about you?"

"Me? I'm just a simple man, here to love ya both, keep ya both as safe as I can, and help ya wherever I can and wherever God in Heaven needs me to be. We'll not be fearin' the banshee anymore, love. Not anymore."

She started to say something more, but he interrupted her.

"I love ye, lass. More than I can say." Then he kissed her, letting his lips and caresses explain how he felt about his second Eilís.

The End?

Glossary

Characters:

-A-

Arnold, Nancy, Mrs.	Principal at the Roosevelt Elementary and Middle school.

-B-

Billie Ray	Female friend of Scanlon O'Brien.

-C-

Collins, Will	Derry's (O'Brien) husband. Twin girls, Kiera and Keena
Cooper, Harry	Farmer and rancher out east on Harrison Road. Wife named Mae.
Cotton, Debbie	Fourth-grade schoolteacher.

-D-

Delany, Sam	Chief of the Roosevelt Volunteer Fire Department.

-E-

Emlich, Pastor	The pastor of the Saints Above Parish Church in Roosevelt.

-F-

Frasier, Carl	Moira Ann's (O'Brien) husband. Two boys.

-G-

Gorden, Mary	Three-year resident of Roosevelt and fifth-grade schoolteacher. Mary is 28 years old.

-J-

Jeff, Bob	Owner of Jeff's Grocery Store in Roosevelt.

-M-

Marrow, Cali	Wife of Lieutenant Robert A. Marrow. Reportedly killed when she was 25 years old. Maiden name Hughes.
Marrow, Robert Alan	Lieutenant with the Ann Arbor, MI Police Department. Married to Cali Eilís (Hughes) Marrow. Killed when he was 29 years old.
Martin, Lloyd	Sheriff in Roosevelt.
Mayer, Seth	Rancher east of Roosevelt, source for firewood.
Morgan, Merril	Brenna's (O'Brien) husband. Three boys.
Morrison, Doc	Town doctor. Wife Bertha.
Morrison, Connie	Doc and Bertha Morrison's daughter. Graduated from high school the previous year. Waitress at Stumpy's.

-O-

O'Brien, Anne	Wife of Devlin O'Brien. Died five years past in a nine-car pileup accident along with her parents in Royal Oaks, MI. Mandy, age 5 at the time, was the sole survivor of those in her car. Maiden name Kelly.
O'Brien, Devlin (Dev)	Five-year resident of Roosevelt, works for Bob Jeff as a stocker in the grocery, volunteer fireman under Sam Delany, and father of Mandy (Amanda) O'Brien. Dev is 31 years old. Married to Anne (Kelly) O'Brien; Widower.
O'Brien, Einri	Eldest son of Gallagher O'Brien. Criminal and murderer, involved in

many Detroit area crimes and murders.

O'Brien, Finnian	Husband of Maeve. Father of Brenna, Derry, Henry, Moira Ann, and Devlin. Died at the age of 72.
O'Brien, Gallagher	Finnian's brother. Father of Einri (EHN-ree), Mikalean, and Scanlon.
O'Brien, Henry	Dev's brother in Brighton, MI. Age 33 years.
O'Brien, Mandy	(aka: Amanda) Only daughter of Dev O'Brien, age ten. Fifth-grade student at Roosevelt Elementary.
O'Brien, Maeve	Mother of daughter Brenna (35) (Morgan), daughter Derry (34) (Collins), son Henry (33), daughter Moira Anne (32) (Frasier), and son Devlin (31). Married to Finnian O'Brien; Widowed.
O'Brien, Mikalean	Second son of Gallagher O'Brien. Einri's brother. Age 30 years.
O'Brien, Scanlon	Third son of Gallagher O'Brien. Einri and Mikalean's younger brother. Afflicted with mental disabilities. Age 28 years.

-W-

Williams, Detective	Investigating detective from Brighton, MI Police Department.

Places and Things:

-B-

Bear Canyon Motel	Roosevelt's only motel, operated year round for hunters in the winter and hikers in the summer.

Betty's B&B	One of two bed-and-breakfasts in Roosevelt. Open year round.
Bill's Outdoor Wear	Primary clothing store in Roosevelt.

-J-

Jeff's Grocery Store	Principal grocery store in Roosevelt. Owned and operated by Bob Jeff.

-R-

Roosevelt, Colorado	Small high country town located in the mountains north of Buena Vista, CO, west of US Highway 24 and south of Colorado State Highway 82 over Independence Pass to Aspen. Elevation 8,873 feet above sea level, population 463.

-S-

Saint's Above Church	Parish church in Roosevelt. Pastor Emlich.
Stumpy's	Stumpy's High Country Café and Saloon. One of two restaurants in Roosevelt.

-T-

Tall Pines Café	The second of two restaurants in Roosevelt.

-W-

Whispering Creek B&B	One of two bed-and-breakfasts in Roosevelt. Open year round.

-Z-

Zeke's Conoco	Gas station and deli on the main highway at the east end of Roosevelt.

Books by Aidan Red:

Fearin' the Banshee

Keeper and His Tiger
(After living homeless to find his parents murderer...)
Book 1: An Unexpected Complication
Book 2: Deadly Undercurrents
Book 3: The Trap

Paladin Shadows Series
Terran Assignment
Book 1: Things Are Not As They Seem
Book 2: When Luck Is Not Enough
Book 3: Fate Has A Different Idea
Terran Recruits
Book 4: In the Wake of Chaos
Book 5: Terran Talents Join Forces
Book 6: New Rules of Engagement
Operation Retribution
Book 7: The Training Phase
Book 8: Taking the Fight Off-World
Book 9: Luring the Prince Into the Open
Garda Nua
Book 10: The Proliferation of Talent
Book 11: When A Planet Is Stolen
Book 12: Right Does Not Ask Permission
Assignment: Casha-Six
Book 13: No Warning
Book 14: The Best Laid Plans
Book 15: A Change of Heart?

More Books by Aidan Red

Eight's Warning
A West's Ghost Ranch Trilogy
(A tale in the world of high octane aviation fuel and restored warbirds)
Book 1: The Past Hunts
Book 2: The Past Attacks
Book 3: The Price of Escape

About the Author

Aidan Red's passion for aviation and aircraft design, engineering, and a deep interest in space and space travel go back many years. An avid reader from an early age, Aidan, with great trepidation, ventured into the world of writing during college. With real world experience in business aviation, Aidan's creative side led him to create an alternate world where the beautiful Riggs Valley was born and Shara's life became chronicled in his epic science fiction series, *Paladin Shadows*.

Paladin Shadows consists of the five triptychs (three-part works), *Terran Assignment, Terran Recruits, Operation Retribution, Garda Nua* and *Assignment: Casha-Six*. In between the Paladin triptychs, Aidan has penned two, three book series, *Keeper and his Tiger,* and *Eight's Warning,* a West's Ghost Ranch Trilogy, and a novel, *Fearin' the Banshee*.

The unpublished books in his various series are scheduled for release on a regular basis in the coming months.

You can visit

www.RedsInkandQuill.com or

www.AidanRedBooks.com

for more information on Aidan Red's books and where to purchase them.

www.ingramcontent.com/pod-product-compliance
Lightning Source LLC
Chambersburg PA
CBHW051442260626
47162CB00001B/206